Audacity

SERAPH

ELODIE HART

ALCHEMY PUBLISHING LTD

Dear Reader

You survived Alchemy...

Now buckle up.

Content Advisory

Audacity paints a picture of sex work that's less rose-hued than bubblegum pink. This is deliberate. It's a fantasy, an exploration of a particular kink through the lens of a woman with a significant amount of agency. It is absolutely not a commentary on the horrific indignities and dangers sex workers face everyday in the real world. If that doesn't sit well with you, please proceed with caution.

This book also contains light bondage, role play, sacrilege, and some group activity before Gabe and Athena find their monogamous HEA.

Prologue - Athena

M oments of note don't always feel noteworthy.

So when a woman whose poise, whose elegance, *would* be noteworthy if we were in any city other than Paris presses upon me a fresh flute of champagne, this moment of my fingers closing around its weighty crystal as my eyes meet hers offers little more than a mild flicker of curiosity.

My first guess—or *assumption*, more accurately—is that she wants me. This I'm used to, from both men and women. Apparently, I give off carnal vibes, even when I'm at my most sedate and polished.

Especially when I'm at my most sedate and polished.

She's eyeing me with a combination of approval and pleasure. It's a *she'll do nicely* look.

'*Vous-êtes anglaise?*' she asks me. Her accent is decent, but there's an unmistakable British roundness to the vowels of her *vous* that gives her away. I get it. It's hard for us Brits to relearn the actual linguistics that will allow us to form authentic French vowels. I suppose she, like most people, prioritises the ability to speak fluently and accurately over the sheer joy of one's mouth speaking the words as they are meant to be spoken.

'I am.'

I leave it there.

She'll tell me what she wants from me soon enough.

'I thought so,' she says. 'You're a perfect English rose.'

She has a cut-glass accent, but it's a trite phrase, and one I've heard a thousand times before. To her credit, she doesn't try to dress it up as anything more impressive than a mere matter of fact. I am, apparently, an English rose. People have catalogued me as such all my life, although if I pressed them on the datapoints that make up that category, I'm sure they'd fumble.

One man even told me I looked like a Rossetti painting, which I frankly found offensive. His muses had decidedly horsey jaws. *Not* attractive. No, I'd rather bask in the heady warmth of being compared to one of Sargent's ethereal subjects in all their doe-eyed, pale-skinned, rosy-lipped glory.

Some of them, like the beautiful Duchess of Portland, even have a beguiling pink flush on their cheeks, almost as if the painter burrowed under all that lustrous oyster-coloured satin to seek out their most intimate parts and made them climax on his fingers for the sole purpose of capturing that shameful, intimate bloom on their skin.

I've got myself off to that fantasy before.

This is also one of my working theories on why people have carnal reactions to me: I look like someone, or something, pristine that they want to violate. To overpower. To smash.

I shrug at this immaculate woman's underwhelming descriptor. There isn't much to say when someone simply states facts at you.

She holds out her hand, her pose at the correct end of the jutting-slash-languid spectrum. Nobody likes a languidly extended hand.

'I'm Camille St John.'

Camille. Maybe she has a French mother. She really should work harder on those vowels. There's no excuse for sloppiness.

'Athena.' I shake. I don't see a reason why I should offer her my surname at this point. That she gave hers freely is not my problem.

She smiles then, and it's a fierce, unguarded smile. It makes her far more likeable. 'God, I love that.'

'Thank you,' I say, quietly amused.

Her eyes dart over my face. I suspect the meekness of my countenance and the unavoidable connotations of my name strike her as incongruous.

'Goddess of handicrafts. Do you crochet?'

Athena. Goddess of war. Of wisdom. Lauded for her resourcefulness. For her lack of promiscuity.

If ever a female-presenting Greek deity was not to be trifled with, it was Athena.

And this woman chose fucking *handicrafts.*

'Interesting that you went there. Do I look like I crochet?'

'You do not. It felt less invasive than asking you outright if you were a virgin goddess. Although the goddess part is indisputable.'

I was right.

She wants me.

I don't usually do women, but she's undeniably magnetic, her dark-hair sleekly centre-parted in a way that would look overly severe on someone who didn't have her bone structure or her skin or her ability to perfect a velvety scarlet lip.

'Again. Do I look like a virgin to you?'

She doesn't answer immediately, instead taking a sip of her champagne as she allows herself to study me. I know what she'll see. My Miu Miu dress is sleek and black and tasteful, hinting at my assets rather than serving them up on a silver platter. My stockings are black and sheer. My Valentino heels are elegant, my Van Cleef bracelet and earrings set—a gift from my parents—an understated addition.

I look like I could fit in anywhere and conduct myself with exquisite social propriety and never, ever disgrace myself unless, or *until*, the right person dragged me into a store cupboard or a disabled loo and put his hand around my throat and forced me to my knees.

Then I could disgrace myself with aplomb.

'You look,' she says, lowering her glass as she continues to survey me, 'like you are not a virgin, countless times over, and like every single man whose path you cross wishes you were with a fervency that takes his breath away.'

That earns her a smile.

Tonight's pleasant soirée in the spectacular surroundings of the Musée Rodin comes courtesy of Swiss bank Loeb, who's hired the place out at no small cost to woo the *crème de la crème* of The Sorbonne's current MBA class. Alas, it's too cold to avail of the pristinely manicured gardens, but I've enjoyed them plenty of times before. The museum is a favourite of consultancy firms and investment banks looking to put on an uncompromising display of the wealth, the luxury, that awaits us if only we choose to sign our lives away to them.

This woman, Camille, is, I assume, part of the Loeb delegation. She's probably flown in from London or Zurich or Geneva to have a crack at us. She looks just as much at home here as I feel. When you've grown up in the embassies of Europe, polished floors and gleaming crystal and sparkling conversation that goes precisely nowhere are second nature to you.

I'm less *interested* in working for Loeb, or any other bank for that matter, than *willing to consider it*. Really, I want to end up in industry. I want to call the shots, not advise people on what shots to call or help them to fund those shots. I put in a management consultant stint at Bain after finishing my degree a year early, and now that I have some consulting experience under my belt, it's time to pivot.

That's what an MBA represents to most of my peers: the vehicle through which they can pivot to a new and equally gruelling sub-sector of the finance industry.

Investment banking is dull and rigidly, endlessly hierarchical, but there's no denying it gives you a solid grounding in the nuts and bolts of how companies work and how their financial systems run. I can put my head down for a year or two if it means arming myself with the tools for a quick ascension elsewhere.

As we size each other up, I take a moment to appreciate how sophisticated Camille looks, how poised against the backdrop of the museum foyer's iconic wrought-iron staircase and monochrome floor. I nod at her shift dress—black and simple, just like mine.

'Celine? That's a Phoebe Philo, surely?'

She may not have a bona fide Parisian accent, but she certainly has the discernment of a local. Many a chic Parisienne will refuse to touch anything designed by the house's subsequent creative director, Hedi Slimane, staying loyal instead to its Philo-era vintage.

She smiles, approving. 'You know your Celine. I'm impressed.'

I shrug self-deprecatingly. 'You can't see a Phoebe Philo piece and not recognise it. It's beautiful.'

'And yet you want to bag a job at Loeb and bury yourself in a grey cubicle twenty hours a day?'

'You're a better ambassador for Celine than you are for Loeb,' I observe, taking a ladylike sip of my champagne. It's non-vintage, but decent. Probably from one of the smaller grower vineyards.

Her laugh is a tinkle. 'Oh, darling, I don't work for Loeb.'

This is surprising. 'Don't you?' I leave the less polite question hanging. *What the hell are you doing here, then?*

'They're...' She glances around the throng of people before lowering her voice. 'They're a client of mine, but that's not why I'm here.'

Again, I stay silent. If she has an agenda, she'll push it.

'I work for an agency. We place people in very senior positions at firms like Loeb.'

Ugh. She's a recruitment consultant. A necessary evil in this world, but horrific all the same. I smile politely. 'C-suite executives, you mean?' CEOs, CFOs, COOs—all roles far too senior to be appropriate for MBA students.

'Executive assistants.' She watches me as she says it.

It takes all my experience of working diplomatic circles not to sneer. If she's sniffing around the soon-to-be graduates of one of Europe's finest business schools, she's wasting her time. 'This crowd may be a little...'

Overeducated. I swallow the word before I can say it, because it smacks of intellectual snobbery.

She raises a shapely eyebrow. 'Overqualified?'

I smile, shrug again. 'Or expensive. Or greedy.'

'Hmm.' She casts her eye around the room again. 'I wonder what they'd say if they knew that almost all of our candidates place with a seven-figure annual package.'

Now she really has my attention, because that is ridiculous. I ask the only question I can.

'How?' *Who the hell pays that to someone who books their travel and compiles meeting notes?*

She takes an almost indiscernible step towards me. 'I could tell you so much more over a cocktail if you signed some paperwork first. We take our clients' and candidates' confidentiality incredibly seriously. But I will divulge this much.

'The agency I run is called Seraph, and the women—and currently it is only women—whom we place have access to the most powerful men in industry. These women are *full service* executive assistants.'

My lips part involuntarily, her meaning landing with me even before she articulates it further.

'Our EAs are all MBA-level qualified, from top schools only, and they bring a whole host of value to their employers in the C-suite... and also in the bedroom.'

There's a pull deep in my core. It's instantaneous. This vision she's conjured up in a single sentence—it's intoxicating. *A whole host of value... in the bedroom.*

'These are busy men, Athena,' she continues. 'They need a... turnkey solution, if you like. They have profound appetites and refined tastes and exacting standards. They need an assistant who is the absolute best of the best at everything she does. Someone whose intellect matches theirs, who can anticipate and meet every need they have.' She pauses, nodding at me meaningfully. *Someone like you.* 'And they are happy to reward that very, very fully, financially, of course. And... with an extraordinary level of access.'

'You're a madam,' I say under my breath. Somehow, it's not a shock.

'I'm a feminist, and the man who owns this company, an extremely influential power player, is a feminist too. Women are still locked out of so many positions of power. There's so much back-channelling, so many old-boys' networks that play out on golf courses from Augusta to St Andrew's. But we have advantages that they don't have, and it's my mission both to facilitate the maximising of those advantages and to ensure that my candidates are exquisitely remunerated in return.'

With a tilt of her head, she delivers the closing shot of her pitch. 'Imagine the *access* that a certain level of intimacy delivers. Imagine having the ear of the most powerful decision maker at any company, because what you give him in your uniquely positioned capacity goes far, far beyond what anyone else, even his closest management team members, can dream of.'

PART ONE

Introitus (Entrance)

CHAPTER 1

Gabe

There is no cocktail of emotions quite like the one that assaults you when you wake suddenly, violently, to find yourself stark bollock naked in front of a woman who has categorically not chosen to share this experience with you.

Horror, humiliation, vulnerability, shame: they all come for me with the adrenaline delivery of an epi pen, while the twin shocks of full-wattage lights and female shrieking have me sitting up on the bed with the gasping drama of a seemingly dead TV villain suddenly come back to life.

She screams in a heavy Eastern European accent. 'Oh no! I'm sorry, mister, I'm sorry. I think it was empty!'

'Fuck,' I mutter, cupping my junk on instinct with one hand as I use the other to shield my eyes against the sudden glare. Where the fuck are my trousers? I glance blindly around the area of floor beside the bed, my eyes landing not on my clothes, as I hoped, but on a used and knotted condom.

Excruciating.

'I'm so sorry. I'm so sorry,' I mutter on repeat with a grating British obsequiousness more suited to pushing past people on a tube escalator than inadvertently flashing someone who is almost certainly not paid enough to deal with this shit.

My mouth is parched. I must have been snoring, because the dehydration is definitely not from alcohol. This sex club, Alchemy, has a two-drink limit to protect everyone who partakes in its delights. Clearly, the only parties not protected from unwanted advances are its poor cleaning staff.

'I'll be out of your hair in just a moment,' I insist, wedging a pillow in front of my dick and using my free hand to bear my weight as I peer plaintively over the other side of the bed.

This is ridiculous.

I feel like I'm starring in an x-rated version of *Mr Bean*.

I'm a thirty-six-year-old man who is now responsible for hundreds of staff members and billions of pounds of assets. It's about time I started acting like it.

'I leave you,' she insists even more forcefully, backing out of the doorway and shutting the door with a firm click.

Heavenly Father, what the hell am I doing?

I collapse on the bed, flinging my forearm over my face to keep the dratted overhead lights out of my eyes. She left them on—smart woman. Probably knew I'd pass straight back out if she turned them off again.

At least there's no sign of the person I fucked earlier this evening. Waking up with her would have been arguably more horrifying than waking up to a traumatised cleaner—especially because I no longer recall her name.

(My fuck, that is.)

Wait—did I finish? I did, didn't I?

The low-grade chafing of my dick confirms for me that no, I did not fall asleep on the job and I remember that yes, I did indeed acquit myself with honours before I passed out. She liked it when I got her on her hands and knees.

She *really* liked it.

I summon the energy to move my arm and drag my hand

down over my face. If forsaking one's vows and leaving the priesthood to assume the management of eight billion crisp British pounds of assets was a common enough occurrence to warrant being a cliché, I would indeed be a cliché.

As it is, I'm simply a laughingstock.

I'm also stiff—not in a good way—and fucking freezing. These beds have satin fitted sheets but no actual coverings—an attempt to prevent dipshits like me getting too comfortable, presumably.

I groan aloud and haul myself off the bed. A glance at my watch tells me it's just after four in the morning.

I am a joke.

The winter sun is a small comfort, I suppose. It's streaming through the windows of my office, hitting my monitor in exactly the wrong place, but I welcome it.

I ended up coming straight into the office when I left Alchemy this morning. God knows, I needed a shower, but I wasn't about to use the room's ensuite when the poor cleaners were waiting to purge the scene of my sins of the flesh. I have a large bathroom and shower here—it's useful when I jog into work—so I washed myself and proceeded to lie wakefully on the sofa opposite my desk for a couple of hours before yielding to the inevitable.

I'd had my sleep for the night.

My Alchemy membership was supposed to be a stopgap for me. An interim measure. My mate Anton Wolff suggested it a few months ago, when I may as well have still been a priest. Casting aside my vow of poverty was inevitable for a man in my position. A necessary evil.

Casting aside my vow of celibacy sat far less well with me... until it didn't. But, much like the money and the whisky and every other numbing technique I've abused since assuming this role, the blessed lustre of my orgasms has faded and now I simply feel grubby. Shame-filled.

It's not exactly a surprise. One of Christianity's foundational concepts is that base, fleeting pleasures will never bring the kind of everlasting peace and joy that spiritual pleasures do. Still, I find myself in some kind of joyless vicious circle where the overwhelm of this new version of my life necessitates constant, aggressive numbing. I'm drowning in this toxic whirlpool of materially-driven stress, and until I find my flippers, I need regular life-aids.

Which brings me to the move I know I need to make. The move that, of all the sins I've committed in the past twelve months, feels grubbier, more exploitative, more transgressive, than the rest.

I reach into my desk drawer and pull out a small rectangle of card, pressing my finger and thumb to diagonally opposing sides and spinning it. It's pale pink and made from heavy card stock. On the front, a pair of intricate gold angel wings and a single debossed word.

Seraph.

Anton passed me this card last week at Alchemy when I was just as exhausted as I was last night. Even more convenient than sex on tap at a club, he argued, was having sex on tap at work. An MBA-qualified executive assistant from Seraph, an agency he founded, would apparently sort me out on every front. She'd service me whenever I needed it, particularly during office hours, and keep me sated enough that eight hours' sleep might become a reality.

The level of fatalism with which I've been approaching many of life's decisions these past few months is frankly terrifying. I'm on a rickety rollercoaster with very little, if any, sense of control over this path along which I'm hurtling. But nothing says *abject moral decay* like picking up the phone to employ a prostitute in my place of work.

I pick up the phone.

My conversation with Anton leaves me jittery. He's promised to put in a call to Athena, his own former EA and the woman whose praises he and his successor, Max, sang that night at Alchemy. According to them, Athena is a walking epiphany: physically sensational and terrifyingly competent on every front.

If she can't or won't entertain the notion of jumping ship from her current employer, a guy Anton quotes as being "a total fucking waste of her body and her personality", he will call the Seraph CEO and have her meet with me to find me the right candidate, a process so daunting that I'm already shitting myself.

It's with fatigue and a growing sense of self-loathing that I drag myself from my desk and over to one of the small rooms adjoining my office. Dad used it as a store room when he ran this place, but a spontaneous and horrifyingly expensive trip to Sotheby's auction house shortly after I took over the running of this financial behemoth had me anointing his store room with a new function.

There it is.

On a table in the dimly lit space sits an illuminated glass case, its contents more nourishing for my soul than any amount of sex or scotch.

Above it, a simple crucifix hangs on the wall.

Before it stands a Victorian leather-cushioned *prie-dieu*, or kneeler.

I shut the door behind me with a soft click and approach the table with reverence. I already feel the softening, the easing of friction and exhaustion and guilt. This is my baptism. It will purify me in the same way that immersing my naked body in the River Jordan would cleanse me of this grimy layer of sin I carry.

It will, in a small way, expunge the lingering memory of the past twelve hours and help to ground me in what is good and true and pure.

It's close enough to nine o'clock. *Hora Tertia.* The hour when the Holy Spirit descended on the feast of Pentecost. The Office of Terce offers guidance and strength from the Holy Spirit for the remainder of the day that lies ahead.

Next to the glass case sits a metal pitcher and matching metal bowl. I filled the pitcher earlier this morning and now I pour the water into the bowl, admiring the shallow, gleaming arc of liquid the jug's generous lip provides. As I prepare to wash my hands before handling the contents of the glass box, I muse at the irony of keeping Terce far more regularly in my new life as a billionaire CEO than I ever did when I was an anointed servant of God.

You join the priesthood for a sacred life, a life of service. And while the sacred remains, the service aspect takes front and centre. Of all the eight Hours I learnt at the seminary, the only ones I kept were the morning and evening ones of Lauds and Vespers respectively. At nine o'clock most weekday mornings, I was mucking in at our parish soup kitchen or wrangling donors for fundraisers.

I was categorically not in a position to keep the Hours in the company of a seven-million-pound Book of Hours from the Italian Renaissance.

But now, here I am, this surreally corporate world allowing me the space for structured contemplation that my actual role as a priest simply did not. While it's by no means a daily habit—I'm a businessman, not a Trappist monk—I find myself nipping in here for the occasional Terce before board meetings, for noontime Sext prayers devoted to peace and strength (often needed *after* said board meetings) or for the perspective on sacrifice that the three o'clock None offers—often before stuffing my face non-ironically with afternoon tea and biscuits.

This ritualistic washing of hands that I insist on adopting may, at face value, be the smart thing to do before touching a priceless artefact, but it doesn't escape my notice that it's grounded in the muscle memory of the Lavabo ritual I undertook every day at Mass before I handled the Eucharist.

I may not be a priest anymore.

I may no longer have the right to perform sacraments.

But this silent, ceremonial handwashing tethers me to this moment. This moment where I've chosen to stay in stillness and humility and prayer. To seek out God's grace, even as the poor, miserable sinner I am.

Hands washed and dried, I don my nitrile gloves and raise the lid of the display case. My previous role required the handling of precious items—none so precious as the Lord's body and blood—but this is the most expensive and creatively impressive masterpiece I've ever owned.

An Italian Book of Hours.

A stunningly intricate book dedicated to the glory of God, its provenance almost as fascinating as its visual riches. It was originally commissioned by the Tornabuoni family, who were major patrons of the arts during the Italian Renaissance, and its still-vivid illumination is a celebration of Florentine flamboyance, with accents of richest vermillion and ultramarine and malachite overlaid with burnished gold leaf.

The conservationists at Sotheby's held my hand throughout the entire process of my taking stewardship of this priceless piece. They arranged for its storage in my office and educated me thoroughly on how to care for and handle it. The expert who led the process told me I was the first buyer she'd ever met who actually intended to use it for the purpose for which it was originally created.

I can't imagine many Sotheby's clients keep the Hours.

The book lies open within this humidity-controlled display case, its spine supported at the requisite one-hundred-and-twenty degrees. I take a moment to marvel at the intricacy of the *bianchi girari*—the white vine scroll work—in the margins as I begin to intone the words that introduce all the Hours.

Deus, in adiutorium meum intende.
Domine, ad adiuvandum me festina.
O God, come to my assistance.
O Lord, make haste to help me.

How many people's gazes have fallen upon these pages? How many people have beseeched God with these words to help them, to bring them strength, in times of distress and fear that we, with the blessings of modern medicine, can't begin to fathom?

I pick up the fine bone handle with which I turn the pages of this ancient book. It's only then that I note the page it's currently open at.

Compline.

The bedtime prayer for protection and peaceful rest.

I pulled a late one at the office last night, trying to make a dent in the infinite void of Things About This Industry I Do Not Know, before ending my working day with Compline.

That was about an hour before my mate Adam Wright called me and dragged me out to Alchemy for drinks.

My prayers to God for a peaceful rest fell on deaf—and almost certainly disapproving—ears last night.

CHAPTER 2

Athena

When Anton Wolff's name lights up on your phone's display, you don't decline the call.

For a variety of reasons.

I pause the documentary I'm watching—*Winter on Fire*, about an uprising in Ukraine a decade ago. It's compelling and confronting in equal measure. Mr Wolff is guaranteed to provide some light relief.

'Anton. Hello.'

'Hello, Athena. How's tricks?'

I can hear the smile in his voice as he drawls my name, and I swear to God my entire body breaks out in goosebumps. I'm a dog whose owner is clanging a bell and offering me a tasty chicken treat.

'Still turning them.' I set down the remote and sit up straighter, shifting in my cashmere cocoon. The sofa is a nest of Loro Piana blankets and throw pillows, all presents from Steve Goodall—the man I currently work for—who is a thoughtful and generous gift giver.

He chuckles. 'That's my girl.'

I would like to clarify at this point that I was never actually in love with Anton while I worked for him—not entirely, anyway. He was merely my billionaire boss who, at more than twice my age, commanded me and used me and consumed me, rendering my seven-figure salary the *second best* thing about working for him.

Not something I can say about my current boss.

Alas, that's not to say Anton can't have my nipples hardening with a phrase like *that's my girl*, because the things I used to do—*willingly*—to earn that phrase in that particularly filthy, intimate tone aren't easily forgotten.

'How's monogamy?' I ask. It still smarts that he kicked me out as soon as his now-wife, Genevieve, rolled over for him. One Wednesday, he sidled off to Cannes with her and his number two, Max, for a recce of her sex club, the one he was investing in, and by the following Monday morning he was grinning and sun-kissed and telling me, kindly but firmly, that our gig was over.

It made for a hell of a nightmare trying to pass things over remotely to his new EA, that's for sure. And, while it's the nature of the job, it can sting.

'Bloody amazing,' he says in that cheerful, larger than life voice of his, and I know that this particular instance of *that's my girl* is a figure of speech and nothing more.

I have to admire his total commitment to this relationship. Genevieve may be his fourth wife, but this one is here to stay. That fact was clear to me as soon as I laid eyes on her. As soon as he lured her into his office and got Max and another colleague to rail her while he let me get him off, I knew that man's heart was toast.

Along with my job.

'Glad to hear it.' I clear my throat. 'What can I do for you, Anton?'

'I have a potential position for you,' he says, and I roll my eyes.

'I have a position, thank you. And I don't need a pimp.'

'Goodall keeping you overflowing with orgasms, is he?'

The derision in his voice is clear. Steve is a thirty-something, socially awkward nerd who runs an innovative hydrogen fuel cell company. I took the role to learn all I could about the renewables sector and because the salary was exceptional. It's easy money in a fascinating space, and the fact that I have to fake it every Monday, Wednesday and Friday when Steve fucks me, missionary-style, on his office sofa, isn't a huge deal.

'That is precisely none of your business.'

It really isn't, and he knows it. He also knows that I'd never allow any indiscretions where my employers are concerned, ironclad NDAs aside.

His voice softens. 'Look. I know it isn't. I've just—I've got a mate who could use someone exactly like you in his life, and I wanted to at least make you aware of the opening. You're far too shrewd a businesswoman not to have an eye on the market at all times.'

I sigh. 'Who is he?'

'You know I shouldn't tell you without an NDA.'

'Your call. But *you* called *me*, remember? And you know I would never repeat our conversations.'

'His name is Gabriel Sullivan. Gabe.'

I frown, trying to place the name. 'Sullivan...'

'As in Sullivan Construction. He's recently taken over from his old man.'

Oh. Now I understand. Sullivan owns half of the London docklands. They're an enormous Irish construction company going back several generations. They went public a few years back, making the family billionaires several times over.

'Does the son run the public company?'

'No. He runs Rath Mor, the family's investment vehicle.

They've got assets of over eight billion. They kept a lot of the land. His brother runs the construction side.'

'So it's a private wealth fund, basically?' I'm familiar with this concept: families so wealthy that they don't go to a Swiss private bank like most normal rich people but manage their assets in-house like a proper investment firm.

'Exactly. Do me a favour. Look Gabe up.'

'Okay. Give me a sec.' I reach across and pull my MacBook onto my lap, typing *Gabriel Sullivan* into the search engine.

Holy fucking shit.

'He's not Steve Goodall,' Anton quips.

'He most certainly is not,' I murmur.

A guy stares back at me from the array of corporate and Getty images the search throws up.

Black hair.

Blue eyes.

Unsmiling.

Cheekbones that could cut glass and ramrod-straight posture.

In most of them, he's wearing some variation of a suit and tie, or suit and unbuttoned shirt.

But as I scroll, one photo catches my eye.

I click into it and Google serves me up the following head-line in the financial section of *The Telegraph*, dated last year.

Gabriel Sullivan is to leave the priesthood and take up the helm of Rath Mor Asset Management. His father, Ronan Sullivan, is due to retire this September.

It's a formal shot, but boy does it hit differently from the others. Gabriel is standing in the nave of a beautiful old church, arms folded and smile absent —so far, so on-brand— in basic priest's garb. He has on a black shirt and trousers and a simple white dog collar. Around him, the space dances with fragments of colour, courtesy of the sunlight streaming through the church's stained-glass windows.

I lean in to study the image. He's arresting and grave, this man of the cloth, and he is hot *as fuck*. So hot, in fact, that the little frisson of pleasure I've felt at speaking to Anton is instantly forgotten.

How does a man go from *that*—a sense of vocation so strong that he's willing to subjugate his most primal desires in favour of a life of service—to paying up for sex on tap?

And what type of enigma does that make him? Do his former sacrifices *explain* his interest in the kind of solution only Seraph can provide, or do they render it wholly *inexplicable*?

Presumably, he once believed in the sanctity of the vows he took. In their ability to hold him and cleanse him and behallow him.

Presumably, that covenant promised him a celestial array of eternal, exalted rewards in exchange for renouncing any earthly worship of money and sex.

Yet he now wants to use his unlimited supply of the former to pay for an unlimited supply of the latter.

There's lapsing.

There's pivoting, even, in one's belief system. One's moral code.

But this guy's one-eighty must be giving him whiplash.

'You've gone awfully quiet,' Anton drawls. 'Like what you see?'

'Hang on.' I stare at the unsmiling eyes of the man in the photo. 'Are you honestly suggesting you want me to fuck a guy who used to be a *priest?*'

'*Used to be* being the operative words. He's a layman now, and you'd better believe he needs some stress relief. We signed him up to Alchemy, but the poor fucker's too exhausted for all those late nights. One of the cleaners stumbled across him at four in the morning the other day—he was out cold in one of the private rooms. I don't know who was more traumatised. Anyway, he needs more of a full-service solution.'

I'm silent, weighing my options. On the one hand, I don't like to turn over my employers too often. It doesn't look good on one's CV. On the other, my agency Seraph, a discreet outfit owned by Anton and specialising in employees like me, could place me at a dozen different places tomorrow if I wanted to. CV optics aren't really a priority.

'Come on,' he says in a wheedling tone. 'Just meet with him. If you're happy with Woodall, then fine, but I'd like to see you have your cake *and* eat it. You're my OG Seraph girl, you know you are.'

'I'm your *only* Seraph girl,' I point out. Anton may have founded Seraph, but he didn't make his first hire—me—until after he'd extricated himself from Marriage Number Three, and he met his wife only a few weeks after I started. 'And don't try to use words like *OG*. You're far too old. It doesn't work.'

'I've got teenage kids,' he retorts good-naturedly. 'I'm cool.'

'You're really not.'

He really is. For his age, anyway.

'What do you say?' he persists. 'If the tall, dark and handsome billionaire doesn't float your boat, you can scurry back to Steve and his godforsaken offices in—where is it? Swindon?'

'Reading.' In a retail park, no less. It's godawful.

He guffaws. 'You don't belong in fucking Reading, sweetheart. Say the word and you could be back in Mayfair where you belong, with a disgustingly handsome man fucking you senseless every day of the week. The guy was celibate for a decade, God love him. Imagine how much lost time he's got to make up for.'

I chew the inside of my cheek.

Imagine, indeed.

CHAPTER 3

Gabe

T he process of laicisation, whereby a priest becomes a layperson again, can be painfully protracted. The wheels of bureaucracy move slowly at the Vatican.

That is, of course, unless you have something with which to grease them.

Happily for impatient bastards like me, hard cash is as much of a lubricant to the machinations of the Church today as it was five centuries ago, when reformers such as Luther grew pissed off with the practice of indulgences—in that case, greasing the wheels of the journey to heaven for you or your loved ones.

Heaven is, I assume, no longer an option for me, but in the end I was laicised relatively quickly: six months, to be exact. In fact, the most excruciating part of the entire process was having to write a letter to my boss's boss's boss—His Holiness the Pope—requesting that I be released from my ecclesiastical duties for good.

As far as resignation letters go, it was a brutal one to pen.

With wheels and palms greased accordingly, I was free relatively soon to sink my selfish bones deep into the swamp of moral corruption, and, appropriately enough, I celebrated the news that I was a layperson with my first fuck in a decade, finding some beautiful woman in a bar in Mayfair when I was out with my reprobate brother.

I did *not* acquit myself with honours that night. I barely had enough time to wedge myself inside her before I was filling my condom like a spotty teenager. The past few months, I've honed my craft—stamina, precision, kinkiness—refining it principally at Alchemy, restoring the lustre after my years-long dry spell had rusted it. My then-new mate, Anton Wolff, whom I'd met at a high-level mixer held by one of the big consultancy firms, told me about this club his wife ran, a club I'd been meaning to try.

A club that could solve all my problems.

It solved most of my problems, except for the obvious one. Complete fucking exhaustion.

So here I am, making my way to the eighth floor of a discreet modern building near the Bank of England to see if I can't shoehorn my personal needs into my working day and procure for myself the layperson's Holy Trinity of sleep, sex and sanity.

Seraph's offices are heavy on excellent views and premium square footage and light on actual personnel. I imagine their commissions are chunky as hell and that little manpower is needed at the management level. The space is almost entirely creamy white marble and glass, and when the unthreateningly attractive receptionist shows me into a meeting room, the vista of the City of London on this cold, crisp morning is simply breathtaking.

There's nowhere like the City, with its heady mix of history and architecture and power and wealth, and to be back in its beating heart awakens something in me. It's so gloriously, unapologetically secular. This most ancient part of

London was built on the greed and ambition of centuries of men—and I do mean *men*.

It's probably intentional on Seraph's part, but simply being here has me morphing into an entirely different type of man from the type I purported to be in my shabby parish in Willesden, North West London. As I stand with my hands in my pockets, gazing out at the very top of the Royal Exchange's famous facade, I observe that this lofty position serves to make one feel entitled.

And if there's anything more entitled than using one's grotesque wealth to purchase the sexual services of a beautiful woman, I don't know what it is.

There's a voice behind me, saying my name in an assured tone, and I turn.

'Camille St John,' she says, offering her hand. She's tall and well-dressed, but somehow austere-looking, with her slicked-back dark hair and black suit. She pronounces her surname in that inexplicably contracted way we Brits traditionally do: *Sinjun*.

I step forward and shake the hand she's extending, feeling a flush of relief that she, like this entire setup, looks professional to a fault and not in the slightest bit seedy. There is absolutely nothing about Camille St John or these lavishly appointed, perfectly situated offices that scream *brothel*.

Just like Anton promised me, this is a classy outfit without the merest suspicion of sex in the air.

Once my flat white has been procured and we've seated ourselves at the small round conference table at one end of the room, Camille clicks on a small remote control, rendering the glass windows completely opaque. It's the first reminder that what we're about to discuss is of a delicate nature.

'Thank you for filling out the questionnaire,' she says.

'Of course.'

The questionnaire was... comprehensive. It covered not only my and my business' professional needs, but my personal needs, too. My car-crash of a sexual history, with its gaping hole. My appetites. My kinks. My expectations of what a Seraph executive assistant could provide. But apparently, I got the abridged version, coming to the agency as I was as a personal friend of Anton's.

I get it, obviously. This is serious stuff, not to be messed with. Still, it's unsettling to know that this stranger knows as much about my sex life as I knew about that of my more communicative parishioners, once upon a time.

'You have an EA currently, I understand?' she asks, glancing up from her laptop.

'Yes, but she's transitioning out. She's been my father's EA for years, and she's decided to take the opportunity to cut back on her workload, so she'll be his PA for this next phase.' I stifle a smile. Dad's ancient EA, Gladys, is pretty much the antithesis of everything I hope to get from my Seraph EA. If a dinosaur could also be a dragon, you'd have Gladys. I've tried to make it work for a good nine months now, but really she's a glorified PA, better suited to booking plane tickets than trying her hand at anything remotely strategic.

'Understood. And can I ask if you see this as a transition opportunity for Rath Mor, too?'

Rath Mór. Great Success. My father dropped the *fada* over the *o* but retained the rest of the phrase to encapsulate the Midas touch that he and my grandfather have had over the decades.

'Most definitely.' I cross my legs. 'My father's way of doing business was old school. Our entire estate management system needs an urgent overhaul, not to mention the hundreds of projects we need to get off the ground.' Projects that keep me awake at night (when I'm not passed out in a sex club, that is). Archive digitisation and sustainability initiatives and real-time occupancy rate tracking and centralised databases and maintenance predictions and upgraded procurement systems.

The vastness, the complexity, of what needs to be done hovers at the edge of my consciousness day and night, singeing my brain with its impossible, overwhelming immensity.

She nods briskly, as though what I've said is something she can easily accommodate. 'One of the main advantages of hiring your EA through Seraph is that they all have MBAs from the top schools. These women aren't just there to book flights—the kinds of projects you've described are their jam. Some of the work they do is more akin to what you can expect from a COO or a chief of staff, and if you have those positions in-house, you can absolutely have your EA work with them, too, if that's what you want. In fact, we find that many of our clients end up hiring PAs or other assistants to take some of the more administrative work off their EAs' hands so they can make optimal use of them.'

She's talking purely about her EAs' day jobs, but I can't help a small frisson at the unintentional reminder that there will be other ways in which I'll want to optimise my EA's time.

'That sounds amazing. My father employed some great people, but I'll want to build my own team, too.'

'Of course you will.'

I'm already drawn to her unflappable air of competence. If nothing else, I bet any of the women on her books can whip Rath Mor into shape with ease.

'If I were to ask you,' she says next, 'on a scale of one to ten, how confident you feel running this business you've inherited as things stand today, what would you say?'

'Six,' I say after a small hesitation. 'I have a business degree, but it's very rusty. I've really only been dealing with parish finances for the past few years. The only reason that number's not lower is because I obviously still have the team my dad built, so to some extent the business can trundle on like it's been doing while I take stock. And I have my dad and my brother around, too, if I really need help. It's a family business. I've grown up around it, so it's familiar to me at a high level, but getting to grips with the nuts and bolts of it is a different ballgame.'

After probably twenty more minutes of working through my business needs, my character and my preferred working methods in broad brushstrokes, Camille taps a nail on the polished walnut of the table and gives me a little smile.

'So, I understand you're particularly interested in interviewing Athena Davenport?'

I instantly feel self-conscious, like I'm some slimy fuck who's trying to backchannel his way into a woman's knickers.

'Well, I mean—I don't know her at all, personally. It's just that she came very highly... recommended by Anton. And by Max Hunter.' My voice sounds strangled even to me. It's unbelievably weird to be sitting here, opposite a total stranger, discussing in polite, professional terms my interest in hiring a woman who we're both painfully aware will be paid to suck my dick in between setting up charitable foundations and automating reporting systems.

It seems Camille can read my discomfort, and a part of me hopes it furthers my case if I don't come across as some slick sexual predator.

'Athena is a very special woman,' she tells me now. 'She really is. She's one of the most articulate, intellectually nimble and generally competent human beings I've had the privilege of working with. And she's always interested in getting to know new sectors, so what I sense feels like a bit of a mess from where you're sitting, if that's not an overstep, would be a dream come true for her.'

I let out a breath. 'You had me at competent,' I joke lamely. 'Is she... available?'

'She's employed currently, but I understand Mr Wolff put a call in to her himself, and she's happy to meet with you.'

Good. That's good.

'Is it helpful if I run through how our process works?' she asks.

'Please,' I say, because this "process" has been shrouded in mystery from the moment Anton set up this meeting, and I find myself totally out of my depth. All I know is that I've already paid six figures to get myself on Seraph's books and that if Athena or one of her colleagues agrees to work for me I will find myself in some kind of professional and sexual nirvana with nary a headache again.

'Of course. In a moment, I'll leave you to peruse Athena's files online.' She nods to the end of the room, where there's a white leather swivel chair and a desk with a large iMac. 'These will include her CV, which I can of course email to you, as well as anonymous references from her previous Seraph clients and a series of photographs of her, including some of an intimate nature.'

The heat rises to my neck at the mere thought of it.

Holy fuck.

'It's our policy not to share any photographs of our candidates digitally, to ensure their complete protection, but you should take as much time as you like in here, and there are tissues'—she nods delicately towards the desk—'should you need them. I've also taken the liberty of pulling two other candidates' files should you not feel as though Athena is the right fit for you or your business at this stage, and you're welcome to access those, too, from the home screen.'

'Thank you,' I say weakly.

'Should you wish to proceed,' she continues, 'we have a strictly prescribed hiring process. At the first stage, you would invite the candidate to your offices, where you can conduct your interview according to your hiring policies. At this point, you are also welcome to have her sit down with other members of your team.

'Of course, this stage is not just a chance to find you the perfect executive assistant but a preliminary opportunity for you to assess the extent of your sexual attraction to the candidate in the flesh. We would ask, though, that all your questions at this point pertain only to her ability to execute her role as executive assistant.'

I nod my understanding. *Got it.*

'You'll understand, Mr Sullivan, that everything we do is geared towards the safety and wellbeing of our candidates. Therefore, whomever you've met with is welcome to walk away at this stage, or indeed any stage.

'If, however, you're both happy to proceed, then the next round of the hiring process is a dinner where you can both discuss the more intimate parts of your proposed contract. Frank communication between the two of you is strongly encouraged at this point to set expectations and establish boundaries. The candidate will be interviewing you just as much as you are interviewing her, and it's my experience that she is far more likely to walk away from this stage than you are.'

'Yeah.' I clear my throat. 'Yes. That's fine, of course.'

'Good. We usually hold these dinners in a private spot in a selection of trusted hotels, and we reserve a suite in the same hotel for your use. Directly after supper, if you're both happy to proceed based on your conversation, you and she can make use of the suite to explore the sexual side of the interview.'

I begin to gape and quickly clamp my jaw shut. Anton mentioned something about this in passing, but still. It's all so... *transactional.* I mean, of course it is. But the idea of sitting across from a woman at dinner when I haven't been on a proper date in donkey's years and spelling out for her all the things I want to do to her before taking her upstairs for a fucking test drive is confronting. It really is.

It's also, for some reason, incredibly arousing.

I have to force myself to ask the next question.

'Is there a prescribed format for that part, too?'

A tiny smile. 'No. That's down to you. We ask that she establish a safeword and that you honour it.'

'Okay.'

'You've already paid your retainer, for which I thank you. You may see and interview as many candidates as you like, but for every candidate you take to the second round, there is a twenty-five thousand pound fee that goes straight to her. This is to ensure that none of our clients take gratuitous liberties with our candidates.'

It makes sense, and I like that they have this measure in place. Ugh. I imagine some dirty bastards would work their way through every woman on Seraph's books otherwise.

'That sounds reasonable,' I say.

'Excellent.' She pushes her chair back. 'Now, unless you have any other questions, I'll pull up Athena's details for you and leave you to it.'

CHAPTER 4

Gabe

Viewing Athena's files is akin to being a lobster in a gently simmering vat of water. At least, that's what I conclude as I look at the Contents page at the start of the document. My journey of discovery will take me, apparently, from her CV and professional references through to something called Intimate References, which simultaneously has my skin crawling and my blood heating. I'm sure it'll fluff me up nicely before I look at the Images section.

As I read through her opening statement and the rest of her CV, it quickly becomes apparent to me that this woman is not only disgustingly accomplished but grotesquely overqualified to assist anyone.

She went to school in a number of European countries—the daughter of two cultural attachés, apparently—and speaks French, German and Italian fluently. After that, she finished up her secondary education one year early at the unimpeachable Cheltenham Ladies' College and read Classics at Balliol, Oxford.

After only two years at Bain instead of the requisite three

years for MBA entry, the Sorbonne accepted her for their MBA programme from which, reading between the lines of her employment history, she was plucked by Seraph.

Camille was certainly telling the truth about Athena's capacity for work that goes far beyond administrative duties. Her CV is a list of her achievements: projects led and foundations established and corporation-wide systems overhauled. I bet she did it all without breaking a sweat. While the company names are withheld, I note that she hasn't worked for many bulge-bracket firms since Bain, Wolff excepted.

Either Seraph doesn't operate within those companies, or it's a function of Athena's own admission in her opening statement: she seeks to gain as much of an education as possible from the access her position gives her.

I choose not to linger on the word *access*.

Her first position was in Paris, it seems. She then worked for a 'conglomerate' which I'd guess was Anton's company, Wolff Holdings. After that, she was at some kind of tech firm and now holds a position in the renewable sector.

There's no doubt this woman would overhaul Rath Mor more quickly than you could say *dinosaur*.

I skim through the professional references. They are as glowing, as grateful, as I imagined they'd be.

The next section—the *Intimate References*—makes for uncomfortable reading. I'm desperate to click through to her photos, ravenous to see what a woman this accomplished, this polished, this adored by Max and Anton, looks like. But I don't. Instead, I force myself to dwell on the pithy soundbites laid out on the page in elegant quote marks, as if I'm reading a selection of verdicts from restaurant critics and not horny businessmen. They're horrifying and arousing in equal measure, a kind of sick boys' club where we're all winking and high-fiving each other over our excellent choices.

"Athena fucks like a dream and took absolutely everything I gave her."

"Athena is that rare woman who is even filthier than me. She led a lot of our fantasies together and pushed me beyond my limits."

I press my lips together. I can feel the judgement radiating from myself at these comments. I can't bear it, but neither can I look away. And with every dirty word I read, my anticipation ramps up.

It's the final review that has my dick thickening in my trousers.

"Do yourself a favour and, more importantly, do Athena a favour. <u>Unleash her.</u> Hiring this woman and just fucking her on your desk twice a week would be a travesty. It would be like buying a thoroughbred and making it do kiddy rides at the fair. THIS WOMAN LOVES DICK. She wants it from you. She wants it from your clients. She wants it from you IN FRONT OF your clients. Ask her yourself. Just promise me you won't treat her like the fragile little rose she looks like, because she will wilt and die."

I hit return, breathing heavily as the screen turns to a white page entitled *Images*. My skin is prickling, my dick now fully hard. What a disrespectful, nasty prick that last guy is. Emotions push through my veins like a twisted, toxic rope. I have no way of knowing whether he's telling the truth, whether he understands or respects Athena's needs at all, but I'm suddenly, uncomfortably, aware that this is the big leagues. This woman is experienced. She's done things I can't begin to imagine with some of the most powerful men in industry.

And if I go ahead with this insane scheme to hire her, I'll have to make it worth her while.

In every way.

I click through, and I almost laugh.

The build-up to this moment has been ridiculous. Athena has been lauded as the most competent employee and incredible fuck, and I honestly didn't know what to expect. Some AI concoction of the perfect woman, I suppose.

But not this.

The young woman gazing back at me from the head and shoulders portrait is beautiful in a way that makes the word feel meaningless and trite. It's clearly a business photograph. Her auburn hair is in an updo loose enough to showcase its natural wave. She's in what looks like a black dress with a modest crewneck, a simple strand of pearls at her neck and pearl studs in her ears. Her makeup is light. Tasteful.

She looks like the daughter of diplomats, that's for sure.

She looks like she belongs in a fucking Ferrero Rocher ad.

But none of that matters, because her face alone is its own best advocate. She's not merely hot or sexy or enticing—she's classically, ethereally, achingly beautiful in a way that appears to be down to the perfect alchemy of her huge hazel eyes and delicate bone structure and shapely nose and rosebud mouth.

It's an elite, untouchable kind of beauty. The kind that would make a man wary even of approaching her if he saw her in a bar. A flawless loveliness that belongs on centuries-old frescos and one that I absolutely cannot square with the filthy, carnal, animalistic things those men said about her.

That this woman sells her body for money is the biggest head fuck I've ever had.

That she sells it for seven figures a year and has men like Anton and Max drooling over her memory years after their paths crossed is marginally less shocking, I suppose.

The next photo is a similar crop, but this time she's makeup free. Her hair is loose, and I can see it is indeed wavy, trailing past the bottom of the image. I'm no expert, but it looks professionally blowdried and very, very glossy. If it wasn't for the thin black bra straps, I'd think she was naked.

Her skin is clear, that rosebud mouth slightly open and just as pink without its light sheen of lipstick. There are the faintest shadows under her eyes, and they make her look even younger. More fragile. That she allegedly enjoys being gang-banged is a thought I can't allow myself to entertain, not when I'm hard like this. And, despite my throbbing erection, I slip into priest mode, asking myself the questions I would have asked about any member of my flock.

Is she vulnerable? Has she had sufficient agency with these men? Does she have someone to advocate for her? To keep her safe?

The next shot is, God help me, a full-length image against a white backdrop: Athena, barefaced and barefooted, naked except for a sheer black bra and what looks like a thong. It's a simple pose, not provocative. She's standing still, hands hanging loose at her sides, feet together. Sheer lingerie aside, there's absolutely nothing porno about it, yet it's oddly confronting.

I think it's the lack of artifice. Once again, she looks young and fragile and untouched, and I have the distinct impression that I'm looking at something—some*one*—I shouldn't. If the effect Seraph is going for is intoxicatingly forbidden, then these people are diabolical indeed.

She's on the slim slide, with a slender waist and fuller hips, but she's not gym-honed at all. Her skin is pale and flawless aside from a smattering of moles on her stomach that look positively decorative. There's little muscle definition. Her breasts are heavy, the outlined nipples full. Her stomach is a soft swell.

A man could lay his weary head between those breasts or on that stomach and feel thoroughly, happily contented.

I let my gaze run over the photo as I palm my dick through my trousers. Suddenly, the box of tissues Camille pointed out makes a lot more sense. There is absolutely nothing about this picture I don't like. No doubt about it, Athena Davenport is a stunning woman.

The arrow at the bottom of the screen is still black. Looks like there are more images to see.

Oh holy fuck.

Dear, blessed Father in Heaven, I know not what I do... because I was *not* expecting *this*.

Athena, perched on a tall stool.

Utterly, wonderfully naked.

She's sitting upright, eyes wide, lips still parted, that same, neutral expression on her face. This time, it strikes me as more disingenuous. More *dangerous*.

Her toes are propped up on the rungs of the stool, her knees wide. That beautiful auburn hair hangs loose, trailing over what are indeed glorious breasts, their rosy nipples now tightly furled.

She's cupping a breast with one hand while, with the other, she reaches between her legs and opens herself up for the camera with her fingers.

I zoom in.

So help me God, I zoom in like a frenzied madman, so I can enjoy the glossy pinkness of her bare cunt, exposed for *me*, for *my* viewing pleasure. I stare at it, palming my cock harder. I absolutely will not be that man who gets himself off in someone's office to pornographic images of a beautiful woman with whom he has not yet entered into a contractual relationship.

I will *not*.

But there's something so deeply arresting about this juxtaposition of Athena's facial inscrutability and the wantonness, the brazenness of her pose.

It feels less like an invitation than a challenge.

A challenge to try in vain to resist her.

And it's clear, simply from the miraculous arrangement of pixels in front of me, that I will fall at that first hurdle.

CHAPTER 5

Athena

The French have two phrases they use when they want to wish someone good luck: *bonne chance*, for when one's fate lies in the hands of the gods, and *bon courage*, for when your success will come down to your personal level of fortitude.

It's the latter I need when I first meet a prospective employer. Not only is walking into the offices of someone who might be your new boss *and* your new fuck particularly surreal, but the interview dynamic is a tough one to get right.

Women often have to fight not to be treated as a sexual object in the corporate world. Most of us would demand, or at least hope, that any interviewer for a new job would focus on our qualifications for the position and not on our looks. In this instant, however, I will sit down with a man to discuss his professional needs and my professional suitability while both of us imagine each other naked on a constant loop.

It's a lot. Even the dress code is a tough one to get right: professional rather than provocative but not totally sexless.

The elephant in the room at first-round Seraph interviews tends to be more of a T-Rex. A T-Rex who asks *does he want to put his dick inside me badly enough to offer me a job* and *can I tolerate being stuffed full of him enough to say yes?*

I'm not sure why I'm nervous this morning. On paper, this is a no-brainer. I've worked for Steve long enough to know that renewables, while superbly positioned for future growth, aren't my jam. The sector isn't for the faint of heart. Someone else comes up with better technology, which they inevitably do, and you're toast.

More pertinently, this guy I'm meeting today, Mr Sullivan, is clearly an upgrade—unless he's been a cleric for so long he's forgotten how to use his dick, that is. Everything I've seen of him online shows me he is hot as fuck. Steve, on the other hand, is perfectly fine but nothing to write home about looks-wise. Our sexual relationship is highly regimented: he has a strong preference for being able to dictate the circumstances in which he gets intimate.

I get it, and I've grown surprisingly fond of him (or as fond as I grow of anyone). He's insanely smart and generous to a fault with his information. I've learned a tonne from him, and I truly relish our intellectual back-and-forths. Sexually and career-wise, though, I'm in a rut. So I should be champing at the bit to get my hands on this job... and this guy.

It's just that going into a new role with a new boss can be fraught. Given the salary I command, I aim to hit the ground running, professionally and sexually. There isn't ever time to get my feet under the table properly, and I find it takes a huge physical and emotional toll on me. Again, it's a lot, and if I take this challenge on I'll have to be even more disciplined with my sleep and nutrition regimes than I have been since I got comfortable with Steve.

This morning, I've taken the step of turning the Eras Tour on on my TV while I get ready. Usually, I have CNBC or Bloomberg on in the background to get me up to speed on any overnight news out of the US and Asia, but today I require a proverbial kick up the arse.

Taylor Swift is not just about the music for me, fantastic though it is. She's a walking, singing example of what we can achieve when we keep our eye on the prize. Her work ethic and her commitment to excellence are second to none. She keeps her head down. She pushes herself. She moves forward. She dreams big. She does what needs to be done, and she does it with boundaries and grace and humility.

So when I'm feeling uncharacteristically vulnerable or apprehensive or my usual drive eludes me, I watch her command tens of thousands of people and I remind myself that star quality might be innate but that hard fucking work gets you what you want and where you want.

This job is a stepping stone.

This *guy* is a stepping stone.

I have a vision, and I'm already so far ahead of the rest of my MBA class in terms of the salary I command and the access I enjoy and the trajectory I have that it's laughable. After another three or four years of doing this, I'll have my pick of C-suite jobs and I won't have to endure years of middle management along the way.

I slide my iPad into my handbag. The car I booked is waiting for me downstairs, and I'm confident the traffic will allow for ample time for me to go over the copious notes I've made on Mr Sullivan's background, the growth and IPO of Sullivan Construction, and the spin-off of the estate into Rath Mor.

One last glance in the mirror confirms all I need to know.

My lipstick is perfect.

And my future is blinding.

There's always a moment in this job: *that* moment when you catch your first glimpse of him in the flesh.

I've seen photos of Mr Sullivan already, obviously, through my research, but it's always different seeing them in person.

Rath Mor's offices are located in a beautiful Georgian building on Berkeley Square, right across the square from the infamous members' club Annabel's. So far, so much better than Steve Goodall's offices in Swindon. The interiors are plush and old school. Their thickly padded cream carpets and wood panels and perfectly lit art scream *private bank,* but the overall effect is less stuffy than reassuringly opulent.

I'd put money on that being a real Twombly behind the reception desk. My parents, who are cultural attachés, were pivotal in making his posthumous exhibition at the Centre Pompidou in Paris happen a few years back.

This guy may have been a priest, but he enjoys expensive, alluring things.

Noted.

I see him a second or two before he spots me. He strides out into the reception area from a corridor on the left at a brisk pace, an unasked question on his face as he looks to his receptionist. And in the moment before our eyes meet, my brain downloads him like a 3D scanner.

Taller than I expected.

Lean build.

Good posture.

That's a custom suit, probably Savile Row, and he wears it *well.*

Somehow, his face looks more open, less intense, than that photo I enjoyed so thoroughly of him as a priest.

Still, I'm not the only one who's tightly wound. I can sense his nervous energy from here.

And finally...

He is seriously fucking hot.

I rise as he turns towards me, preempting him, smoothing the skirt of my dress over my thighs as I do.

'Ah, Athena,' he says, clocking me. There's no way to miss the rapid—and likely involuntary—sweep he does of my body before meeting my eyes. He approaches, hand outstretched, with what I know he intends as a reassuring smile on his face. 'So good of you to come in. How do you do?'

I know this guy comes from new money, from at least two generations of proudly self-made Irishmen. Perhaps that explains his friendliness, but in this instant the elite education his family wealth has afforded him at Ampleforth and then Durham University is also evident.

Socially assured, but with that Irish charm?

It's a deadly combination.

We shake. 'Thank you so much for having me, Mr Sullivan,' I say, my voice clear and steady. 'It's wonderful to meet you.'

I've been in training for moments like this my entire life. Every gala I've attended in the kind of icy imperial splendour that only Vienna can boast; every visiting cultural delegate with whom I've had to make sparkling small talk; every opening night at L'Opéra in the presence of artists and money men alike: they've all taught me how to produce precisely the right social reaction for every given situation.

'It's Gabriel or Gabe, please,' he says, turning and gesturing towards the corridor from which he appeared. 'Don't make me feel any more like my father than I already do.'

He takes my coffee order and relays it to the receptionist before ushering me down the corridor and through an antechamber featuring an empty desk to his office. I take it in quickly: it's a large, well-lit room with the same panelled walls and cream carpet as in reception, except that these walls are painted a rich midnight blue. I assume that space we just came through is where I would sit if I worked here. There are two doors off to the right, both shut.

I'm here to sell my powers as an executive assistant, but I can't help but run through in my mind how the sexual side would work. The partition between this room and my area is glass, but the door and wall leading out to the corridor are solid. It's a good start. His desk is huge and solid oak, with presumably ample room for me to slide underneath it if I wanted to suck him off, and there's a large sofa against the far wall.

I've worked with worse.

At his signal, I take a seat in front of his desk and cross my legs, placing my handbag on the ground next to me. I've opted for my interview staple of a fitted navy shift dress in supple wool crepe from Victoria Beckham. It's just as formal as a suit, and squarely work attire, but the exquisitely sharp tailoring is most definitely cut to celebrate a woman's body.

The main agenda of this meeting may be defined, but there's a shitload of subtext, and I intend to make that subtext speak very, very clearly. I have good reason to be confident about my prospects if I nail this morning's interview. Camille reported back to me that Mr Sullivan—Gabriel—emerged from perusing my portfolio somewhat gruff of voice and with his overcoat held firmly in place in front of his crotch.

So he was turned on, but he didn't avail himself of the tissues. How very Catholic of him. Every sperm is sacred—isn't that how it goes?

I've also seen the full notes from their meeting. I know how out of his depth he feels, and I sympathise. He's emerged from what was supposed to be a lifelong vocation only to spearhead a company that's loaded with potential but is really a bit of a mess. He was probably severely institutionalised in the priesthood, and I imagine his business degree feels far, far away.

All I have to do, therefore, is wow him with my understanding of his needs and my business acumen and persuade him that I can take every single professional headache off his plate—and that's all before we get to the next round—the part where I fuck him free of every *personal* headache, too.

CHAPTER 6

Gabe

I f this was a usual type of interview, I'd be berating myself for objectifying my interviewee quite so shame-lessly. As it is, I allow myself to be just a little transfixed by the assured, beautiful young woman sitting in front of me.

I draw the line at pulling up that provocative image of her naked and holding herself open from my spank bank, though. That's a bridge I absolutely will not cross this morning.

Even so, it's the oddest thing to know that she's essentially interviewing to fuck me as well as to work for me. It feels equal parts miraculous and profoundly wrong that a princely sum of money is all that's required for me to get intimate with her.

Because there is no denying she's a prize of the greatest magnitude, but it's my bank balance, rather than my worth as a man, that will ultimately dictate my success here.

I really must concentrate, because I am in dire need of a fine strategic brain to assist me with the multitude of responsi-bilities I face, and while the team I inherited is perfectly fine (the ancient Gladys aside), I'm yet to make a senior hire since I took over.

Putting the right team around me is vital to the success of

this legacy I'm stewarding, and everything coming out of Athena's mouth tells me she could do this job standing on her head. She'd preempt everything I need; I can just tell. She'd nail her allocated workload, and it wouldn't surprise me if she jumped into a whole host of extra projects just for the thrill of it.

Still. It's surprisingly hard to concentrate, surprisingly difficult to separate my search for the perfect executive assistant with the strictly off-limits part of this interview: the knowledge that I'm essentially sizing someone up to be my main fuck buddy for the foreseeable future.

Athena's beauty, you see, is the kind that's impossible to ignore. It's everything her portfolio promised and more, because static images can never compete with the perfection of features like these when they're in motion.

It's not just the size of her big, thickly lashed hazel eyes that's captivating but the way they shine when she summarises a particularly taxing analysis she undertook recently on hydrogen fuel cells.

It's not just the lustrousness of her long, thick auburn hair, but the way she keeps flicking it impatiently over her shoulder as if it's cramping her style.

It's not just the lushness of her body, swathed in enough expensive wool to be perfectly professional, but the expressive grace with which she uses her hands to hammer her points home.

It's not just the pink rosebud mouth, which was appealing enough in the photos but now undulates in a way far more sensuous than her businesslike delivery probably intends.

That's the thing. This woman is not flirting in the slightest. She's solely in business mode, and it's compelling. It's compelling partly because of her staggering looks, which feels unfair to her because her allure in this moment is so much more than that.

She's not manic—not in the least bit. She's far too assured for that, too self-controlled. But there's an energy there, a drive that's impossible to miss. She's dynamic in a way that's seriously impressive. The extensive prep she's done for our interview shows, and her enthusiasm is undeniably infectious. In this moment, she's every inch the star MBA student from one of Europe's best schools, and I know she's exactly what this fucking place needs.

That her face and her voice and her body are one bewitching siren's call should be beside the point.

Should be.

But she's not a stereotypical MBA student, and this is not a stereotypical position, and those looks of hers aren't incidental. They're integral to this pitch she's making to me that she's worth a salary tens of times higher than this position would otherwise warrant.

None of this is to judge her. Lord, no. After all, she's playing to her strengths in spectacular style. She's the real deal, the fantasy that's equally intoxicating to the businessman in me who's drowning professionally and to the flesh-and-blood man.

One thing has quickly become clear. This role will morph into something far beyond its basic requirements if Athena takes it on. I may not be experienced in business, but I *am* experienced in people. If an individual as promising as her shows up, I'm going to maximise her potential.

In the day job, that is.

I've been sitting perfectly still, fingers interlaced over my stomach, listening to her speak for a couple of minutes. Listening is another area of expertise I honed during my previous career, but rarely is it as pleasurable as this. Rarely in my parish prayer meetings or in the confessional was I this avid.

'It's clear you're incredibly capable,' I say now, 'and that you like to get your teeth into things. There'll be a lot of that here. We're very much still in a transition phase, and I'm finding myself so busy fighting fires and improving on the most glaring problems that I haven't had much of a chance to get on the front foot with what's really the fun stuff—that is, building out how I want this estate to function for the next generation or two.'

'I can definitely help with that.'

'And I'd love your help. Once you had full access, how would you go about identifying which projects we should prioritise?'

I can see the machinations whirring in her head as she tilts it. 'Well, the most efficient way would be if I drew up an initial, high level transition plan within a couple of weeks of starting. And then—'

'What would happen if we took a bit more time?'

She frowns. 'In my experience, expediency is the preferred route, as long as it doesn't risk sloppiness. And it sounds like we have no time to waste, if you're still feeling like you're on the back foot after almost a year in the role.'

I smile inwardly at her use of *we* and lean back in my chair, studying her intently.

'I'm a very patient man, Athena. Expediency isn't always the best route. Sometimes, taking it slowly is far more rewarding.'

I pause. Sink my teeth into my bottom lip.

She stares at me, pressing her palms to her thighs, the silence stretching between us like a taut, living thing.

'After all,' I say after a moment, 'nothing is more important than getting the job done properly, is it? I don't like a rushed job. I'm nothing if not... thorough.'

Our gazes are still locked, and I'd swear I'm responsible for that flush on her cheeks. If I've managed to fluster the professional with a couple of unfairly made innuendos, then I'm less rusty than I thought.

'Absolutely.' She shifts slightly in her chair before clearing her throat. 'Yes, I—of course. I'd aim to be efficient while prioritising excellence and, um, rigour above everything else.'

I shoot her what I intend to be a smooth smile. 'Excellent.'

CHAPTER 7

Gabe

If I'm still slightly embarrassed by how quickly I called Camille after Athena left my offices yesterday morning, then I'm also ecstatic at how quickly Camille called me back to confirm a dinner with Athena tonight.

Even if she'd looked like Gladys, I would have got down on my knees and begged her to take the job and put me out of my misery.

As it is, I'm thrilled to report that she looks nothing like Gladys and is, if her presence across the table from me is any proof, open to taking this process to the next round.

Upstairs.

We're dining in an intimate alcove in the excellent seafood restaurant at The Montague Hotel in Knightsbridge. It's an elegant, discreet restaurant, perfect for clandestine dates or morally ambiguous 'job' interviews. Around us floats a soundtrack of dinner jazz and low voices and cutlery being employed.

I was waiting at the restaurant's bar when Athena arrived, a fact that seemed to surprise her. It was worth it to enjoy the view of her walking across the stylish space in a dress that's far sexier than the one she wore yesterday while being far too classy to hint that her profession might be the oldest one of all. It was black lace, hitting just below the knee and fitted enough to showcase her fantastic curves. I didn't miss the appreciative, curious glances she got from both men and women, and the hit of intense smugness I experienced when she stopped in front of me and allowed me to kiss her on both cheeks was decidedly unchristian.

'You know,' I say conversationally once our champagne has been poured, 'you're the first woman I've taken out to dinner for years and years. Aside from my mother, that is. Oh, and the Mother Superior from our local convent in Willesden once or twice.'

She gives me a sardonic smile. 'I'm honoured.'

'Don't be. Mum tells me my dinner conversation is terrible. But I'll try not to talk about Scripture too much tonight.'

'That would probably set the wrong tone,' she muses.

There's a pause while we each take a sip of our champagne. She's surveying me with something akin to low-level amusement, I think. It's as if she can smell my nerves, as if she knows exactly how apprehensive I am about this conversation. I'm sure she's not apprehensive at all. I'm hoping this is very firmly in her comfort zone—in fact, I'm counting on it.

'I hope you can tell me how the fuck this thing is going to work, because I haven't got a bloody clue.'

She sets down her glass, narrowing her eyes. 'Please tell me you're not talking about your dick, because that would be very disappointing.'

I bark out a shocked laugh, both at the fact that she's gone there so soon and at her perfectly deadpan delivery. My guffaw is loud enough that a woman at the nearest table glances over in alarm.

'No. I'm pretty well versed in how that works.'

'Are you sure?' She arches a perfectly groomed eyebrow. 'You can take the guy out of the priesthood...'

So this is how it's going to be. I needn't worry about transitioning from our mostly formal conversation yesterday to something darker and hotter and slicker, because she's already setting the tone. It makes sense, I suppose. I'd hardly expect her to clutch her pearls.

'I promise. Anton's had me in training for this. *Hard.*'

At Anton's name, something flickers across her face. Agitation, maybe. She looks a little flustered. 'That's one hell of a visual,' she murmurs, and I shake my head, diverted.

'He signed me up to Alchemy.'

'Oh, yes. That'll do the trick.'

We're silent again for a moment, then she says, 'In terms of how this works, the answer is that it works however you'd like it to work, and it can be fluid.'

I nod. 'Without breaking confidentiality, can you give me any idea of how you've managed in the past?'

'It really depends on my employer. I've only had four placements so far. Some of them liked the kink factor, obviously. As in, the actual fact that they were paying me to fuck them whenever they wanted was the primary appeal.'

I nod again, reaching desperately for my champagne flute. Jesus. Having this conversation sober and dispassionately and face to face with this beautiful, sexy woman will be harder than I've anticipated. I wonder if she can see how out of my depth I am.

'Often, I'm a tool. An upper or a downer. In the same way that leaders with a lot of responsibility might deal with it by snorting coke, or drinking too early in the day, or having a masseur or a chiropractor or a PT, depending on how health-conscious they are, other guys use women like me to screw it all out of their system. They need to fluff themselves up before a big meeting—they fuck me. They need to celebrate a win or get over a bad meeting—they fuck me. It's amazing just how many professional headaches can be eliminated by an excellent blowjob.'

She pauses, and I focus very hard on not reacting outwardly, because the fact that my reality will soon consist of a woman who looks like Athena getting on her knees for me whenever I want during the working day is really breaking my brain.

'Some guys want me as a trophy. And,' she continues with an elegant little shrug, 'some guys just want efficiency. Or productivity. The ones who are less patient than you, naturally.'

She gives me a teasing smile that I find I like a lot. She didn't smile much yesterday, but she's undoubtedly more mellow this evening.

'You talked a good game about productivity yesterday, Athena. But the way you look is going to be by far the biggest risk to any productivity I might have.'

'You'd be surprised.' She licks her lips. 'Don't underestimate me—or yourself. All those transition reports I said I could draw up for you? You can read them while I'm under your desk, sucking yo—'

I lean forward, cutting her off. When I speak, my eyes are on her little pink mouth and my voice is lower, gruffer, than I've intended. 'If you think I'd be able to focus on *anything* but you when you were getting me off, you are far more naïve than I thought you were. Remember what I told you? Sometimes slow is way better.'

The smile she shoots me is self-satisfied. 'So that *was* an innuendo yesterday. You were fucking with me. I couldn't be completely sure.'

I sigh. 'A parish priest has to be almost as patient as a lifer in prison. I was telling the truth. I am a patient man.' A pause.

'But yeah, I was fucking with you. Just a little bit. I wanted to see if I could get a rise out of you.'

'I like that.' She hesitates and looks down, twirling the stem of her glass between her fingers. 'As soon as you said that, I imagined your mouth between my legs and your hand on my stomach, holding me down while you took your time with me.'

A muscle clenches, low and insistent, in my belly.

I realise she's paid to do this. I realise it's her job, and she's very, very good at it. I realise she's essentially an echo chamber for my ego and my desires.

But God if it doesn't feel real when she says things like that.

More pertinently, real or not, it seems like it's going to happen tonight.

'Good. I wanted you to imagine that, because I was imagining that too.'

She looks up at me, her face rapt. 'I was a little worried you'd be holier than thou.'

I roll my eyes. 'The fact that I'm trying to hire you suggests otherwise.'

'Touché. And now that you've brought it up, why don't you start by telling me exactly how a man who used to be a priest comes to an agency like Seraph. Maybe then we can work out how "this thing" is going to work. It might give me a starting point for how I can help you, at least.'

'Did Anton tell you anything?' I ask, watching her face. 'I know he put in a call.'

Her mouth twists in amusement. 'He said you were struggling with burning the candle at both ends—you traumatised one of the cleaners at Alchemy, I believe?'

I suck in a rueful breath through my teeth. 'You could say that, yeah. Anton and Max suggested I might do better to optimise my workdays, shall we say. They both spoke very highly of you.'

She shoots me a proper smile, and it is absolutely dazzling. 'Ahh, Max. He's a bad, bad boy.'

If the nostalgia she seems to be indulging in behind that smile is any indication, she really does enjoy the sexual part of her job. That should assuage my lingering guilt over paying this woman for sex, but I do *not* enjoy the pique that hits me right in my gut. 'So I've heard. Totally reformed now, of course,' I add hurriedly, lest her stroll down memory lane turn X-rated. 'Completely loved up, twice over.'

'I saw that. Wonders will never cease. But yes, those two definitely knew how to "optimise" their working day. And you want to do the same, I assume?'

I hesitate. 'I won't pretend this is a no-brainer for me. From celibacy to paying for sex is a far bigger moral leap than I could ever have seen myself making, and I'm working through a lot of shit related to that. But'—I sigh—'I'm damned anyway. I'm very far from celibate these days, and the Seraph proposition is extremely attractive. As are you, obviously.'

She leans forward, giving me an excellent view of the shadow of her cleavage. 'Gabriel. I can't pretend to know what you've been through during this transition but I can assure you, there's no need to feel any guilt on my account. This is purely transactional, just like you hiring me as a regular EA would be transactional.

'If anything, this should *relieve* you of any guilt you have around going after sex. You don't have to pretend you're going to call someone, or worry about leading her on. You're paying me. The boundaries are very clear, and I'm a professional. I can look after myself. You don't need to cuddle me after sex, or send me flowers, or worry about me falling for you. You fuck me, you pay me, that's that.' She sits back in her seat. 'When you think about it, it's pretty refreshing, actually.'

I smile at that. 'That's reassuring, thank you.'

'My pleasure,' she says coquettishly.

'Can I ask you a question? I realise you may not give me a genuine answer, but if you feel you can be honest, I'd appreciate it.'

'Of course. Honesty is very important.'

I'm galvanised by her response to Max Hunter's mention just now. She doesn't seem traumatised by whatever the fuck he and Anton did to her. On the contrary. 'Do you enjoy the sexual side of your job, or do you merely tolerate it? Is it just a means to an end?'

She gazes at me and worries her bottom lip between her teeth in a way that tells me she's giving my question serious consideration.

'If you want full honesty, then it's both. It's a rung on a ladder that everyone has to climb, only my ladder is steeper and gets me much, much further than most people's. But I enjoy the climb very much, and I've chosen this stage in my career very intentionally. I haven't been forced into it at all. I get unimaginable access to powerful, inspiring men and I learn more than I ever could as a graduate trainee.'

I watch her lips move as she enunciates the next part more deliberately. 'And, for the most part, I enjoy fucking powerful guys. I fucking love it. It turns me on to have them use me, to know that everyone wants a piece of them and they want *me*. These are men who command people's attention effortlessly, but I'm often the centre of *their* attention. Does that answer your question?'

It's answered my question so fully that I'm semi-hard under the table now. I believe her. She's bloody convincing.

'What do you enjoy the most?' I ask her, my voice low and rough. The restaurant around us is forgotten. There's only Athena and her beauty and her wantonness and her candour.

'I'll enjoy whatever you enjoy,' she recites, and I scoff.

'Athena. I wasn't born yesterday.'

'Fine. I told you. Being used. It's the filth of it that does it for me most of all. My current boss is very... sweet. Respectful. He worships me, which is lovely, but there's not much throw-down. I'm happy there, but I'd like to try a new sector. Which is why I agreed to meet with you.'

I don't let my eyes stray from hers, even for a second. 'I think we established yesterday that my company would present you with plenty of intellectual challenges.'

'Yes, we did.'

'So that's a given. Now, forget the sector for a second and *tell me what you like.*'

So help me God, I want to imagine it. I've met this woman twice and she's already got under my skin. I'm aware I have my work cut out.

How the hell can a guy who willingly abstained from sex for years begin to satisfy a woman like this, who is so in touch with her needs?

But I already know I want to. I already know *this* is what will be the kindling in my relationship with Athena, however transactional. This is what will bring purpose to my days:

Challenging her.

Commanding her.

Conquering her.

My tone has her huge eyes widening. It's almost as if she needed to hear that a man she must be thinking of as too virtuous for his own good is capable of speaking to her like that.

A server materialises with our Achill oysters and places the platter deferentially on the stand between us. When he's left us, I nod at her to continue.

'I like being your... property, I suppose,' she says more quietly. 'I love putting my business brain to good use while all the time knowing that I'm at your beck and call, that you'll treat me like nothing more than a set of warm, tight holes when I least expect it.'

I swallow at her debasing, hypnotic words. 'Go on.'

'I love that you can just shove me to my knees whenever you like, or prop me up on your desk and play with my pussy for hours while you make calls, teasing me and teasing me, but I can't make a sound. Or that you can lock your office door and get me on my hands and knees and fuck me, literally whenever you want. And my absolute favourite thing would be being your trophy.'

I shut my eyes for a moment, steeling myself to make it through at least the starter of this meal before shooting my load. I'm rock hard now. She mentioned the term *trophy* earlier, and I have a horrible feeling I know just where she's going with it.

'Tell me more about that,' I say, my throat tight with desire.

She pauses and picks up an oyster, adorning it with vinaigrette and lemon juice before raising her chin and tipping one down her throat. She swallows it whole—shocker—and I watch like a filthy pervert as the pale column of her throat contracts around it.

She licks her lips. 'Those are truly excellent. As I was saying, the trophy thing really gets me off. Think about it— what's the point of spending a million pounds a year on me if you don't get to have a little flex to your friends? I'm your biggest status symbol and your most lethal secret weapon.'

Under the table, I wipe my palm down my wool-covered thigh. I'm sweating. 'Go on.'

'If you want to show me off, you can. Play with me in front of your investors. Get me to strip. Lay me down in the middle of the fucking boardroom table and use me as a sushi platter for a lunch meeting—I'm down with it all. Think of how jealous they'd be that you have a fuck toy like me and they don't. Think of the bragging rights. Let them get stuck in, if you're feeling kind.' She lowers her voice until it's barely more than the most filthy, suggestive whisper. 'Or if a counterpart isn't playing ball, that's when you wheel me in. You can use me as a carrot, if you like. Get me on my knees in front of them and they'll sign whatever building permit or God knows what else you want.'

My mind is reeling. A woman more intelligent, more highly educated than the vast majority of the people I've interacted with—both within the Church and outside it—is hitting me with shot after depraved shot of sin and corruption and deviance and exploitation. The part of me that has always taken the pastoral needs of his flock to heart is horrified, but there's a darker, baser, part that's downright desperate for a better glimpse of this twisted dynamic she's describing.

I couldn't give a fuck about bragging rights—exploiting a woman like *that* to "flex", as she puts it, is anathema to me.

But the rest of it is hot as fuck.

Why is that?

Why is the picture she paints of me using her and enjoying her publicly and passing her around my friends so intoxicating? It's the power dynamic, I suppose. It's far less about establishing superiority over any business associates than it is about establishing power over her. Of being her master, of having such a spellbinding, impressive woman willing to do all of those things at a single command from me.

The realisation disgusts me, even while it has me hardening, impossibly, all the more. But what she's saying shouldn't come as a huge surprise to me, given that anonymous review that still burns my retinas.

THIS WOMAN LOVES DICK.
She wants it from you.
She wants it from your clients.

She wants it from you IN FRONT OF your clients.
Ask her yourself.

The shock, therefore, lies in hearing it from her own pretty little mouth. *This is what she wants.*

I asked her to tell me, and she's telling me. And I'm judging her, probably because of some antiquated, misogynistic assumption that women can't have obscenely high IQs *and* adore getting dicked down and probably also because I'm so terrified of how much *I* want everything she's just described that I daren't allow myself to believe that she might want it too, just as badly.

If Athena is telling the truth, then it seems like I may have to get used to her taking me to places I didn't even know to conceive of before.

As problems go, that's a high quality one.

CHAPTER 8

Athena

By the time we've finished our main course, my thong is soaked through. It's partly the topic of our dinner conversation that's done it, naturally. Recounting all the things that get me off the most in this unique role of mine turns me on every time, and I can only hope he's been listening as attentively as he seemed to be. Not sure I've ever met a guy who's as good and patient and thorough a listener as Fr Gabriel, although calling him that is *not* helpful to my current state of arousal.

I was brought up in a firmly atheist household, even if it was one that could fully appreciate the glory of Renaissance-era religious art. So I've spent very little time dwelling on priests or priest kinks or anything of that ilk aside from occasional musings on what a waste enforced celibacy is for *anyone*.

But give me a truly good man at war with his inner demons and I am a puddle on the floor. So watching Gabriel get quietly, steadily, involuntarily turned on by our conversation has been a truly exquisite sight to behold. It's hot as fuck when a guy is trying to uphold his morals while you bash them down, piece by piece, until they're useless rubble on the floor.

Right now, Gabriel Sullivan is that guy, surrounded by the pointless debris of *his* ethics and totally defenceless against *my* lack of them. And I want him like this. I want him so addled with desire, so tightly wound by the awful, relentless needs I've stirred up that he'll be unleashed when I get him upstairs.

He smiles tightly at me when the server has cleared away our plates. It's the smile of a man whose blood flow has vacated the top half of his body. 'Would you like to see the dessert menu?'

I'm the only dessert menu this guy is going to need this evening.

'I'm fine. Why don't we continue this conversation upstairs?'

Gabriel has fine blue eyes, like the true Irishman he is, but right now they're practically all pupil. 'Are you sure? You don't—wouldn't you like some time to think about it?'

'Believe me, I've had all the time I need. I'm perfectly sure. I want you to take me for a spin, Gabriel.'

He closes his eyes for a second. Gathering his inner strength? Praying to a God he almost certainly still converses with? I'd feel bad for the guy if I didn't know for sure that his evening is about to get a whole lot better.

When he opens them, there's a level of intent in their blue-black depths that he hasn't allowed himself until now. He's been the perfect gentleman, but it looks to me like he's about to turn full predator. I shiver a little.

'Apparently I should ask you for a safeword,' he says, his voice strangled.

I smile at him. 'Minerva.'

'Minerva.' He tries it on for size, but the halting way he says its syllables tells me he's missing the context.

'Minerva is the Roman equivalent of the goddess Athena,' I tell him, and his face brightens.

'Got it. I'm not so strong on my polytheistic gods.'

'I wouldn't expect you to be.'

'I can recite the names of Roman Catholic saints and martyrs ad nauseam, though,' he says. 'In fact, I've been reciting some of them in my head tonight in a vain attempt at staving off my—well. I'm sure you can imagine. Let's get you upstairs.'

He keeps a chivalrous hand on the small of my back as we walk through the beautifully festive hotel lobby to the lift. Around us, gold- and red-decked Christmas trees stand like sentinels, while fairy lights twinkle softly from wreaths and garlands.

I like the light weight of Gabriel's touch, and I fucking adore the anticipation that's coursing through me. I love that we look like a well-heeled couple, retiring to our suite, and that no one but us knows this esteemed gentleman is paying me five figures so he can rampage all over my body.

So far, we've talked dirty but played nicely. The gloves are about to come off—alongside every other scrap of clothing—and I'll get to see what this guy is capable of.

I really, really hope Catholics are as kinky and depraved as they're supposed to be—especially ones who have years of self-denial and shame and guilt to make up for.

We're not the only ones in the lift. Gabriel positions himself behind me in the back corner and puts his hands on the dip of my waist before sliding them down to bracket my hips and tugging me back against him. It's an assured move, a possessive one, even, and it feels so good after having only had handshakes and cheek kisses. He scoops my hair out of the way and dips his head so he can bury his face in the side of my neck.

He inhales hard.

'Those fucking photographs,' he growls in my ear, low enough so only I can hear. 'Have you any idea what they did to me?'

I giggle and push back against what is definitely a semi. 'I have some idea, yes.'

One of his hands slides around so he can palm my stomach, gluing us together. I've never understood why, but having a man's large hand splayed across my stomach, even through clothing, has always given me enormous pleasure. It feels anchoring and safe and, in this case, ominous in the sexiest possible way. Already, this feels less like an audition and more like a scorching one night stand with a tall, dark and hot-as-hell stranger.

'They gave me an idea,' he whispers enigmatically, and then we're excusing ourselves and easing our way out of the lift.

Gabriel swipes the keycard and holds the door open before following me into the suite. It's a beautiful space, all plush fabrics in neutral shades. The lamps are lit, and the bed is turned down. Clusters of candles in votives are lit, too, their fragrance heady. Jasmine, maybe.

I turn to him. 'Did you ask them to do this?'

He hesitates. 'I popped up here and lit them before dinner. I wanted the right atmosphere.' There's a self-consciousness to his tone that stops me from telling him he doesn't need to bother with details like this for an escort. The only motivations I need are money and this man's looks, but his having pulled out all the stops speaks volumes as to his character. I hate to admit it, but I'm touched.

So, instead of dismissing his efforts, I give him a smile. 'Thank you. It's perfect.'

'I'm well aware you're auditioning me far more than I'm auditioning you at this point,' he says gruffly.

I begin to demur. 'No, not at all.' But he shakes his head.

'It's true. And if you do agree to take this position, then we'll be building a relationship. It may be one that's transactional in nature and a little... unorthodox, from my end, anyway, but it's a type of relationship, nonetheless. And I want to make sure you understand from the outset how much I'll respect and value you.'

In my audition with Anton Wolff, he made me roll a condom on him as soon as the door clicked shut behind us before shoving me up against the wall and fucking me so hard and fast we both saw stars, but this works, too. Every word out of this man's mouth tells me what I already know: his integrity is irrefutable. That box is well and truly checked in my head. I'll be safe with Gabriel.

Which *means* I can have all the fun in the world teasing him, tormenting him, until every chivalrous instinct is buried under raw, primal need and he's driven purely by his dick.

'I appreciate that,' I tell him softly. 'I can tell you're a good man. But I want to see what you're like when you're bad, so tell me about this idea you had.'

'It can wait a moment,' he says, tugging me towards him with one arm banded around my waist and the other hand in my hair. Then his mouth is on mine, his lips soft and firm all at once, and I open for him right away. He slides his hand down to my bottom and grips hard, grinding against me as his tongue, taut and insistent, finds mine.

He asked me towards the end of dinner if I allowed my employers to kiss me.

'This isn't *Pretty Woman*,' I told him. 'For what they pay me, they can do whatever they like.'

I get the intimacy thing. It's undoubtedly intimate having someone's tongue inside your mouth, but like everything else I let these men do to me, I can handle it. Besides, I adore kissing, and Gabriel, it seems, is an excellent kisser. The way he uses that hot, hungry mouth of his on me is ardent and accomplished and sensual, and for the hundredth time since he told me yesterday how much he likes to *take it slow*, I can't wait to have it between my legs. If he eats pussy as skilfully, as carnally, as he kisses, I won't be faking anything.

I yield to the kiss, slipping one hand into his hair (short, soft) and allowing the other to roam up his back and across one shoulder. As I suspected, he has the leanly muscled physique of the naturally athletic. I bet he was captain of every team at prep school. This guy has Golden Boy written all over him. As it is, his delts flex under my touch in the most gratifying way before I squeeze his tricep (hard as fuck, if you must know).

It seems he likes my touch, because he angles his head, deepening our kiss, grinding me against his now fully hard dick in a manner that's thorough enough to obliterate any concerns I may have had about him packing anything subscale down there. The little noise I make in the back of my throat isn't remotely strategic—it's a natural reaction to a beautiful man tongue-fucking your mouth and dry-humping your pelvic bone as your needy nipples rub against his chest.

And I need more.

He breaks the kiss, pulling his face away with a jagged exhale while his hand lingers on my bottom. 'Fuck, you're beautiful. And you taste just as delicious as you look.'

I place my palms flat on his—excellent—pecs. 'You going to let me take care of that now?' I ask with a nod at his erection.

'Nope. There's something else I need you to do for me first.'

'Anything.'

He licks his lips, surveying me. Is there anything more arousing than seeing yourself through the eyes of a man who wants you so badly he can scarcely breathe?

I don't think so.

'I need you to take off all your clothes,' he begins. 'Every last scrap. Shoes, stockings, the lot.'

'Mmm-hmm.' I'm enjoying this already.

'Go get one of those stools'—he nods at the bar area behind me, where I vaguely noticed that a couple of bar stools stand—'and put it in the centre of the room, facing me. Then I want you to sit in it and arrange yourself *exactly* as you were in that photo in your portfolio. You understand me?'

CHAPTER 9

Athena

I can't be sure how fully Gabriel understands this about me yet, but orders make my knees tremor and my pussy drip.

Give me a command, and I positively ache to obey.

Say it in *that* voice, the voice that smacks of need and thinly-held vestiges of self-control, and I'm practically coming before you've even touched me.

And look at me in a way that suggests you're doing it not because you know I'll get off on it but because I'm your little fuck toy and you can do whatever the fuck you want with me, and I simply may not survive.

But I'll let him find all that out for himself... the fun way.

Instead of spontaneously orgasming in front of him, I let the corners of my mouth curve upwards into a seductive smile and turn slowly.

'Unzip me?'

He inhales sharply as he drags the zip down over its metal teeth. This is the first time he's unwrapped me.

'Thank you,' I say as he gets to the bottom. Another turn has me facing him.

I shimmy a little, and my little black dress sinks to the floor in an expensive pile of Italian silk and French lace. This dress always pulls its weight at this stage of the process.

Equally expensive is my gorgeous Dior lingerie: slate-grey satin with a black lace trim. A large part of my brand, my allure, is appearing exclusive. Expensive. Out of reach, if you like. It gives men a far greater thrill when they actually get me.

I afford him a good look as I step out from the puddle of my dress and kick off my heels. Without them, I'm a good four inches shorter, and it throws the power balance further off kilter. He's watching me in silence, his face almost stricken.

I look up at him through my lashes. 'Can you help me with my stockings?' I ask him, putting a hand on his shoulder and holding up one leg.

'Of course,' he murmurs, fiddling a little with the suspender clip at the front before it releases and he moves to the back. He glances at me and I nod my permission before he rolls the stocking down my leg and pulls it off, making quicker work of the second one.

'Thank you,' I purr before taking a step backwards so he can better enjoy the show. I lose the suspender belt and fix my eyes on him as I reach behind to unclip my bra. I love my breasts. They're full and round and soft and gravitationally superior. I slide the bra off, and he makes a noise at the back of his throat that's very promising indeed.

When I hook my thumbs into the side of my thong and tug that down, exposing my almost-bare pussy with its neat little landing strip, his lips part. Our eyes meet once more before I turn away in search of the bar stool. This way, he gets to assess me from behind, to learn the way my hips sway and my arse cheeks move as I walk away from him. I fetch the stool and set it right in the centre of the room.

He watches avidly with those dark blue eyes as I climb

elegantly up. He's shoved his hands in his pockets, a move that tells me he doesn't trust himself and which serves to put even more pressure on the fabric straining around his erection.

I love that he's still.

I love that he's watching me, that he can't take his eyes off me. Not for a second.

I love that he's clearly been thinking about that photo of me since he saw it last week and has had the ingenuity to recreate it.

The stool has a padded seat covered in silky damask. I shimmy forward slightly until I'm comfortable. My hair is cascading down over my breasts. I shake my head to get it off my shoulders and give him a better view. Then slowly, deliberately, I cup my breast, resting my forearm on the arm rest.

I balance my toes on the stool's rung and open my knees.

I reach down and find my pussy. God, I'm slippery.

I hold myself open and look straight at him. 'How's this?'

'It's perfect,' he says on an exhale. 'You're fucking perfect, aren't you?'

'As long as I'm what you want, that's good enough for me.'

He shakes his head. 'Stay still for me so I can enjoy you.'

He's motionless, too. His face is rapt as he simply drinks me in. If it wasn't for that aggressive-looking erection, he could still be a priest, standing in front of Raphael's Aldobrandini Madonna for the first time, lost in the rapturous stillness that truly great art provokes.

I wonder if he's musing on what to do with me.

I know exactly what I *want* him to do with me.

His eyes flit down to my glossy burgundy toenails and back up, his gaze sliding over my body. The total silence in the room adds to the weight of anticipation I feel in this moment. I can hear my heart thumping in my ear canals. I'm aware of every ragged inhale and exhale I take travelling through my nostrils. The room is warm, but I'm covered in goosebumps, and my nipples are already painfully taut.

He draws closer and I tilt my head back so I can gaze up at him. His first touch is that of tugging my hair fully off one shoulder. The warmth of his fingertips has me wanting to arch into him like a cat, but then the same fingertips are trailing down over my collar bone and further south until he finds the breast I'm not cupping.

It's already so intense: this silence; his proximity to me; his torturously light touch. So when his fingers close around my nipple and he pinches it, hard, it takes me by surprise. I let out an involuntary whimper, my body reacting instantly. Sex hormones lace my blood with what feels like opium. My biochemistry is already screaming.

'Fuck,' he grits out. He rolls my nipple between his fingers without loosening his grip. I could come just from this.

'It's so pretty. God, I could play with these all night.' He reaches up and gives my other nipple the same treatment. Pinching it hard. Rolling it. I let my mouth drop open as I gaze at him, at the workings of his jaw as he explores my body. More gently, he takes the hand cupping my breast and lowers it to my thigh so he can weigh both breasts in his hands, squeezing them as his thumbs work my nipples.

'I could do this to you in the office, couldn't I? I could just play with you whenever I wanted to.'

'Yes—' I gasp. 'Yes, you can do anything you want to me. I told you, I'm your fuck toy.'

He pushes them together, assessing my cleavage. 'I'd love to see these around my dick. I can't imagine how good it would feel.'

'I want to do that for you,' I tell him, trying not to squirm on the seat. He's ordered me to stay still, after all. But the sexual energy coursing through my body has me lit up from the inside.

'God, we'll never get any work done,' he huffs. 'I told you. The way you look will be a major, major problem. Now, let's see the rest of you. Keep holding yourself open for me, that's a good girl.'

He releases both my breasts, and I pout, but my fingers keep a grip on my slippery pussy. With one hand, he grips my chin firmly so I can't look away from him.

And the other?

It skates down over my stomach, causing a fresh outbreak of goosebumps, and then he's sliding his fingers down my landing strip. When they hit my clit, I gasp, my eyes widening, and he grins wolfishly. 'God, I love that.'

He finds my entrance and pushes two fingers in hard. Our faces are so, so close, and the satisfied gleam in his eyes as he feels me from the inside is almost as hot as the sensation of being filled up.

'Jesus Christ,' he says, and I mentally clock getting a former priest to blaspheme as a pretty positive sign. 'You're so ridiculously wet, and *so* tight.'

'I've been like this the whole way through dinner,' I tell him.

'Have you now?' He shoves his fingers in deeper and crooks them right as his thumb finds my clit again. It's perfect, just perfect, and I'm so wound up and so close that I might embarrass myself by coming before he's even got started with me.

'Shit,' I say, letting out a shuddery breath.

He gazes at me intently. 'You okay?'

'Just trying to hold off,' I pant.

'Let's slow it down then. I want to have way more fun with you.' With that, he lifts his thumb off my clit and bends to kiss me as he fucks me in a leisurely fashion with his fingers. I clench around them as I kiss him back, trying to communicate with my lips and tongue just how aroused I am. Naked and writhing on a stool while a gorgeous, powerful, fully-dressed man samples my body is pretty much nirvana for me.

CHAPTER 10

Athena

He pulls away, releasing my jaw and withdrawing his fingers before lowering himself elegantly to his knees. He leans in to inspect my pussy, so close I can feel the torturously light kiss of his breath on my exposed flesh. I'm so wet now my fingers are losing their grip.

When he speaks, the timbre of his voice is as low, as rough, as I've heard it so far. 'I want to get an invoice from the hotel later this week to replace the fabric on this stool because you've ruined it so thoroughly with the mess you've made.'

He glances up at me, and I stare back at his beautiful eyes and ravenous expression and sensual mouth. Arousal is coursing through me, treacle-thick and heady. I need that mouth on me *now*, but I'm also beginning to realise that I've seriously underestimated this guy's capacity for filth, and it's the most glorious kind of epiphany. I already know that I'll let him do whatever the fuck he likes to me when he has me in that office.

'That won't be a problem,' I tell him. 'Permission to show you?'

A curt nod.

I slide my fingers inside my body, avoiding my clit, which is an unexploded grenade in this moment. I am absolutely soaking. I pull them out and wipe them on the damask, leaving a slick streak that darkens the cream fabric.

'Perfect,' he whispers. 'Obedient little thing, aren't you? Keep your hands on the armrests.'

It seems he wants to reward me, because he leans in and takes one nipple in his mouth, groaning deeply as he sucks on it. It's so fucking good, and I want to clutch at his head and hold him to my breast so he can suck for dear life, but my obedience is more important than my pleasure just now.

Besides, I have a feeling he'll make it worth my while if I'm a good girl.

So I do my best to arch against his mouth as my hands claw at the ends of the armrests, and I take the agonised arousal he's provoking in me and I revel in it.

After sampling my other breast, he pops off and kisses down my stomach, putting his hands on my knees to hold them further apart. Oh please oh please oh please.

For a moment, he just kneels there and stares. Then he says in a voice laced with hunger, 'I've been imagining what this little pink cunt would taste like since I saw that fucking photograph.'

How can a man who, until recently, used his words to turn bread and water into the body and blood of Christ and to extol the glory of God have such a filthy mouth? Didn't he have to unlearn all that shit at the seminary?

His mouth is about three inches from my poor, throbbing pussy. I love that he's been imagining this, that I've been an actual fantasy for him rather than just some candidate who passed muster.

I don't speak. I can't. I sit there, thigh muscles straining beneath the firmness of his grip, and I watch as he shoots me one last filthy look before dipping that dark head and taking his first lick. It's long and thorough. He licks me from my entrance to my clit before murmuring his approval, and I buck. Oh God oh God oh God.

Another lick. 'Fucking delectable,' he mutters gruffly, and then he's leaning in and really going to town on me with decadent pulls of my clit before he makes his tongue taut and indulges in some excellent tongue-fucking. My entire pussy is pulsing so hard that all I can do is gasp and moan and hold onto those armrests for dear life.

'I'm not going to last,' I manage. 'It's too—I'm too turned on.'

'*Good,*' he growls. 'Don't move a muscle.' He releases one knee so he can drive a couple of long fingers back inside me, thrusting and crooking and twisting so perfectly that I bite down hard on my lip to stop myself from rutting against his face like the greedy little whore that I am.

The look he gives me as he glances up, his beautiful mouth wet with me and his eyes the dark, depraved eyes of a man on the brink, makes me shiver. He may be the one calling the shots, but I'm getting every single thing I want from this little scene, and I'm *not* talking about the twenty-five grand that landed in my bank account this morning. Although, the fact that he's paying me for this, that he's *this* desperate to get me alone and naked and at his bidding in a hotel suite, is disgustingly arousing all on its own.

'I can't wait to see you come,' he mutters as I stare down at him. 'You're so angelic looking. I can't wait to see what you're like when you let yourself go.'

'You'll find out in about twenty seconds,' I promise him, and he lets out a pained laugh.

'You certainly know how to galvanise a fellow. Okay, sweetheart, let's see it.'

With that, he lowers his head and gets back to work, really letting me have it. His fingers burn as they work in and out of me; his tongue laves my clit with licks that would be rough if I wasn't so ridiculously soaking. It's almost perfect, except—

'Permission to play with my nipples,' I ask him.

'God, yes,' he groans. With a relieved exhale, I reach up and pinch my nipples, closing that sacred circuit and ramping up my pleasure tenfold. I'm so close. I'm *so* close. He angles his head so he can keep licking me as he watches me play with my breasts, his eyes flashing with delighted disbelief. If he likes this sight, he'll soon be able to enjoy it every single day if he wants.

The thought of Gabriel instructing me to sit on his desk and get my tits out, to tug and pinch and play while he reads or takes calls or fondles my pussy is so incredibly stirring that it sends me over the edge. I pinch my nipples harder and widen my legs as much as humanly possible as he works every fucking nerve ending in my pussy with his clever fingers and magical tongue.

In my experience, the men who employ me get off on two things. They love having me be a quiet, submissive, pliant little mouse while they build me up, but they *adore* it when I finally fall apart.

I think it comes back to that decorous appearance of mine. My looks, my clothes, my demeanour, my intellect—all of it screams *untouchable*, so when I'm screaming and writhing and begging, when my eye makeup streaks and my lipstick smudges and my pale skin is stained with that unmistakable flush of orgasm and, more often than not, branded with some-one's mouth or teeth or cum, it sends them fucking feral.

Because they haven't just fucked a woman.

They've claimed one who seemed out of reach.

Not merely claimed her, but conquered her.

And their egos tell them they've won a glittering prize.

Happily for everyone involved, I love both aspects. I love submitting; I love trembling with the sheer effort it takes me to stay quiet and still like a good girl; I love how all that energy I'm repressing adds to the build.

And I love coming apart and casting off that demure persona and letting out my greedy, wanton little inner slut. Believe me, I adore the effect these men have on me as much as they do.

So when the almighty cacophony of Gabriel's fingers and tongue and my own fingers builds and builds and crescendos into a climax so powerful it should shatter every mirror, every window, in this suite, I let my little slut out, letting go of one nipple so I can push my fingers through his short, dark hair and crush his mouth to my rapacious pussy and milk every fucking drop of sensation he's willing to provide as my whimpers turn into cry after cry and heat, heady and powerful, pulls me under, to a place where I'm neither my appearance nor my profession, but merely a woman.

A woman in a state of ecstasy so transcendent, it almost makes me believe in a higher power.

CHAPTER 11

Gabe

I've broken her, and it's magnificent in the same way that witnessing an all-powerful wave crest and break and dissolve into a mesmerising froth is magnificent.

She's magnificent.

This assured young woman who has not put a foot wrong since we met yesterday, whose every word and gesture have been premeditated and purposeful and flawlessly delivered, has her hand clamped around my head, smashing my mouth against her cunt, her astounding body wracked with sobs, with shudders, as she rides out the mother of all orgasms against my tongue.

If I wasn't already reeling, drunk on her scent, I would be now. I can feel her inner walls convulsing around my fingers as I work my tongue as roughly as I can against the slick button of her clit. It's fucking soaking down here, her arousal coating my fingers and dripping down over my knuckles.

Even when I order her to make a mess, she's an over-achiever.

I groan against her flesh, lapping her up, drinking her in greedily as her orgasm ebbs away. My cock is an iron bar in my trousers, reducing my headspace to one single thought: it needs to replace my fingers, to push into that tight channel that's so ridiculously, so thoroughly primed for me.

She loosens her grip on my head with a shaky, self-conscious little laugh that has me easing my mouth off her pussy and kissing her inner thigh before raising my head so I can take her in. She's looking down at me, those huge hazel eyes glassy. Her hair and makeup are still immaculate but she looks softer, somehow. More vulnerable.

I ease myself gingerly to standing, my agonisingly hard dick jerking in outrage at the friction of my trousers against it. 'You taste even sexier than you look,' I say, sliding my hands under her jaw and tipping her face upwards, 'and that's saying something, believe me.' After I've kissed her, fleetingly but sufficiently for her to taste herself on my lips, I help her off the stool.

'Look,' I say, pointing at the stool's fabric seat as I band my other arm around the soft skin of her waist. 'What a very messy girl you are.'

I'd love nothing more than to throw her on the bed and stay fully clothed as I rail her, but I'm conscious this is as much of an audition for me as it is for her. It's only fair she sees the goods before she signs on the dotted line.

'Undress me quickly so I can get inside you,' I tell her instead. 'I'm about to shoot my load after that.' The look she shoots me is downright lascivious as she gets to work, unbuttoning my shirt with swift movements and tugging the tails out from my waistband. She makes quick work of it, and it's off in a moment.

'Let me take the edge off,' she purrs, unbuckling my belt. 'I'll suck your dick now and then you can take your time fucking me.'

I groan, because my dick would like that very much. But I've obsessed about this over the past few days. 'I told you I was a patient man. I'd very much like the first time you suck it to be when you start working for me. If you take the job, obviously.'

She gives a little moan. 'Mmm, that's hot. You can get me on my knees as soon as I walk in the door, for all I care.' She accompanies this by sliding her dainty little hand into my unzipped trousers and palming me through my boxers, and *booooly fuck*. If I'm not inside her in the next thirty seconds I'll die, I'll actually expire, so I assist her by means of shoving my trousers down and hopping around as I clumsily wrench off my socks and shoes. My final move is to send my wallet, into which I've stuffed a few condoms, flying onto the bed.

When I'm standing straight again, she steps right up to me so she can run her lips and nose along the ridge of my shoulder before sliding her hand inside my boxers and wrapping it around my cock.

'Fuck,' she says against my skin.

'On the bed,' I growl. *'Now.'*

She releases me. 'How do you want me?'

Dear God. 'On your back, so I can see you.'

I lose the boxers as she trots over to the bed, arranging herself prettily on her back. I waste no time in climbing on and ranging over her. My dick may be pointing angrily at her, but I am a master of delayed gratification. And taking in the astonishing beauty of this naked woman lying splayed beneath me on the sumptuous white bedlinen is gratifying indeed.

She's staring up at me, her eyes flickering from my face to my erection and back again, her expression playful and curious. I reach out and caress her breast, allowing my hand to skate downwards over the curves of her body until it rests on her hip. She is every lonely, starving fantasy I've ever tried to stifle throughout my years of pledged celibacy.

The male of the species is shown from the very first pages of Genesis to be pathetically ill-equipped to withstand temptation. This Eve, with her perfect body and entrancing eyes and silken tresses, is the ultimate seducer, and every glorious curve is as ripe, as decadent, as that forbidden fruit must have been to Adam.

As we gaze at each other she moves her leg, stroking the arch of her foot along my calf. 'I'm not just saying this, but you are fucking gorgeous. You must have had women throwing themselves at you after Mass every day of the week. I know I would have.'

I laugh and reach back to grab her ankle. 'The women of my parish had a healthy respect for the office of the priesthood.'

She wrinkles her sweet little nose. 'Ugh. How revoltingly virtuous. And it's their loss. Because I'm the one who's got you naked. You going to show me what damage you can do with that thing? Or are you just going to make me stare at it all night?'

I shake my head as I release her ankle so I can reach for my wallet. She is a piece of work, and if I should be deluded enough to think for a moment I'll be calling the shots with her, I suspect I'll only have myself to blame for the fallout.

'I'm absolutely not going to make you stare at it all night, no,' I say as I rip open the foil of one condom and pinch the tip. 'I'd far rather be buried deep inside you.' I pause, grimacing as I roll the latex over my terrifyingly engorged crown. 'But I've been looking forward to this moment, in a way, since Anton and Max sang your praises, so I'd like to savour the moment, if that's okay with you.'

She's not looking at my face. Instead, her eyes are glued to my dick as I sheath it. 'If you're asking whether I can wait a few more seconds until you unleash weeks of anticipation and years of tragic celibacy on my body then the answer is yes, I can certainly accommodate that.'

Despite myself, I grin. She's funnier than I expected,

which makes sense, because a person this smart would of course be witty. Besides, in this profession she presumably needs a decent sense of humour.

'You're very intense,' she notes, cocking her head to one side. Her eyes have, amazingly enough, travelled back to my face. 'I can't wait to see if you're this intense when you fuck.'

'I absolutely am,' I assure her as I wedge one arm under her and flip her over. She goes with a little squeal of surprise but scrambles to her knees like the pro she is.

'You wanted intense,' I say by way of explanation, and she makes a pleased humming sound.

She's waving that lovely pale bottom in my face, her bare cunt pink and glistening and marvellous, and all of it it is a red rag to a fucking bull. Before she can reply, I notch myself at her entrance. 'This okay?'

'God, yes,' she moans with a little shimmy of her hips.

'Good,' I say and I push in. I move harder than I usually would, but she's like the Niagara Falls down here, so I'm assuming lubrication is not a problem.

It strikes me in this moment, as I wedge myself inside her inch by excruciating inch, that it is apt indeed that she's named after a goddess, because I've had sex—plenty of sex—since I threw myself head-first down my rabbit hole of sinful secularism, but Athena is on a different level.

I'm unsure just how fucked up it is that the most transactional—the *only* transactional—sex I've had is shaping up to be the least perfunctory by far.

Perhaps in this, as in all things, you get what you pay for.

She's shaking as she takes me in. I release my dick, which is now wedged far enough inside her to direct itself, and grip her hip as I run my other hand down the delicate ridges of her spinal column.

In this moment, as I bottom out, they seem as sacred as a rosary.

A man could find peace here, buried astonishingly deep inside her while his fingers move along the exquisite knots of her spine just as they might slide over prayer beads. Even with the torturous burning of my need for release, my arousal flying around me like a maelstrom, there's a kind of peace here, a hyper-presence at the heart of this storm.

We Catholics have a rich history of finding stillness in the confrontation of physical discomfort. Is my desperate need to rut and rut until I've emptied myself inside the vessel of Athena's opulent body any less effective than whips or hair shirts or hot coals?

I don't think so.

But being on the cusp of fucking Athena senseless is undoubtedly a pleasure of the flesh, and I'd do well to luxuriate in it, to soak myself in every last drop of the filth and depravity this moment offers.

And I do. I fucking do.

'I'm going to move,' I tell her, dragging my fingers back down over those rosary beads so I can grip both hips, because there is a time for praying, and there is a time for acting.

'Do it,' she begs. Her voice and her warmth and the tight glove of her body are enough to send a fellow insane. I pull out and drive back in, the glow of pleasure lighting me up as I bottom out again. She shunts forward with a small moan before righting herself and pushing back against me.

Fucking hell.

I brace on one hand so I can explore the lavish weight of her tits as they hang free. Her nipples are still rock hard, and I pinch one before caressing her whole breast.

'Mmm,' she whimpers.

Something godless and feral and base comes over me: a surge of satisfaction that I am inside this most glittering prize, this most magical woman. 'Fuck, you're worth every penny,' I grit out as I ram into her again.

'Better make good use of me,' she says, breathing heavily. 'Think about how crazy that photo of me holding my pussy open for you made me, like it was an invitation. *And now you're inside it.*'

'Fuck, yeah,' I agree, driving mindlessly into her. That fleeting moment of stillness has shattered and my dick has taken over.

'You just bought yourself one of the most exclusive whores in the country,' she continues, standing her ground valiantly as I fuck her, 'and you can do *anything* to me. I can't wait for you to tie me up and show me off and debase me and do whatever the fuck you want.'

A sickening arousal courses over me. 'You like that? You like being reminded that you're a whore while I fuck you like this on your hands and knees?'

'I need it,' she admits brokenly.

I didn't know absolution could be like this.

What kind of fucked-up paradise am I in, I wonder as I fuck her and fuck her and fuck her, where absolution comes from the acknowledgment that I can, in fact, lean into every filthy, debasing urge I have because it's not only what she likes but *what she needs?*

Dear Lord, I am so fucking damned.

'I'm going to spend every day until you start this job thinking up ways to put you to work,' I tell her with the bravado of a man so galvanised by the high of imminent orgasm that everything seems possible and permissible. I reach forward with one hand and wrap a thick rope of her beautiful hair around my fist, angling her head to one side so I can see the workings of her jaw and throat as her own pleasure grows.

'Oh God,' she moans. 'Please do. You can do anything.' Her words, her breaths, are growing more ragged with each thrust. 'Oh fuck—fuck, I'm—'

And she lets herself go.

The pure joy and relief I feel as she convulses around me, giving me her blessing to let myself hurtle through galaxies filled with white-hot pleasure, is indescribable. I'm aware of the low, bestial noises I make as I rut and rut and empty and empty, of the soaring, wondrous, light-filled euphoria coursing through me.

As I come down from my impossible high, I release her hair and smooth my hand down her back. All thoughts of prayers are gone—I don't fucking need them.

I ease carefully out of Athena's body and help her onto her side. 'Wait,' I tell her, clambering off the bed with my fingers holding the condom on. 'Don't move.'

In the bathroom, I dispose of the condom quickly and grab her a robe. I have no idea if a woman who's been paid for sex has more or less post-coital vulnerability than other women, but I'm not about to take any chances. After the mother of all orgasms, I'd like to think my despicably base urges are sated and I can think and act like a man for whom compassion has been his literal job.

When I come back through to the main suite, she's lying on her side, facing the centre of the bed, one leg pulled up and one laid out. She looks otherworldly beautiful, pretty fucking satisfied, and not overtly self-conscious.

'Hey,' I say, climbing on and laying the robe over her before I lie down to face her.

She gazes at me through her thick eyelashes, giving me a dazed little smile. She looks like she's momentarily lost a couple of IQ points, which I'm unfeasibly pleased about.

'That's very thoughtful, thank you.'

'I didn't want you to feel uncomfortable, so...' I trail off and prop myself up on one elbow so I can enjoy the view. 'Are you feeling okay?' I ask.

A little laugh. 'Uh, yes. I am *very* okay.'

My parents definitely didn't raise me to employ high class

hookers in my workplace, but neither did they raise me to treat any woman with less than the full respect she merits. And Athena may have got off on being spoken to like a whore just now, but it's clear to anyone who meets her that she is an incredible woman who deserves to be treated like the goddess she is.

As far as I'm concerned, the moment we both come down from our orgasms is the moment that demeaning talk stops and I demonstrate the full force of my esteem.

'Glad to hear it,' I say now. 'That was...' I blow out a breath. 'Fucking spectacular.'

'Yeah. It was hot as fuck.'

'Excellent.' I clear my throat as I lay a hand on her hip through the robe. 'So the obvious question is, when can you start?'

She laughs, but there's a pleased flush on her face that I really like. 'I've got the job?'

Now it's my turn to laugh. 'You've got the job, a million times over, if you'll take it. I'm so fucking sold it's not funny.'

She sits up, letting the robe slide off her, and I admire the generous swell of her breasts, the perfect pinkness of her still-taut nipples against her creamy skin. She gets her arms through the sleeves of the robe and pulls it loosely closed around her, leaving it untied. I rise reluctantly to sitting and place a spare pillow over my dick, because it seems she's already shifted into work mode.

'Okay,' she says, eyes narrowing as she surveys me. 'Let's do this.'

'Really? I passed?' A broad grin splits my face, and she shakes her head at the sight of it.

'Let's just say you scraped through. By the skin of your teeth.'

Those two toe-curling orgasms I gave her tell a different story, but I'll let her have this.

'Glad to hear it. So when can you start? What's the score with giving notice?'

She screws up her face. 'Technically, there's no notice period. That's to protect the Seraphim if we want to get out of a position quickly. But I'd never do that to my current employer, so let's say a month. I owe him that, at least. I'll hand in my notice as soon as I receive your formal offer letter.'

She'll have that letter in her inbox by tomorrow, if I have my way. 'A month. Jesus, kill me now.'

'You'll survive. I'm sure your current EA—Gladys, wasn't it—can jerk you off if you get too wound up.'

'Please don't even joke about that.'

'Well, you can take yourself off to Alchemy. Try to stay awake this time. You're a big boy, you'll handle it. And I'd like to start reading up on the business in more detail while I'm working out my notice. I'll sign an NDA with the offer letter so you can share your data with me.'

'Sounds good,' I say forlornly. A whole fucking *month*.

'It'll fly by, especially with Christmas.' She pats me on the shoulder as she slides off the bed, wrapping her robe more tightly around her. 'Besides, you told me you like taking things slow. Remember?'

CHAPTER 12

Gabe

Debussy observed that it's the space between the notes that holds the music, and, in my previous vocation, I often observed something similar. It was the pauses, the voids, when my heart felt fullest and God felt closest.

While I delight in my faith's love of pomp and ceremony as much as the next Catholic, I've often wondered if those early Protestants, those first solifidians were onto something. They proposed the concept of faith alone—*sola fide*—being enough.

A void entreats us to fill it, you see. A nullity invites prayer in a very different way than the heart-swelling, gladdening triumph of soaring voices or the towering, almost architectural layers of organ music do.

Some of the times I've communed most effortlessly with God have, in fact, been when my faith stepped in, in all its unfathomable, swirling, glorious abundance, to fill a void. There have been a couple of instances at the end of Good Friday services, even, when I've undertaken that systematically solemn act of stripping the altar.

I've removed the altar cloth, leaving the altar itself as bare and desolate and hopeless as that cross was when they took Christ's body down from it. I've snuffed out candles and shrouded crucifixes in the bleakest, blackest cloths and had my altar boys bear away armfuls of flowers, and I would swear on the relics of any saint that, on an occasion that should feel starkly grieving, I have found myself aglow from within.

It's almost as if, having extinguished the ever-burning sanctuary light by the tabernacle, I have obliterated every last visual trapping that tethers us poor, blind sinners to the path, to the truth, leaving one last thing.

Faith.

As if it's only when everything else has been brutally gutted that I can find the space to feel, to hear, to see that faith, small and quiet, but palpable and brave.

The more I sink into this quicksand of lay life, especially *my* particular brand of lay life, with its money and trappings and equally shiny cars and women, the more I become numbed against that plucky, lambent faith. The more I become deafened to its quiet voice.

If I have earthly riches beyond what is probable or decent or fair, there's a spiritual paucity in my life these days that my fleeting moments with my rosary or Book of Hours simply cannot fill, and I feel it like an itch, like the abrasive reminder of a horsehair shirt.

It's ironic, perhaps, that I should spend the anniversary of Christ's birth musing on the odd but certain comfort that celebrating His death has brought me in the past. I went to Midnight Mass last night, not at my old parish—no fucking way—but at Farm Street in Mayfair. If the sprawling, gilded Brompton Oratory is where you'll see London's Spanish and French and Italian populations decked out in all their finery, Farm Street is where that small and curious cultural minority flocks: upper class English Papists.

Midnight Mass tends to give me what daytime Mass on Christmas Day does not—peace and quiet, a hushed solemnity, an understanding that we are gathered in the middle of one of the darkest nights of the year to celebrate Christ's birth on the very cusp of that miraculous day.

Sadly, my attendance there last night was steeped in pragmatism, as I was required this morning at my parents' house out near Newmarket, just past Cambridge, for a day of revelry, Sullivan style.

Let me state for the record that if nature likes to claim it abhors a vacuum, it hasn't met my family. Voids are anathema to the Sullivan clan, and voids in conversation are deemed almost as intolerable as voids in wineglasses.

This year, like every year, I will not spend the Lord's birthday cultivating enough space to hear my flame of faith flicker bravely into being.

Not on your life.

I'm currently sitting on an overstuffed floral sofa, nursing a pint of Black Velvet in an old silver tankard while trying valiantly to pace myself ahead of what I know will be a long and boozy lunch. My beverage may sound luxurious but, at half Guinness and half champagne, is absolutely fucking lethal, not to mention a spectacular waste of vintage Bollinger. Why they don't use bog-standard champagne for these I've never understood.

I have my tankard angled towards me so no one can see its contents. If Dad thinks it looks too full, he'll be pissed off that I'm not pulling my weight. If my brother Brendan thinks it looks too empty, he'll try to top me up. Thank God it's opaque.

Mum's on straight Bollinger, as are most of the other women in the room—mainly local friends of my parents. Given our proximity to the famous Newmarket racecourse, the crowd around here is seriously horsey. The only people not getting stuck in are a few designated drivers, who are on low-alc beers. If I didn't require social lubrication quite so desperately to get me through the rest of the day, I would have volunteered to ferry people home. As it is, my plan is to maintain a steady low-level buzz and avoid attention where possible.

'Come and chat to us, for fuck's sake, Gabe,' Dad booms in a thick Dublin accent from the huge stone fireplace where he and Mum are holding court. My parents' high social standing around here is well deserved and easily explained: they're fucking loaded, highly sociable, and way too generous when they host—which is a lot.

Not to mention, this house we grew up in is gorgeous. Over-furnished, but gorgeous, and a far cry from the slums near the Dublin docks where Dad grew up as a young lad, where the privy was out the back and he, as the eldest boy, had the great fortune to get the first go in the warmish, cleanish bath water when the seven kids had their weekly washes.

Apparently, his youngest brother, Niall, grew up knowing only cold baths laced with his six older siblings' piss. Poor fucker.

I force myself off the sofa and amble over to the gaggle of men and women at the fireplace with a smile I hope belies my reluctance. Gerald, one of my parents' three lurchers, presses his long, shaggy face to my thigh and I reach down to rub him sympathetically between the ears. He, too, hates a full house.

'Here.' After a cursory glance at the two-inch gap in the top of my tankard, Brendan tops me up with two hands, pouring draught Guinness from a can with one hand and Bolly with the other.

'Try doing that after dinner and see how much you spill,' I tell him, and he grins broadly. 'You're on.'

Brendan and I are what's known impolitely as *Irish twins*. I arrived eleven months after him, a fact that makes me very fucking angry on behalf of my mother. Not even in my days as a priest have I ever been comfortable with the Church's take on contraception. There are some areas where pragmatism and compassion and human fucking decency trump ancient theological tenets, and birth control is one of them.

It's often said that I should have been the eldest—I am, after all, far more responsible than Bren—but I don't necessarily agree. He's the doer, I'm the thinker. And while I was enjoying a profession where thought was integral, Brendan was working his way up in our family's core construction business, assuming the helm before the IPO a few years back and proving himself.

He's impressively smart and impressively driven, but when he's not at work he's terrifyingly basic. Or base, perhaps. Both or either.

I say that with love, but it's true.

Case in point: the wink he gives the young woman who's handing around the canapés. She can't be more than nineteen or twenty, and my brother's winks are lascivious enough to knock a girl up. I shake my head at him. It's a good-natured shake, but still. I'm sure it delivers a message.

'Loosen the fuck up, Angel Gabriel,' he says, slamming the Bollinger down on a side table. 'It's Christmas Day, for fuck's sake. Jesus Christ.'

'Language, Bren,' Mum says, tutting.

'Our Brendan has women coming out of his ears,' Dad tells his cronies proudly. 'What happened with that blonde you met at the two-thirty last Saturday? She was pure class.'

'A gentleman never tells,' my brother says with a grin that suggests neither he nor the blonde he picked up at the races behaved in a remotely classy way. 'But what about Gabe? I hear you've got a smoking hot new assistant, mate.' He accompanies this tidbit by shaking his fingers out and pretending to blow on them.

Bloody Gladys. She met Athena briefly last week when the

latter came in to pick up some paperwork. Apparently, reading annual reports over Christmas is my new EA's idea of a good time. Anyway, I assume Gladys blabbed.

'She's extremely highly qualified and I think she'll be a great fit,' I say with all the moral outrage of a man who absolutely does *not* know just how lovely a "fit" his employee's pretty pink cunt is for him.

'*And she's hot,*' my dickhead brother pushes.

I frown at him. I'm a former priest, for heaven's sake. I can keep up the self-righteousness all day long. 'She's attractive, yes. But that's not why I hired her.'

'Nobody'd blame you, son,' Dad says. 'God knows, no one would begrudge you a pretty face to look at after all those years of keeping your dick dry.'

Mum, whose face is turning gradually redder with every champagne top up my brother provides, looks like she might actually fall down dead from the shame of it. It's bad enough, in her eyes, having a former priest in the family, without one's spouse bringing it up in front of all the neighbours. 'Ronan Sullivan, that's a shocking, sinful thing to say. You know Gabriel only left to take over the reins so you could sit on your arse all day and gamble.'

'Ay, thanks, son,' Dad says, not remotely bothered. 'You're doing a grand job. I'm very proud of both my boys. But your Mammy and I wouldn't mind some more grandchildren before we die of old age. Unless you want us to leave everything to Elsie.'

Elsie, my sister Mairead's eldest, is a holy terror.

'Better get Bren on the case. I'm still getting used to being allowed to date,' I say weakly, earning a dirty cackle from my brother, who knows all about my little Alchemy habit. He's asked me to put him forward for membership, and I've refused point blank. The last thing I want is to bump into my degenerate brother stark naked and slap bang in the middle of an orgy on a random Thursday night.

Although, if things work out well with Athena, I won't need my membership much... unless I want to take her there and have some playtime with her. Her CV did say she was into group fun, after all.

Now there's a thought.

One thing's for sure, though. I have no intention of letting my brother anywhere near Athena or the little secret she and I are hiding.

Mum's saying something.

'Hmm?'

'Try and stay sober till we sit down for lunch, will you?' she mutters in my ear. 'I'd like you to say Grace.'

This time last year, I was saying Mass.

Now, I'm demoted to saying Grace for a bunch of rich pissheads, and I have no one to blame but myself.

I pat the sparkly lavender tweed covering her arm. 'Of course,' I say absently.

It might be the only thirty seconds of contemplation I get today.

CHAPTER 13

Athena

Tonight is New Year's Eve. We're planning on ringing in the new year by eating nachos and listening to Madison Beer and Olivia Rodrigo and Gracie Abrams, because when one of you is eight years old, you're not letting anyone else dictate the playlist.

I was supposed to be hosting, but instead we're hanging at my best friend Marlowe's tiny flat. Her daughter Tabby is usually the first to accept an invitation for a sleepover at mine, but not this Christmas.

The reason: last week, Father Christmas delivered the most spectacularly girly tent mankind has ever seen to Marlowe's living room, and there's no way Tabby is leaving it, even for one night.

The tent, bedecked and bedazzled way beyond anything Tabby asked for in her letter to Father ChristmAas, mysteriously showed up in their living area on Christmas morning. (In reality, I'd paid through the nose for a handyman to dress up as Father Christmas—just in case Tabby woke up—and put the tent up late on Christmas Eve). It's now sitting pretty where it belongs, in Tabby's bedroom, as are we. Marlowe and

I are shoehorned into the tent alongside Tabby, a can of Sprite, two glasses of champagne, and a bowl of seriously tasty cheese and onion crisps. Good times.

When Marlowe mentioned that Tabby had asked Father Christmas for a tent and she was stumped as to how to make it super magical, I may have hijacked the operation slightly. Tabby had, to be clear, requested "a tent as cool as the one from *The Holiday*" which I, naturally, sniffed at.

Don't get me wrong—it's a cute tent and a stunningly well crafted scene, but why think small when you can create something extraordinary? Marlowe is far too linear, God bless her. Too constrained. She's also skint, with every last penny of her savings ring-fenced for a cause far more critical than a tent.

Which is where godmothers come in.

I immediately contacted the personal shoppers at Harrods, who were happy to commission and furnish a bespoke four-sided but compact tent for Tabs. When Marlowe hit the roof which, predictably enough, she did, I had one rejoinder.

'This isn't about a tent, you realise. You could have gone to IKEA for that.' Like everything else in her flat. 'This is about ramming home a *very* important message to a sick little girl—that sometimes, in a world full of shitty disappointments, sometimes, just sometimes, life not only delivers but blows your fucking mind. It's always worth believing. If nothing else, I want to help you teach her that.'

She hugged me then, and we both cried a little.

I know I can be overbearing, and I know a part of Marlowe disapproves of my irresponsible spending habits—especially when it comes to Tabby—but whatever I can do to help drum an abundance mindset into that fiercely intelligent little brain I'll consider time and money well spent.

Not to mention, the tent is fucking amazing. It's been crafted from a double layer of ivory cotton embroidered with gold stars. The fabric of its ceiling is gathered into a central point from which hangs a battery operated rotating disco ball (no cutout paper stars for us). There's even a beautifully carved, hot pink lacquered cabinet housing Tabby's medication. It comes with a sturdy heart-shaped padlock, the key to which Marlowe is wearing around her neck.

But my favourite part of the whole setup is the child-sized sleeping bag-slash-camp bed inside the tent, made from palest pink faux fur with an integrated memory foam mattress, so she can camp out here in grand style.

'Go into the living room,' she orders now with an imperious wave of her hand. 'I want to play doctors and nurses and you're taking up all the space.'

'Right you are,' Marlowe tells her with a kiss to her forehead. 'Call us on the walkie talkie if you want company.'

'Don't forget to take her temperature,' I say, nodding at the doll who's supposed to be incapacitated.

I clamber inelegantly out on my hands and knees and blow Tabs a kiss before following Marlowe through to the small kitchen-cum-living room. To her credit, she's done as good a job as she can with the place. It's pretty and homely and, most importantly, safe. Or as safe as it can be in New Cross, which is a total shithole.

Because I spent Christmas with my parents in Cologne and thence took a cheeky couple of days to myself at Baden-Baden, today's been my first in-situ experience of the tent. I'm absolutely thrilled at how delirious Tabby is with her new home. All little girls deserve to dream big, especially the ones who've already had to endure shit most adults can't imagine.

Hopefully, that tent will be a refuge for Tabs. She can dream big in there, but she can also make herself small and secure when she feels the need. She can rest there when she's exhausted but she still feels like playing. It's an investment in her joy, essentially, and I can't think of a better way to spend my excess cash.

God knows, I understand better than a lot of people the power of having a sanctuary that's all yours, a restorative haven where you can shut the door and heal from all the craziness.

As I told Tabby earlier, every princess needs her castle, and every great warrior needs her retreat.

'Okay,' Marlowe says, fiddling with her walkie talkie to ensure it won't transmit anything indecent to her innocent, sleeping little girl, 'spill the tea.'

We're sitting curled up on her (IKEA) sofa, having eaten our body weight in nachos and switched to red wine. Tabby is out cold next door, so this is our window to have a good old gossip. Marlowe and I have been best friends since we met in the Sixth Form at Cheltenham Ladies' College, to which she'd won a full choral scholarship.

I assess her with amusement. She's perfectly lovely, a natural blonde thanks to her Dutch mother and who boasts what Anne Shirley would definitely have deemed an *alabaster brow.* Honestly, given the crap she eats, it's completely unfair, but given the rest of her life is a steaming pile of horseshit, I'll let her have her great skin and her amazing daughter.

'On what?' I ask innocently. 'Baden-Baden? Yes, I had a colonic. Yes, it was life-giving. No, I did not befriend or even see Victoria Beckham.'

She sighs. 'On the new gig. The new guy.'

Now I grin. 'Marlowe Winters. You can't handle the tea, and you know it.'

She screws up her face like she's bracing for impact. 'I can. You can tell me. I won't freak out. Have you slept with him? You have, I assume?'

'Yes, I've "slept with" him.'

'Mmm-hmm. And how was it?'

'It was excellent, thanks for asking. Very, very promising, especially considering the guy used to be a priest.'

She giggles bashfully. 'God, it's so weird. You just, I dunno, turn up for dinner and then go upstairs and shag him? Isn't it awkward?'

'You are ridiculous. I wouldn't even get dinner out of them if I went on Tinder.'

'True.'

'And no, it wasn't awkward, because we used the dinner to discuss our... expectations, and he is really fucking hot, so I was turned on way before we went upstairs.' I pause. I'm mean, but she's so easy to rile. 'And then he made me strip and pose naked on a stool, holding my pussy open so he could go down on me. Then he fucked me from behind on the bed. So, two orgasms. That's very respectable for a first time, you know.'

'Oh my *God*.' She sets her wine glass down on the floor so she can bury her face in her hands as she drums her socked feet on the floor. 'That's mortifying! I would literally *die.*'

I grab a cushion and swipe her with it. 'It's not mortifying! And it's not even kinky. I'd say that's a pretty vanilla night. It was hot, we both had a good time. What's the issue?'

She raises her head, her face stained bright red. She has second hand embarrassment, and it's adorable and hilarious in equal measure. 'I just can't imagine it! Like, standing there and stripping on demand for some guy you don't know from Adam, and then letting him stick all his... body parts inside you!'

'That's generally how sex works, babes,' I remind her gently. It's been a while for Marlowe. She, who was the best of all the good girls at school, got totally fucking seduced by her professor in her first year of uni. Seduced *and* knocked up. That'll quash your faith in men just as quickly as it'll quash your career prospects, and once you find out your newborn daughter has a rare congenital heart defect?

Well, that's the death knell to any kind of social life more exciting than evenings on the sofa with me or the occasional event I drag her to.

It's not her fault she's severely out of practice.

It's not her fault she's only slept with two or three guys.

And it's definitely not her fault that she's been dealt blow after blow by the universe. If she were a Bible character, Marlowe would be Job—with smaller pores.

'I know.' She grimaces again. 'It just sounds so... confronting.'

I reach down and hand her back her glass. 'Lucky you're not a hooker, then.'

'I'll drink to that,' she says, and she does. 'So, you're excited about this gig, then?'

'I am, actually.' I'm counting down the days until I finish with poor old Steve, in fact.

'Because it's a new sector? Or a new dick?'

I nearly spit out my wine. 'Marlowe! You dirty little slut.'

'I am not the dirty little slut in this room.'

'Fair. And it's both, if you must know. I've been reading up on the estate. It's fascinating. They're one of the highest value landowners in the UK. And there's so much shit to clear up. I'm absolutely *itching* to get to work.'

'And the guy?' she asks slyly.

'Well, he told me he was going to spend these few weeks thinking about how to put me to work, and I don't think he meant pulling reports, so that's a big fat Happy New Year to me.'

'Oh my God,' she whispers. 'Would you have guessed he used to be a priest?'

I take a sip of my excellent St Emilion as I consider her question. Marlowe and I operate on a silent understanding that I bring the wine when we hang out so she doesn't have to overextend herself and I don't have to drink cheap vinegar.

'Not necessarily. If anything, he was less priest-like than I expected.' *Especially in the hotel suite. Especially when he was ordering me to make a mess of the stool's fabric.* 'But there was something... contemplative about him. He's a lovely guy, but I suspect he overthinks everything.'

'Did you find out why he left the priesthood? It's weird, no? Going from being a priest to paying someone like you to shag him at work?'

It absolutely is. 'Only the official line—that his dad was retiring and he basically swapped one sense of duty for another and picked up the baton of the investment vehicle. They were adamant about keeping it in the family, apparently. And he claims he's hired me as a pragmatic measure, so he can fulfil his needs without burning the candle at both ends.'

For some reason, a visual of him waking up, naked and disoriented, in the bowels of a sex club tugs at my heart a little. Poor fucker. At least there'll be no need for any of that when I'm around. I'll take care of all his needs and then some.

'But you think there's more to it than meets the eye,' she insists, her eyes wide with the promise of salacious gossip.

I waggle my eyebrows at her over-dramatically. 'I'd put money on it. Not that I'll be able to tell you any of it. NDA, remember? Now, I have something for you while I've got you to myself.' I reach down and pull a large envelope out of my handbag. 'Just keep an open mind, okay? That's all I ask.'

Marlowe's scarcity mindset may be completely under-standable, justifiable even, but it's a vicious circle. She needs to start thinking big if she's to conquer the next round of chal-lenges that face her and Tabby.

She slides the brochure out of the envelope and stares down at it. 'No.'

'Babes, it's not impossible. Please.'

When she glances up at me, her blue eyes are limpid with tears. 'It is impossible.'

It is a glossy brochure for the paediatric cardiology services at Duke Children's Hospital in North Carolina, one of the best hospitals in the world at treating conditions like Tabby's and, as it's becoming alarmingly clear, her greatest hope right now. Far greater than the wonderful but limited capabilities of our National Health Service, anyhow.

'I can pay,' I insist. 'We've been over this.'

'A single operation would cost *a hundred grand*,' she hisses. 'It's not an option! The doctors at Great Ormond Street have told us they're doing their best to put her forward as a research case. That's honestly all we can hope for.'

But it's not enough.

'It's not,' I say evenly, 'because I can pay. Jesus Christ, babes, what the fuck else is a better use of my money than my goddaughter's life?'

Tabby, who was born with a congenital heart defect called Tetralogy of Fallot, has already survived two open heart surgeries in her short life: one at birth and one when she was three. Unfortunately, she's on the brink of outgrowing the valve inserted during her last surgery, and her medical team at Great Ormond Street—London's preeminent children's hospital— has recently grown concerned that her heart function is deteriorating more quickly than they would have expected.

Long story short, it's a fucking nightmare—a ticking time bomb, more like—and one we could get in front of if Marlowe would set aside her fucking pride and let me help.

'You earn that money with your *body*,' she says with gritted teeth, tears sparkling on her lashes. 'You let men do unthinkable things to you, and honestly? I admire the hell out of you for doing it. But you earn every penny of that money, and there's no way I'm taking any of it.'

'We both know US medical expenses are a black hole,

honey, especially for the kind of surgery Tabs needs. It wouldn't just be one surgery, you know that. It would be a bottomless pit. There's got to be another way, we just have to find it.'

I shoot her a glare to communicate that this conversation isn't over, but she looks away to stuff the brochure back into the envelope.

There will be another way.

There always is.

Marlowe might just have to stop thinking like the good, rule-playing girl she is and assume Athena Davenport levels of Machiavellian strategising to pull this particular rabbit out of a hat.

PART TWO
Offertorium (Offering)

CHAPTER 14

Gabe

This time, I'm waiting for her at reception when she steps out of the lift on the third floor. I greet her with what I hope is a warm smile and a firm hand-shake, and I send up a fleeting prayer, the tiniest plume of celestial smoke, that my delight that the moment has finally arrived isn't written too clearly on my face.

When we walk through to my office, Gladys' former desk in the antechamber is clear except for a monitor and keyboard and an oversized vase bearing the most decadent array of flow-ers, their greenery tumbling wantonly down the sides and their heady, musky scent filling the air. My personal assistant, the achingly competent George, has aced his mandate to ensure Athena's floral arrangement packs a punch.

'Welcome to Rath Mor,' I say with a feeble gesture at the flowers.

'Thank you. They're beautiful.'

'Come on through, why don't you, and have a seat while you tell me how your Christmas has been.'

She perches on the cream sofa, knees and ankles pressed daintily together, and I take the compact armchair opposite her, allowing me a good look at my new prize. Because if someone who looks like *that*, who is as intelligent as that, and whose job description now includes letting me use her whenever I want isn't the most dazzling prize, I don't know who or what is.

Her dress is a silk shirt-waister, ivory coloured with a delicate print of semi-furled ferns. Despite the fabric-covered buttons that run the gamut from her breastbone to a few inches above her hem, it's beyond reproach. The fabric, which moved like water as I led her through to my office, now falls modestly from her knees almost to her ankles. There are pearls at her throat and in her ears, and her auburn hair is glossily, perfectly coiffed. The overall look is perfectly demure—at least it would be on anyone who didn't look like Athena, because this woman could be dressed for Antartica and she'd still scream sex to anyone who looked at her.

Rather, she'd scream *you want me but you can't have me, because I am legions and galaxies out of your league.*

Unless your pockets are deep enough.

I love it, though. I love that everything about her is exclusive and elevated and extortionate. I rejoice in the certain knowledge that the Athena who sits before me, poised and intoxicating, is a different creature from the one I've had the good fortune to unravel, twice now. That when you stroke her and lick her and fuck her and whisper filthy words to her, she's every bit as wanton in that moment as she is buttoned up in this.

A man would do terrible things for a glimpse of that woman beneath the ice queen facade. Those glimpses are the most delicious forms of foreshadowing. Of foreplay, even. So when she leans forward after a few minutes of small talk, my entire adrenal system marshals itself.

She begins innocuously. 'I've done some reading on the priesthood over Christmas.'

I narrow my eyes. 'Is that so?'

'Mmm-hmm.' She crosses her legs, the silk flowing around them as she does. 'I thought it would be helpful to understand where you're coming from. But I had a question.'

'Go for it.'

A little smile. 'I bet you know where this is going.'

I shake my head, amused. 'I wouldn't presume to know what you're thinking, Athena.' I'd never be able to keep up.

'When you administered Holy Communion,' she asks, her voice low and melodic, 'would the members of your congregation kneel for you?'

My pulse kicks up a notch, though I have no idea why. 'Not in my parish. That only happens in churches where there's an altar rail. They just formed a standing queue.'

'Oh.' She deflates a little. 'And would they take it in their mouths? I mean, would you put the Host directly on their tongues?'

'Only for some of the older or more traditional parishioners, usually. The practice of taking it in the hand has been permitted by the Holy See for fifty years or more, now. Why do you ask?'

'I was trying to visualise how it would have been when you did it. I was trying to imagine you giving me Holy Communion, and how it would have worked.'

I smile. It seems a sweet, if random, line of questioning. 'If you'd lined up to receive a blessing, I would have asked you to simply cross your hands over your chest and I would have made the sign of the cross on the top of your head. I couldn't have administered the Holy Eucharist to you as a non-Catholic.'

She nods. 'I see. So, let me get this straight. Do you mind humouring me for a second? Will you stand?'

My brow furrows as I get to my feet. I have no idea where she's going with this. Her tone sounds innocent, intellectually curious, but something tells me she has an agenda here.

She, too, rises, standing in front of me. 'So I would have done this?' She crosses her hands diagonally over her chest in an X.

'Yes. Now bow your head.'

She does, and I use my thumb to make the sign of the cross over the silkiness of her hair. When she tilts her face upwards, I see how close we are.

'So if there was no altar rail,' she muses, gazing up at me through her eyelashes, 'then it couldn't have gone like this, if I'd ever decided to come into your church and trick you into thinking I was a baptised Catholic.'

Before I can understand what's happening, she's sinking gracefully to her knees before me, the silk of her skirt billowing around her like a parachute. I stare down at her with some twisted mix of fear and fascination as she raises her hands in front of her, joining them in prayer.

'And if most people take it in their hands,' she continues, 'then you would never have been in this position, where a young woman was kneeling before you, with her mouth open and her tongue held out to receive the Body of Christ, but all you could think about, as you made your pilgrimage along the altar rail, was how easy it would be to slide your cock in there instead and really put her to the test.'

I'm thickening instantly, at her awful, disrespectful and downright sacrilegious words, even before she closes her eyes and opens her mouth and sticks out her little pink tongue just enough that yes, it fits how people have traditionally received the Host, and yes, I can see how right she is, how staggeringly easy it would be to unzip myself, to give myself a couple of pumps before brushing past her plush, waiting lips and onto that expectant, welcoming little ledge her tongue is providing.

As I stand there, staring down at her and reeling at the skill with which she's just unrolled a canvas and shown me a world of possibility painted on its front, she opens her eyes and fixes their hazel orbs on me.

'No, I don't suppose you did. Even if the thought ever crossed your mind, I know you would never have acted on it. You'd never have put your own needs first, would you?'

'No,' I mutter, because she seems to be waiting for an answer. 'Of course not—the idea of it is unfathomable.'

She nods and parts her hands, placing them on the tops of my thighs so they bracket the straining fabric of my suit trousers. 'Of course it is. But you're not a priest now, Gabriel. You're a layman, and you're allowed to do whatever the fuck you want. And I suspect you still need to be reminded of that every now and again.'

She pauses, and I slide my hands beneath all that hair so I can cradle her jaw. Her skin is so soft under my thumbs as I stroke it, her lips so supple as she speaks.

'So how about I pretend I'm one of your penitents, and I've come to receive Holy Communion, but you know I'm not Catholic. You know I shouldn't be trying to disrespect this sacrament when I'm just some terrible sinner, a random little slut, and you decide to teach me a lesson. Because the only thing I'm worthy of swallowing down is your cum.'

I inhale harshly, my dick throbbing behind my zipper. 'Jesus Christ, Athena.'

'If I've driven you to blasphemy already,' she muses, fingers hovering over my flies, 'then I must be doing something right. How about it? Want to play?'

My thumbs drag over her jaw as I gaze down at her.

Who is this she-devil who, with a few expertly crafted sentences, has taken all that I know to be true and noble and sacred and turned it into something that is quite literally intoxicating, but whose poison I am apparently powerless to resist?

How can she take what was, for me, the single biggest privilege of the priesthood—the God-given ability to turn bread into flesh and wine into blood, *Christ's* blood—and set it alight, torching it so it burns in my veins like the basest kind of addiction and smokes out every last drop of good sense, of propriety?

And how the actual fuck will I withstand her unholy charms if, at eight-thirty on a Monday morning, she already has me incapable of doing anything but accepting this infernal little proposition with indecent verve?

Forget Jack Nicholson and his well-meaning soundbites.

This woman makes me want to be a far, far *worse* man.

When I speak, I barely recognise my own voice.

'Do it.'

CHAPTER 15

Athena

Is there anything more gratifying than arousing a decent man so thoroughly that he turns feral before your eyes?

I think not.

I suspect, from the shocked and even dismayed expression on his face, that he has quite literally never had this thought before I planted it, that he never sullied the responsibility of his former vocation with impure thoughts about his flock.

But I *know*, from the heat in his eyes and the set of his jaw and the bulge in his trousers that he has well and truly taken my little fantasy and run with it.

Whether he likes it or not, he's back in his vestments just now, standing at an altar rail with a golden dish of sanctified wafers, while before him a russet-haired enchantress extorts him with her mouth to besmirch his vows and take his pleasure.

Do it.

Amen to that, Father Gabriel.

I've been looking forward to this since my audition, and I'll bet he has, too. After all, he told me to save this treat for my first morning, didn't he? And I'm nothing if not obedient.

I unbuckle and unbutton him before drawing his zipper down, slowly, slowly. The fabric of his trousers strains as his thumbs drag over my jaw, his fingers flexing on my neck and in my hair. I won't be happy until they're digging into my skin and holding my head in a vice so he can fuck my mouth.

His breathing is ragged as I shove his trousers around his ankles and edge the waistband of his grey boxer briefs down. Oh, sweet Jesus, there he is, and my mouth is watering already. He's fucking huge, just like I remember: hard and male and angry, his lovely straight cock so engorged it's shiny.

I lick my lips.

Before I put my mouth on him, I want to make sure he is absolutely in this little fantasy with me. I hold my hand out, palm up, supporting his cock, and he shivers at the contact. I can smell him, clean and musky. He smells of soap and skin and box-fresh, unsated arousal.

'Imagine it,' I whisper. 'Just like I told you. I'll be waiting for my Holy Communion. That's your signal to do whatever you like to me, *Father*.'

With that, I let my eyes drift closed and I open my mouth and slide my tongue out, and I wait, an invitation made flesh, mere centimetres from his lovely dick. I can feel the pleasing silkiness of my tongue's underside against the soft pad of my lower lip. I hope what he sees is equally alluring, because I can lead the horse to water, but I can't make him shove his cock in my mouth.

I may be the temptress masquerading as a fuckable penitent, but this doesn't work unless he makes the proactive decision to violate me in the coarsest way.

His breathing is already ragged as he contemplates this buffet of temptation, and I wonder if he's more concerned about indulging in a deeply transgressive fantasy or fucking his actual new assistant's mouth in her first ten minutes on the job.

I hope it's both.

He'll realise, in about five minutes flat, that when it comes to me, nothing lies on the other side of acting on his basest instincts but sheer ecstasy.

Then he withdraws one hand, brushing the crown of his dick over the very tip of my extended tongue with the most featherlight touch, almost as if he's allowing himself to answer his most burning question: *what would it feel like?* There's no precum quite yet, but that gossamer swipe feels like a threat, and I want him to jam the whole fucking thing so deep inside me that I can barely breathe.

He groans audibly—a good man, a still-holy man, driven to darkness by the promise of a warm, wet mouth. Still, it feels to me that he needs a little shove over the edge and into the abyss.

'Give me what I deserve, Father,' I whisper hoarsely. 'Please. I'm only asking you for what I deserve.'

'Jesus fuck,' he rasps. Now, I'm no Catholic, but that particular juxtaposition feels like another level entirely of profaning the Lord's name. He fists my hair hard with the hand still on my neck and then, *then,* he shoves that glorious organ so hard, so fully, inside me that I let out a strangled, involuntary moan of pleasure.

'You want what you deserve, hmm? This is what you deserve, you little fucking vixen, for committing sacrilege and making me remember what a pathetic flesh-and-blood man I am when I should be doing God's work.'

He puts his other hand back on my neck, his strong fingers more a vice than a cradle around my jaw, and for a long moment we simply stare at each other, I gagged and subservient, he splendidly aflame. I exhale slowly through my nose as I find his ball sac with one hand and press the palm of my other hand against the rigid, hair-strewn muscle of his quad.

Then he moves, and his groan as he slides his length slowly out of my mouth and surrenders to his desire is the best kind of defeated. His eyes drop to where my lips are closed around his crown, and I have the distinct pleasure of seeing raw, animalistic need etched on his gorgeous features. I give his tip a decadent swirl with my tongue, and he shudders. When he ruts back inside me, it seems something shifts for him. He may still hate himself for wanting this—and resent me for provoking him so effectively—but it appears he decides to chase his prize.

'Slap me on the thigh if it's too much,' he grits out, and then he's fucking my face in fine style, hips pistoning and his dick, impossibly, ominously hard, driving in and out.

This is my Eden: on my knees at a powerful man's feet, my elite education and dazzling business brain forgotten, in his mind, in favour of my unctuous mouth and sinful tongue. I abandon his sac—the rhythm is too punishing—and get a good grip of his arse with both hands, revelling in the way his glutes contract with each merciless thrust.

'I have never, ever fantasised about violating a parishioner like this,' he tells me, and he sounds really fucking pissed off, 'until *you* showed up. And God knows, I'll never, ever be able to un-see this.'

I moan my approval around his cock.

He works me, and I take it valiantly, breathing hard through my nose as my mascara runs and my saliva escapes, sluicing him with moisture. It's slippery and messy and fucked-up, and I adore it. My clit throbs more every time he twists my hair and plunders my face. I give myself over to the sensation, closing my eyes and focusing on surviving the onslaught as he hardens even more, thrusts even more aggressively.

And then: 'Coming, *God*,' he groans, his manners intervening as he loosens his grip on my head and tries to pull out, but I dig my fingers more firmly into his arse and hold on tight, and then he's erupting down my throat in warm gushes, his body wracked with convulsions and his breathing frantic. I wait until he's emptied himself before pulling off him just enough that I can swallow, and then I proceed to lick him clean.

He stands there, sighing out his pleasure, his fingers teasing my hair as he watches me minister to him. When I look up at him, there's nothing but a quiet, replete kind of reverence on his face. He stills as our gazes lock, and I have the oddest realisation that in any analogy where this guy is Jesus, I am most definitely Mary Magdalene, the blow job I just gave him the most pornographic take possible on washing his feet.

There are acts of service, and then there's the epic servicing I just provided.

Nevertheless, I feel nothing but satisfaction as he helps me to my feet. His gaze drops to my painfully hard nipples, which are forging a path through lace and silk.

'Did that really turn you on?' he murmurs, searching my face.

'God, yes.' I dab as delicately as I can at the saliva pooled at the corner of my mouth.

'Show me. On the sofa. Turn around.'

I take this to mean that I should kneel up on the sofa, facing the wall, so I do. I gather my skirts all the way up to my waist and spread my knees wide, turning my head so I can watch him take in my mostly bare bottom in its ivory lace thong and suspender belt.

He crouches to hoist up his boxer briefs and trousers, fastening the latter blindly, his eyes firmly on the view in front of him.

'Bend over for me,' he says, and I do. I lean forward and rest my forearms on the back with the generous silk of my dress gathered in the crook of one elbow.

His touch, when it comes, is a fingertip drawn straight down the centre of my thong. I shiver at the sensation, which is delicious and yet nowhere near enough.

'Absolutely soaked,' he observes neutrally as he bends to kneel behind me on the floor, putting himself level with my pussy. 'That really did turn you on, you dirty girl.'

He hooks his thumbs through the sides of the thong and peels it down, leaving me bare and glistening and right there in front of him. His breath is a teasing warmth on my sensitised flesh.

'I have been looking forward to this for the past month, you know that?' He slides a leisurely finger inside me, and my greedy, greedy flesh contracts around it. 'How many guys have you fucked since I last saw you, Athena, hmm?'

'Only one guy right before Christmas, and my old boss,' I manage. 'During my notice period.' I'm perfectly still on the sofa, braced for whatever touch he'll give me.

'Really? No one else? You expect me to believe that? You must have men coming out of your ears.'

'I'm extremely selective.' It's true. I'm highly selective about who I fuck in my personal life, and when I'm in a professional relationship that's sexually rewarding, I don't tend to sleep around much. I don't need the extra orgasms, and I'd rather keep myself under-serviced and hungry for whatever my employer sees fit to give me. It makes the dynamic more charged.

Ironically, I'm not selective in a professional setting. If Gabriel rounded up his entire team and got me to work my way through the lot of them, I'd luxuriate in the whole sordid process. It's the kink factor rather than the guy, or guys, that does it for me in that context.

'So you've had a few orgasms, then.'

'Only self-administered ones, really.'

'Your old boss didn't make you come?'

I hesitate, torn between breaching Steve's trust and gaining Gabriel's. 'No.'

'Why not?' He adds another finger, and the stretch is glorious.

'Too vanilla.'

There's a ghost of a laugh. 'Too vanilla. Got it. I must remember that. Is this "too vanilla" for you?'

'No, it's—it feels really good.'

'But you need more.'

'Mmm-hmm.'

'Luckily for you, I've thought about this cunt far too much over the past four or five weeks,' he admits, and with that he twists his fingers inside me and his lips meet my clit.

It's more of an obscene open-mouthed kiss than a lick, and it has me practically jumping off the sofa. My whimper must tell him exactly what I think of it, for he hums his approval against my flesh and proceeds to lick me harder, his tongue doing lavish laps as he finger-fucks me slowly, deeply.

I kneel there, head bowed, the crown of my head resting against the wall of his office and the stretched elastic of my thong digging into the sides of my knees as Gabriel pays homage to my clit. His entire face is buried there, it feels like, his nose pressing just south of my entrance and his lips and tongue working every surface millimetre of the miraculous nervous system that's giving me such intense pleasure. I was close before he laid a finger on me, whipped into a heightened state of arousal by the savage way in which he used my mouth, but now that he has *his* mouth on me, I'm lost to everything that is not chasing the beautiful, shimmering rainbow of this orgasm to its very end.

'I'm going to come,' I gasp with difficulty. 'I'm going to— oh God, I need it as hard as you can.'

With a savage growl, he amps up the intensity of his finger-fucking and the tautness of his tongue, laving my clit with deadly precision and the perfect pressure: just the right side of *too much*. Those licks send me hurtling over the edge, and I shove my knuckles into my mouth as a blistering heat courses through every last vein and my entire body ignites into wondrous nothingness.

He licks me through it, sliding his fingers out as I come down and pressing a kiss to my clit before pulling away from me. In one swift move, he's collapsing on the sofa beside me and wrapping an arm around my waist so he can right me and tug me sideways onto his lap.

My most toxic trait as a sex worker is my love of aftercare. I absolutely don't require it—it's crucial for my mental health that I can look after myself after any kind of transactional sex, no matter how immersive or explosive—but I truly enjoy it.

I'm unsure if it's my love of being adored, or the need for some human connection to bely the commercial nature of what's just gone down, but I am a veritable kitten after a good orgasm or two. I love being petted, and cuddled, and praised. Some guys aren't interested, obviously, but some enjoy it. I suspect they even find it gratifying to see me soft-limbed and pliant and sleepy. Given the way Gabriel looked after me last time, fetching me that robe, I suspect he's in the camp that recognises its importance, even if he doesn't explicitly get off on it.

Nevertheless, I'm experienced enough at reading cues to understand that, given the way he's looking at me and the way he's sprawled, sated, on the sofa, he wants a moment before we move onto logins and phone-answering protocols.

And the way he's looking at me is hungry and not a little awe-struck. He tugs off my thong, which is still tangled uncomfortably around my knees, and smooths the silk of my dress over my legs, restoring my modesty. Our faces are so close, and I take the opportunity to gaze down at him, at the fans of dark lashes around his eyes and the sex-swollen lips.

'Fuck, I think I need to go to confession after that,' he mutters, and I laugh, because he sounds positively sheepish.

'How so?'

'I've never done that to a woman before.'

'Done what? Let her perform fellatio?' I find Latin always makes everything sound classier than it actually is. *Fellatio* originates from the past participle of *fello*: I suck. Pretty accurate really.

'I've never... fucked her mouth like that. It was pretty aggressive. Are you okay?'

I lick my lips. 'Do I look like I'm not okay?'

'No, but...'

'Gabriel. You abused my mouth, and I fucking loved it, as you know, because you got to find out for yourself just how hopelessly turned on I was, didn't you?'

He hesitates. He has one arm banded around me, and he reaches the other up to play with a tendril of my hair. 'I suppose so. But why a beautiful woman with the world at her feet wants me to abuse her at all, I'm not entirely sure. I'm in uncharted territory here.'

'Because it's kinky. Because it's subversive. Because I'm a relentless Type A in every other part of my life, as you'll soon see, and it's exhausting, and my way of balancing that is to have men dominate me and turn me into a little plaything, and it feels fucking wonderful. Does that reassure you?'

His face is so serious, so intense. This man listens with his whole body.

'I'll have to take your word for it.' His hand is deeper in my hair now. I adore having my hair played with. 'But I need to be absolutely sure that you'll advocate for your needs when you deem it necessary.'

'Gabriel, don't for a moment mistake my submission for a lack of confidence. I have more boundaries than Oprah. I promise you, if I'm unhappy in a situation, you'll know about it. But right now, I am very happy. This morning has gone down *exactly* as I intended so far.'

'Is that a fact? I'm as shocked as fuck.'

That gets him a laugh. 'Think of it as an icebreaker.'

'And then some.'

'Now that we've fooled around in your office, it's game on. Just remember, you can do what you like to me, whenever you like. *I want this.* I want to be your little whore. That's what I signed up for, remember?'

He frowns. I suspect words like *whore* make him uncomfortable when he's not in the throes of orgasm. No matter. We'll get him comfortable. Meanwhile, he's looking at my mouth like a starving man.

'If it's game on, may I kiss you?'

It's sweet that he asks, after everything we've just done. 'You may.'

His lips and tongue are supple, the touch of his hands proprietary, and he tastes like me. Now *that's* a turn on. How many women does this guy have to fend off every time he walks into a club or a bar, or even out of this room?

I bet he's inundated, and he's wearing *my* pussy all over this sexy face of his.

If that isn't a win for a Monday morning, I don't know what is.

CHAPTER 16

Athena

After Gabriel has fed me excellent coffee and I've borrowed his en suite bathroom to fix my hair and makeup and change my thong, he takes me for a tour.

This family office has two primary functions, as I understand it: managing the substantial and mainly urban land-based estate underpinning the Sullivans' astonishing wealth, and managing the family's other investments across all asset classes like any other private investment firm.

The business, therefore, is divided down the middle, the staff split between estate management and wealth management functions.

'Is there a philanthropic arm?' I ask Gabriel as we turn out of our little enclave and down the art-adorned corridor onto the main floor, so generic it could be any bank or consultancy firm. Heads turn as we approach. Also generic is the buzz of energy—or perhaps nerves—that always arises when the CEO shows his face on the floor.

'Those efforts still operate under the umbrellas of their divisions. There's an urgent need to extract them and establish a formal foundation, but it's been on the back burner as I try to get to grips with everything. I'm hoping we can breathe some new life into it. We're having a meeting about it next week, in fact.'

It makes sense. I know he's been overwhelmed. I nod. 'Of course.'

He stops by one of the first cubicles, where a fair-haired man a couple of years older than me is sitting, and slaps the back of his chair heartily.

'And this is George. My PA, my saviour.'

The PA-EA relationship can be a little fraught some-times if boundaries aren't clearly drawn. It will help, of course, that my desk is next to Gabriel's office and George's is out here, although I'm sure that positioning has more to do with my being here to covertly fuck the boss than anything else.

George gets to his feet, and we shake. 'Thank Christ you've arrived. I've been counting down the days.'

'I hired George as soon as I came on board,' Gabriel tells me. 'He wiped the floor with poor Gladys. But he's right. We've all been counting down the days.'

He smiles at me, his smile laced with the memory of us shoving our sex organs into each other's mouths just now. I catch a glimpse of George's stricken expression and instantly understand two things. He has a definite thing for Gabriel, and Gabriel, God bless him, is utterly oblivious. George can hopefully be an ally for me, as long as he can control whatever jealousy might arise over my presence. Meanwhile, he's managed to school his features and is now looking me over appreciatively.

'That dress is fabulous. Etro, perchance?'

I shoot him a genuine smile. 'Bingo.'

'God, that's impressive,' Gabriel says, scanning my dress in bewilderment. 'I've never heard of them. Um—can I assume you two will sit down for coffee at some point and hash out your working relationship? I think it makes sense.'

'Definitely,' I say. That's a priority. I may also have to take George under my wing and ensure he doesn't work himself to the bone for his delicious, oblivious boss. His demeanour has *eager puppy* written all over it, and something tells me service is his love language.

Coffee agreed, we move on. This floor is the estate management floor, and I'm encouraged to see a pretty equal balance of men and women. I assume Gabriel inherited the majority of employees from his father's tenure here. There are some definite characters.

The Finance Director, Old Jim, strikes me as a probable crony of Sullivan Senior. His real name is James Flanagan, he's a Dubliner, and he's sixty if he's a day. He has the bulbous nose and reddened face of a seasoned whiskey drinker, but I bet he's sharp as a tack. I could do without the lascivious look he gives me, though. Revolting.

Gabriel's Chief of Staff, Eleanor Whitmore, is Flanagan's opposite—old money and probably Oxbridge educated like me—but I doubt she'll give me an easier ride. She tells me she's worked for the Sullivans for twenty-five years, and it sounds like a warning not to tread on her turf.

God, I love it when people think they can manage me. I'll eat this woman for breakfast if I have to, even if she tastes like she looks—tough as old boots.

'I very much look forward to working together, Eleanor,' I tell her with a steely poise that reflects every ounce of my breeding.

'Ah!' Gabriel says with what sounds like genuine enthusiasm as a younger woman approaches. 'This is Torty—Victoria Spencer-Wells, the estate's Head of Stakeholder Relations. Torty, meet Athena.'

Torty may as well have a flashing neon sign above her head

that says *The Wannabe Future Mrs Gabriel Sullivan*. We eye each other up.

She's pretty enough, in that insipid, blonde, slightly inbred way so typical of the English upper classes. I went to school with a million versions of her. She's probably around thirty, but she's dressed like she's ready for a life of Range Rovers and shotguns and Labradors in a little cashmere sweater and a tweed pencil skirt. In my book, tweed is not okay unless it's Chanel or Balmain and extremely sparkly.

Torty's tweed is none of the above.

By far the most interesting thing about her is the naked panic in her expression as she shakes my hand, like I'm a threat she didn't see coming and one against which she has to fashion an immediate neutralisation plan.

'Welcome to Rath Mor,' she murmurs, shaking my hand a little too firmly. Subtext: *Back off, bitch. I have dibs on him, even though I know I'll never, ever get him.*

'Thank you so much,' I coo with my most beatific smile. *I've already had his huge cock in two of my holes, and he fucking loves it. Move aside, love, while you still have some self respect.*

One floor down, on the investment side, things get more interesting. A cursory glance tells me that the team here is MBA-heavy and that most of these people could be working for bulge-bracket banks or consultancy firms if they wanted to.

It's hard to describe *how* I know, exactly, except to say that there's a palpable hunger among the staff here. I've been in enough sleepy old-school investment firms—mainly on visits with my various bosses—to identify the mix of smugness and apathy that comes with working for a second- or third-tier firm. You know, long lunches and piss-taking and clocking off early.

I don't get that vibe from these guys at all. I bet they work sixty-hour weeks and are, for the most part, ruthless as hell. I allow myself a contented sigh, because these could be my people. I thrive in environments like this, and it makes me miss Bain.

Gabriel talks me through the layout with accompanying gestures. This floor is arranged by asset class: fixed income, equities, currencies, commodities, money markets, alternative investments. The layout is more open-plan here, with desks laid out in long rows. I spot dealer boards full of buttons so the dealers here can call their brokers to put on trades. Befriending these guys could be beneficial for my investment portfolio.

Gabriel claps his hands and asks for everyone's attention for a moment.

'Good morning,' he says. His voice is clear and loud, his stance relaxed. I suppose years of saying Mass will strip you of any self-consciousness. 'I hope you all had a cracking weekend. I'd like to introduce you all to my new executive assistant, Athena Davenport. I'm extremely excited to have her on board. She'll be sitting right outside my office upstairs, so please feel free to pop up anytime and make her feel welcome. Thank you.'

The employees themselves are eyeing me and Gabriel with acute interest. I can positively feel the hostility radiating from some of the women in particular, and I have to hide my smile. If we think this is anything more than a jungle and we've remotely evolved past being primates, situations like this are here to remind us otherwise.

I know how I look.

I know the message that sends to men and women alike.

It's exactly the message I want it to send.

And, if some of these women can't deal with it, if they incorrectly assume that Gabriel is fair game, that's not even the slightest bit my problem.

Sure enough, the primates begin to rise from their seats

and shuffle this way, ostensibly to say hello and really to check me out. The guys are first, coming in strong with handshakes and what they think are charming smiles. Some of them are decent looking, some not, some are actually pretty sexy. But how any of them could think they stand a chance when I'm standing next to the greatest prize in the entire building is baffling.

Interestingly, Gabriel seems less oblivious in these circumstances. He edges closer to me, his hand going discreetly to the small of my back as I smile and shake and say hello. When one particularly tall, particularly hot Dutch guy introduces himself as Dirk and smiles at me like I'm his next meal, Gabriel's fingers trail oh-so covertly south, pressing lightly into the cleft of my bottom.

The message: *Remember you're mine.*

Mmm. He's learning. I reward his delicious little show of possession by throwing a dazzling smile his way before giving Dirk short shrift. Not going to happen, pal. Not in any lifetime. I'm sure he has a Porsche or a Ferrari. I'm sure he wows his women with top restaurants and fine wines. But the poor guy has no way of knowing just how far short he falls of my average fuck. I don't dip my toes outside of the C-suite.

'That woman Torty wants your babies,' I tell Gabriel as we stroll back to the lift.

He laughs easily. 'Don't be ridiculous. No she doesn't.'

'She does. She hates me already with a passion she didn't know she had in her until just now.'

He stops and turns with a frown. 'I'm sure that's not the case, but if anyone gives you any hassle, I want to hear about it. I would never, ever stand for that in my workplace.'

Oh, sweet, sweet man. 'I promise you, anyone who underestimates me does it precisely once. You have nothing to worry about. But it's adorable quite how many future Mrs Sullivans there are wandering around down there. Perhaps you can get

George to research countries where polygamy is legal if you don't want to break too many hearts.'

His face softens. 'I know you can handle yourself. And I could say the same for you.' He holds out a hand, gesturing for me to enter the waiting lift. 'I had to swat them away like flies. Fucking Dirk Jansen.'

I smile as I back up against the wall of the lift, arching my back and enjoying the ravenous way his eyes roam over my body. 'They can look, but you're the only man who gets to lay a hand on me. I really liked it when you reminded me of that back there. How does it feel to know that you can touch me whenever you want, wherever you want?'

He takes the bait, stepping forward as the doors close and sliding his hands around my waist. He dips his face, seeking out my neck and inhaling hard. I have my scent custom-blended, and it seems he approves.

When he speaks, his voice is muffled and, I think, a little bashful.

'It makes me feel like a fucking king.'

This is it.

This is the way to intoxicate him.

That this beautiful male specimen has spent the past God knows how many years in a willing state of poverty and celibacy, of eschewing worldliness in favour of being spiritually replete, is staggering to me.

Because he *is* a fucking king.

And I'm going to waltz in here day after day, looking my absolute best, and show him, with every weapon in my arsenal, that I am here for one reason and one reason only.

To serve this king of mine.

CHAPTER 17

Gabe

I take Athena to The Wolseley for lunch, a move dictated primarily by my wish to make her feel welcome and partly by a baser desire to show her off.

This beautiful space, once a prestigious car showroom and now a brasserie, has always been one of my favourite places to eat. When I was still a priest, I'd come here with Dad and Bren on their dime—my self-imposed ban on supplementing my meagre salary with family money didn't extend to the odd excellent breakfast.

I adore the atmosphere here. The interior is somewhat masculine, all Art Deco features and magnificent chandeliers and monochromatic marble flooring and soaring ceilings: a church to the fine art of dining. The vibe is reminiscent of those wonderful European Grand Cafés, with a menu to match.

Once we've ordered—kedgeree for me and French onion soup for Athena—I revel in the warmth that comes from having the undivided attention of hands down the most beautiful woman in a bustling restaurant.

'What?' I ask, amused at the way she's been appraising me.

She shakes her head. 'It just staggers me that you were ever a priest.'

'Why is that?'

'Well, for one, you're wearing a five-figure suit. For another, you seem far more at home at Rath Mor than you let on when I interviewed. And you seem fond of the finer things in life.'

I laugh. 'Maybe I'm just highly adaptable.'

'Maybe.' Her narrowed eyes tell me she's not buying it.

'Look. Rath Mor may only have been spun off a few years ago, but this has been my family's business since before I was born. I've always had a foot in both camps. Uncomfortably so, perhaps.'

'You must have been the wealthiest priest outside of the Vatican.'

'Not in practice. I didn't take a penny of my family's money.'

'Could you have? You took a vow of poverty, didn't you?'

'It's not technically a vow, more like a solemn promise. I could have taken some money, certainly, but it would have been in pretty bad faith, don't you think? It would have diminished my ability to align with my parishioners, in any case.'

'And what about now?' She takes a sip of her sparkling water. 'Did you—'

We're interrupted by a guy who approaches with an apology that sounds totally fucking phony to my ears. He's tall, with light brown hair. I'd put money on him working at one of the many hedge funds in this neighbourhood. He's staring at Athena as though the Virgin Mary herself has just graced him with an appearance.

'So sorry to disturb,' he says suavely. 'I just wondered—are you two together? Because if not, I'd love to—'

'We're together,' I say in my best *don't even go there* voice, at the same time as Athena says, 'I'm not interested.'

Her voice is polite but dismissive. She has no interest in him. She doesn't seem tickled by the blatant play he's making for her, but neither does she seem at all taken aback, and it makes me wonder quite how often she gets hit on.

'Is that normal?' I ask her once he's backed away with a sheepish smile and an apology. 'Do people really come onto other people like that, when they're quite obviously at lunch with someone else?'

She shrugs. 'You'd be surprised. It's a jungle out there. Count yourself lucky you were free of that element for a few years.'

I suspect that little interlude has less to do with the jungle and more to do with Athena herself. I suspect if I were a different type of man and I saw her in a restaurant, I'd take one look at her and deem her worthy of breaking any sort of social codes to have a crack.

She really is that exquisite. She's applied fresh scarlet lipstick that makes her mouth look like a beautifully wrapped present, and I know all too well what a gift it really is.

'*Anyway,* I was just about to ask you if you'd done any financial damage since you came back over to the dark side, before we were so rudely interrupted.'

I consider. 'I decorated a house. That was the biggest one. And I bought a Book of Hours.'

That has her attention. 'Really? What kind?'

'One from the Florentine Renaissance. I saw it in Sotheby's and couldn't resist. It's really—well, it's beautiful.'

'I adore religious art,' she confesses. 'My parents did six months in Florence. It wasn't long enough, and I was at uni, so I didn't get enough time there. But I love that that was your big splurge.'

'It's at the office. You know the door next to my bath-room? It's in there. I'll show you when we get back.'

She leans forward, head tilted. 'Do you actually use it for praying, or is it just because it's beautiful?'

'Both. It's an exceptional work of art, but I've found I engage with it in a way that really enriches me, you know? There's something about referring to a centuries-old source to help me pray. It feels, I don't know…'

'Elevating,' she supplies, and I grin.

'Exactly. It elevates the experience of praying to a whole different level. That's one element of Catholicism I've always felt comfortable with, actually—the role of beauty in cele-brating the glory of God.'

Her face is interested, open, as I speak.

'So your faith is very much intact. You haven't thrown out all your old beliefs—just your vocation itself.'

'Very much so, yes.'

'I was curious. Because you hired me, obviously. So there's a conflict there. Is that a fair assumption?'

'That's correct,' I tell her. 'And, if you can believe this, the conflict comes less from hiring you, in particular, and more from navigating this intensely secular lifestyle in general. Hence, the Book of Hours acts like an anchor. It helps to tether me to what's important. It allows me to tend to my spir-itual health.'

She says nothing as we're served our food, but I can practi-cally see that extraordinary brain of hers whirring.

'What is it?' I ask with a smile.

'I have an observation,' she admits, 'but I can't think of a way of asking it without it being incredibly insulting.'

'Well, now you have to ask it. I'm intrigued.'

She hesitates, which I suspect is unlike her, and sets down her soup spoon. 'I realise your family is Irish, so Catholicism was deemed normal for you, but you're obviously an extremely cerebral man, and I can't for the life of me work out how you've fallen for the whole organised religion thing. From where I'm sitting, it's quite obviously a construct, an exercise in mind control. I mean, it's so ridiculously over-engineered! I just can't square your intellect with a faith so strong that you gave up everything to serve it.'

She sits back, as if the conundrum of my belief system has actually defeated her fierce, presumably atheistic, brain, and I grin.

'The entire answer to your question, Athena, lies in your use of the word *faith*.'

'Yes, but, it's so far-fetched. Why not give the gift of your faith—and your service, for that matter—to something more deserving?'

I study her. I've had this conversation more times than I can count, of course, mainly with parishioners who've felt lost or doubtful or even deceived, but periodically with fellow clerics, shooting the theological breeze over beers on our nights off.

'What makes something deserving of our faith?' I ask her quietly.

'Well, believability, for a start. I have a theory that organised religion was made complex for a reason. It was world building on the scale of epic fantasy, if you like. Tolkien had nothing on the Old Testament. And I understand that it served a critical role—not just the church as an instrument of the state, as mass crowd control—but to give people purpose and meaning and comfort.

'But we're not wretched, terrified peasants now. We're highly educated, sophisticated beings with far more agency over our own existence, so for the love of God, why would we still choose to believe all that?'

Her argument doesn't offend me. Not in the slightest. And I have no intention of going on the defensive. The bottom line is that we are both perfectly entitled to our views, no matter how obtuse we may deem each other for not sharing those views.

'One of the gifts of having a soul as well as a brain,' I begin, 'is the ability to believe in things we cannot see or prove. Like gravity.'

She groans. 'If you tell me you're a gravity denier, I'm getting up and leaving right now.'

'Of course I'm not a gravity denier! And I don't believe God created the world in seven days either, if that makes you feel better. But I do believe that this universe of ours, that operates in such perfect homeostasis despite its complexity, can only be the creation of a benign God, and everything else I believe stems from that.'

'You sound like a humanist,' she says, picking up her spoon and dipping it into the amber-coloured liquid.

'I believe in very many things that humanists don't. I believe that Christ rose from the dead to grant us eternal life, and I believe that every time I stood on that altar, I had the unutterable privilege of transforming bread and wine into His flesh and blood.

'But, perhaps most importantly, I believe that God's grace is the most precious gift He can give us. To be imperfect and know that you are still worthy of love... to receive love so great, knowing you absolutely haven't earned it nor can never, ever earn it? That, for me, is probably the most beautiful and mystical thing about this faith of mine.'

She stares at me, spoon suspended. It's as if I've knocked the wind out of her sails.

'The Stoics would have said that was a lazy argument,' she counters eventually, but she doesn't sound as though her heart is in it. 'Giving up on being the best version of yourself because you'll be loved anyway? What a cop out.'

'Ah, yes. The Classics scholar speaks.'

'At least they didn't need the carrot of heaven or the threat of hell dangled over their heads to be good people. They believed in self-improvement for its own sake. And self-sufficiency.'

'St Augustine was a bit of a Stoic, now you mention it,' I muse. 'Before his conversion, I mean. "Lord, make me chaste, but not yet."'

She laughs, looking delighted. 'Did you just make a sex joke about St Augustine? That prayer could be a good one for you, come to think of it. You might want to hold onto that. But honestly, they're worlds apart.'

'Not really,' I press. 'There are a lot more parallels than you'd think. Yes, we have miracles and divine grace, but you could argue that both philosophies carry a mutual respect. Stoics and Catholics alike are urged to examine their conscience on a daily basis. Our cardinal virtues are definitely rooted in Stoicism. And—my trump card—both are massive on suffering.'

She throws her head back and laughs, and it's a truly privileged sight to see her beauty animated through mirth.

'Okay, okay,' she says, reaching for the bread basket. 'So Catholicism is Stoicism with miracles. Got it.'

'And grace. And redemption. Don't forget those.'

As we continue with our meal, Athena excoriates me for the way the Church has bastardised Classical Latin over the ages. I counter fiercely with what I believe to be an intellectually robust defence: namely that in the aftermath of the Roman Empire blowing itself up, Church Latin has been responsible for keeping this most solemn and noble of languages alive to this day, albeit with a healthy dose of creative licence.

She doesn't buy it.

It only strikes me after we've returned to the office that my soul is feeling as replete as my belly.

CHAPTER 18

Athena

The next afternoon, I swing by George's desk and out we sashay to find a suitable venue for our introductory coffee. My initial agenda has shifted somewhat, because Gabriel has decided that George should be the only person at Rath Mor who knows the full extent of my job description. He argued at lunch yesterday that we'll need George on board for 'logistical help'—that is, booking hotel rooms.

Gabriel actually suggested that he tell George, a proposal I instantly quashed. Only one of us is aware of his PA's gigantic crush, so only one of us has the emotional intelligence to handle this gently.

'Oh darling,' he says, giving my powder blue Chanel shift dress an appreciative once-over, 'you are most definitely *not* Gladys, thank fuck.'

'I certainly am not.' I smooth down my dress, which Gabriel has already removed once today, and wonder idly if I should go show that Torty woman what tweed is supposed to look like. For his part, George looks fabulously fashionable in perfectly cut chocolate-brown trousers and a chunky cream sweater.

'The Ritz?' he suggests as we meander down Berkeley Street.

'It would be rude not to,' I agree.

We settle on a well-stuffed sofa in the iconic Rivoli Bar. Its walnut panelled walls and gold Art Deco flourishes feel decadent, even in the middle of a January afternoon.

'The thing you need to know about our Angel Gabriel,' George begins conspiratorially, 'is that he's shockingly bad at looking after himself. I don't mean he's incompetent—he lived by himself for years, obviously—but he doesn't put himself first.'

I refrain for now from saying that Gabriel has indulged in quite the act of self care by hiring me. Sex on tap aside, I can well believe it.

'Go on.'

'You can take the man out of the priesthood, but it's a lot harder to take the priesthood out of the man, if you catch my drift. He's still a giver. He chats with everyone in the office like he's hearing their confessions. And that recurring Wednesday lunchtime meeting in his calendar? That's him trotting his lovely arse down to a soup kitchen off Ladbroke Grove.'

'He volunteers at a soup kitchen?' I ask. I don't know why I'm surprised. It makes perfect sense, but it's so... grass roots. Hands on. I assumed he would just throw money at these kinds of things.

'He *funds* the soup kitchen, and yeah, he volunteers there. A priest mate of his runs it—Father John. He was struggling to keep its doors open, so Gabriel stepped in and promised unlimited funding.'

'Got it. What else should I know?'

'He forgets to eat lunch unless I put it in front of him and stand there menacingly while he eats, and even then, he eats for fuel during the day. He's definitely too low-maintenance for a billionaire. It's most disappointing.'

'How much have you had to bling him up?' I ask, my eyes narrowing. I'm beginning to wonder if Gabriel would still be living like a priest if left to his own devices—seven-figure religious artefacts aside, obviously.

His grin is devilish. 'Quite a lot. I'm *very* good at spending other people's money. I worked for the Royals before this, you know. Tight-fisted gits. So the suits are my doing. He was wearing high street suits when I came on board.' We both shudder. 'I tried to get him to go down the Tom Ford route— he has that fabulous, rangy body shape—but he ended up going to Savile Row. Still, he cleans up well. And his house has been a whole thing. What a fucking palaver.' He puts up his hands in a show of resignation.

'How so?'

'Well, he took on one of his family's properties—nice place in Manchester Square. You know, just by the Wallace Collection? Anyway, it had great bones but inside it was like something out of an Eighties bonkbuster. Strictly between us, Maeve's taste—that's his mum—runs a little nouveau, bless her. So I took over the interior design project. We haven't done much structural, but it's been a gigantic ball ache. It's just about done now, and it's fucking fabulous, if I say so myself. Not a gold carriage clock in sight.'

I giggle. George is my kind of person: whip-smart and judgmental as fuck.

Also: that's good intel about the house. Manchester Square isn't too far from the office. Could be good for the occasional fuck.

When the server comes, I put a hand on George's arm. 'I vote we have a proper drink. I have something to tell you, and I'm not sure coffee's going to cut it.'

We order—champagne for me and an old fashioned for

him. Once our drinks have arrived, he sits back, nursing his cocktail and appraising me.

'Let me have it, you little beauty. Jesus, I may love dick but you are frankly stunning. Honestly. You've put a few noses out of joint in the past twenty-four hours, believe me.'

I smile with satisfaction. 'About that.'

'What about it?' He sits up straighter.

I pull a pen and a sheaf of papers out of my Birkin. 'New NDA. Sign first, then I'll tell you.'

He sighs as he slides the papers towards himself. 'Another fucking NDA. This had better be worth it.'

'Oh, it definitely will be.'

He signs with a flourish and picks up his tumbler. 'Well? Shoot.'

'Gabriel hasn't just hired me as his EA,' I begin, watching his face for a reaction as he takes a sip of his old fashioned. 'He's hired me to fuck him.'

He claps his free hand to his mouth and jerks forward, coughing violently. I remove his drink from his other hand. 'You okay?'

'No.' He rasps out the word and continues to cough. 'Nope.'

I wait until he has his choking under control. 'Look. I know you're attracted to him. I'm sorry.'

He jerks his head up. 'Seriously? You barely know me!'

I scrunch up my face in sympathy.

'You think Gabriel knows?'

'Please,' I scoff. 'He's clueless.'

Relief flashes across his features, followed by hurt. '*He's hired you to fuck him.* Does that mean what I think it means?'

'It means I'm what's known as a "full service" EA. I meet the professional and sexual needs of extremely powerful men within their office hours. It's highly efficient.'

He's full-on gaping at me. 'Hoooly fuck. Is that actually a thing?'

'It absolutely is. A very discreet, very expensive thing.'

'Hang on. Let me get this straight. So you're telling me our precious Priest Boy hired himself a... oh my God. Oh my *God*. This is better than Fleabag!'

I bark out a surprised laugh. 'You're taking this a lot better than I expected.'

He visibly sags. 'Oh, please. It's not like I thought I had a chance. I know he likes women. Loves them, if the amount of times I've booked him a private room at Alchemy is any sign.'

'I heard he traumatised a cleaner there,' I say with a smile. 'That's when he decided to hire me.'

'It was a low point, that's for sure. Do you know what he did, though? He had me chase Alchemy for the cleaner's details and send her a huge bunch of flowers and a grand's worth of Tesco vouchers. How sweet is that?'

I roll my eyes. Of course he bloody did. 'Ridiculously sweet. God, he's a good man.'

'He is one hundred percent Jesus in this scenario,' George confirms. 'And you know what that makes you, right?'

'Let me guess. Mary Magdalene?'

He nods. 'That is correct.'

'I'm the fallen woman, the whore who tries to corrupt him.'

'The whore who *sees* him,' he corrects me. 'And who *falls for him.*'

'Well, that's not going to happen. I'm just here to keep his mind clear and his dick wet.'

He flops dramatically back on the sofa. 'Jesus Christ. Pun intended. You lucky, lucky bitch. I can't bear it.'

'Is this going to be a problem for you and me?'

'No.' He shakes his head and presses his lips together before continuing. 'Alas, my love for him is as selfless as it is unrequited. I just want to see him happy and well looked after. And if it has to be anyone, I'm glad it's you, because you literally couldn't be any hotter, and you're also a total badass, which I really like. Plus, I bet you're as good at blowjobs as I am.'

'I absolutely am,' I agree.

'Have you fucked him already?' He turns to look at me. 'You have. Of course you have. Fuck, you've already had the privilege of seeing him naked.'

Yes, I have, and it's a fine, fine sight. I usually take great pleasure in knowing that these incredible men want *me* and no one else, but I hate this for George. He's a lovely guy who cares about Gabriel a lot, and it's shitty. 'For what it's worth, I'm sorry.'

He waves my apology off. 'You can make it up to me by getting knocked up, because you guys would make the most gorgeous babies, and also please marry him and shove your big fat diamond in the faces of all those horrific Sloane Rangers who drool over him at work. I'd pay good money to see that.'

'I can confirm I have no intention of compromising my birth control or marrying the guy, but I promise you, my only objective is to make him happy.'

'Yeah.' He looks me over. 'God, you'll definitely do that. I have to say, the man has impeccable taste, even if he doesn't appreciate your Etro and Chanel game. I love that he hired you. I've been dying to see what kind of women he goes for, but honestly? I can't fault you.'

I smile at him. 'Why, George, that's very touching. Thank you.'

'So where do you do it? Have you been booking the hotels? Because I can take that over for you, obviously.'

'My agency booked a hotel suite for my audition,' I tell him, 'but today and yesterday we've just done it in his office.'

He presses his fingertips to the bridge of his nose and

exhales long and hard. 'There is so much to unpack in that sentence that I have total overwhelm. Why is it so hot that he auditioned you? Right, that's going straight into the spank bank—with him auditioning *me*, obviously.'

'Obviously.' I shrug. 'I think that one will work well for you.'

'And you have an agency?'

'I do. Seraph. They make sure everything's above board. I wouldn't do this on my own. They're amazing.'

'Seraph,' he muses. 'That's an angel, right? I love that for you. Are there loads of these angels around?'

'Seraphim, we call ourselves. And yes. Next time you meet a CEO with his attractive young EA, you can speculate as to the nature of their relationship.'

'I will. I absolutely fucking will. And you've been shagging him in his office while we all sit around the corner, totally oblivious. Excuse me while I die of jealousy. But it's now making a lot more sense as to why he asked me to get a remote control lock installed on the outer door last week.'

I laugh. 'He used that this morning.'

'I bet he did, the dirty bastard. Right, well we can do better than that for you, my dear. I assume you'd like to fuck the delicious Mr Sullivan in an actual bed from time to time? I can set that up for you. What's your preference? Claridges? Here is nice, too. If you leave it to him, he'd probably book some budget horror.'

'Let's do Claridges. It's closer and less of a circus.'

'Agreed. Discretion will be your friend. Although you should know that money is already exchanging hands around the office over how soon you guys will fuck. Everyone's watching you, just so you know.'

'Don't worry,' I promise, 'I've got this. I'm so discreet I could be fucking the king himself and no one would know.'

He chortles, delighted. 'Stranger things have happened at

Buckingham Palace, let me tell you. And I promise I'll be discreet, too. You don't help plan three royal weddings and not take a vow of silence. But this is the most delicious secret *ever*. Do you know what the best bit is? Everyone in the whole fucking place is positively jostling to put a ring on that man, and you just want his dick.'

'Abso-fucking-lutely,' I tell him. 'Now, why don't you give me the lay of the land? Aside from the fact that everyone's already sticking metaphorical pins in me, tell me what else I need to know.'

'I wouldn't assume they're metaphorical, darling. There are probably a few dolls in desk drawers doubling as pin cushions already. But let me see.' He takes a thoughtful sip of his drink. 'Generally, Gabriel is well liked. Adored, even. I wasn't here during his old man's reign, but I think he got pretty lazy towards the end. I mean, wouldn't you, if you were that loaded? He was way more interested in the gee-gees than the estate, apparently.

'But there's some definite frustration among the ranks that we haven't seen big changes yet. I think they all expected the Angel Gabriel to turn things around immediately, but you can't turn the Titanic overnight, can you?'

'Exactly,' I murmur, making a mental note of that. For God's sake, Gabe's been a priest for a decade. It's not like he's come straight out of an MBA. They need to cut the guy some slack. 'What would you say the biggest issues are in terms of what they want changed?'

'Well, most of it goes over my head, but it seems there's a view that they should either start managing other families' assets or cut back the investment management team, which is a bit bloated. But the lack of a foundation seems to be the most egregious issue. It's not like the Sullivans don't give a shitload to charity—they really do—but it's not a cohesive strategy, you know?'

'Gabe mentioned yesterday that the foundation was a matter of urgency for him.' This is excellent. I was integral to the creation of a foundation for my first boss in the tech sector. It's definitely an area where I can add value.

'It is, but good luck putting a rocket under Eleanor Whitmore's arse. She's supposedly leading the whole thing but her approach to our "charitable projects" as she calls them, is very *champagne socialism*, if you catch my drift. She still thinks it's 1985 and she's running the charity committee at her son's prep school. But don't let the pearls fool you. She's got teeth, and she doesn't like to be challenged.'

'Roger that.' I make another mental note. It doesn't get more juicy than structuring a foundation. It's any MBA's wet dream. I'm not about to let some old fart decked out in the family pearls get in my way. 'Is that woman Torty involved? She's in charge of stakeholder relations, correct?'

He pretends to shudder. 'Yes, and she's smart, and definitely hungrier than Eleanor. But she's a ghastly name-dropper. She's all *Cadogan* this and *Grosvenor* that. She'd love to think the estate is all about preserving gorgeous old buildings when really, the docklands is still a shithole. A lot of those communities are still seriously deprived. I think she needs to learn to read the fucking room. Oh, and she needs to find someone else to fixate on instead of drooling all over the lovely Gabriel. She's been circling him like a posh shark for months.'

I sigh. I have faith in Gabriel and I want to help him achieve whatever vision he has for this great chunk of London that he owns. But without the right team, his job—*our* job—will be a lot more difficult.

'What else?' I push. 'What about Old Jim?'

'Old Jim is a ghastly old lech, and fuck knows how he's not on the liver transplant list yet. He's a functioning alcoholic. I wouldn't know a P&L from a balance sheet, but apparently he's excellent at what he does—when he's sober. Greedy old fucker, though. I can't imagine he'd be the biggest fan of increasing our charitable efforts.'

'He will when I wow him with tax efficiency possibilities,' I say with confidence. I allow myself a sip of crisp, cold champagne. Delicious. 'George, you're a star. Will you be my spy?'

'Sure,' he agrees easily. 'I'll be your eyes and ears on the floor while you're busy getting fucked over the boss's desk. Just... look after him, okay? He's still new to this world. It's a lot. He's a good man, and that heart of his is like an open church door. Whether he knows it or not, he needs nasty little bitches like you and me to protect him from that lot... and from himself.'

CHAPTER 19

Athena

This risk I'm taking isn't merely ill-advised.

It's quite possibly a sackable offence.

The unofficial, unspoken mandate I've assumed is that I'm here not merely as a vessel into which this good, devout man can pour his baser urges but as a siren. A corrupter. Someone to help him cross that chasm between where he stands, suspended in a kind of spiritual no-man's land, and that carnal, flesh-loving kingdom that the rest of us inhabit so freely.

It's not that I want him to forsake his beliefs. It's already clear to me that his faith, his moral code, is what sets him markedly apart from all the other powerful men I've ever served. It's that I want him to commit to the path he's taken. I want him to revel in the lushness of this sensual playground; I want him to behave like a free man, a joyful sinner, and not a saint who's lost his way.

But there's holding Gabriel's hand as he takes those first cautious steps onto what must still feel like the least convincing of bridges, cobbled together from rope and planks and knots, and there's disrespecting his faith and using my body to profane the very things he holds dearest.

He reminded me yesterday evening as we left that he had an early breakfast meeting today but that he hoped to be back in time for Terce, which is apparently the 9am prayer to the Holy Spirit.

God knows, he'll need him this morning.

As I wait, I gaze down at the *horae,* or Book of Hours. I've seen a couple before in the flesh, most notably at the Biblioteca Nazionale in Florence. I may not have a religious bone in my body, but my entire skeletal system is artistic, and this ancient manuscript awakens in me that rapture that I'm privileged enough to call familiar. The sense of awe, of disbelief, is there, as is the kick at being alone to commune with a truly great piece of art. The still-vivid illuminations may not move me to prayer, but they make my soul sing.

I shake my head slightly so my waves tumble silkily down my back. I took even more care with my appearance this morning than I did yesterday, tonging my hair before applying a scented oil that I know brings out my natural auburn high-lights and achieves a rich gloss. The primping routine doesn't come from a place of insecurity—I have no doubt how attracted Gabriel is to me—but from a desire to delight him. Entrance him. Remind him that I'm the most dazzling prize of all and that *he's* the man who deserves me.

I've knelt on harder surfaces than the leather of this *prie-dieu,* worn smooth by the knees of a century or two of sinners. Still, it's not the most comfortable of positions, and I'm a little on the cold side. This temperature-controlled room is not the ideal place to be naked.

On the plus side, my nipples are perfectly tight little peaks and the multi-million pound view in the display case in front of me as I wait could be far worse. I may have accused Catholi-cism of being over-engineered yesterday, but this intricate manuscript has me delighting in the bells and whistles the Church has seen fit to weave into the fabric of the belief system it promotes. The page is already turned to *Hora Tertia* —the third hour. Gabriel allowed me the pleasure of donning the nitrile gloves yesterday and turning the pages of this fragile manuscript in readiness for his morning prayers.

As the modest wall clock in here shows eight-fifty-five, there comes the distinctive click of Gabriel's office door opening, and my heart rate kicks up right on cue. He's unlikely to miss the way my dress and lingerie are laid across his sofa—the most intimate kind of invitation. I roll back my shoulders and assume my position of prayer, my palms and fingertips kissing chastely before me.

I can hear the muffled sounds of him moving about in his office, and then he's opening the door. There's a harsh intake of breath, and then my favourite kind of curse from this man's lips: blasphemy.

'Jesus Christ, Athena.'

I turn to look up at him, quite aware of the timeless contradiction this image must portray: the whore on her knees in front of a priceless religious artefact, and seemingly in prayer, for once. It also strikes me that, in here, I'm not the most expensive of his possessions. Nor am I the most *recherché*.

He's removed his coat, but a camel cashmere scarf still hangs around his neck. His eyes are glittering, his nose red-tipped from the cold, and there's something about the loose-hanging scarf and the neat punctuation of his tie below his Adam's apple that evokes his former priestly self in whatever his vestments are called.

But there is nothing priestly about the way he's taking in my naked body.

Nothing priestly at all.

'If it's too much, tell me and I'll go get dressed. I don't

want to offend you.' My voice is assured. Unhurried. I have no intention of making myself feel as though I'm on the back foot here. This is a calculated move on my part, after all.

He doesn't reply, merely takes a step towards me, reaching blindly for the door handle and pulling the door closed behind him. From this angle, he looks huge. Hulking. His presence looms over me, and I feel alone with him in a way I haven't yet —not yesterday morning, and not in that vast hotel suite, certainly. That was a playground and this is a priest's cell, confronting in its compactness.

There's nowhere to run in here.

'It seems we have very different ideas about our morning practices,' he deadpans, strolling over to the small sofa that takes up the entire length of the far wall. My eyes follow him as he whips off his scarf and peels off his suit jacket. After his initial profanity, his voice now gives little away—less than his actions, certainly.

'I thought perhaps we could combine them.'

A small bark of a laugh. 'You thought I should bury myself deep inside my beautiful, beautiful whore while I pray to the Holy Spirit for fortitude.'

He's turned to me and is unbuttoning his cufflinks. *Very promising.*

I hold firm. 'I thought it might be a novel way to elevate the act of prayer.'

'Elevate. Not desecrate?'

'Sometimes they can feel very alike.'

'Don't I know it.' He takes a few steps towards me, tossing a cufflink down on the table. 'You filled my water jug.'

'Yes.' Yesterday, when he showed me the the *horae*, he explained to me how he washes his hands before praying, a practice harking back to his former Lavabo ritual.

'Thank you,' he says softly, dropping the other cufflink so it clinks against the wood of the tabletop, just next to the trio of condom packets I've laid out. 'It's always important to wash one's hands before touching anything this exquisite, isn't it?'

I stare up at him wordlessly as he stands beside me and rolls up his cuffs. Their snowy whiteness is the perfect frame for the architecture of his body: that olive skin and soft, dark hair; the pleasing substance of his wrist bones and the taut flex of muscle in his forearms. I haven't seen him naked for over a month, which is probably why his little performance feels as erotic as a Victorian damsel unbuttoning her glove so that her suitor can kiss her wrist and a damn sight more ominous.

Perhaps he's not prepared to admit verbally that he's on board with fucking me here in his sacred space. Maybe he'll just show me instead. Besides, if I'm not mistaken, there's a definitive bulge growing beneath that flat stomach and shiny belt buckle.

I watch as he pours the water in a steady arc, as it sluices cleanly into the metal bowl, as he sets down the jug and proceeds to wash his hands. Slowly. Methodically. He's not ignoring me so much as silently accepting my presence, it seems. There's something pleasingly austere about the juxtaposition of his beautiful hands and this cold, clean water. No soap. No bubbles. This isn't an indulgence—it's an act of service.

I observe the whole thing like an adoring puppy who's hypervigilant of her master's needs. It's only after he's reached for the pressed linen cloth and dried his hands with efficient strokes that he glances up at the clock before looking me in the eye again.

'Time to pray, I think.'

I suspect other women may have grown increasingly uncomfortable during this encounter. I, on the other hand, am perfectly content. Gabriel hasn't kicked me out, which means he's happy with—if taken aback by—my presence. My nakedness. I have visual proof that I'm affecting him. If anything, the past few minutes have felt like foreplay, if foreplay was a game of chess.

I've made my move.

He's had his deliberation time.

Now it's time for him to make *his* move.

CHAPTER 20

Gabe

'Legs apart,' I tell her as I come to stand behind her. 'Lean forward for me.'

If I thought she was dangerous on her knees for me yesterday in the middle of my office, in here she's downright lethal. I take in the sight of her: burnished waves and creamy skin and the violin-shaped silhouette of her body that's surely as hardwired into our beauty-seeking parts as the Fibonacci sequence. Her bottom is pale and pert and so inviting as to feel like home for my angry, pulsing dick.

She obliges as if she's a good girl and not the intoxicating little sacrileger that she is, and I sink slowly to my knees. The kneeler on this thing is generously proportioned, but it's a tall order to get two adults stacked one behind each other on it, and when I kneel, my wool-clad legs straddling her bare ones, it has the effect of pressing her front up against the wood and every perfect inch of her back up against *me*.

I take a moment to drink her in. Usually when I'm in here, my mind is on the beautifully inscribed words in front of me and on the grace I seek, but today my senses are spilling over with the blessings of this beautiful woman. Instinctively, she tips her head to the left so I can lay my cheek against hers as I peer over her shoulder to the prayer book. I inhale luxuriously, her heady floral scent enveloping me. I already equate it with the most decadent kind of sex.

My fingertips trail up the sides of her body with the lightest of touches, moving up over the goosebumps on her thighs, her hips, and lingering at the dip of her waist before I bring my arms up. An ill-advised glance over her shoulder shows me her breasts smushed together and two hard, pink little nipples on full display.

I set my elbows on the cap rail so my arms are framing hers, and then I join my hands in prayer around hers. Her steepled fingertips are freezing. I cage her in more firmly with the sensitive skin of my bare inner forearms against her outer forearms. She shivers in the cradle of my body, leaning back as much as she can against my chest.

She feels tiny and fragile like this, and her shiver serves as a timely reminder that she isn't just the fierce warrior queen whose role she plays so convincingly but a young woman who must have her own demons, her own insecurities, no matter how skilfully they're buried. Her taking this step, waiting in here for me like this, touches me in a way I can't quite articulate.

The realisation has me speaking more gently than I may otherwise have done when I begin to intone the opening to all the Hours.

'Deus, in adiutorium meum intende.
Domine, ad adiuvandum me festina.'
O God, come to my assistance.
O Lord, make haste to help me.

How fucking ironic that I should be praying these words while my body is wrapped around that of a young, shivering, perfectly naked woman for whose very presence, nakedness, I am paying through the nose. I recall our jokey conversation about St Augustine yesterday at lunch.

Lord, make me chaste, but not yet.

I'm self-aware enough to know it's highly improbable that I'll want any divine intervention against the very venal sins Athena and I are hurtling towards in my private and previously sacrosanct space.

I pray the Hymn of Terce aloud, pausing before I launch into the Psalms to whisper into Athena's ear. With my head turned a little, my lips brush the delicate shell of her ear.

'Did you know that Terce is essentially a prayer to the Holy Spirit to ask for moderation and control of one's earthly passions?'

I can't see her smile, but I can certainly hear the pleased note in her voice. 'I did not. How fitting.'

'Fitting? Horribly ironic, more like.'

'Maybe your God has sent me to tempt you. Did you ever think of that?'

'If he has, then I'm screwed.' I allow my lips to linger in the hollow below her cheekbone for a moment before turning to face the book. I don't need it as a prompt, and if I did, its ornate calligraphy would fall well short of easy legibility.

At Terce, I tend to say a selection of lines from The Book of Psalms that I know by heart, lines that bring me comfort and strength. Only, as I recite them today, I feel every word as an admonition, as excruciating as if I were flogging myself as I recite them:

'Turn my eyes from looking at worthless things.
Turn away the reproach that I dread.
Let my heart be blameless.'

When I set this time aside in an otherwise full calendar, when I turned the handle of this door, my intentions were pure. This was to be my moment, in a life sliding alarmingly towards total secularism, to check in with God. To ask for His grace. To connect with Him, really. And now, with my senses as full of this naked temptress as my arms are, my prayers sound disingenuous to my own ears.

I want it all. I want to commune with God and His son and His Holy Spirit, and I want to bury myself deep inside Athena's body, a body that feels extraordinarily sinful and yet has been created in God's likeness.

It's a body so beautiful that I could happily never come up for air.

I want spiritual rapture *and* bodily rapture, it seems.

What would happen if I tried for both? God won't rain His wrath, His vengeance, down upon me. This ancient manuscript won't combust into flames. He gave man Free Will for a reason.

'Keep your hands like that,' I murmur, sliding mine down over her wrists, her forearms. I move further south, splaying my fingertips over the whisper-soft skin of her stomach and enjoying far too much the way the muscles below it contract under my touch. With my other hand I stroke that silken nook running along the underside of her breast, and it seems to me that she braces for more.

I pinch her nipple. She whimpers, and it's a rallying cry that has me rolling it, kneading her breast.

'So we're "elevating" my morning prayers, are we?' I ask softly, and she hums her answer. 'Let's see.' I let the hand on her stomach drag south, over the tidy strip of hair that covers her pelvic bone until my fingers find her wetness. 'Dear me, you have been looking forward to this, haven't you? Such a greedy girl that you couldn't let me have my fifteen minutes with God first, hmm?'

'I wanted to see you praying,' she gasps out as my fingers work their way past her clit to her entrance.

'That, sweetheart, is bullshit. You could have done that

fully clothed from the perfectly good sofa over there. No, I think you wanted to *feel* me praying, isn't that right?'

I'm so hard now it's ridiculous, and her *yes* is strangled as she grinds that delectable little arse against my cock and attempts to impale herself on my fingers.

I continue to recite my psalms as I oblige, jack-knifing a couple of fingers deep inside her body while my other hand tends to her breasts, pulling and plucking at her impossibly stiff little nipples.

'*Instruct me in your statutes, Lord, that I may follow them.*'

She's arching in my arms, trying to spread her legs and getting precisely nowhere because they're caged in by mine.

'Fuck me, Athena, you're making it very difficult for me to concentrate,' I growl before nipping at her jaw. It's true. My soul has officially gone offline, and the only thing my chimp brain can focus on is how tight, how slippery, her cunt feels around my fingers.

I absolutely have to replace them with my cock. I pull my fingers out and get unsteadily to my feet before hauling her up and turning her to face me. She gazes up at me, eyes glazed and cheeks flushed, and it once again hits me how extraordinarily perfect she is. If I ever had any doubts that this little minx wanted more from me than just a hefty salary, those doubts are ether now, and it causes me to wonder just how much further I can push her.

How much further *she wants me to push her.*

'If you want my cock, you'd better get a condom on me, quick,' I tell her, my fingers flexing around her upper arms.

'I want your cock,' she snaps back, and then she's biting her lip and wrestling my belt and zipper open with none of her characteristic finesse. When she has my erection exposed and free, she rips a foil packet. We both watch as she rolls the condom on, and it takes every remaining trace of discipline I have not to push her down to take it in her mouth.

'Stand up on the kneeler,' I command. 'Bend over—brace your hands on either side of the display case. I need this fast and hard.'

Her face collapses a little at that last part, like it's the best thing she's ever heard. 'God, yes, me too.'

I take a step back, my trousers and boxers around my ankles, so I can enjoy the visual feast that is Athena stepping up onto the kneeler, bare feet apart, before folding herself elegantly forward so her stomach rests on the smooth ledge of the cap rail and her palms hit the table just beyond it.

'That's it.' I place a palm on each perfect white cheek, spreading them so I can enjoy the sight of her well-prepped cunt, pink and glistening and inviting, and the darker, more forbidden hole above it.

If anything is forbidden when it comes to this woman.

I grab my cock for the first time since I entered this most excellent trap and allow myself to trace a line with the tip down through her folds.

The breath she lets out is shuddery. 'Oh, God.'

'Praying now, are we?'

I notch myself at her entrance and take her hips, and Christ is the feeling of wedging myself inside her is an earthly paradise so sublime it could have me forsaking any more illustrious versions of heaven. I grunt out the next lines of today's psalm, the act of sullying these holy words only making my physical pleasure keener. Sharper.

'Before I was afflicted, I went astray,
but now I keep your word.'

The irony. Fuck, I've bottomed out in her. I pause for a second to wallow in the sheer delight of it, Athena's groan telling me we are both very much on the same page. I pull out and really let her have it, keeping one hand gripping her hip while I use the other to burrow under her arm and find one perfect breast.

I'm a man lost to everything but his basest needs and to this beautiful, writhing woman's ability to speak to them. The white-hot ecstasy coursing through my veins feels like the most lethally addictive opioid, a drug so strong I know it will pull me under and fill my lungs with its glorious toxins.

We come together like this, with me rutting into her with every animalistic urge I have and grunting out the basest, most transgressive take on psalms penned by King David himself and meant for the glory of God as she swallows my prayers with her cries.

I'm quite certain I've desecrated the Office of Terce on this January morning, but fuck if it doesn't feel like the kind of exaltation most sinners will never know.

CHAPTER 21

Athena

'I f you want me to stop, you really are going about it the right way,' Gabriel murmurs against my clit.

I pant against the smooth white sheets of our discreet bedroom in Claridges, willing myself to stop wriggling. This is absolutely not the type of establishment to rent rooms out by the hour, but it turns out it absolutely *is* open to accommodating local businessmen who choose to make a permanent standing room reservation.

All the more convenient for said businessmen to get their assistants naked and begging in their lunch hour.

I send up a mental prayer of thanks to the efficient George even as I grit my teeth with frustration, my hands flexing uselessly in their silk ties. 'I didn't know former priests could also be sadists.'

A little laugh against the skin of my thigh. 'Oh, they absolutely can. And they're *definitely* masters of being masochists, which is why I'm not balls-deep inside you already, sweetheart.' He uses two fingers to part the lips of my pussy so fully that even the warm whisper of his breath on my flesh risks sending me over the edge. 'Now tell me just one of your favourite memories and I'll let you come, and all this misery will be over.'

Ever since I ambushed him in his prayer room last week, something has flipped. It's as though he's let himself go willingly to the dark side with me. As though he's yielded to that inexorable downward pull I represent towards a dark underworld that, in his previous life, represented mainly a threat to his parishioners.

What that has meant is that he's started to take the lead more in our sexual relations. Whether it's because he finally understands that *I'm* giving him permission or because he's finally given *himself* permission, I'm unsure.

Neither am I complaining.

Except for now, when this orgasm is as alluring and as inaccessible as the mirage of an oasis in the desert.

He has me naked and trussed up, spread eagle style, on an oak four-poster in Claridges. Our new arrangement lessens the risk of us being caught at work and allows us to get far more adventurous (though I'd argue that sex on a wooden *prie-dieu* was pretty enterprising of us both). He's naked too, a beautifully wrought arrangement of tanned skin and hard muscle and dark hair crouching over me as he toys shamelessly, relentlessly with my body.

I need him to let me come, and *then* I need him to lay all that delicious weight over me and crush me as he fucks my brains out. He, however, has other ideas. He's the seasoned CIA operative to my detainee, only his favoured intelligence-harvesting technique is orgasm denial.

'I've signed NDAs,' I say weakly.

'Don't care. I don't need names, just generalisations.' He slides a single finger so slowly, so carefully, inside my body, and it's nowhere fucking near enough, and I just want to howl. 'I'm still plumbing the depths of you, Athena, and I feel like I haven't even started.'

He's not talking about the depths his finger is exploring in such a torturously leisured way. He's talking about the depths of *me* and my sex drive and my tolerance for depravity. And I get it, because I know he feels on the back foot with me. I know he feels out of *his* depth, like the sex we've had so far has been firmly in the shallows.

I won't admit it to him, but a part of me feels conflicted. I was pretty open with him at that interview dinner, but I understand that I've operated in environments he can't even dream of. He knows I'm dirty, but he has no idea, really, of the things I've done over these past few years while with Seraph. Of the kinds of men I've been with. And there's some small, dark part of me that doesn't want this former man of the cloth judging me for that.

It's as though he can read my mind. 'I want to go places with you, if that's what you want. I want us to have some fun with this. I just—I'm still trying to map you.'

In the end, it's this sweetness, this vulnerability, that hits the spot. A beautiful man taking the time to map out the lush kingdom of a woman's desires is the dream, and Gabriel is offering to chart the heady highs of my dreams and the verdant valleys of my desires and, possibly, even the caves where my kinkiest fantasies lie—caves that may from the outside look dank and moss-laden and forbidding but are, when an intrepid explorer shines a light on them, beautiful inside.

Incandescent, even.

Because when my desires are illuminated, they cease to be dark caves and instead become softly radiant rose quartz formations, and milky selenite columns, and blood-like garnet, and swirling emerald malachite, and even amethyst geodes, their violet reflections as richly pigmented as light filtered through stained glass.

I look along my body at my intrepid explorer, at the plumpness of his lower lip and the quiet intensity in his eyes, at the manly heft of his shoulders between my legs, and then I let my head flop back down onto the pillow he's thoughtfully stuffed behind me.

'There are so many.'

'Give me one that plays on a loop in your head.'

I sigh. 'Once on my birthday, my boss at the time wanted to do something special for me.' It was my first boss, a kinky fucker who worked me *hard*.

'Go on.'

'He stripped me naked and blindfolded me and put a big red bow around my neck and tied me to a high stool—a bit like the one you used in that hotel suite—and he invited some of his mates and business associates into his office at lunchtime.' I pause, remembering how confronting and fucked up and indescribably arousing it was. 'Um, he had a table next to me covered in loads of sex toys and a sandwich board, like the ones you see in hotel lobbies telling you where your conference is. It said in big letters *IT'S MY BIRTHDAY. MAKE ME COME.*'

Silence. Gabriel shifts on the bed, his finger flexing inside me. 'Jesus Christ, love. And they did?'

I give a little laugh. 'They certainly did.'

The memory of that day crashes over me, a wave of disbelief and wonder at the things my boss let them do to me—the things *I* let them do to me. It has my desperate arousal ratcheting up impossibly further. I feel as though every inch of my skin is on fire. I ache everywhere. I want Gabriel to make me come, but if he could find ten friends to help him then that would be excellent.

'And you were okay with that? Weren't you scared? Did they treat you well?' There's concern in his voice, but the gruffness I hear tells me this is turning him on far more than he'd like it to.

'I was terrified at the start,' I admit. 'I was worried it would be really overwhelming. And it was, obviously. But I was also so aroused—I was whipped up into this whirlwind of anticipation, and it was just so incredible. I really trusted my boss, and he was engineering the whole situation, and they all knew my safeword, so... yeah. That's one of my dirty little secrets. Best birthday ever.'

It really was. The fact of being naked and spread open for these powerful men to play with in the middle of the working day, to be the only person they were focused on, to be a body with a set of holes that they were allowed to tease and fuck with all manner of silicone toys so that I came over and over and over...

That was a cave of amethyst and labradorite and quartz, the subspace that followed as blankly, blissfully tranquil as the ocean bed.

Apparently, I'm not the only one affected by my sordid little story, because he extricates his finger and crawls up my body, laying his weight on me. His latex-sheathed dick jerks between us, and the way he's pressing down on my pelvic bone is really fucking unhelpful, but it's his face that's the most distracting thing of all.

Those black-lashed eyes.

That plump lower lip.

I may be the whore in this room, but *he* looks like sin.

'So you loved it,' he mutters, his gaze dancing over my face.

'Mmm-hmm.'

'Ever been gang-banged?'

'Yep.'

He closes his eyes for a brief moment as if drawing strength from some inner well before fixing them on my mouth. 'Let me guess. You loved that, too.'

'I adored every second of it,' I whisper.

'Clearly, I need to up my game.' He braces on one arm and reaches between us so he can position his dick at my entrance.

The feel of that bluntness poised against me has me inhaling shakily. 'They warned me, you know. Your previous employers. It's in your references, how much you love dick.'

He pushes inside me desperately, without finesse, as if he won't survive a single second more outside my body. His groan is so low, so *male*, and the sensation of him filling me up as I lie here, spreadeagled and helpless on this bed, has me on a precipice. I love that he's compiling his filthy mental dossier on me. I love that each new insight may be making him bolder, braver, giving him more ideas for how to profane me.

I want him to feel like he has *carte blanche* to do with me as he pleases. Because yes, I love dick. There is no denying that.

He bottoms out in me, and there's a moment where we simply stare at each other. Restraints aside, this is pretty vanilla fucking, especially in light of the story I just told him, but nothing about the way he lowers his mouth to mine and kisses me feels vanilla. I suppose it's because we're both so hopelessly aroused by the image I've branded onto both of our brains, but having his tongue in my mouth and his dick in my pussy feels like exactly the right amount of overwhelm.

Forget blindfolds and faceless guys and silicone toys: for some unknown reason, Gabriel Sullivan is hitting every spot in this moment, in this luxurious, light-filled hotel room.

He releases my mouth and braces on his forearms so he can start to move inside me, every thick stroke of him teasing me higher, our eyes locked. But with my legs outstretched like this, I can't tilt my pelvis enough to get the friction I so desperately need against my clit, and I let out an involuntary squeak of frustration. He halts immediately, his dick pulsing inside me.

'What's wrong?'

'It's nothing—I...' I trail off. Sometimes, in the heat of the moment, it's easy to forget quite how much these men are paying for the privilege of fucking me. For six figures *a month* I can suck it up and forgo the occasional orgasm.

'Tell me.' He puts his weight onto one arm so he can slide a hand over my breast, and I shiver.

'We're all good. I promise.'

His look tells me he's not buying it, but he pulls out slowly and slams back in, and I grimace as I try and fail to roll my hips. I'm so turned on that it's impossible to focus on anything else but my shimmering, elusive orgasm.

He stops again immediately, looking between our bodies.

'You can't come like this.'

'I can come on my back,' I admit, 'just not with my legs stretched out like this.'

'Fuck, I'm so, so sorry.' He looks utterly horrified, and I hasten to reassure him.

'Gabriel, I'm your employee. This is precisely what you're paying me for. This is about you, not me.'

With a grimace that tells me what he thinks of *that* comment, he reaches between us to secure the condom and pulls out of me, scooting down the bed and untying the silk ties with rapid tugs. Once both of my legs are free, he turns to crawl over me again. I bend my legs luxuriously, the soles of my feet sliding over the cotton sateen of the sheets, and he snags one ankle, cuffing it before sliding his hand up my calf. My thigh.

He opens his mouth, hesitating before speaking. 'You are, without a doubt, the most beautiful woman I've ever had the privilege of being inside. You're probably the most beautiful woman I've ever laid eyes on, in fact. I look at you naked and I know, I just *know*, that you were created in the likeness of God Himself. Every single hair on your head is astonishing. So you honestly think I could fuck you without caring whether you're enjoying yourself?'

I stare at him wordlessly, unclear as to why my eyes are

beginning to sting. His face is so full of intent. He's beseeching me to hear him, and I do, and God knows, my self-confidence is pretty high, so why hearing those words from his lips feels like the most moving kind of benediction I have no idea. Perhaps it's that, by bringing his beliefs into it, he's elevating this far beyond what it is—great, if transactional, sex. He's elevating me beyond being a *genetically* blessed woman who's excellent at what she does into some *divinely* blessed creature.

'Forget the money, Athena. Making you feel good—seeing you come—is so intrinsic to this whole thing we're doing that I have no earthly idea where your pleasure ends and mine begins. None at all.'

He releases my leg and lowers himself so he's ranged back above me. As he slides back in, I fold my legs up further and tilt my hips so my greedy clit can rub against his pelvis. I simultaneously love how powerless the restraints make me feel while wishing fervently that my hands were free to roam through his hair. To tug his face down to meet mine. To dig into his arse and push him even deeper inside me.

At least he doesn't deprive me of his mouth. He dips his dark head again, and I open for him, savouring the feeling of his tongue entangling with mine as he fucks me, slow and deep. Frantic though we both are to come, he takes his time, and I force myself to take mine too, to drink in every last drop of this intensity.

For some reason, the way he's fucking me feels filthy. It's the leisurely drives of his hips, the rough grind of his pelvic bone against my thrumming clit and his hair-dusted pecs against my nipples, the sensual laps of his tongue. As the pleasure ratchets up and up inside my body, I abandon myself to it, the heel of my foot digging into his arse cheek as his kisses swallow up my cries and mine engulf his grunts.

Why is it that moaning into another person's mouth is so

unspeakably hot? Maybe it's knowing that they're greedily taking all your noises for themselves. These sounds I'm making are meant only for him, after all.

He breaks away enough to whisper brokenly, 'I fucking *love* that you love dick. God, the things I want to do to you. Every time I think there's a limit, you and your filthy little fantasies remind me there isn't.'

My body is a whirlwind now, a maelstrom of sensation far too powerful to withstand. A storm rages inside me, sweeping through me, rendering me incapable of anything other than riding it out until it's wrung me dry. I usually close my eyes when I come—shutting off my sight heightens my other senses, of course—but I can't look away from his hooded eyes and lust-clenched jaw. He's my co-conspirator as much my captain in this moment, as helpless to withstand this as I am.

The alchemy, the sorcery, our bodies are weaving together has brought this good man metaphorically to his knees, and I hope it feels like a prayer to him, because this miracle of sweat and skin sure as hell feels like the closest thing I can imagine to a spiritual awakening.

I can't. I can't hold on. I'm—

'Gabe,' I gasp out, 'Gabe.' It's a warning that comes too late, because I'm splintering, shattering into nothingness, a force that feels positively atomic detonating inside me with shock wave after perfect shock wave rippling through my body, and I am nothing but smoke and light; I'm outside my body and yet conscious of nothing else *but* my body.

Nothing else, that is, but the man above me and inside me, feeding off my orgasm as he explodes into his own cataclysmic climax.

I have no earthly idea where your pleasure ends and mine begins.

That stinging in my eyelids returns as I wrap my legs around him as much as I can, cradling him through his orgasm as he fucks deep into me before his thrusts subside. He holds himself there, and I turn my head to the side as he buries his face in my neck, peppering my skin with kisses.

His hand is wrapped around my wrist and I stare at it with blurry vision, at the beautiful dark hairs on his wrist and the long, slender fingers, at the short, square nails. I swallow, attempting to quell the low-level panic bubbling up inside me. *This is good,* I tell myself. *You had fan-fucking-tastic sex with a total god who is paying through the nose for you and who seems deeply invested in your wellbeing. The chemistry is off the charts. This is a* good *thing. There are no problems here, so don't invent issues where none exist.*

I'm quiet as he tugs at the sashes around my wrists, pulling the bows open easily, and collapses next to me, pulling me towards him. I go willingly, rolling onto my side and burying my face against his chest as I attempt to get a handle on this perplexingly emotional reaction I'm having to an excellent fuck. He throws a leg over me and bands an arm around me, his palm pressing between my shoulder blades to keep our bodies flush.

It's not until our breathing has regulated that he murmurs, 'I really, really liked it when you called me Gabe.'

CHAPTER 22

Gabe

'Have a seat. There's something I want to show you.'

I pat the edge of my desk, just next to me, scooting out my chair as I do. Athena laughs as she rounds the desk.

'Again?'

I shake my head, unable to stop my grin. The young woman in front of me is flawless in a fine black sweater, a slim-fitting black leather skirt that hugs her hips enticingly, and what can only be called fuck-me boots. She's always the epitome of class—she's probably the best-dressed woman in the entire firm—so no one would believe I had that shiny ponytail wrapped around my fist this morning as she sucked my cock under this very desk.

Nobody but me, that is, and I'll never forget it.

'Something *else*,' I tell her as she perches elegantly on the edge, crossing her ankles. I hand her a large cream envelope with the Alchemy crest embossed in the corner. 'Take a look at this.'

This is an invitation, issued only to a small subset of Alchemy members, bearing a moody photograph of an ancient mist-shrouded castle and debossed with two words in gold foil:

PRIMA NOCTA.

As she turns it over and slides out the thick piece of card, I watch her intently for a reaction. She's still pretty implacable —when I don't have her on the brink of orgasm, that is—but I'm getting to know her tells, and I'm dying to see what she thinks of this invitation.

Since she recounted that absolutely filthy tale a couple of weeks ago about her birthday treat, if you can call it that, from her old boss, I've been in something akin to emotional turmoil. Sex with Athena is gratifying beyond anything I could have imagined, and she seems to enjoy it, too. But I knew when I hired her that she had what appeared to this former priest to be perilous appetites, and it seems I'm terrified that I alone won't satisfy her as much as she needs and deserves.

I'm terrified she'll walk.

It's true that she's got stuck into her work here with the skill and low-level aggression I'd expected, and she's mentioned a few times that she's far happier here than she was in her former position. It seems inconceivable that the steady string of orgasms I deliver to her on a daily basis are anything but real, but I have to remember that she's exceptionally good at what she does. If she wasn't satisfied, I wouldn't necessarily know.

The safest option is to keep up with her. To anticipate those very particular needs she has, and to fulfil them.

It may be a straightforward strategy, but it's bloody terrifying.

So it's with some wariness that I watch her now, hoping I haven't misjudged this situation.

She takes the invitation in with narrowed eyes. It arrived earlier by courier, but Cal, one of Alchemy's cofounders and their head of events, mentioned it to me in passing a few days ago when I was at the club. (It was a chaste evening. Drinks with the boys only. I have absolutely no need for The Playroom these days.)

'Prima Nocta,' she murmurs. 'This is an event they're doing?'

'Yeah. They've hired out some Norman castle in Essex for it. It's their first big themed popup in the UK—sounds like it'll be very *Game of Thrones*.' It also comes with a price tag that would cover a family home in most parts of the country, but I'm not about to tell her that. 'Are you familiar with the concept?'

She looks up then, and the dazzling smile she shoots me leaves me in no doubt at all as to her views on the topic.

'*Jus primae noctis* is the correct term,' she says, and I nod.

'The law of the first night. Got it.'

She's still smiling. 'The French call it *le droit du seigneur*. The right of the lord. I've always found that hot as fuck.'

'Tell me about it,' I say. The small amount of googling I've done has made me seriously uncomfortable, but this isn't about me.

'Well, there's absolutely no historical evidence that it was an actual thing, but it's amazing how much it's come up in different cultures, all the way from ancient times to medieval. The Irish have mentions of it, the French, the Chinese, the Ancient Greeks, Gilgamesh—even the Holy Roman Empire.'

I'm unsure whether to be impressed by Athena's encyclopaedic knowledge or deeply unsettled by her familiarity with this kinky rabbit hole. 'Go on. Can I touch you?'

She frowns. 'Of course.'

Every time I want to lay a finger on her, I ask her first.

Every time, she reminds me I can do what I like.

I'll never stop asking.

I slide my hand under the hem of her skirt and stroke her knee through the fine nylon of her stockings. 'Tell me what turns you on about it, and then I'll tell you what they've got planned.'

Her face lights up like a child at Christmas. 'The bare bones of it are pretty horrific, actually—it supposedly gave kings or overlords the right to bed the brides of their serfs on their wedding nights, or whichever ones they fancied the look of, anyway.'

'And that does it for you.' It's not a question.

She sinks her teeth into her full, pink bottom lip before answering. 'The fantasy version does, anyway. The idea that I'm some innocent virgin who has no clue about sex and is supposed to marry some useless serf, and then he takes me to his lord's castle, but the lord drags me off and ravages me however the fuck he wants, and he just takes and takes because it's his feudal right, and shows me what it can really be like? My God, it's the dream.' She actually flushes, right there on my desk, and I can see what a powerful fantasy this is for her.

Maybe, just maybe, this is something I can give her.

Something that her gang-banging, sex-toy-toting bosses of old can't.

I slide my hand up her inner thigh. I have to say, she paints a far more alluring picture of the whole thing than that horrifying Wikipedia page did. With a few effortless brush-strokes, she's painted a picture I didn't know to want until now: me in my castle, in my robes and my furs, and Athena, jarringly lovely, in a white gown that speaks of her purity and on the arm of another man who's desperately in love with her, *mine* to take and plunder and shatter so thoroughly that her poor, toothless husband will never, ever be able to satisfy her.

'It can be a reality, for one night.' My fingertips find the lace top of her stocking and she shifts forward, opening her legs as much as she can, which is not very far at all.

Her eyelids drift closed, eyelashes fluttering. Her voice, when she speaks, is breathy. 'Tell me.'

I'm about to tell her. In fact, I'm about to check how wet this conversation already has her before taking it any further, but a movement in front of me catches my eye.

Fuck's sake.

It's my fucking brother.

I hastily remove my hand from between Athena's legs and grab the invitation. Luckily, she's facing away from the open door and her stance, although perhaps a little familiar, doesn't suggest that she's doing anything more than perching on her boss's desk, having a catch up. I stuff the invitation under a folder on my desk. That is most definitely not for my brother's eyes.

He breezes through Athena's antechamber and into my office, coat slung over his arm. He looks far too cheery and smooth as fuck, and I see the moment his eyes alight with interest on the back of her head. I also clock the moment she turns to see who's interrupted us and Brendan's face goes from curious to downright feral in half a second.

Again, *fuck*.

'Hi,' I say curtly, but he's not looking at me.

Of course he's not.

'You must be Athena,' he says, flinging his coat unceremoniously on the sofa and not bothering to disguise the beeline he's making for her. My eyes meet hers in a silent moment of resignation—my fingers are still warm from her skin and were so close to being wet—before she pushes herself off the desk and stands to greet him.

'How do you do?' she asks, extending her hand. I watch her for any sign that she's falling prey to his infamous charms. Our mother may insist, with the hopeless bias that mothers have, that both her sons are equally good-looking, but there's no denying that my brother has had far more practice over the past decade of honing his skills—both in bed and out of it.

'I'm doing a lot better now, I can tell you that much,' he says, fixing that easy grin of his on her.

Nothing. I see nothing on her face but polite implacability. My little ice queen isn't giving him an inch. Perhaps it's because she's in her place of work or perhaps because, when you look like Athena, having men hit on you is the most banal of occurrences. I don't really care. All I know is that she's categorically not letting him see the version of herself who whispered *tell me* just now as she widened her legs to accommodate my searching fingers.

This kind of possessiveness is puerile in the extreme; I know that.

I couldn't give a flying fuck.

'So,' Brendan presses on, 'is this one treating you well?' He slides his hands in his pockets as he continues to take her in.

I know what he can see.

I know all too well.

Chasing hot women is one of my brother's favourite pastimes, but Athena's beauty isn't just "hot". It's astonishing. It's the kind of beauty that inspires paintings and poetry and could ruin a man forever.

'He's treating me very well indeed, thank you,' she tells him. Her tone is blandly polite, but the quick flick of her eyes to me is all the filthy subtext I need from her. I suppress a grin.

'Glad to hear it.' Bren is a dog with a bone. 'Hey—would you like to go for a drink sometime?' He shoots her what I know he considers to be his killer smile.

Her reply is like whiplash. 'I would not. Gabe, I'm ready to head out when you are.'

If I wasn't so pissed off with my brother, I'd be struggling to keep a straight face. It's so fucking typical of him to waltz in here and proposition my employee, even if he couldn't possibly know the details of our relationship. But she showed him with that briskly schoolmarmish putdown.

I think I'm in love.

'Bren, stop harassing my assistant. Let's head over, shall we?' I push myself abruptly up from my chair. 'Athena, take the time you need.'

This evening is the opening of a new exhibition at the Royal Academy: *Eden's Echo*, a horticultural art exhibition. Bren and I are representing the Sullivan family, which is a longtime patron of the RA, and apparently Athena is also going along with a friend who works there.

'I'm all good,' she says. 'Just let me grab my bag.'

She strides coolly across the room and discreetly shuts the door in the middle of the glass wall that separates my office from hers. We both watch her go.

Brendan exhales theatrically and shakes out his hand as if he's been burnt. 'Jesus fuck. You sneaky, sneaky bastard. You'd better put a ring on that, or at the very least, fuck her. She's *insane.*'

I shake my head in a show of disapproval as I walk around him to follow Athena. There's no upside to responding to those lewd comments.

Especially given how on the nose they are.

CHAPTER 23

Athena

I t's raining, which gives me a socially acceptable pretext for taking Gabe's arm as he holds his umbrella over both of us (but mainly me). Happily for my high-heeled boots, it's a shortish walk down Berkeley Street toward Piccadilly, where the Royal Academy dominates in its grandiose home, Burlington House.

Less happily, the walk is long enough for me to conclude with certainty that Gabe's brother is vapid at best and an arrogant dick at worst.

I suppose the upshot is that I definitely ended up working for the right Sullivan brother, although I have no interest in analysing why walking through Mayfair on Gabe's arm is so gratifying. The conversation is mainly small talk, though there's some chat between the guys about how things are going over at Sullivan Construction, of which Brendan is the CEO.

Brendan does eventually add some value by offering to check our coats and umbrella in at the Royal Academy's cloakroom when we arrive, thus giving us a moment of privacy to continue the conversation he interrupted earlier. I lean back against a pillar and look up at him.

'So, you're thinking of accepting that Prima Nocta invitation?' I enquire in a studiedly casual tone I'm sure doesn't fool him for a second.

He hesitates, eyes boring into mine. 'Only if you're interested. I wouldn't want to do it with anyone else. It's on a Saturday, though.'

And that's the crux of it. Even in this most transactional and carefully boundaried of relationships there are bound to be moments where one or both of us are tempted to cross those boundaries, and this is one of them.

Both sides of my role are strictly workplace-related. I'm on the clock as much as any other employee. I'm there to assist him and to relieve his stress, slake his needs, when he's at work. Simple as that. I'm not there to date him or escort him to events, to be his arm candy or his convenient weekend fuck. All of those things remain rigidly beyond the scope of our arrangement.

You could argue, though, that this explosive, fearsome chemistry between us should also lie beyond the scope of our arrangement. Satisfying my employer is one thing, as is tolerating him and getting off on our dynamic.

Being moved to tears and snorting the scent of his skin as he holds me after sex are other things entirely.

All of which is to say that I understand his hesitation here. I understand it perfectly.

And yet... *prima nocta* with Gabe.

Role-playing the virginal bride of another man only for Gabe to seize his right to me.

Seeing him dressed in rich furs as he exercises his *droit de seigneur* over me.

Having this experience with him, so far removed from

anything we've done in his office or that hotel room, is far too enticing an offer to refuse.

After all, I've already promised myself I'd serve my king well. What better expression of that oath than this?

I let my lips curve up into a mischievous smile, noting how his expression clears at the sight of it. 'We should do it.'

Before we even meet up with Marlowe, I'm already anticipating that Brendan will hit on her, just like he hit on me.

There's no denying that the guy is disgustingly attractive, just like his brother. Like Gabe, he has that classic Irish colouring of almost-black hair and blue eyes. Like Gabe, his beard is dark and well-manicured. He's bigger than his brother, who's more on the lean, athletic side. I suspect Brendan lifts some serious weights to achieve shoulders that broad. He's wearing the hell out of his suit, and I bet he has to fight women off.

Despite all that, there's something about him that leaves me cold. I've known too many men like him. Fucked too many guys who are drunk on their own Kool-Aid, who've lost touch with the essence of themselves.

The false gods of wealth and power can be both glittering shields and unreliable mirrors, which makes me marvel all the more at the integrity, the humility, that Gabe exhibits every day.

It seems his faith has him moored in still waters.

I've been wandering around the exhibits with Gabe and Brendan. I've spotted Marlowe from afar a couple of times, but she's firmly on duty, schmoozing with patrons of the RA.

It makes me reluctantly glad that I didn't come along by myself.

The paintings themselves are wonderful. Monet's garden at Giverny was, of course, the starting point for this *Eden's Echo* exhibition, but the RA has flexed its considerable muscles in borrowing pieces from Bonnard and Le Sidaner, Nolde and Sorolla.

While I've been fortunate enough to see some of these paintings in their permanent homes around the cultural capitals of Europe, there's a deep gratification in seeing them clustered together to provide a joyous explosion of florals and colours in one of the bleakest months of the year.

I find myself slipping into curator mode as we peruse the exhibit. I'm talking Gabe and Brendan through a lovely oil of Louis Comfort Tiffany by Sorolla, one I've never seen in the flesh before, when Marlowe catches up with us. Her long blonde hair is gathered up in a low, artfully messy bun with escaping strands, and she's wearing a maxi dress printed—appropriately enough—with winter florals that I bought her for Christmas. As usual, she looks ethereally, naturally beautiful.

I hold my champagne flute off to one side so I can hug her. She has a pretty pink flush on her face that tells me she's in her element. Her role as mother to Tabby is by far the most important role in her life, but it's as gruelling as it is pleasurable, and it takes its toll. Seeing her here this evening with her work hat on makes me really bloody happy.

'It's gorgeous,' I tell her. 'Just gorgeous.' But she's looking beyond me, mischief dancing in her blue eyes, and I know she's dying for an introduction to Gabe. I sigh and relent.

'Marlowe, allow me to introduce my boss, Gabriel, and his brother, Brendan.'

Gabe extends his hand and steps forward with a smile I know is as genuine as it is warm. It's a smile hewn from years spent greeting parishioners and making the most marginalised, the most destitute, feel welcome.

'Gabriel. So good to meet you, Marlowe.'

'I've been dying to meet you,' she confesses to him with a sideways grin at me, and I roll my eyes.

'That's quite enough of that. And this is Brendan.'

I gesture his way, bracing myself for some sleazy line. But he's staring at my best friend with what looks like shock, his mouth hanging slackly open. I frown at him, but Gabe beats me to it, nudging him lightly on the arm.

'Bren. Mate.'

Brendan jolts, some champagne sloshing over the edge of his flute and onto his hand. He swears softly before finally, tentatively, extending his unscathed right hand to Marlowe.

When her hand closes around his, his eyes actually flutter shut for a moment.

'Lovely to meet you, Brendan,' she says with her usual friendly ease.

He coughs. 'Um. Yeah. Hi.'

This is the guy who propositioned his brother's employee within ten seconds of meeting her.

This is the guy who's spent the past half an hour swaggering around the Royal Academy like he owns it and flashing his predatory grin at every female with a pulse.

So who the fuck *this* version of him is, I have no clue.

CHAPTER 24

Athena

This model of fucking at work isn't just time-efficient for Gabe—yes, he has me calling him Gabe now. It's working very well for me, too. I get an excellent orgasm or two during office hours, and it means I can spend my evenings getting to grips with my new EA role instead of swiping right or hitting up bars so I can get laid.

God knows, I need all the time I can get to do a deep dive on this foundation thing. I've spent the past few days pulling together a detailed briefing pack for Gabe ahead of his meeting with Eleanor and Torty. The proposed agenda is to take the first steps towards implementing a formal foundation structure under the umbrella of Rath Mor, but I'm damned if I won't provide Gabe with as much detail, as much analysis, as humanly possible. His parents and brother and sister will be in attendance too, giving him four more reasons to bring his A game.

If I'm right, the Old Guard won't fail to underwhelm with their proposal, which makes me intent on arming my boss with as compelling a counter argument as possible. My instincts tell me that Gabe's background of community stewardship and pastoral care will give him a very different vision of his future foundation from the one Eleanor and her cronies present.

And guess what? I'll bend over backwards to make his vision a reality, even if I suspect I'll have to intervene on occasion to ensure he doesn't give every last penny away. There's a way to do this that's hard-headed and practical while being innovative and sustainable, and I already feel excited about the idea of being in a position to affect change for good. I'll throw every single thing I learnt during my time as a management consultant at this, that's for sure.

In the days before the meeting, I run myself ragged, hunting down the owners of every last piece of information I need and seemingly interacting with most of the estate management team in the process.

The brief Gabe has given me is limited to compiling current state analysis—that is, a picture of where things stand right now—but I'll be damned if I don't go back to him with all the extra material he didn't know he wanted or needed. And that's precisely because the current state analysis makes for bleak reading.

I've mapped—with difficulty—the places to which the Sullivan family donations are currently going, and the picture is piecemeal as fuck. I've compiled an audit of all their current charitable initiatives as well as historical giving platforms under Gabe's father. I've got to grips with the current decision-making process where charitable donations are concerned (in a nutshell: random) and I've proposed a list of inefficiencies that I see with the process.

To be honest, the only real area that *isn't* inefficient is taxation. Rath Mor's charitable endeavours seem to be an exercise in optics, and offsetting tax, and little else. It's not that the family doesn't give away a lot of money. They really do. It's simply that their giving appears spontaneous and reactive and the very opposite of strategic.

By virtue of the insane value of the land this family owns, it's one of the biggest landowners in the UK. It has an incredible opportunity not just to part with money but to transform entire communities and create an innovative blueprint for responsible land ownership around the world.

If I'm being completely honest with myself, the fact that they're even contemplating doing this in-house is insane. With the amount of money in play, they should absolutely be farming this out to Bain or McKinsey or another bulge-bracket management consultancy firm. Any of these guys would lose their shit over this opportunity. I should make this clear to Gabe, and I will. Just not yet.

I want a chance to sink my teeth into this first.

If my first impressions are correct, the bar for making an impact on this front is very fucking low.

In the end, my brief to Gabe extends far beyond its initial remit. I complete my current state analysis (dismal) and then some. A benchmarking exercise against other UK family foundations proves equally depressing, so I perform a deep dive into the state of the London Docklands, where the bulk of the Sullivan family's wealth is tied up.

This land in South East London is incredibly valuable but, as George pointed out, far less developed than the likes of Kensington and Chelsea, the preferred base of the aristocracy for centuries. By contrast, the Docklands are home to some of the most diverse and deprived boroughs in the entire UK.

I pull a tonne of demographic data on the Docklands, and it makes for tough reading. One of its more infamous boroughs, Tower Hamlets, has one of Britain's highest incarceration rates and highest proportion of social housing. Its green spaces are woefully inadequate. This is a dream of a regeneration project across all fronts.

It's not all bad news. The grassroots efforts in some of these communities are truly inspiring. There's hunger and activism and a real, screaming need for change. And while I'm sure there's no one in this firm more conscious than Gabe of the struggles the poorest people face, I also suspect his experience has left him ill-equipped to affect change at any scale greater than the parish level.

Money will talk to so many stakeholders here in a way that a Catholic priest could only dream of and pray for. If Gabe is undertaking this project from a place of compassion, of positivity, then I am absolutely going to weaponise his agenda with every gun in my arsenal.

So, once I have a clearer picture of what we're dealing with, I take the initiative to include an entire section on inspirational precedents. There's no bloody way I'll allow the likes of Eleanor and Torty to be the only ones painting a picture for Gabe.

My devious form of visual overriding comprises examples of successful projects across environmental, social impact and community contexts. I would imagine Eleanor is already all over the more glamorous cultural preservation projects.

I reference projects ranging from the High Line and Industry City in New York to Barcelona's 22@, which is a fantastic example of the kind of regeneration that can be carried out on industrial land. In my view, these are precisely the kind of precedents the Sullivans should be homing in on, rather than what the likes of the Cadogan and Grosvenor Estates are doing in London's swankiest areas.

Finally, like the good little Bain-trained management consultant I am, I crunch more numbers than these guys could ever want or need at this stage in the creative process. I keep them as high level as possible, but I want everyone at that meeting to understand that philanthropy and smart business don't have to be mutually exclusive.

I lead with the tax benefits, obviously. But there are plenty of sustainable funding models with which any self-respecting MBA will be familiar, and a lot of the projects I'm proposing we consider would be prime recipients for government grants. I finish up with some high-level risk analysis based on the information I have at this stage.

Put that in your pipe and smoke it, Eleanor.

It's really fucking good.

'This is really fucking good,' Gabe says in amazement. 'You know it's about a million times more detailed than I asked for, don't you?'

We've made some cups of tea, locked his office door and curled up on his sofa together. My shoes are off, one stockinged foot folded beneath me and one outstretched. Gabe takes it and lays it in his lap so he can knead it. This is some oddly intimate hinterland between the two parts of my role, but the feeling after a day in heels is utterly glorious.

I resist the urge to moan in pleasure and instead look him dead in the eye. I won't mince my words. 'Look. I want you to have all the information when you go into that meeting, and fuck knows, the information isn't easy to come by in this place.

'You may think you're at a disadvantage when it comes to huge-scale business decisions like this, but you have a perspective that no one else in that room has, and that's one of humanity and compassion. From what I've seen, this is a once-in-a-generation opportunity to have serious, massive impact, and I'm damned if I'm not going to arm you up so you can advocate for yourself and for all the people whose lives could change if crusty old farts like Eleanor step aside and admit that *noblesse oblige* and fucking charity balls aren't the way to affect change.'

He laughs. 'Wow. You're my pet piranha, aren't you? My secret weapon.'

'You'd better believe it,' I retort. 'Wait until you see my teeth.'

George's warning about Eleanor flashes into my mind. *Don't let the pearls fool you. She's got teeth, and she doesn't like to be challenged.*

That makes two of us, buddy.

He laughs, then says, 'I'll send this to my family today. They'll be blown away.'

'Good. That's good. Get them on board with your vision before they've even walked into the room.'

'*My* vision?' He holds up the pages of what should be a briefing document and instead is a solid pitch, and I have the good grace to laugh.

'Our vision.'

'That sounds more accurate. But I reckon Dad'll love this stuff. He grew up on the Dublin docks. He'll get it.'

'And your mother? *God* that's good,' I moan as his thumb circles my instep hard.

He lays the briefing document down and circles my ankle with his other hand. 'She'll agree with the core of it, I think. I mean, it would be hard not to. But she loves Eleanor.'

'How? *Why?*'

He purses his lips before answering. It's something he does a lot. He's never in a hurry, never one to say something without measured consideration.

'Validation, I suppose. Having people like Eleanor on

board credentialises my parents. They may be very wealthy, very successful, but there's a part of them that still sees themselves as interlopers. You know what London high society is like—it's a melting pot of old money and new. Eleanor provides that old-money gloss that they feel gives them some respectability.'

'That's ridiculous. From the sounds of it, your parents are about a million times more impressive than her.'

'Maybe so.' He strokes his fingers along my foot, his grip deliciously firm. 'But sometimes it seems as though they're still trying to find a way to belong. Even after all this time.'

CHAPTER 25

Gabe

I 'm perched on the front edge of my desk, rereading Athena's epic briefing document when she turns up for work on the morning of the foundation meeting. I let my gaze track her as she reverently places her oversized handbag on her desk and saunters through to my office.

'Wow.'

'Thank you. Good morning.'

'Pulling out all the stops, I see. I recognise that dress.'

It's the navy one she wore to her interview here, the one that somehow makes her look like a boss and a sex kitten all at once. It's formal enough to be parent-friendly, but in this ravenous man's eyes it showcases every delectable curve.

She smooths her hands over her hips as she approaches. 'I thought you might like to take it off later.'

I let the briefing tome fall to my desk and hook her around her waist with my arm, tugging her closer so she's standing between my legs. She is simply bewitching.

Every weekday, she is mine to do with as I please, and it's a privilege I take great delight in. That said, the more we mess around, the deeper I fall into this yawning abyss of need. Every fuck, every intimacy, feels like a silken strand of Athena's web, ethereal-looking but alarmingly strong, and this little fly is as disinterested in resisting as he is powerless.

We're almost nose to nose. 'Actually, I'd like to take it off *now*. I'm feeling... antsy, I suppose. I rarely enjoy these sit-downs with my family. I'd like to take the edge off.'

I run my fingers down the length of her exposed zip until I can cup her arse, and she tilts her head so her lips are against my ear. Her voice is low, seductive.

'Not on your fucking life.'

I jerk back. She's never once declined my advances since she started here, and she's perfectly entitled to, obviously—I just didn't see it coming. Not from her body language.

'No?'

'Gabe, if you think I'm going to let you throw away that edge before this meeting, you're sorely mistaken. You need to hold on tight to whatever edge you have with both hands.' She slides a hand around the nape of my neck. 'Think about it. You're like a happy baby bear when you've just had an orgasm. An entire SWAT team could rampage through this place after you've come and you'd be totally oblivious. There's no way I'm letting you go in there like that.'

I stare at her in disbelief. 'That's not true!'

She smiles sweetly. 'Oh, darling. It's very true. And very endearing.'

'I distinctly remember you telling me at our first dinner together that one of your services is fluffing your bosses before big meetings,' I counter mulishly. I'm not letting this go. Not unless she tells me she doesn't want this, in which case I'll obviously drop it immediately.

She throws back her head and laughs. 'You're so right! I did. But some guys get off on that. It gives them extra Big Dick Energy to swagger into a meeting, knowing they've just railed their assistant. It *gives them* an edge. That's not you.' She jabs me in the pec. 'You'd let everyone walk all over you if you went in there having just shot your load.'

I scowl at her, which is childish, but I'm absolutely not about to admit that she's right. (Probably even more childish, come to think of it.)

'Instead,'—she licks her lips sensually—'you should walk in there thinking about the kind of prize you might get later if you smash the meeting. And by *smash*, I mean following your own agenda and not letting anyone else railroad you with theirs. I've told you before, I make an *excellent* trophy.'

It's with Athena's seductive promise ringing in my ears and far too much unresolved "edge" still coursing through my veins that I lead her into the main conference room down the corridor. The room is empty, but the screen dominating one end is already live. On it sits the opening slide of Eleanor's powerpoint presentation in our standard template: *The Rath Mor Foundation: The Future of Philanthropy.*

Athena scoffs. 'Future, my arse. You should know that if she's used clipart, I won't be responsible for my reactions.'

'God, you're a tough woman. She must be in her late fifties. She's not exactly Steve Jobs. Give her a break.'

She laughs. 'Never. What's your plan, again? Say it.'

'Appeal to their hearts *and* their business brains,' I parrot. 'Stay true to my vision. Don't let myself be railroaded.'

'Excellent. Remember, channel that edge.'

'Fuck knows, there's enough of it, thanks to you cock-blocking me,' I grumble.

When my family members show up a few minutes later with Eleanor and Torty, Athena and I are sitting side by side, the picture of professional decorum. This is good practice for us. We spend so much time alone together that it's hard sometimes to remember to act like colleagues in front of the broader team. We rise. Greetings are given, introductions made.

'New season Oscar!' Athena gushes at my mother as they shake hands. 'Oh God, that's divine.'

'Thanks, love,' Mum says, looking genuinely touched. 'You've a great eye.' She's wearing a pink dress and matching jacket that I haven't seen on her before, and she looks lovely. Dad's taking her out to lunch after this meeting—I suspect they're making a day of it.

'Is that Victoria Beckham you have on there?' she asks, nodding at Athena. 'Sure, isn't it absolutely gorgeous on ye? You've the figure for it.'

I think my mother would actually drop down dead on the spot if she knew the real nature of Athena's role at Rath Mor, but there's no denying she appears charmed at first glance. It's hard *not* to be charmed by Athena. Her combination of looks and intellect and polish is nothing short of deadly, something my family is about to experience first hand.

Athena and my father exchange a hearty hello before she leads Mum over to the sideboard to fix her a coffee, giving my brother, who goes in for a double kiss, short shrift. Unbothered, he throws me a wink that says he's still tickled by quite how attractive my EA is. I notice the tight smile and curt nod Torty throws Athena as the latter passes her a coffee cup, and recall what Athena said about Torty disliking her and wanting my babies in equal measure.

The thought makes me deeply uncomfortable. She's suggested "mentoring drinks" after work more than once, and I've politely but firmly fobbed her off each time. She's a nice woman; I wish her all the best. Interest from well-meaning, hopeful but ultimately unappealing women like Torty is one of the main reasons I joined Alchemy.

If I thought the thrills it provided were gratifying, I had no clue.

Nothing and nobody is more rewarding than Athena Davenport. Even in here, making what amounts to friendly small talk with my mum and my sister Mairead, she positively dazzles. It's impossible to focus on anyone or anything else when she's in the room. I have a slight pang at the realisation that this may be precisely why the likes of Torty feel threatened by her.

It must be impossible not to.

'Our objective today,' Eleanor intones with her signature gravitas—and glacial pace, 'is to take the first steps to formalising how we would like the Rath Mor Foundation to look as we take our charitable initiatives through to the next generation under Gabriel's capable stewardship.'

She looks to me for agreement, and I nod before catching Mum's eye. She's smiling. She and Dad are so excited about this—we all are. This is to be a Sullivan family endeavour, an opportunity to harness this extraordinary wealth we've—*they've*—amassed and put it to seriously impactful work.

'Might I suggest that we look to cover the following issues?' Eleanor continues. She pronounces it with an *s* sound rather than a *sh*, something that always makes my skin crawl for unknown reasons. When she clicks through to the first slide, Athena kicks me under the table, because the "iss-ues" are surrounded by a glory of clip art. I shake my head to communicate that I am moderately amused and have no intention whatsoever of disclosing that fact.

But I'm not amused as I scan Eleanor's agenda.

Preservation.

Business Support.

Community Outreach.

Cultural Partnerships.

'The wonderful thing is that there are some very illustrious precedents here in London,' she continues smoothly. Below the silk scarf knotted around her neck, her more-than-ample bosom rises and falls alarmingly as she speaks. 'The Cadogan and Grosvenor estates are excellent blueprints for the kinds of philanthropy you may want to lend your names to. I feel that looking to the most established models is wise here.' I notice Mum smiling and nodding as she follows along. I swear she'd follow Eleanor off the edge of a cliff if she had the opportunity. 'I've taken the liberty of asking Victoria to overlay, if you like, the main tenets of those models with what the Rath Mor estate could apply to its land. Starting from scratch would be overwhelming and risky, in my opinion.'

Torty nods and opens a folder from which she gathers a sheaf of papers. 'It's merely a starting point, but it will give us a helpful top-down view of how these estates allocate their funds and what they consider the most compelling priorities.' She tosses her hair self-consciously. 'I actually went for coffee with Serena Cadogan last week and she was *so* helpful in passing along some tips from their key stakeholders. Why don't I pass these around?'

She goes to rise from her chair. I exchange a brief, loaded glance with Athena, who purses her lips together in unspoken disapproval, and hold out my hand. 'Torty. Wait.'

She freezes and sits fully back down. I hesitate, then push my own chair back and stand, thrusting my hands into my pockets. 'Listen. I don't mean to overrule either of you—I'm well aware we've asked you to kick off this meeting, Eleanor. But I don't want to waste people's time here. And I think we should start in the spirit that we mean to go on.

'At the end of the day, the Sullivans are builders, not dukes. We're new to this, and we can build whatever we want. We don't have centuries' worth of expectations defining how we should act. So we should *absolutely* be tearing up the rule book here'—I pick up Athena's briefing pack and brandish it for effect—'and writing our very own.'

Gabe

Eleanor interrupts, frowning at the briefing pack. 'May I ask what you have there, Gabriel?'

'I asked Athena to pull together some thoughts for me and the family,' I reply smoothly. 'I wanted to be fully briefed to ensure we got the most out of this time.'

Her eyes narrow, and I suspect she's thinking that the beautiful, spiral-bound pack I'm holding represents far more than "some thoughts".

'Someone from Torty's team would have been delighted to do that for you,' she presses. 'They're far more familiar with our charitable works than Athena would be, having joined us so recently.'

She smiles at Athena, but it doesn't reach her eyes, and it bothers me. We're trying to do some good here. I don't have any tolerance for territorial bullshit—we've got enough on our plate without having to manage easily-bruised egos.

'That's extremely kind, but briefing me ahead of key meetings is precisely what my EA should be doing. And sometimes it's good to get a fresh perspective on an old problem, isn't it? Besides, Athena is my secret weapon in this instance. She spent several years as a management consultant *and* she has an MBA, both of which make her perfectly suited to this kind of research.'

I see my mother's eyebrows arch in pleased surprise at Athena's impressive background. She definitely favours a strong pedigree in people as well as horses.

Before I can continue, my sister leans forward and taps her copy of the document. 'I totally agree. To be honest, I was absolutely dreading this meeting until I flipped through this thing. It was very bloody inspiring. Nice work, Athena. Eleanor—we can continue with your powerpoint if that's what you'd like, but we should just use this as the starting point for any sensible discussion, if you want my opinion.'

Mairead runs the stud farm within my parents' stables. It's an extraordinarily successful business. My sister has not only a strong nose for business but, predictably enough for someone who spends her days focused on equine erections, an even stronger nose for horseshit and time wasters.

Unfortunately for Eleanor, Mairead can tend towards seeing her as guilty of both of those things when their paths cross.

'Thank you,' Athena says quietly to my left as Eleanor glares at Mairead and then Athena, her body stiff with betrayal.

'I must say, I feel quite on the back foot here. Next time you request that I chair a meeting and then see fit to create your own agenda, Gabriel, I wonder if you'd be so kind as to furnish me with a copy ahead of time?'

'Absolutely, Eleanor.' I hold my arms wide to show her I mean no harm. 'And this was certainly not meant to be an alternative agenda—I merely asked Athena to pull together some information to get me up to speed. She went above and beyond, and I was impressed, so I had some copies couriered to the family to give them some background.'

'Why don't you go on with your presentation, Eleanor?' Mum asks, eyes darting between me and Eleanor as if she's watching a tennis match.

'Please do. Perhaps you can summarise where our philanthropic works stand at the moment, Eleanor? And then we'll get down to the business of wiping the slate clean and taking it from there.'

I hope my subtext is clear. If what's to follow on the screen is nothing more than a rehash by Eleanor and Torty of what their blue-blooded friends over at Grosvenor and Cadogan are doing, we'll be aborting their powerpoint pretty damn quickly.

Fifteen minutes later, my fears are confirmed. Following a summary from Eleanor that put a more positive spin on the same current numbers that Athena pulled, Torty is now walking us through a proposed foundation structure that, as she puts it, borrows from the supposed best practices of her favourite references.

It's becoming increasingly clear to me that Torty sees our "stakeholders" as parties with whom we should curry favour: local government; local businesses; high-profile individuals. The diagrams she's created fail to speak to any of the more disenfranchised members of our society, and the irony is sinking in, slow but deadly: in some misguided attempt at gaining social currency, my father has populated this firm with some fearful snobs who are frankly out of touch and tone deaf.

Around the table, my family members look disengaged at best and bored at worst. I can practically feel the disapproval radiating off Athena next to me. I've got to put an end to this bullshit. I hold my hand up again.

'Thanks Torty, but I'm going to stop you there.' I get to my feet again. 'Look, I think we're all clear on the fact that what's worked in Belgravia won't work in the Docklands, and that we have an advantage in that respect. Dad, you and Grandad grew up piss-poor. And when you came over to the UK, you didn't ask for permission. You watched, and you listened, and you built. That's what we should be doing.

'I'll be honest, I've been flailing a bit since I took the reins here, wondering if I'll ever find that sense of purpose I struggled to find even as a priest. And you know what? This is the first time I've felt that flicker. We've got an opportunity to use our wealth and our street smarts on an almost inconceivable scale, so let's have some fun with it, for God's sake.

'This isn't about handouts. It's about giving people back their dignity and power and connectivity. I've seen the good that one stable community space can provide. Building sustainable change takes time, a *long* time, but none of us is going anywhere. Athena proposed three pillars—let me see... Ah, yeah. Here we go. Cultural heritage preservation, which I feel like you're very strong on, Torty, but that needs to look very different in this area. Urban community development— that's everything from housing to small business support. And finally, but critically, environmental sustainability, right down to ring-fencing more green space and even urban farming. Here.' I push my briefing pack in Torty's direction. 'You and Eleanor should take a look. I'll share with Athena.'

I sit back down, and we begin to tentatively throw ideas out. My brother's knee-jerk reaction is to fight for any land that's been earmarked for development but could be sequestered for green spaces instead. But he's quickly placated by the potential to showcase Sullivan's sustainable building practices and to extend affordable housing initiatives further.

Mairead makes the case for the environmental angle, stressing the importance of getting kids outside and moving their bodies and, ideally, connecting with nature, with animals. She's all over the idea of urban farming projects while Eleanor, seemingly noting the change in the room's energy level, takes copious notes.

'You know, I like this,' Dad says, throwing his glasses down and rubbing his eyes. 'It feels more right, I suppose. I'm glad Old Jim's not here, because he'd try to remind me that this is an exercise in divestment and estate planning, and it's really not. Not for me and Maeve, anyway. It's about giving people a bit of fucking human dignity and getting our hands dirty.' He slaps the table. 'I think that's what we've been missing, and fuck knows, the Sullivans have never been afraid of getting their hands dirty. You know what I mean?'

'I think the issue is that the people in these areas have problems we can't even imagine,' Mum says, covering Dad's hand with hers. 'You know, drugs. Gangs. Knives. We're so out of our depth, so the safe thing to do has always been to throw money at the problem and stay well away.'

There's a silence that's uncomfortable and thoughtful in equal measure, because she's right, and her explanation is as good as any as to why we haven't delved deeper before.

'Athena had some thoughts on that side of things,' I say with a glance to my left. 'Do you have anything to contribute?'

When she speaks, her voice is quietly assured. 'As someone who is very much removed from this and is viewing it mainly through a management consultant lens, I'd agree, Maeve, that it would be very ill-advised to think we can wade in and throw around a bit of white saviourism and magically solve people's problems.

'But at the same time, if you look at the root causes and the appeal of gangs, which I'm sure is something Gabe knows more about than me given his pastoral work, there are elements you can weave into your infrastructure that might help. They may be as basic as donating funds to the local schools to allow them to do more work, but it could also be twenty-four-seven safe spaces, late night sports programmes, mentorship from reformed gang members... there's a lot you can do. The key, I think, is ensuring that these are led by people in the community itself.'

'You mentioned that a lot of these endeavours could be covered by grants?' I prompt.

'Yes, absolutely, making your investment stretch further and work harder. I realise that a lot of the problems you'll be facing are very modern problems,' she says, addressing my parents, 'but you have deep pockets and a whole world of expertise at your fingertips, should you want it.

'I promise you, there will be solutions that are just as radical, just as extreme as the problems themselves, and there are many, many experts who'd kill for a chance to work with you at the cutting edge of impact investing, because that's what you're proposing here. Some of the examples I've included have revolutionised entire communities, and there's no reason you can't shoot for the stars here, too.'

I wish I could squeeze her hand and tell her how much I'm in her thrall every time she opens her mouth, but I can't. Instead, I double down on her message.

'Athena's right. This is a huge, ambitious vision, and it'll take more than a village. Honestly, I'm feeling pretty daunted. I'm not sure parish bake sales have prepared me for this kind of scale.' My brother snorts. 'But no one's suggesting we effect change overnight. The Sullivans are excellent at building juggernauts. That's what we do. We use the best people and the best materials and the most revolutionary processes—and that goes from building insulation to horses' balls. If we take the values at the core of our businesses and we apply them to this with the help of experts in these fields, who knows what we can achieve.'

'Hear hear,' Dad says, slapping the table for good measure. 'Fuck knows, you're right. We didn't get where we are by being copycats. If we do this, we do it right and we do it our way. Now, I have a beautiful woman to wine and dine, so Maeve and I will leave you to thrash out the details.' He pushes his chair back and nods at Mum. 'You ready, darlin'?'

'You're a good boy,' Mum tells me as she stands. I see in her face the first inkling of approval since I left the priesthood.

CHAPTER 27

Athena

What do you get when you cross a group of thirsty Seraphim with a platinum Amex?

A *very* large cocktail bill.

At least that's the way it's looking.

It's my turn to fund the Seraph drinks this evening. As the latest of this highest order of angels to start a new job, I'm putting my generous sign-on bonus to good use behind the bar of the new and sinfully decadent Bar Noir at the Montague Hotel in Knightsbridge.

'When the Clase Azul is flowing on someone else's dime, the Seraphim flock,' I observe. 'It's busier than the gates of heaven tonight.'

In reality, I couldn't give a shit about the bar tab. It's Friday night, and I'm with some of my favourite women in the world. My friend Sophia has even flown in from Monaco for the occasion. She calls our monthly drinks *essential self-care.*

'St Peter must be lonely tonight,' she muses. 'I wonder if he ever resorts to his own hand.'

I shake my head. 'You're dreadful. How did you get out of work early, anyway?'

'Thad fucked me over lunch for good measure and then helicoptered me to Nice so I could catch his PJ over. You know me, I'm all about efficiency. *Yamas.*'

'*Yamas,*' I say, holding up my shot of Clase Azul in response. We clink carefully and then down our drinks. Tequila this excellent requires no accoutrements.

Soph is Greek-born but was educated primarily in the UK and US. The daughter of a prominent shipping family, she works for another Greek shipping magnate, Thaddeus Karavitis, and spends most of her time with him between Athens, Montenegro and Monaco. Karavitis may be in his early sixties, but he's arguably the kinkiest bastard of any Seraph client. God knows, he works Soph hard, and God knows, she bloody loves it. He may have a wife and four kids, but she's more like a paid mistress than an EA, from what I can tell.

The lifestyle seems to suit her. She's a lush beauty, all huge black doe eyes and pouty lips and incredible tits.

'Nice.' I tell her. I lean in and sniff her neck. 'You still reek of sex, you dirty bitch.'

She throws her head back and cackles delightedly, earning amused glances from the rest of our little group. They all know what she's like.

'You know it. I just had time to spritz some perfume on before I got on the chopper. He's fucking insatiable. That man pops little blue pills like they're Skittles.'

'I bet he can't keep his hands off you. And you're indecently tanned for January,' I say, looking her over. She could never in a million years be accused of looking slutty, but her wardrobe is definitely more flamboyant than mine. It makes sense, given her jet setting lifestyle, that she's less about demure Max Mara and more about the fun brands: Dolce. Cavalli. Versace.

'Thad and I went sailing in the BVIs for a week after

Christmas,' she confesses. 'I was topless or nude on the yacht most of the time. He likes me tanned.'

'I bet he does,' I murmur, giving her exposed décolletage a once-over. Her golden tits are nestled like puppies into the low V of her gorgeous red silk dress. I'm not really into women, but Soph and I have fooled around once. During my brief stint with Anton Wolff, Karavitis invited him onto his yacht when it was moored in Montenegro. Let's just say the two tycoons put their heads together and decided upon watching me and her get each other off with vibrators before they got in on the action.

I can confirm that Karavitis is an excellent poster boy for Viagra.

I can also confirm that Sophia's puppies feel as fantastic as they look.

In theology, Seraphim are the order of angels closest to God's throne. The name Seraph, therefore, is fitting in more ways than one. Not only do our combinations of fierce intellects and ethereal polish merit it, but our positions afford us that same proximity to myriad seats of power across Europe and the US.

Icarus showed us that those who fly too high can get burnt, so Soph's definition of these meet-ups as *essential self-care* is on point. Fuck knows, it can be intimidating, exhausting, managing these titans of industry, these entitled men-children who aren't used to being told *no* and who expect it all.

Our NDAs purposely extend to individuals outside the Seraph organisation only. Camille structured them so that we could share details of our work within the group on a confidential basis. Our positions in our respective firms are necessarily isolated and overly focused on one person. The Seraph sisterhood provides a safe place, a support network, a sense of belonging. There's no rivalry, only camaraderie.

In a society that would shame us for our career choices while bleeding out with envy at our bank balances, we have this group of likeminded women to cheerlead and commiserate, to share seduction hacks and horror stories alike. No one fluffs each other up like Seraphim. We even have an online chat devoted solely to swapping tips for our investment portfolios, because the Seraphim are raking it in.

When we're all sitting in a black and gold alcove with a shot glass and champagne flute apiece and a bottle of Clase Azul sitting pretty in the middle of our table, Camille raises her flute with her trademark poise.

'To the Seraphim: may you rise ever higher... and take our clients with you to heaven.'

'To the Seraphim,' we all chorus, flutes held aloft.

'To the angels who guard the gates of power,' Sophia offers.

'To celestial bodies and earthly pleasures,' I counter, and she snorts.

'To vertical integration and horizontal negotiations,' quips our friend Bree, a gorgeous Black woman with a Stanford MBA and a body that's frankly ridiculous.

The rest of us laugh, and Camille's mouth twists in amusement. 'To burning bright and keeping secrets.'

'Amen to that,' I say firmly, and Bree's head whips around. She doesn't miss a trick.

'Oh look! The hot priest has converted her already! That's so sweet. Christianity is a good look on you, honey. Do you guys pray together, too?'

I roll my eyes to conceal the fact that a memory is searing itself onto my brain.

Gabe's clothed body wrapped around my naked one,

pumping me from behind as he recited The Book of Psalms in a way that was conflicted and filthy all at once.

'I only know one way to pray,' I retort, 'and it always ends in a celestial moment. For everyone involved.'

'But it's going well?' Camille asks, her face serious now. 'I have to say, of all the guys who walk through our doors, he seemed like one of the most thoroughly decent.'

The girls are watching me like hawks. I need to be careful here.

'It's going really well,' I tell Camille briskly. 'He's a lovely guy, like you say, and the company is fascinating. There's so much to sink my teeth into.'

'I bet there is, you horny little slut,' Soph mutters beside me, and I turn and glare at her.

'I meant overhauling their charitable efforts and building a proper foundation, airhead.'

'I'm looking him up,' Maya, another Seraph, declares, bending her head over her phone. 'What's his name again?'

'Gabriel Sullivan,' Camille supplies unhelpfully. She shoots me another of her enigmatic smiles. 'He really is *very* attractive. And you know he came in and asked for Athena specifically.'

'What can I say?' I pretend to admire my glossy maroon nails. 'My reputation precedes me.'

'Well, if he wanted to be well and truly corrupted, he went for the right Seraph,' Maya muses, then sits up straight. 'Holy shit! He's fucking *gorgeous!*'

She turns the phone around, and fuck. It's that photo of Gabe in his dog collar—the one I found so arresting during my initial Google search. The one where he's ramrod straight and unsmiling and bathed in rainbow light diffused through his stain-glassed windows. Glancing at it now, having fucked him several times, knowing how hooded those astonishing eyes go right before he comes, knowing the sounds of disbelief

and awe he makes when he first pushes inside me each time…
it's a whole other level of affecting.

'Jesus fuck,' Sophia says, peering in for a better look. 'You
jammy bitch.'

'Please tell me he dresses up as a priest for you,' another
Seraph, Claudia, pleads. 'For the sake of women everywhere.'

I manage a laugh. 'No—I haven't—he hasn't dressed up.
It's still a big deal for him, I think—he's still very much in
transition to being a lay person.'

'Hiring yourself a Seraph would be an effective way to
speed up that transition, I should think,' Claudia says.

'You need to get your kink on and explore the priest
thing,' my friend Talia pipes up. 'Claudia's right. Think of the
stuff you could do! Oh my God, it could be so hot.'

'I don't want to offend him,' I protest, ignoring the fact
that I profaned his sacred little prayer room without a second
thought—*and he let me*. I'm aiming to convey discretion. I
feel odd discussing my working relationship with Gabe here,
with these shrewd, exacting women, and I'm not sure why. I
never had any problem regaling them with outrageous tales
about Anton or moaning about how boring Steve was. I tell
myself it's because Gabe is new to this world of… sin, essentially. He's a good man undergoing some serious shifts in his
lifestyle.

He's not fair game.

Not like the others.

Bree cocks her head and surveys me, her expression
shifting from amusement to concern.

'Any other recent fucks you want to fill us in on?' she asks
with a gentleness I don't like. The vast majority of us are in
non-exclusive contracts with our bosses, which means they,
and we, are free to screw around as long as we use protection
and get tested fortnightly. We can even have boyfriends, if we
like. I definitely enjoyed the benefits of no-strings-attached sex

when I was working for Steve Goodall, but it hasn't even crossed my mind since I've started with Gabe.

'No,' I say weakly. 'He keeps me... busy.'

He keeps me so awash with orgasms that I have no need to go looking for D.

It was the same with Anton, I remind myself. When you're in a sexually gratifying dynamic with your boss, there's no need to go looking elsewhere.

I'm aware of the girls exchanging some concerned glances.

'It's okay if this one's different, honey,' Bree says now. 'You know that, right?'

'It's—he's not!' I splutter. 'I've only been there a few weeks, okay? The first few weeks are always intense.' There's intense, and then there's the memory of Gabe looking up at me as he ate me, claiming his "prize" after our successful meeting about the foundation, but nobody here needs to know that.

She pats my knee. 'Of course they are. You do you, okay? Now, let me tell you about my most recent trip to La Perla with Robert. They closed the place down and smuggled us in the back.'

Bree works for a very senior Member of Parliament, a man who holds the nation's fate in his hands and has such a penchant for dressing his beautiful EA in expensive lingerie that they go to underwear stores at least once a week. Or so it seems, anyway. As she talks, I allow myself to relax, grateful for the elegant way she's steered the conversation away from Gabe.

I may be enjoying my time with him a little too much, but I'm barely capable of admitting that to myself. There's absolutely no way the topic of me and him is open for discussion among this group of badass women whose brains, looks and ambition have them unabashedly, systematically, sleeping their way to the top.

The hilarious banter continues, interrupted only when a group of what look like crypto bros at the bar send a server over with a bottle of Dom Perignon, complete with sparklers, to our table. They've been leering all night from a safe distance. There's much cheering from them when the cork is popped, and a couple of decorous nods of acknowledgement from us, but not much more.

We don't want to encourage them, after all.

One, we're here strictly for girl time.

And two, they could never afford us.

CHAPTER 28

Gabe

I feel like a schoolboy.

I'm sitting at my desk, earbuds in and pen at the ready and a snowy-white new page open in my notebook.

I'm ready to learn.

The meeting I'm about to jump into is a Zoom the Alchemy team is running to brief its members on the protocol for their upcoming Prima Nocta event. I have no intention of letting Athena overhear a word of it—I want to preserve as much of the mystique as I can until Saturday night comes.

While my desk faces away from my windows and towards the glass partition between my desk and hers, hers is at a forty-five degree angle in the direction of the outer door. As I wait for the hosts to start the meeting, I gaze at the mass of glossy waves that tumble down her back, at the glimpses I catch of her profile whenever she turns her head. She must feel my eyes on her, because she twists around so she can smile seductively at me.

'Just shout if you need me,' she calls through the open door.

I grin back. 'I will.'

It could be any regular Tuesday and any regular exchange between a CEO and his EA... except we both know it's not. And while I don't intend to shove my cock down Athena's throat while listening to the Alchemy founders speaking, I still marvel at the fact that I *could*.

I'm also not above doing it as soon as the call ends.

Zoom informs me that the meeting is about to begin, so I turn my attention back to my monitor. The pop-up window shows Gen Wolff, one of the club's cofounders and its CEO. She's also the wife of my mate Anton and a force of nature. Today, she looks every bit as polished and glamorous as she usually does, her pale blonde hair swept back off her face.

'Thanks for joining us,' she says crisply. 'As you're all busy people, we'll get started. This call is specifically for those of you who've opted to play the role of feudal overlords at the upcoming Prima Nocta themed event. Actually, all of you here identify as male, so I may refer to you in terms of gener-alised male pronouns on this call.

'That's in contrast to your so-called brides on the night, who we'll be referring to as virgins. While the dynamic of Prima Nocta is traditionally a male-female one, we have a few different takes on that tradition happening next weekend. Some of you have opted to have multiple virgins brought to you, some of you have signed up for this at the behest of the women in your life, who've requested multiple lords for the night. Of course, some of you will take a male or non-binary virgin, and many of you have requested that we provide "guards", who will all be Alchemy hosts, to either watch or assist with the deflowering process. All of which subversion I applaud most thoroughly.'

She shoots the camera a dazzling smile. She looks genuinely thrilled that her members are rising to the occasion.

I have a fleeting flash of panic. Jesus. Multiple lords. Perhaps I should have asked Alchemy to commandeer a few other guys and give my beautiful assistant one of the gang-bangs she apparently enjoys so much.

But I talk myself off the ledge. I get the impression that it's the historical kink factor that has Athena so worked up over this particular event. It's the idea of casting aside her brains and her success and her agency for one evening and allowing herself to be completely dominated that appeals. If I play my part right, I can make this a fuck she'll remember.

Gen keeps talking. 'My co-founder, Cal, is going to lead most of this call. He's organised the bulk of this event. In a moment, he'll take you through the logistical aspects as well as giving you more historical context and advice for your roles. But I wanted to step in first, to share a few perspectives with you.'

She pauses. 'We've had a few members raise questions over the ethics of this kind of role play, and I'm well aware that for those of you who weren't familiar with the term and went straight to Wikipedia, you were confronted with the fact that they'd put it in their *Violence Against Women* section. That's a highly problematic red flag if ever there was one, so I want to be extremely clear.

'When we look into new themed nights, we often do it in response to requests from our members, and that's because our members have *incredibly* rich imaginations, and we're privileged that when you want to act out your most extreme fantasies, you come to us. So let me tell you this. Prima Nocta, or some version of it, has been requested many, many times since we opened the doors of this club, okay, and the *vast* majority of those requests have come from our female-identifying members.

'We have a rich history of political incorrectness,' she

continues. 'Hello, Slave Night?' She grins, and so do I. I haven't braved Slave Night at Alchemy, but I can only imagine the kind of depraved shit that goes down. 'And that's because so many of our darkest fantasies *are* politically incorrect or downright transgressive, but when we act them out in a safe space, with other consenting adults and clear boundaries, they can be extraordinarily powerful.'

She's right, of course, and I'm certainly guilty of applying my own Good Boy, hyper-Catholic brakes when it comes to anything remotely taboo. I've known for a long time, since before I left the priesthood, in fact, that those same kinks that are so steeped in shame and guilt and even fear are the ones whose transgressive allures turn me on.

I've already taken the biggest, most terrifying step of all. I hired a woman whose depraved mind and beautiful body can act as the most transformative portal to this dark world of pleasure... if I allow her to take me there. My next step is to find a way to sit with the inner conflict to which Gen is alluding, to be able to acknowledge the forbidden nature of some acts while accepting that, with Athena's enthusiastic (and hopefully noisy) consent, there is no actual harm in partaking in them.

'I'll vouch for the fact that there are many fiercely bright, strong, powerful women among our members at Alchemy,' Gen goes on, 'and I promise you that these women understand very clearly the pleasure that total submission can bring in a sexual context while holding onto their power very ably outside of the bedroom. That's an important distinction, and one I'd urge you to reflect on as you carry out this charade.'

I let my gaze wander over to my beautiful assistant. I'm equally in awe of her intellect, her fire, her appetites. I jot down a note.

Powerful in life / submissive in the bedroom

It makes sense, of course. Athena is the most Type A of Type As. Of course it's logical that she gets a kick out of being dominated. What I still haven't entirely worked through in my mind is whether the blind need I have to be the man who can do that for her is sick or healthy.

Maybe it's sick, and maybe that doesn't matter. Maybe the only thing that matters is respecting Athena enough to listen and act when she advocates for her own desires, no matter what kind of perverse thrill I get out of our arrangement.

Gen's speaking again. 'My advice to you is twofold. First, heed the information yielded to you in the questionnaire that your partners or guests have completed. We'll send these to you after the call. The questionnaires are intended to furnish you with as much insight as possible into how they'd like your evening together to go, without ruining the magic or the sense of surprise too much.

'Second, lean into the spirit of this thing. This is our first immersive offsite experience, and the scale of it is ambitious. It's really about casting aside your everyday persona and *having fun*. Newsflash: it's not every day you get to act out a fantasy of playing a villainous medieval overlord. So do it with gusto! The more you and your fellow role-players let go and get stuck in, the more memorable it will be for you all. Or so we hope, anyway.

'While this group will obviously be the dominant party in your personal role plays, there is an element of vulnerability for both parties. Very few of us play-act these days. We're all far too serious and busy and important to pretend to be knights or princesses or evil kings or whatever else takes our fancy.

'That is to say, mutual trust is needed here when you and your partner or partners are role-playing in a scene this intense.

The very nature of it is an act of vulnerability. But if you take the leap together, our hope is that it will bring you great pleasure. So please consider this your reminder to act your part as if an Oscar depends on it and, for God's sake, have a ball. With that, I'll hand you over to Cal, who has some truly excellent—and worryingly well thought-out—suggestions for how a predatory feudal overlord might act.'

CHAPTER 29

Athena

I've been to my fair share of boundary-pushing parties, from themed events to full-on orgies.

Given the kinds of men I've worked for, that should be no surprise.

But I have never, and I mean never, taken part in something quite as immersive as this. The scale of the Prima Nocta event is off the charts. I feel like an extra in *Game of Thrones*.

I completed my questionnaire, and I attended a Zoom call for tonight's "virgins" hosted by two of the Alchemy founders, Anton's wife Genevieve and her colleague, Callum.

Having the wife of the guy who not only owns my agency but used to pay through the nose to fuck me talk us through the delights that awaited me was interesting. On one infamous evening in Anton's office, he let two of our colleagues fuck Genevieve because she wouldn't let him touch her, instead using me to take the edge off for him as he watched her get spit-roasted on his office floor. I may have been blindfolded for all the good parts, but holy fuck was that night electric.

Any woman who has the self-control to hold off on Anton Wolff like *that* deserves serious kudos, in my view. It's no wonder that he proposed with indecent haste after she finally yielded to his considerable charms. Watching her today, I'm reminded that she's my kind of woman. In another lifetime, we would have been friends, I'm sure of it. Rarely have I seen that level of badassery outside of my circle of Seraphim, and I admire her just as much for fronting an outfit like Alchemy as for getting a guy like Anton Wolff to fall head over heels in love with her.

At any rate, she and her indecently attractive colleague, Callum, did an impeccable job on the Zoom of talking us "virgins" through what to expect tonight on a strictly need-to-know basis. They explained that they were intent on furnishing us with enough details to assuage any anxiety or uncertainty we may have had while holding enough back so as not to spoil any of the surprises in store for us tonight.

Let it be said that I had zero anxiety or uncertainty and that, while I usually loathe surprises, sexy surprises are absolutely fine with me. The more the merrier.

Bring them on.

Still, it's with more trepidation than I expected that I look around at these atmospheric surroundings. This is a *lot*. I haven't seen Gabe since we finished work yesterday and I skipped off, giddy as a schoolgirl over what lay ahead. We've travelled here separately, and the ninety-minute car ride from West London gave me plenty of time to close my eyes and ponder my fate tonight.

The experience started as soon as we reached the castle gates to find routes marked *Overlords* and *Virgins.* God knows what the driver must have made of it, but he's deposited me in a clearing manned with guards, and I'm shivering at the loss of the nice warm Mercedes and twenty-first century life—both its comforts and its securities.

We've been instructed to wear casual clothes, so I've turned up in athleisure wear and my enormous Moncler that is more duvet than coat. I hug myself as the guards, in a combi-nation of chainmail and leather armour, run their hostile gaze over me. A few of them hold the leather leads of Irish wolfhounds who stand still. The dogs are trembling, despite the lit brazier nearby. Poor beasts.

'Declare yourself,' one of the guards barks. Hastily, I hold out the piece of parchment that was delivered to the office this week, my name beautifully inscribed on it.

'Athena Davenport.'

He jerks his head in the direction of the tents. 'To the bathhouse.'

The tents are a hundred or so metres from where we're standing. I pick my way down a path that's been laid with rushes and which is illuminated with flaming torches mounted on iron brackets. Indeed, the vast sweep of the main drive is lit like this, and the effect is certainly dramatic. In the distance, the castle itself has been anachronistically uplit with red lights, but I doubt any of my fellow revellers will mind, because the effect is hauntingly fabulous.

I can't get over how atmospheric it all is. It's a clear, cold night and the moody beat of distant drums pulses through the air. The sky is dark above me and azure over to the west, but there's a smoky haze from the numerous braziers dotted around the campus. Even the scents are alien—cooked meat with, I think, spices, and the earthy scent of horse shit. I really do feel like I'm in one of those full-immersion folk villages.

There's a gaggle of women outside the cluster of tents signposted as bathhouses, huddled around a brazier wearing the beige-brown bonnets and rags of servants. They are uniformly stout and ruddy-cheeked and I marvel again at the level of detail that's gone into this event. As I draw closer, I see a large wooden board propped up against the nearest tent. It bears a list of names, including mine, and I point at it.

'Hello—um, I'm Miss Athena Davenport?' I say,

parroting the format of my name on the board. We were advised on the Zoom that we'd first be washed and given a change of clothes in the manner that a lowly bride might have been, but I don't know much else aside from the fact that I won't have to endure any sham wedding ceremony to my village 'husband'. Lack of self assurance is never a problem for me, but I must admit to feeling a little uncertain right now. What I *am* sure of is that every last detail has been contrived to make me feel exactly this way, to stoke that sense of vulnerability, of anticipation, and it's really bloody clever.

One of the servants jerks her head towards the tent entrance, but the gesture is far cheerier than that of the guard.

'In ye go, dearie. Let's get ye washed.'

Inside, the tent is far warmer than it should be, and far grander than I expected. I suspect the Alchemy crew has found a way to marry the needs of its high-maintenance members with adequate historical accuracy. The canvas walls and wooden floors are covered with Persian rugs, and in front of a freestanding copper tub lies a bear-head rug that I sincerely hope is fake.

The tub itself, I'm thrilled to see, is filled with water hot enough to have steam rising thickly from it, carrying the scent of roses and whatever other herbs are floating with the rose petals on the surface.

'What are ye waiting for, duckie?' the woman asks me, flapping her hand. 'In ye get! Do ye know how much wood we had to burn to heat this water?'

I stand still for a second, uncharacteristically frozen as I realise she means for me to strip in front of her. I understand privacy is a modern construct, and I'm hardly a blushing virgin, but still. I can't help but feel as though this is one more sneaky move on the organisers' parts to ratchet up that insidious feeling of exposure, of vulnerability. In any legend about

Prima Nocta, no matter how fictional, any woman in my position would have felt that terrifying powerlessness at every turn.

She slides my coat off my shoulders and lays it on a nearby wooden chair. 'Best make haste before your bridegroom appears. His Lordship won't be happy at all if another man sneaks a look at his goods, not even your own husband.'

That galvanises me. I'm not in the habit of honouring random guys with the gift of my nakedness. I shoe off my trainers before tugging off my clothes, one layer at a time. She watches me unabashedly, as I unclip my bra and pull down my panties.

'What lovely full hips you have,' she says cheerily. 'May you be blessed with many healthy children in your lifetime. His Lordship will have his fill of you tonight, I'll warrant.'

The significance of her words hits me. Of course. Historians believe that the idea behind Prima Nocta was to give the overlords the chance to spread their seed. If they could impregnate brides before their new husbands had a chance to get to them, they could stamp out the advancement of other or lesser tribes.

The thought is both chilling and impossibly arousing. Within the next hour, "Lord Sullivan" will be tasting his new wares and exercising his feudal rights over every inch of my body. God, I can't wait to see him in all his seigneurial glory.

I push the thought away as I sink down into the warm, scented water, holding my hair out of the way. I'm not some strong, present-day woman, so confident in the power of her sexuality that she's forged an entire career from it. I'm a frightened young woman, a virgin who is impossibly ignorant of the things men do to women to create heirs and sate their bodily appetites. In order to wring every last ounce of pleasure from this evening, I need to lean the fuck in.

'What is he like? His Lordship?' I ask. This was one of the suggested questions we were given in our information packs.

Apparently, the actors we will meet on our way to be deflowered have all been briefed on us and our "Lords" for the night.

She comes around so she's behind me and, lifting my hair, ties it up in a rag before draping it over the edge of the tub so it won't get wet. It's a gesture I'm grateful for. I may be wearing almost no makeup except for blusher and mascara, but I carefully blowdried and tonged my hair this afternoon. I'll be the most well-groomed virgin in this place tonight, right down to my very modern Brazilian.

'You'll have heard that he's a very handsome man,' she tells me, stroking my hair as I allow myself to sink down further in the water until only my head and shoulders are above the surface. Rose petals and stems of lavender float around me.

She picks up a little bowl filled with a pale substance. 'Almond paste, to cleanse and smooth the skin. Go on, take a little. Very handsome, as they say, with hair blacker than a raven's feather and eyes as blue as the summer sky.'

I begin to smooth the paste over my arms. It's a mild exfoliant, and it smells wonderfully of almond oil.

The maid lowers her voice and whispers right into my ear. 'But they also say that he is a cold man, hungry for power and as greedy for women as he is for gold. Even so, he rarely exercises his *droit de seigneur*. Those at the castle say he insists on having only the most beautiful maidens, and when he gets them, his appetites are voracious.

'God knows, you are a rare beauty, as rare as I have seen. I will send up a prayer for you tonight, dearie, because he may not have his fill of you before daybreak. Make sure to wash between your legs so that his His Lordship might find you pleasing.'

CHAPTER 30

Athena

The simple white garment of linen and crocheted lace in which the maid dresses me is more nightgown than wedding gown. I'm naked underneath, and every move has the fabric abrading my nipples. The cloak is faux-fur and hooded but insufficient against this frosty night. The gravel of the driveway is cold and sharp through the thin leather of these weird little slippers they've given me.

I'm freezing my tits off, but I feel alive. Vitality is coursing through my veins almost as thickly as arousal. That bath was the perfect portal, winding me backwards through the centuries from my world of Moncler and Mercedes to this incarnation of me as an ingenue (complete with miraculously intact hymen) on the threshold of learning what it means to be a woman of greedy flesh and heated blood and thumping heart.

The Athena who awaits the horse-drawn cart that's trundling up the driveway has no agency and little power, aside from the effect her physical assets will have over the man who presumes to overpower her.

My skin is clean, softened with almond oil. The maid's

seductive words washed over me as potently as the water she sluiced over my back when she bade me lean forward. By lamenting my likely fate tonight, she ignited that life force inside of me, the one at the very essence of who I am in every incarnation.

I may be a virgin tonight, but I'm a woman, too, and the very helplessness of this scenario I find myself in roils deep in my belly in a way that feels remarkably like desire.

I'm back outside my cave, as dusky as it is daunting.

Will its shadows consume me, or will its crystalline walls light me up?

The carriage draws up. I hug my cloak around me as I gaze at the passenger. These really are the most impractical garments if you want to have use of your arms.

A guy around my age—my brand-new husband, presumably—stands as it comes to a halt and then proceeds to drop down from the cart. He's nice looking, with sandy hair and the wholesome face and decent build of a kindly village lad who probably hoes potatoes and lugs bails of hay around. Twenty-first-century Athena would eat him for breakfast, but I force myself to gaze at him with affection.

'My love,' he says, holding out his hand. I can see his reaction to me written all over his face, and I doubt it's the result of his acting skills, decent though they seem.

I take his hand, and he helps me up into the cart. It's modest and open, with hay strewn over the wooden seats— hay that does absolutely nothing to ease the jarring discomfort as I sit, the hard wood digging into my sitz bones. He jumps up beside me and takes the reins. The carthorse trots on, and I instinctively grip the bench, because this thing has zero suspension.

The castle lies only two or three hundred metres ahead down this wide, straight approach, the way lit on both sides by hundreds of tall torches, their flames and smoke warping in the wind and filling my lungs with their scent. Thanks to the way the castle is lit, I can see the colourful heraldic flags adorning its entrance. The whole effect is fabulously over-dramatic and steeped in gravitas.

The castle draws nearer. Up close, it's even more impos-ing. More forbidding.

'I had hoped he would spare you,' my bridegroom says, glancing my way. His hands are light on the reins. 'But it seems he is a lusty dog baying for blood. I am powerless to protect you, but I promise I shall still love you, even if a man far greater than me has presumed to steal your virtue.'

'Thank you,' I murmur, as a chainmail-clad guard with another wolfhound stops in front of the cart, holding his hands up.

'Halt! Proceed no further!'

My husband stops the cart, and two more guards approach my side of the vehicle immediately, their faces in shadows below their chainmail. Behind them stands a cluster of drummers drumming slowly in tandem. Their instruments hang suspended from their necks. With the sounds echoing off the castle walls, the effect of their sticks against whatever animal skin their drums are made from is as ominous as it is atmospheric.

'Declare yourself!' one of the guards shouts.

'Miss Athena Davenport,' I say, my voice clear.

At that, he nods. 'My Lord Sullivan has been waiting for you. Come, make haste.'

With a last glance at my groom's stricken face, I descend carefully from the cart.

'Godspeed,' he murmurs, and I nod, though I suspect he can't see my acknowledgment from beneath the oversized hood of my cloak.

Behind me, his cartwheels crunch over the stones as four guards flank me. They're fucking huge in their armour, each holding a silver shield and a lance. In their midst, I am tiny and defenceless, Red Riding Hood amidst four silver wolves.

A shiver goes through me, and it's not from the bitter cold of this night. It's a shiver of anticipation, of the very particular frisson that comes when you know viscerally you are safe and yet *feel* so unsafe, so prettily precarious.

It's the frisson that only the prospect of a beautifully orchestrated scene can offer. For what is a scene but the most mystical fairy tale for adults, brought to life with sensory details that are both achingly inventive and unimaginably sweet?

'This way,' one of the guards barks, and together they march me to the castle entrance.

The enormous doorframe dwarfs even the guards. The stone-floored hallway is rich with tapestries and lit with hundreds of candles on iron sconces, their wax sagging and dripping so prettily. The air is heavy with beeswax and a heady, sexy scent that I'd swear, if I wasn't bang slap in the midst of the Middle Ages, is Diptyque's *Baies* candles.

On both sides are heavy carved oak doors, shut tight, and ahead of us, a wide oak staircase, more heraldic banners fluttering colourfully above it. The guards lead me to the staircase, and I gather up my cloak and skirts and ascend carefully. The steps are shallow, but it's dim in here and my hood is constricting my vision. I have the oddest feeling of being marched to my execution, when really, only great pleasure awaits me.

As we climb, the faintest sounds of a woman's moans carry on the air like a whisper of candle smoke, and that insistent pull deep in my belly only intensifies. *That will be me in a few moments.* It's a carnal sound, a promise of unknown delicacies behind closed doors.

When we reach the top of the staircase, the guards process along the corridor before stopping at a doorway at the front of the palace. Through the narrow windows along the front wall, I can make out the fuzzy torchlight that lights the driveway. I stare at the carvings on the door, my heart thumping as though I've just run up fifteen storeys instead of walking painfully up one.

One of the guards uses his fist to thump three times on the door, and through the slab of wood comes the muffled response.

'Enter.'

It's Gabe's voice, but it's not. This voice is more imperious. More impatient.

Two guards move in front of me and open the door with a flourish, pushing in. The other two position themselves behind me. One prods me in the back, and I realise I've been standing frozen. I stumble slightly. My pulse is pounding in my ears, for some reason.

This is Gabe.

This is a role play.

And yet I can't help but feel in this moment like a sacrificial lamb.

I advance slowly into the room as the door clanks shut behind me with an ominous thud of finality. The chamber is huge, with high ceilings. Rich tapestries hang from the walls, their jewel tones long faded. Beneath my leather slippers is a layer of rushes. My first impressions are of flickering candlelight and long shadows, of some ephemeral quality of solemnity.

Then I see him.

Fuck.

Fuck.

Fuck.

Just as it was with his voice, it's Gabe and yet not Gabe, because the man standing before me in the centre of this room, as strong and grounded as a great oak, has the kind of entitlement my Gabriel has never embodied. He's removed and kingly and imposing... and so, so gorgeous.

For a moment, it's me and him, taking each other in in these fantastical guises, and it's the oddest, oddest thing.

It's as if we've both hurtled back in time to the Dark Ages where we've found each other again.

It's as if our paths are meant to cross in every century, however impossible that might be to fathom.

Until his voice cuts through the thick silence as coldly, as harshly as a scythe might cut through a wildflower meadow.

'Bring her closer. Let me see.'

CHAPTER 31

Athena

This lord's bedchamber is as richly appointed as my first impressions suggested. Behind him stands a majestic four-poster bed: a great, hulking thing carved from oak. Its heavy hangings are a deep red, and a thrill courses through my body at the thought of the guards closing them around us so it's just me and him in a womb-like space where he can consume me entirely.

The guards ahead of me move forward until they're in front of him. They stop and move to the side to give their lord a clear view of this virgin they've brought to his bedside. We stare at each other again, and I take him in.

His hair is more tousled than I've seen it, his beard less neatly clipped. He's in a fine doublet made from burgundy-coloured velvet and punctuated with a wide leather belt. His breeches look like wool; his long boots are black leather. I spot several chunky rings on his fingers.

I bet they'll rub against my clit when he explores his new plaything.

'I said, let me see. Take down your hood.' His voice is

brusque, his entire demeanour straddling that line of bored and pissed off.

'Yes, my Lord.' I reach up for my hood and slowly slide it off my head. I'm not sure if it's my words, or the full sight of my face, but he swallows hard, his eyes roving over me before jerking to one of the guards behind me.

'Take off her cloak.'

They both step forward, crowding me as they attempt to undo the horn and leather closure of my cloak with their free hands. Their proximity has me shivering in delight. I couldn't be more aware of the things I agreed to in my questionnaire, but I have no idea at all of what Gabe has planned for me tonight.

Even so, when they slide the cloak off me, leaving me in a so-called gown that's little more than an expanse of muslin, the full significance of this situation hits me.

I'm alone in a room with five men, the overlord in front of me even more intimidating than his armed guards.

I'm hyper-aware of my nipples, hardened beyond all decency by arousal and something approaching frostbite, poking through the thin fabric. I'm conscious of my growing slickness, of the tremors of my thighs as they press together. I'm aware that his lordship can already see far too much of the bride he's wrenched from her groom, all for the lordly pleasure of shattering her innocence and pumping her full of his seed. He can already see far too clearly how nubile she is, how ripe for plunder.

He steps forward, looking me over in a haughty way. It's as though he's been born to it, as though he's been raised his entire life seeing everything and everyone as his property. His gaze rakes over my face, over my breasts. It floats downwards, taking in the way the fabric skims my hips, and I wonder if the maid was right, if he's assessing my worthiness for his seed.

'Take off your shoes,' he orders, and I toe them off.

They're barely worthy of the term *shoes*, but barefoot, I feel even more exposed. He stares at my feet before wrenching his eyes from my body and glaring at one of the guards in front of me.

'Remove her dress. I want to see.'

Despite myself, I freeze. I can still hear the drummers' tattoo, low and insistent, through the windows. It sounds to my jacked-up nervous system like the beat of danger. Of sacrifice. It sounds like the beat to which blood is spilt and lives are shattered.

This is it. This is why I'm here, and the Athena of this millennium rejoices while her thousand-year-old ancestor shrinks. I need this so badly. I need them to tear my dress from my limbs so he can feast upon me, to consume me so mercilessly that I'll never be the same again.

Beside me, two of the guards grab at the slit of my gown's neckline and yank, hard, and the fabric rips with a sinister shriek. I gasp involuntarily. The curtains have opened on the spectacle that is my body, leaving me perfectly, nakedly on display as they slide the remains of the gown off my shoulders and it drops to the ground behind me.

I'm hyper-conscious, my senses on fire. The warm air kisses my skin just as his gaze sears it. I stand completely still, arms by my sides, as he takes me in. He reaches up and scratches at his beard, and it seems to me he's struggling to contain himself.

He may think he's bringing this maiden to her knees, but I'll be damned if I haven't brought him to his by the end of our night together.

His voice, when he speaks, is a bark.

'Leave us.'

CHAPTER 32

Gabe

This would be an excellent time to call on God's grace, because the sight of this beautiful woman standing naked in front of me, awaiting my bidding, has thoughts so forbidden, so intoxicating, coursing through me that they may well take me under.

The guards clatter out. The thud of the door closing behind them has us alone, and it seems to me the air thickens.

I've met this woman in another lifetime. She wears many guises. She's an angel who pretends to be a whore—or maybe it's the other way around—but tonight, she's a virgin.

Whatever guise she adopts, she is the most beautiful human being I've ever seen. When God created her in His likeness, he gave her wide-set hazel eyes and the creamiest skin. He gave her a mouth a virgin has no business having and hair that is a sheet of silk and breasts that are full and round and lush, with the prettiest little pink nipples.

This particular combination of features may be enough to send a man to hell all on their own, but it's the significance of her standing here before me in this particular incarnation that may well finish me off.

Tonight, I am a man who wears his entitlement like a second skin. Not content with my title and my wife and my lands, I may exercise my birthright to take any woman in my realm as I please, to fuck her and impregnate her and extend my noble bloodline.

Because every single one of them belongs to me, just as every man and horse and dwelling here in Essex belong. To. Me.

I scarcely know what to do with her first.

To her.

In this moment, she is a foreign land, but by the end of our evening together, I will know the hills and valleys of her sweet virgin terrain. I will be as intimately familiar with the music of her cries as with the velvet wetness of her cunt. I will undo her so thoroughly that I'll ruin her forever. She'll beg me not to make her go back to her useless, nameless husband.

She'll be a woman, and he will still be an ignorant boy.

A step forward has us a foot apart. The way her rich chestnut hair falls softly over her shoulders has me wanting to dip my head and smell it as fervently as it has me wanting to use it for a fine bridle around my fist.

'What is your name?'

'Athena, my Lord.'

'A godless name. Are you godless, Athena?'

'No, my Lord.'

'Have you ever let a man do godless things to you? Ever let that new husband of yours touch you?'

She shakes her head vehemently. 'No, my Lord. No one has touched me.'

'Good.' That's very, very good. She is as unsullied as she looks, her body a virgin canvas, her skin a blanket of fresh snow for my fingerprints and my teeth.

'You are mine tonight. My property. Do you understand?'

'Y-yes.' Her eyes are astonishing, her pupils huge. She's

shivering, her body bracing for impact. I stand before her in my rich robes and my tall boots and revel in the fact that she's the most perfect sight I've ever seen.

I can wait no longer.

'That means I can do this to you, and you will let me.' I reach up and pinch her nipples lightly, fleetingly. It's a threat and a promise and a tease, and I watch in something approaching awe as her eyelids flutter closed and her lips part as though I've turned a key in a lock. She lets out a faint, shuddering moan that I decide I like very much indeed.

'Any pleasure you feel tonight is for me. Understand?'

She nods, opening her eyes and fixing them back on me. They're almost all pupil.

I pinch her nipples again, rolling them between my fingers. They're impossibly hard—whether from cold or anticipation, I'm unsure. 'Mine.'

'Argh—yours.'

I take a moment to knead her breasts, to weigh them, to toy with her nipples. She sways a little, breathing fast, as a flush of arousal builds on her cheeks.

'Open your mouth.'

She opens it immediately, affording me a lovely view of even white teeth and her pink, glistening tongue. A tongue that will work very well on my cock. I release one breast and grab a fistful of silken tresses so I can angle her face up to me. Then I bend my mouth to hers so I can kiss her.

The kiss is harsh, invasive. It's far less a sign of affection than a foreshadowing of how thoroughly I intend to explore her holes tonight. I fuck her mouth with my tongue as I hold her in place by her hair. Her arms flutter at her sides as she lets me, but I don't miss the low moan she makes into my mouth.

I release her and trail the back of my hand down between her breasts, my knuckles gliding over the impossibly soft skin of her stomach as I revel in the view of her blown-out pupils and laboured breathing. 'Mine.'

She nods her agreement.

'Widen your legs.'

She does. Such a good girl—so eager to please.

I pause. It's the headiest moment. I'm suspended in the most captivating form of anticipation before I touch her.

By the looks of things, so is she.

I move my hand lower and slide my fingers through her slippery wetness. My little so-called virgin is absolutely fucking soaked. This space between her legs is astonishing: warm and drenched; the most hospitable of terrains for a man.

'*This* is mine,' I remind her. 'It's for *my* pleasure.' I stroke her there lightly, enjoying the slipperiness of her flesh as much as the way her face contorts in sheer delight at my touch. Still, our eyes are locked, and I muse that there may be no greater pleasure than stroking a beautiful, naked woman at leisure and watching her arousal build. Her mouth is working, her jaw tensing, her legs shaking.

'Hold onto me,' I command her, and she grips the wide sleeves of my doublet to steady herself. 'Do *not* look away while I explore my new pretty little plaything.'

She nods again, biting down on her lip as if to hold in her whimpers. But when I push two fingers deep inside her she cries out, whether in shock or pleasure I do not know. Her flesh is molten and devastatingly tight and my poor, aching dick longs to wedge itself deep inside that space and never come up for air.

I fuck her like this for a moment or two, my fingers merciless, watching her plush lips form a perfect *O* as I do, making sure I don't touch that glossy little button that is already so swollen.

Even so, my little virgin is having far too good a time. This is about *me* and my seigneurial rights.

I pull my fingers out and she blinks, bereft. 'On your knees,' I drawl before sucking my fingers into my mouth. She tastes like the most erotic dream.

I knew she would.

She scrambles prettily to her knees.

'It's time for you to serve your lord, to show me what a loyal servant you are. Do you understand?'

'Yes, my lord,' she whispers, looking up at me.

'Good. Wait.'

I unbuckle the heavy silver clasp of my belt and discard it before unfastening my doublet and taking that off, too. She waits patiently on her knees, looking up at me like a penitent so pure she has nothing at all to confess, and I soak it up, this power imbalance: me in my fine leather boots and her, naked on her knees in supplication with that plush pink mouth ready to take away all my earthly woes.

Just the sight of it has me fumbling with the fastening of my breeches and shoving them down, along with my linen undergarments, so that my tortured cock springs out, thick and hot. Without a word, I close my hand hard around the back of her neck and thrust my length deep inside her mouth.

Fuck, it's a wet, lush paradise. She struggles for a moment, eyes wide and arms flailing, before her palms land on my thighs. I allow my fingers to move in her hair as she accommodates me.

'Take it all,' I say, and she moans around my length. It's a wonderful sound, muffled and anguished and desperate, and it has me pulling out so I can drive into her.

This won't take long, but it will take the edge off enough that I can play with my latest amusement for longer before I take her virginity in the fullest possible way.

I show no mercy, pistoning in and out of that blessed mouth of hers as she does her best to take me. Tears are soaking her pretty lashes and running down her cheeks. The huge fire on one side of the room burnishes her hair as she moans and gasps and sucks, and I'm only partly conscious of my own bestial grunts as my orgasm gathers heat and mass so violently that, before I know it, I'm bracing myself for the storm to break.

A primal bellow breaks from my throat as it does. I grip her hair even more tightly, holding her against me. For a moment, my entire body goes rigid as my soul bolts, soaring through the air in pure ecstasy as I let myself loose. I thrust and thrust into her warm, willing mouth, this orgasm ripping through my body like wildfire, consuming everything and sparing nothing.

It's the first way I've plundered her heavenly body tonight, but it won't be the last.

CHAPTER 33

Gabe

When I haul her to her feet, her eyes are glazed and her mouth is swollen and her cheeks are wet and her hair is tangled and her legs are coltish.

She's less perfect this way, but somehow even more beautiful.

I gaze down at her and swipe my thumb over the wetness of her full lower lip, marvelling at the extraordinary pleasure her mouth just afforded me.

'That was very, very well done,' I murmur, and her face softens, mouth curving up at the corners.

'Thank you, sir,' she whispers against my thumb.

'Now I can enjoy you properly.' I smooth her hair with my other hand. 'Get on the bed and spread your legs for me like a good, brave girl.'

Her face contorts a little, as though my suggestion that she'll need courage is less of a threat than a very alluring promise, but she nods and turns, clambering up onto my enormous bed and arranging herself on it. She fans her hair out before lying back fully, arms out to the sides, legs parted, knees drawn up a little.

The very picture of surrender.

My modern-day self knows too well how much more experienced Athena is than me. How much more radical, more comfortable, in her sexuality. I've undoubtedly been the (grateful) recipient of her experience as well as her expertise, but tonight she's giving me something I hadn't thought to want before yet now crave:

She's offering me the privilege of "taking" her, of shattering her maidenhood and, in the process, being the first man to show her the extraordinary things of which her body is capable.

None of it's real, of course. Just like I wouldn't presume to believe it's all real in my office, either. She's the consummate professional, an incredible actor.

Still, it *feels* real, in this candlelit room in this ancient castle with armed and chain-mail-clad guards outside. She wants this evening to be real just as badly as I do—far more badly, in fact. And when I make her come with my mouth and my dick, the honour of being the agent of her irrefutable pleasure will be real enough for me.

I hastily remove the rest of my clothing and jump up onto the bed so I can crouch over her, revelling in the sight of her laid out on this rich damask coverlet. With my hands on her knees, I push her legs further apart and stare at that patch of flesh, rose-coloured and unctuous and forbidden.

Flesh that will soon belong to another man but tonight belongs to me to enjoy.

To do with as I please.

I slide my fingertips inwards from her knees, and she shivers. The skin of her inner thighs is as impossibly soft as the surface of a freshly plucked rose petal, and as unblemished.

'Your husband won't do this to you,' I observe aloud, using my index fingers to hold her so carefully open. The act reminds me of tugging apart a ripe fig and admiring its rich terrain before burying my face in its luscious flesh. 'He'll take one look at you naked and probably come in his breeches like a juvenile. Or if he lasts long enough to notch himself inside you, it will be fast and desperate and lacking in finesse.'

I use my thumb to trace her wetness through from that exposed button to her entrance, and her moan is gratifyingly pained. 'And it's a shame, because your body is a beautiful instrument which, when played by a master musician with the right kind of finesse, can make truly exquisite music.' I allow myself the luxury of sliding my thumb inside her body, just for a moment. Just to remind myself of the pleasures that await me.

She pushes against me, her body sucking me in greedily, and I tut.

'You're an innocent maiden, Athena, not a greedy little lightskirt. Act like it. Do you know what your duties are to your husband?'

I keep my thumb precisely where it is, tearing my gaze away from her sweet cunt and up to her face. She's breathing heavily.

'To obey him, sir, and to allow him to... take liberties.'

I hum my approval. 'Indeed. But tonight, your duties are to yield every inch of your skin and every hole in your body to me in every single filthy way I choose, whether I'm using my fingers,'—I slide my thumb out and back in—'or my prick, or my mouth.'

She stares up at me, eyes wide, lips parted, skin flawless, this lovely, lovely creature arranged in my bedchamber for my delight with furled nipples and tight cunt, and I can wait no longer to feast on her.

'*Do not move an inch.* Understand?'

'Yes, sir,' she manages.

I push myself onto my stomach and reach up to take one nipple firmly in my grip as I bury my face in her glorious wetness and kiss that clit as ardently as I kissed her mouth earlier, laving it with my tongue, lavishing it with attention.

She practically shoots off the bed.

'This is pleasure, Athena,' I say against her flesh. 'This is pure, godless, pleasure of the flesh, and you'll almost certainly never experience it again in your marriage, so lie back and surrender to the pleasure that only your lord can give you. Say *yes, my lord* if you understand.'

'God, yes my lord.' She pants the words out.

'That's it.' I release her nipple and drag my hand down her body, splaying it over her stomach so I can hold her down. I replace the thumb inside her with two fingers and begin to fuck her hard with them as I lick her with masterful, relentless strokes. Every peasant in my realm can copulate like the farm animals in my endless fields, but *this* is what will give this maiden an experience as unforgettable as it is unique.

The young woman before me may not understand this for some time, but by taking my fill, my ownership, of her pleasure, I have prevailed upon her far more thoroughly, more indelibly, than if I had overruled or terrorised her.

Her utter capitulation is my sweetest victory.

CHAPTER 34

Athena

His fingers are savage, his tongue a wicked instrument of the hellfire whose flames are licking at my very core. He is *feasting* upon me as he might feast upon capon or boar or partridge—ravenously. Unabashedly, with carnal, male noises that flood me with shame and heat until I do not know which way is north.

Even the way he has me arranged—pinned down and spread open like a butterfly—is all-consuming. It's all for him —he has made that very clear—but in commanding me so fully he has turned my world upside down. If his words are true and I am never to experience this pleasure again, if this lordly, entitled way he's overpowering me is never to be repeated, then I may as well die tonight.

The heat builds. My head spins. At my sides, my hands grapple uselessly against this fine fabric. My body is a whirlwind of confusion and delight, the sounds I seem to be making quite as mysterious as the sensations that prompt them.

I need more.

My brain doesn't understand this, but my body does, and

it pushes against his dangerous tongue and skilful fingers until he's laughing cruelly and getting to his knees.

He's a dark, lordly figure before me, his muscles lean and his hair black and his skin as sweat-slicked as a farmer's is in a field, and he's holding that huge thing that I took in my mouth, and it's as angry and powerful as it was earlier. I watch with fascinated misgiving as he rolls something onto it and ranges his hulking form over me.

His body is the result of centuries of noble bloodlines, and it is a thing of great, masculine beauty and fearsome power. My mother warned me only that it would hurt the first time.

She did not tell me that a man would pin me like a butterfly and use his mouth on the most private, most sacred part of me and make me cry out.

She did not tell me about the heat. The need.

He braces above me on one elbow and lifts my leg over his shoulder, his muscles bunching beneath my calf. I feel swollen and achy where his mouth was; I feel half-crazy with some mysterious need. He's pushing against my entrance now, pushing in, and the force of his blunt instrument as he breaches me is so intense and so shocking and so invasive that yes, I might die from the pleasure of it.

Every part of my body is screaming. I'm delirious with overwhelm as he stretches me and stretches me, huge and endless, until he pushes so deep inside my body with a grunt that I'm sure he will split me in two.

'This is what it means to be with a man, Athena,' he tells me, looking into my eyes. In this dim light in this canopied bed, his eyes are diabolical black pupils with the loveliest rings of purple-blue that recall dusk on a clear night. 'This is what it means to give yourself to a man in every way, and I will be the first, and likely the last, man to watch you give every morsel of your flesh over to this pleasure. You will experience the miracle of heaven on earth, and I will be your only witness.'

He begins to move in great, greedy shunts. Every time he drags himself out of me, I want to die, and every time he pushes deep, so deep, inside me, that silent screaming inside me begins anew. With my leg over his shoulder, his body is rubbing at that same place that his mouth teased so mercilessly, and with every rub, the heat grows more insistent.

I do not think I can overpower it.

I do not think I can survive it.

'That's it,' he croons, his mouth so close to mine, his breath hot on my face. It's only when he says this that I understand how my sounds have turned from kitten-like mewls to full cries, and I am powerless to stop them. Trapped like this beneath him, impaled by his very body, they are the only outlet I have for this strange, animalistic need building inside me.

'You can't fight this,' he grits out, and I understand that he is a mind reader, too. 'You can't outrun it. Surrender to it. Give it to me. It's mine, do you understand? Every single piece of you is mine tonight, so *give it to me.*'

His thrusts grow more frenzied, and that friction of my flesh against his body grows more frenzied, too, and his own moans grow deeper, more pained. He grips my thigh to anchor me as he drives and drives and drives, and the strange, molten heat inside me builds so impossibly that it feels as though a cannon will explode inside my body.

All I can think is *this* and *him* and *yes* and *more*. This is a terrifying alchemy, my body its vessel.

The cannon is released. I am a ball of iron and metal, soaring through the air into realms so distant I could not have imagined them. My entire body is a furnace, wholly alight, its heat source this lord and the mystical acts he can perform with his body.

It seems my flames ignite his, because he goes rigid and curses before thrusting into me, over and over, with cries that would terrify me if I did not understand that they come from the same place as my cries.

He was correct.

I could not outrun it.

In surrendering everything to him, I set myself free to soar.

CHAPTER 35

Gabe

'Permission to break character.'

I mumble the words against her breast, and she giggles, her hand running up and down my bicep. 'Hi.'

'Hi.' I pull my face away enough to look at her. 'You okay?'

'Define *okay*. Am I now considering running away with you to some grubby D&D community where you can exercise your feudal rights over me on a daily basis? Absolutely.'

'Ah, the simple life. Having a toothsome wench like you to cook and clean for me. I dunno—could be a lot worse.'

She swats me on my bicep. 'I wouldn't call me toothsome if you value your testicular health.'

'So punchy after an orgasm.' I stroke the soft skin of her back. 'Might need to give you another one.'

'Do you want the virgin or the whore this time?' she asks. Her tone is jokey, but there's something else in her voice—something vulnerable—that gives me pause and has me choosing my words carefully.

'Deflowering the virgin was far too much fun... but now

I'd like to be with the strong, incredible woman who shows up at my place of work every day and owns every single ounce of her sexuality. Because *that's* the sexiest thing to me.'

She swallows, her enormous eyes drinking me in. 'So the whore, then.'

'Don't call yourself that. I just want you.' I pause to tuck a lock of silken hair behind her ear. 'The real you.'

We stare at each other for a moment, and it seems she's as transfixed by me as I am by her. Then she eases herself upright so she can straddle me. I'm hard for the third time—which I'm pretty fucking impressed by, though I can hardly take credit for my anatomical triumph.

It's all her.

It's difficult *not* to be hard around this woman.

She reaches across the bed for one of the anachronistic but definitely mandatory condoms and rips it open, and as she does, I admire the view of her body, arching and twisting, her breasts high and full and glorious, her skin so creamy it could make a man weep. It's the perfect foil for her russet tresses.

She really is a beauty for the ages.

None of that compares, though, to the sight of her taking me in her hand and proudly, unapologetically, lowering herself onto me. Watching my cock disappear inside her body will never, ever get old. *Feeling* it is even better. And when she begins to move, it's magic. I lie back on the pillows, delighting in the sight of her using my body, taking what she needs from it.

Athena. It's inconceivable that she could have any other name. She's a goddess: carnal and majestic and fierce, with a life force flowing through her veins that fills me with awe.

I push myself up to sitting, bracing on one hand so I can band the other around her.

That's better.

'Wrap your legs around my waist,' I tell her. She does, and I can't hold back my smile.

When we're in the office, she's on the clock.

This evening, we've been playing a game. A very immersive, sexy game, but a game nonetheless.

But in this moment, we are ourselves, and her beautiful breasts are smushed against my chest, and there's a softness, an honesty, in her eyes as I close my mouth over hers that makes my heart hurt. It strikes me that for a woman like Athena, who needs walls as strong as those of this thousand-year-old castle to withstand the physical vulnerabilities she endures on a daily basis, letting a man into her emotional headspace is the bravest of acts and the greatest of gifts.

I kiss her like this, letting my hand wander over her hair and skin as our lips slide and our tongues dance and our hearts beat against each other's chests. For her part, she cradles my face in her hands as she kisses me, her fingertips caressing my jaw, my beard, my hair.

With her hands occupied and her legs wrapped around me, she's fully impaled on my dick, her entire body weight pressing down so hard that it feels as though I'm touching her womb. I'm throbbing, but I'm patient. My dick is itching to move, to rut, and yet my soul is at peace, far more focused on the sounds of our lips and the warmth of her breath and the impossible softness of her skin under my fingertips.

She shudders into my mouth. *'God.'*

'What is it, hmm?'

'I was just thinking I could come like this, just barely moving. It's ridiculous. But I'm so full of you, and the pressure is... mmm, it's amazing. And the way you're kissing me— I feel completely surrounded by you.'

That it's not just me is indescribable. This feeling is the very opposite of loneliness. It's beautiful, human connection, not just of our bodies, but of our souls.

'See if you can come this way,' I murmur. 'I bet you can.'

She rolls her hips around me, and it's music. It's a fucking *hymn*. 'Fuck, Gabe.'

'I know, sweetheart. I feel it too. Just take your time. Feel your way to it.'

Her hands move on me, sliding through my hair, down my back, as she continues to rock, to roll her hips in the most seductive way. I'm so deep inside her, and with the absence of those desperate, animalistic thrusts from the last round I can observe and enjoy and really *feel* every tiny spark of magic that ignites when she moves her flesh against mine.

Everything is dialled back and amplified all at once. My two previous orgasms have stripped me of that blind hunger, allowing me the willpower to revel in every second of this build. Our hymn has begun quietly, softly, but I have no doubt it will be the most magnificent *Gloria* when we finally explode.

I continue to focus on this woman in my arms, on the way her body fits around mine, on the tiny, wonderful aftershocks that cascade through my nervous system with every cant of her hips. Her sighs become throaty little moans offered up like prayers into my mouth, her rocks grow more desperate, and the heat at the base of my spine swells.

I love the intimacy of this, the quietness, everything stripped away except for us, our naked, entwined bodies the cradles for this communion of our souls. If fucking Athena in full role play mode was Easter Sunday Mass, filled with pomp and splendour, a golden, jubilant celebration, then this intimate coupling has me back at that bare Good Friday altar, where the absence of noise creates space for all that is pure and true.

It creates space for faith. For trust. For the belief in something bigger than ourselves.

Athena falls apart around me, pouring her quiet sobs into

my mouth, the fluttering of her inner walls so softly intoxicating that I'm powerless to do anything but follow her over the edge. I brace myself as hard as I can on my hand and shunt up into her as her flesh engulfs me and my mind goes blessedly, euphorically blank of anything but sheer sensation.

It's funny how the quietest moments can clear the decks, making space for new beginnings.

Athena

From the unwieldiest, most haphazard beginnings, Gabe and I begin to build this idea of an actual, formal foundation. It takes shape slowly but steadily, emerging from the cauldron of the Sullivans' well-meaning charitable efforts in a form that's commercial and inspiring and sustainable... and, dare I say it, viable?

I haven't had this much fun since I had to build a "lean startup" as part of our MBA course. A group of us mocked up a fintech platform that connected female entrepreneurs with female angel investors. I got so intellectually invested that I almost wished I'd had the chance to build it out. It wasn't the altruism that hooked me—unless I'm giving head, I don't have an altruistic bone in my body—but the untapped market potential. So many brilliant female entrepreneurs get overlooked by traditional funding models.

It was simply good business sense.

Anyway, this foundation reminds me of that. I've been obsessively focused on the access, the exposure, this career can offer since I took Camille's bait that evening at the Musée Rodin. That can mean learning directly from men and women at the highest levels of management, but what I'm starting to understand is that it can also mean grass-roots experiences. The opportunity to make suggestions that will be heard and considered and even actioned. The chance to be a player in the game.

I've always said I want to *do*, not to advise. I want to be instrumental in shaping a company's fortunes, in forging its DNA. And this audacious plan to take a blank sheet of paper and put hundreds of millions of pounds to work in changing lives on the ground, *in a real, tangible way,* has given me the biggest commercial boner of my life.

I feel as though I'm thrumming. I'm in a constant state of inspiration. The more engrossed I get in assisting Gabe in thrashing the shape of this thing out, the more the neurons fire in my brain. And the more they fire, the more my entire body acts as a conduit. It's like he could plug me into the mains and make this entire dream a reality by virtue of this insane electrical charge I'm transmitting.

He teases me about it—mercilessly, in fact—but he's fired up, too, to an extent he claims not to have experienced since he walked away from his vocation. He's essentially cut Eleanor and Torty out of the project, telling them with his signature blend of charm and sincerity that we're still very much at the brainstorming stage. While I have no qualms about demanding facts and figures from them when we need them, he and I have found that keeping the circle small allows us to foster that element of playfulness, of free-thinking, that's so crucial at this stage. We're a tiny and highly excitable incubator, basically.

In the weeks following that initial meeting with Gabe's family, he and I have made it our mission to get out and about as much as possible, walking the streets in the areas where his family's land is situated. It's not continuous but instead is focused on huge lots where his grandfather's construction business built enormous complexes and negotiated land as part-payment in a way that then was risky and now seems incredibly prescient.

The River Thames meanders into London from its eponymous estuary in the east. It flows past Essex on its northern banks and Kent to the south. As it does, it forms a curious U-shape in which lies Canary Wharf, the weird and soulless extension of the City's financial district. While Gabe's grandfather wasn't involved in the development of Canary Wharf in the Nineties, he already owned a lot of the land around it, on the north side of the Thames.

And while a good proportion of the Docklands area has been gentrified, behemoths of the Industrial Revolution such as warehouses and factories converted into aspirational apartment blocks, far too much of it is still underinvested and desperately poor.

Gabe's security detail takes us to these areas by car, but he insists that nothing engenders understanding like walking the streets. It's the same reason, he claims, that our police force patrols communities on foot and priests and nuns must be present in the same communities. You can have MBAs coming out of your ears—I think that was a dig at me—but if you don't take the time to observe first-hand, to talk to the people who have built their lives here, you'll never have an edge.

And you'll never understand what is needed.

My (private) response to that is that this former priest is happy as a pig in shit on these missions of ours. We turn up at senior centres and he does the rounds, smiling and shaking hands and actually, truly *listening*. I swear, presidential candidates would kill for this man's devastating brand of ego-free charm. We visit state-funded nurseries and crèches, and he wants to play with every child.

Those visits elicit a strange cramping in my general ovarian area which I try not to examine too closely. Any female observer would have the same reaction.

His sister Mairead accompanies us on a couple of these trips, her focus squarely on green space and sports. I find I like her a lot. She's refreshingly direct—a quality I rate highly—and clearly cares a lot about getting more kids outdoors, but her arguments always sit squarely in the practical realm. Never do I have to reel her back in from some outlandish or unfeasible suggestion.

Brendan joins us on other outings. Of course, Sullivan Construction has built most of the buildings we visit. I find I prefer him in work mode. He's still a super-confident guy, comfortable taking up space in a way I don't believe Gabe is, but here his confidence comes from vast experience and what I'd deem street-smarts. He's savvy, with great judgment, and it seems to stem mainly from sound instincts.

As we carry out these field trips, our mission grows clearer, like a photograph emerging from a bed of chemicals in a dark room. Gabe's an old-school pen and paper guy—he claims it helps him think more clearly—so we devote a wall in his office to an over-engineered montage of photos and maps and sketches and inspirations and faces and one-word prompts and question marks that could be straight out of a TV police procedural.

A business within a business. A non-profit that asks the right questions and thinks smart and stays nimble and helps to fund itself and changes thousands and thousands of lives, transforming education and community and career prospects.

It's business school crack, that's what it is.

Between the field trips, and the endless hours speculating and imagining with Gabe, and the even more endless hours of admin and research that precede and follow every one of our sessions, and the rest of the day job that I still need to keep a firm handle on—oh, and all the epic, epic fucking—it's a lot. This evening, I've dragged myself to a power yoga class at the very swanky gym on Berkeley Square that I joined when I started at Rath Mor. I treat exercise as low-level maintenance. I need to look good and have stamina for this job, but beyond that I don't care for it much. I'll never be an exercise queen.

Yoga's the best of a bad lot, I suppose. At least I always step off the mat a marginally less aggressive version of the Athena who stepped onto it. Also, I get to work every large muscle group in my body at the same time as clearing my mind, which the efficiency-lover in me applauds.

It's around nine when I get back to the office. I had fully intended on leaving my laptop at work for, you know, basic mental health and boundary reasons. But I inevitably found myself mulling over some of the ideas we've been tossing around for reinventing community spaces, and I want to ponder them further in bed.

I'm surprised, when I round the corridor from reception, to see light from Gabe's office flooding through the door-frame. The man himself is in situ, speaking to an older woman who's sitting across from him on the same sofa he likes to fuck me on, her back to me. Even so, I can see—and hear—that she's weeping copiously.

It's Mary, a sweet Irish woman who I've met a couple of times when I've stayed late. She does the evening cleaning shift with a handful of others, from what I understand.

I catch Gabe's eyes and make an alarmed grimace. He presses his lips together and gives me a little nod that says *hi there* and *I've got this.* I return it and turn away from them, sliding behind my desk. If Gabe's been working late, then I want to check my emails on my laptop before I head home so I can ensure he doesn't require anything from me.

When he speaks, his voice is a low, reassuring murmur. It's definitely his priestly voice, and I'm sure it's soothed and healed countless parishioners over the years. 'This is not something for you to grieve, Mary. I know it must have come as a shock, but—'

'But the *shame* of it!' Her cry is explosive, her accent thickly West of Ireland. 'The *shame*, Father!'

That almost makes me snort. Dear Lord. Gabe can walk away from the priesthood, but clearly the poor man will never be able to truly walk away from the confessional. By virtue of his past experience and sweet nature, he's eternally doomed to be a kindly ear for anyone looking to unload. And in this moment, he's not a billionaire whose cleaner has cornered him but a man of God holding space for someone in spiritual need.

He clears his throat but doesn't correct her, which is kind of him. I log in to my laptop while blatantly straining my ears, because this sounds juicy.

Shame?

I'm a whore.

I know all about the dangers of taking on other people's shame.

'Mary. If I may say so, this isn't a matter of shame but a matter of love. Please, I beg you, don't jeopardise the wonderful gift of love that you and your son share because you feel judged by other people. Because I promise you, God will not judge you for this.'

'But the Bible says homosexuality is a sin!' she protests, her voice shrill.

Ahh. So that's it. Her son has come out, and his Catholic mother has hit the roof.

'Well, the Bible says a lot of things about homosexuality,

the vast majority of which we disregard these days.' Gabe's tone is patient, but I can detect the wry undertone.

'So it's not a sin? Peter isn't a sinner?'

Jesus Christ. No wonder he walked if this is the kind of conversation he had to have over and over, every single day.

Gabe forges gamely on. 'You see, sometimes we have to take a step back from dogma that has been dictated to us from a very different place and time, and we have to look inside our own hearts. Because I believe, even as a man who committed the terrible sin of leaving the priesthood, that when we truly look inside our own hearts, we know.

'And that knowing is very important and very powerful. We know what love looks like, and we know what's right and wrong. And I don't for the slightest second think that loving the people your heart tells you to love can be anything but beautifully, perfectly right and also profoundly spiritual.'

My fingers are poised over my keyboard, but I've given up all pretence of doing anything but listening. In fact, I bow my head as Gabe's beautiful words pour over me.

I've fucked some of the most powerful, dynamic, eligible men in this city.

I am carnal and materialistic and relentless.

And the one man who touches my carefully, consciously, comprehensively boundaried heart is *this* man.

I'm basically falling for Jesus.

Fuuuuuck.

Mary is still crying. I don't know where Gabe gets his patience from, I really don't. I'd be tempted to slap some sense into her and tell her to go home and give poor Peter a hug.

The man is a saint.

'Tell me about Peter,' he says conversationally. 'Tell me about what he was like as a little boy. What was he into?'

His chair creaks, and I imagine he's sitting back, stretching out those long legs and interlacing his fingers over that flat stomach of his like he has all the time in the world for her. Like he's not overworked and exhausted.

'Oh my God, it was all about trucks and cars for him. Vans. Lorries. Toy ones and real ones and storybooks about them. Anything with wheels. He'd play for hours and hours, God bless him.'

'I was exactly the same. It's lovely, isn't it, to see little children at play? Such innocence. Such *focus*. It's awe-inspiring, really, to see how transporting these passions can be. And tell me, Mary, did you ever try to get him to lay off the cars and focus on something else? Did you ever say, *no, Peter, cars aren't for you. Why don't you spend more time on football? I'm sure you'll like it better when you give it a chance.*'

She gives a huge sniff. 'God, no. He was useless at football, God bless him! He couldn't kick a ball to save his life. It was cars and trucks all the way until he discovered computer games.'

I brace for Gabe to deliver his spiritual sucker punch. I can see where this is going, even if Mary hasn't cottoned on yet.

'Of course it was. Because he loved them. He was acting with his heart and soul when he played with trucks. *He was listening to his own truth and acting on it.*' He lowers his voice, and I have to strain to hear. 'And that is precisely what he's doing now. I'm not a parent, but from where I'm sitting, your *only* job is to embrace your children's ability to feel and act and speak from a place of truth and to *love* that true essence of them. That's it.'

When Mary has taken her leave with a watery smile at me, I push my chair back and sprint into Gabe's office. He's sitting in the chair, watching me, his face pale and drawn.

I waste no time. This man gives everything to others, he bleeds himself dry for them, and I will bleed myself dry for him. I climb onto the chair and straddle him, cradling his head in my hands so I can kiss him with every ounce of the emotion I'm currently feeling.

He makes a pleased, surprised sound in his throat as my mouth finds his and wraps his arms around me.

'You're such a good man,' I whisper against his lips. 'You're *such* a good man.'

With his fingertips, he traces the bumps of my spine through my dress, one by one.

He calls them his rosary beads.

He calls *me* his rosary.

Says I was sent to him as a channel for his prayers.

His voice is soft when he speaks.

'If you knew what I had planned for your birthday, you wouldn't say that.'

CHAPTER 37

Athena

On your birthday, you dress up.

That's my rule, anyhow.

You dress up particularly carefully if your gorgeous boss has been dropping intriguing hints that he has something special planned for you. I know he plans to take me out for dinner this evening—he's already asked my permission—but I suspect he has something else up that Italian wool sleeve of his.

Today, therefore, I'm in a frothy silk Gucci dress whose powder blue georgette complements the dusky tones of my hydrangeas perfectly. Gabe may have instructed George to change my desk's floral arrangements weekly, an indulgence that pleases George and yields me no end of pleasure, but he's pushed the boat out for my birthday, with masses of blue and white hydrangeas, white snowberries, and green-grey eucalyptus.

Regular check-ins from Gabe and a thoughtful gift from George aside—a gorgeous coffee table book devoted to the Birkin which will go perfectly in my flat—my day has proceeded much as usual. I sit in my finery and work away on the foundation, eager for the hours to tick by and my surprise to unfold.

Christopher Marlowe's famous *Doctor Faustus* quote, lifted from Ovid, goes thus: *lente, lente, currite noctis equi*— slowly, slowly, run, horses of the night. I feel the opposite. Quickly, quickly, run, horses of the day, and pull the hand of time around that clock face, for God's sake. Gabe hasn't even touched me today, despite telling me how exquisite I look.

Mid-afternoon ticks by, then late afternoon. I've tried asking George if he knows what my surprise is. The upshot is that he does, but that he has no intention whatsoever of telling me. Smug, discreet bastard.

It's late afternoon, and all that stands between me and sinful freedom with Gabe is a meeting he's put in the diary with some individuals he's hoping to sound out about the foundation. Apparently, they're all business leaders who may sign up to collaborate with us on various social and environmental initiatives. I asked him if he wanted me to put together any briefing notes for the meeting, but he said he had it all in hand.

At just before five o'clock, he swings past my desk, tugging on his suit jacket. 'I'm going to go greet our visitors. Follow me up in ten minutes, why don't you?'

I do as he says, checking over his inbox one more time before I leave my desk. With any luck, we can both head out right after we've wrapped this meeting up.

One floor up from Gabe's office is the hospitality suite, where a variety of meeting rooms of various sizes are situated. It's decorated just as beautifully as our floor, with plush cream carpets and perfectly lit oil paintings. When I enter the appointed meeting room, I count Gabe plus four other guys, all in suits, standing around and making small talk. The large projector screen is on, showing the generic Rath Mor screensaver, and the blinds have been shut, giving it an intimate atmosphere on this bright spring evening.

'Ah,' he says as I shut the door behind me, 'everyone's here. Good.' He walks over to me and puts a hand on the small of my back, which is more familiar than he'd usually allow himself to be in front of strangers, but I like it. 'Gentlemen, this is my wonderful executive assistant, Athena.'

They stop talking and come forward to shake my hand one by one. As they do, I can't help but notice they're all indecently hot. If I'd known all philanthropists were this attractive, I might have exercised my charitable muscles a long time ago. I note their names. James. Seb. Benedict. Gus.

So far, so aristocratic.

'Let's get started, shall we?' Gabe asks, gesturing to the boardroom table. I could swear I catch a hint of nerves in his voice, which is odd.

We all take our seats except Gabe. He leans forward and hits a button on the desktop monitor. A new slide flashes onto the huge screen—a name and an image.

The name? *PROJECT MINERVA.*

The image is undoubtedly the goddess Minerva, or Athena, recognisable from the armour, shield and spear with which she's usually portrayed.

I frown in confusion.

Gabe walks around to where I'm sitting and lays his hands on my shoulders, his fingers massaging them through the silk. 'These gentlemen aren't here to discuss the foundation, you see, sweetheart. They're here to help you celebrate your birthday.'

The effect on my autonomic nervous system is instantaneous. My body stiffens and my heartbeat ratchets up and my palms go clammy. Suddenly the air feels charged in a way it didn't a moment ago, and I know beyond a shadow of a doubt that when he mentioned his plans for my birthday last week in his office, *this* is what he meant.

Quite what he has in store for me, I haven't yet worked out. As my body reels in the most intoxicating way, my usually agile brain is scrambling to catch up.

'*What?*' I whisper, trying to make sense of it all.

'I didn't know what to get you, you see. I thought, *what do you get a beautiful, successful woman who can buy herself whatever she needs? What does she adore more than anything else in the world?*'

I can see the answer imprinted in my mind's eye before he even says it. It's as clear to me as the knowing smiles of the guys around the table as they watch me react to this bombshell.

'I know you love dick.' The word gets caught in his throat, like he's had to force himself to say it. 'You've told me. Your previous employers have told me. And I've proceeded to ignore those signs, until now, because I just couldn't bring myself to— anyway, I brainstormed with the team at Alchemy and we came up with a very special workplace scene to celebrate *you,* and your birthday, and your needs, and your incredible, incredible body.'

'Oh my *God*,' I whisper.

It's all falling into place. I remember how much I harped on about it during that audition dinner. He's asked me outright before if I enjoy being gang-banged, and I've given him a pretty resounding *yes.* He's read the reviews from my previous employers, too. He's under no illusions as to the extent of my appetites.

But here's the thing. I know Gabe would never in a million years pander to them in a real-life work setting. No matter how confident he was of my position, he would see it as utterly disrespectful to me and to any other parties. He's not like some of the guys I've worked for. He'd never use me as a trophy, never put me in the centre of some power-play or manipulation and bid me be his puppet.

I know all that, and I'm fine with it, because what Gabe and I have is frankly extraordinary. You can work for a guy like Anton or my first boss, Thierry, who know all the tricks and aren't afraid to push the envelope, or you can work for a guy like Gabe, who takes confessions in his office and for whom every fuck is an opportunity to worship me. I've made my peace with that, and the sex is out of this world, every time.

So to know that he's been thinking about this, that he's been mindful of my fantasies all this time and has willingly stepped so far out of his own comfort zone to serve them up to me with a big birthday bow, in the safest and most tightly orchestrated manner he can conceive of while staying true to my fuck-the-assistant fantasy, is blowing my mind.

It is blowing. My. Mind.

He's even branded the entire event around my safeword.

Minerva.

I still haven't said anything else. I'm too shocked. Gabe takes advantage of my relative and uncharacteristic silence to slide his hands down the front of my Gucci until he's palming my breasts from above, and my nipples react instantly, tightening into needy little buds as much at his overt display of sexual proprietorship as at his touch itself. My mild-mannered, deeply spiritual boss has orchestrated a birthday gang bang for me, and he's feeling me up in front of said "gang" to show them who I really belong to.

Every male pair of eyes at the table is staring at his hands on my tits right now, and fuck, it's like a shot of heroin. Gabe's doing my favourite thing—wheeling me out like a dazzling trophy, the ultimate fucktoy—and it makes me realise how much I missed this, how addicted I am to this feeling. If I give him the nod, in a few minutes I'll be theirs to do as they like with, but really, the power is all mine.

I let my head fall back against his stomach, gazing up at him through my eyelashes. 'More,' I whisper, and he obliges. I'm in no hurry for things to escalate. Let me sit here for a moment with one man's hands on me and every other man watching as avidly as Greek and Roman nobles watched lions and bears and slaves tear each other apart.

He stares down at me, and even upside down I can read his face. It's astonishment, and respect, and desire. He knew all this about me, but he can't quite believe it's happening, can't quite believe I'm sitting here in a three-thousand-pound dress, arching my back and letting him toy with me in front of this rapt audience.

'What do you think?' he asks me gruffly.

I straighten my head up. 'Yes. To all of it.' I meet the eyes of the guys around the table one by one. In a few minutes, they'll have their fingers and tongues and dicks inside me, and it's so perfect I can barely stand it. One of them—James—has his elbows on the table and is leaning forward, his eyes fixed on my tits. He's practically drooling.

Behind me, Gabe releases my breasts and returns his hands to my shoulders. 'You don't even know what the plan is yet,' he says, sounding amused.

'I don't care. I'll say yes. But tell me.'

'Well, Benedict here is going to MC. He'll be calling the shots. He's way better at this stuff than me. Benedict? You want to fill her in?'

CHAPTER 38

Athena

Benedict gets elegantly to his feet and puts his hands in the pockets of his suit trousers, clinking his keys as if he's about to deliver a best man's speech at some society wedding. He's tall and broad-shouldered with dark blond hair and an easy air of entitlement that does it for me every time.

If Gabe found these men through Alchemy, they're guaranteed to be filthy bastards, the lot of them.

Gabe withdraws his hands and turns away from me. I hear the soft click of him locking the door and, a moment later, the door of the little drinks fridge beneath the sideboard being opened.

Meanwhile, Benedict runs his tongue along his bottom lip before he speaks, considering me with narrowed eyes. 'No nice birthday party is complete without champagne, is it? Or some good old British party games, for that matter.' He begins to pace. One of the other guys, James, leans back and crosses his arms, smirking.

I'm the only person in this room still ignorant of what

exactly *party games* entails. But I suspect I'm about to be enlightened.

'Let me see,' he continues. 'Blind Man's Buff, which for today's purposes we should probably rebrand as the somewhat less pithy but categorically sexier Blindfolded Woman in the Buff. Always a classic. And of course, Pass the Parcel and Musical Chairs—we have a rather clever way of combining those two, actually. And guess who the parcel will be? Why you, my dear.'

He winks at me, and I watch him, transfixed, as Gabe deftly uncorks a bottle of champagne and sets about filling the half dozen flutes he's brought over. It occurs to me that he's glad of having something to do while Benedict sets this filthy scene with such aplomb. Beyond Gabe's obvious nerves just now, I have no way of knowing what his attitude is to any of this. None at all.

I raise my eyebrows at Benedict's declaration that I will be some kinky little parcel, and he smirks.

'All clear so far? Excellent. So what I'd propose, after we've toasted your good health, is that we get you blindfolded, strip you naked, tie you up like any self-respecting parcel... and have at you.'

His depraved words have my blood heating and my pussy throbbing.

'Have at me, how?' I ask him. I'm proud of how clear my voice sounds. How assured. I want these men to know I'm no pushover, to know that when I submit it's because *I want this* so very, very badly.

'Well, we'd like to get to know you first. Have a little play. See how beautifully we can make you come. And then we'll arrange all these lovely chairs here in a circle over there and take a seat and get our cocks out, basically. We'll put on some nice tunes, and we'll pass our delectable little parcel around so we can all have a turn. Every time the music stops, you move onto the next cock. And so on and so forth until everyone's had a prize.' He leans forward conspiratorially. 'That's an orgasm, to you and me.'

'Yes, I got that, thank you,' I say, an icy attempt at concealing the searing heat coursing through my body. I'm in danger of sweating through this dress. The guys around the table are smiling at me, my co-conspirators in a filthy game while my boss's hundreds of employees work away below, utterly oblivious. I have the sudden, semi-hysterical thought that if Torty Spencer-Wells walked in on this little birthday orgy, she'd probably clutch her pearls so tightly she'd garrotte herself.

'What do you think, sweetheart?' another of the guys asks me.

I glance up at Gabe as he slides a champagne flute over to me. He's glowering at him, his jaw locked. 'Her *name* is Athena,' he reminds them. 'And her safeword is Minerva. And let me remind you, every second of this is for her. She comes first, figuratively and literally. Got it?'

He looks down at me, and I see a world of emotion in his eyes as he raises his flute. 'To Athena.'

'And to all who sail in her,' one wise-arse bats back cheerfully. The air of tense solemnity in the room shatters instantly. Gabe snorts despite himself, and I giggle as the other men guffaw. I mean, the guy's not wrong.

Especially not this evening.

Gabe is the one to blindfold me. He kisses me gently on the lips before moving behind me and securing the ends of the blindfold above the base of my ponytail. I wore my hair up this morning, slicked back into a ponytail and then curled in large, sleek waves. It's now looking like that was quite a practical move.

I love on so many levels that I'll be blindfolded for this scene. It will add to the power imbalance, making me feel more helpless, and to the suspense. It will free up my other senses to take over, to feel everything even more keenly. And it will certainly allow any lingering inhibitions I have to fly right out the window.

'You say the safeword and everything stops.' He kisses my neck before lowering the zipper at the back of my dress.

With my world now one of darkness, the sensation of my skin being bared is heightened. Gabe gently undoes the little buttons at my cuffs, and then he's sliding the dress off my shoulders so it sinks to the floor in a frothy pile of silk. There's the distinct clink of champagne flutes being deposited on the table. I can feel the other men in the room drawing near, predators approaching at the first signal that their prey is exposed. I hope they're enjoying the sight of me, blindfolded and in pale blue La Perla underwear, still in my sheer stockings and heels.

If they do, it's not for long. Gabe unhooks my bra, but someone else in front of me slides it off my arms, and then my thong is hooked at the sides and pushed down, my suspender belt unfastened, stockings rolled down. I'm bidden to step out of my heels, and my wrists are bound behind my back with a length of fabric, forcing my shoulders back and my breasts forward.

A voice rings out behind me, authoritative and clear, generations of aristocratic entitlement bred into it. With my sight removed, I could well be a nineteenth-century courtesan, fair game for some noblemen at Whites or Boodles or another of those exclusive clubs where the only women allowed were the ones paid for their services.

'The lady has been disrobed, gentlemen. Let the games begin. Get her up on the table.'

The lacquered wood of the conference table is cold and smooth against my bottom. They set me right on the edge, so I'm less sitting than perching, my legs spread and feet planted on the ground, my knuckles grazing the surface of the table.

I wonder if this pose will remind Gabe of my audition, or whether he's too busy battling a whole maelstrom of emotions to make the connection.

There's a pause, during which I hear only our breathing and the pulse of the music someone's turned on—an aria over a sensual beat. I'm suspended between apprehension and anticipation. Then, presumably, a silent signal, for they begin to touch me.

Hands everywhere.

Cuffing my ankles.

Sliding up my calves.

Grazing my inner thighs.

Caressing my forearms.

My biceps.

Brushing over my stomach.

Then one of them takes my jaw between his thumb and forefinger and tilts my head.

Someone licks down my neck.

Palms are pressed to my breasts, ghosting over my nipples before pinching them. It feels so, so good that I arch my body, sliding my hands backwards on the table for purchase and letting my head hang back.

Three fingers are pushed imperiously into my mouth, and I suck obligingly.

'That's a good girl,' someone mutters, and then the same fingers pull out and find my entrance, driving in hard. I whimper at the welcome invasion, revelling in the stretch as well as in the knowledge that I have no clue which of them has his body parts inside me. I can sense them closing in, all of them, the scents of cologne and body heat and champagne crowding me.

I spread my legs wider to take the finger-fucking this guy is giving me. Someone kneads one breast, plucking at the nipple, as someone else bends and sucks hard on my other breast.

My tits are being worked by two different men, my pussy by a third, and it's glorious. It's just *glorious*. I moan softly to show quite how well their efforts are landing.

'Look at her take those fingers,' Benedict drawls. 'I think that's earned her some clit action, don't you? And some arse action.'

'Hang on,' someone says, muffled, and there's movement around me. I sense that one of them has got to his knees. Judging from the way the fingers inside me flex, it's the same guy. Next thing I know, his tongue is on my clit, rough and hungry, and I full-on cry out as I abandon myself to this sensory overwhelm.

Someone clambers onto the table behind me, holding my ponytail aside so he can kiss my neck and massage my shoulders. It's Gabe! I recognise the imprint of his mouth and beard on my skin. I hum in delight.

'You're doing so well,' he croons in my ear. 'So fucking well.' He tugs my jaw away from whoever was holding it and comes in for a hungry kiss, fucking me slowly and deeply with his tongue. I give him my best moan, right into his mouth. His view over my shoulder must be pretty full on right now as he watches his mates go to town on me.

I am lapping this shit up. Full body massages need a new name, because *this* is what I call a full body massage: men crawling all over me, kissing my skin and laving at my clit and fucking me with their fingers. Their bodies may have formed a shield around me, but the predators are within.

'Budge,' Benedict says. 'I'm taking her arse.'

My legs are stretched wider, one knee pulled up, and I brace myself harder on my bound hands. There's some jostling for position, then comes a spitting sound, and a finger is probing me back there. Fuck—it's been a while. I've had a lot of anal in the past, but not for some time, and Steve and Gabe haven't even gone there with their fingers.

Benedict's finger is thick and lubed up with saliva, but it's a tight fit, and the filthiness of being worked in all three holes at once while my clit and nipples are tended to in sync is the best, most incredible, most full-wattage onslaught I've had in a long, long time.

'Fuck me, you're tight, you filthy girl,' he drawls.

I'm so glad I'm blindfolded, because it's affording me the necessary clarity to focus on the sensations that are building at alarming speed inside my body.

The dirty thrust of Gabe's tongue in my mouth.

The insistent pumps of those three fingers in my pussy and that one up my arse.

The blessed friction of the tongue on my needy, needy clit.

The fine handiwork that's going on on my nipples, which are being sucked and pulled and pinched.

And that's before I even consider the rest of it—the strokes and kisses on my limbs; the heat of having five guys crowded around me; their mutters of appreciation and approval and disbelief; the sultry beat of the music and, over it, a female vocal that now sounds less operatic and more orgasmic.

I'm in a sensory paradise, and it's so *much*, and I never want it to stop. I sit there, my legs spread as wide as I can get them as these guys pet me and touch me in the most sickeningly arousing ways.

But it has to stop, because this level of stimulation is so rare and so beautiful, its flame so impossibly bright, that it must ignite in glory before flickering out.

I know it must, but in this moment it's blinding, and I'm gunpowder facing a lit match. My cries grow so loud that Gabe's mouth is unable to swallow them up, the men's words of encouragement and exhortation grow gruffer, filthier in my ears, and I give myself over to this chemical reaction that can only end in utter combustion.

As my breathing grows more frantic and my body begins to shake, Gabe releases my mouth. 'She's coming,' he tells them, and I swear they ramp up their ministrations on every erogenous zone in my body.

I erupt in an orgasm of cataclysmic proportions, shattering so brightly that my *petite mort* really does feel like dying, like having one's soul catapulted straight into the stratosphere.

My coming down is assisted with strokes and praise. I am beautiful; I am incredible; I am a filthy whore; Gabe is a lucky bastard.

'Jesus fucking Christ,' Benedict says, withdrawing his finger from the most forbidden nook in my body. 'I assume you're as wet as we are hard. Objective achieved. Move the chairs, quick guys.'

'She's fucking soaking,' one guy says next to my pussy—James, I think? He, too, pulls his fingers out of me, and I feel instantly bereft. Whenever I have a clitoral orgasm, I always need to be filled up pretty much immediately.

Luckily for me, there are four hard dicks ready to do just that. Five, if Benedict gets involved.

'Right, gentlemen. Chairs. Condoms. You know the drill. Quick.'

As the others step away from me, Gabe holds me from behind, wrapping his arms around me. His knees are either side of my bottom, anchoring me.

'You okay? That was fucking incredible.'

'I'm great.' I sound like I've run a marathon. In front of us, chairs are being moved and zips and condom packets alike ripped. I imagine our guests sitting in a circle, fully clothed, dicks hard and out, waiting for *me*. I feel like the greediest birthday girl who's ever lived, and I fucking love it.

He kisses me on the cheek before releasing me.

'Fucking hell,' he groans, and I smile to myself. I assume he's getting an eyeful of his dick-tastic meeting room. 'It's like being back at school.'

I wonder if they got up to this shit at the seminary, too... although they were probably pretty short of women there.

'Right,' comes Benedict's voice from right in front of me. 'It's time for our little mashup of Pass the Parcel and Musical Chairs. You ready, princess?'

CHAPTER 40

Athena

Gabe leads me to what I assume is the centre of the room and then abandons me with a kiss.

'Blindfolded woman in the buff,' Benedict murmurs from behind me, taking my shoulders. 'God, I love it when the reinvention is better than the original.' He spins me gently before walking me forward for a few steps. 'Music.'

Instantly, the orgasm vocals stop and the distinctive beat of Billie Eilish's *Bad Guy* comes on. I smile, because this song absolutely nails both the kinds of men I like and the kind of woman I am.

It would definitely make Gabe's mama sad if she knew the kind of woman her son was fucking.

In any case, the beat gets right under my skin as I stand here naked and unseeing in front of this circle of gorgeous, aroused men. I'm about to be used, passed around them like the most mesmerising prize, but if they don't understand that every single part of this scene is for *me* then the joke's on them.

I land in front of one guy, my hands feeling for his shoulders, my thighs brushing his knees. He's removed his jacket, and his shoulders are broad under the lustrous cotton of his shirt.

'He fucks you until the music stops,' Benedict tells me over the music, and with that the guy grabs me with two hands on my waist, pulling me towards him. I go, widening my stance so I can straddle him, looping my arms around his neck for balance and dipping my head to his neck as he swipes the tip of his latex-clad dick through my wetness. He's a big guy. Gus, maybe? I don't know, and I don't care, because the not knowing whose dick I'm allowing inside my body is the hottest part of this.

That, and the certitude that Gabe and the others are watching right now, dicks out and ready, waiting for their turn with me.

He still has one hand on my waist, his fingers digging in hard, guiding me downwards. I lower myself onto his thick cock, gasping at the instant, glorious fullness of it, at how dirty it feels to be impaling myself on this stranger for our mutual pleasure. How shameless.

'Fucking hell.' His voice is a grunt. 'Jesus *fuck*, you're sexy.'

Behind me, Benedict grabs my ponytail and twists it around his fist. 'Ride him.'

I do, focusing on nothing but the tension on my hair and the burn in my quads and the rough drag of this guy against my inner walls as I move. The friction is excellent, the feel of his powerful body thrusting up into me fantastic. I can definitely come like this. I just need—

The song cuts out abruptly, and Benedict tugs at my ponytail. 'Up.'

Fuck.

'You've got to be fucking *kidding* me,' my fuck buddy pants out as I ease off him.

The guy sitting next to him has me bend over the chair as

soon as a new song starts up so he can take me from behind while Benedict holds the chair steady to prevent us both from crashing forward. It feels so utterly filthy to be ploughed into like this, my hands white-knuckling the chair back and my tits bouncing freely as the others look on.

This guy may not have the girth of the last one, but he's fucking me like he's paid for the privilege and he's intent on getting every drop of value from this coupling. Or maybe he just wants to shoot his load before the music cuts out and avoid his friend's fate. Either way, his hard drives are hitting the spot, and I teeter on this knife-edge of arousal they've had me on until I'm shuddering and gasping and pleading with him, with whoever's controlling the music to just, please, let me have this.

They do, and the orgasm rips through me like a fire in an oxygen chamber, consuming everything in its path. I press my blindfolded forehead into my knuckles as I ride out the climax, the man behind me fucking me roughly through it until he goes impossibly taut before jerking his own orgasm into the condom. When he's done, he slides out of me, leaving me bent over and panting. I'm vaguely aware that his buddy who got short-changed before him is jacking himself off noisily next to us.

The song stops.

'Well, we all enjoyed that little spectacle,' Benedict tells me, sounding a little less in control as he helps me upright. 'How are you feeling? You want a break? A drink?'

I shake my head. 'No. I'm fine.' My second orgasm has me blanketed in an aura of calm and warmth and wellbeing. I have no intention of quitting now.

There's also no way I'm taking a break until I've found myself on Gabe's lap.

Guy Number Three turns me around so I'm facing outwards, my legs stretched open and my feet planted on the outside of his. He undoes my bindings so I can fit more tightly against him and rubs my wrists. When I sit on his cock, it burns my swollen flesh in the best way. He has me do the work of raising and lowering myself as he plays with my tits, plucking at my nipples as if he can make music from them.

Crisp cotton and hard muscle brush my back, his breath is hot on my neck, and the fabric of his open zip abrades my clit every time he bottoms out in me. God, this is good. This is really good. I love how he's holding me open for the rest of the room to enjoy, and the way he's working my tits is giving me so much extra stimulus.

I've always been greedy when it comes to sex, and my body is screaming *more, more, more.* It doesn't know when to stop.

It's incapable of walking away from something like this.

I hear a squirt of what sounds like lube, and then: 'Get me off,' Benedict orders, materialising somewhere in front of me again and taking my hand. He wraps it around his dick, which is huge and hard and bare and lubed-up, the heat pulsing off it.

Poor Benedict. Such a sexy, accomplished MC and so patient. He deserves to get off, too. I slide my index finger through the mess of precum and lube at the tip and then work his length with smooth, assured pumps, all the while maintaining my rhythm of bouncing on this other guy's cock. Benedict groans and slides two fingers inside my mouth. I suck hard, using my tongue as much as I can. I bet he wishes I was sucking his dick right now, but I can't bend that far in this position.

Instead, I focus my energy on making him feel good with my hands as I soak up the sensory assault on my nipples and my pussy. I have a sudden and unexpected flashback to that time in Anton's office, when he had me blindfolded while he watched the soon-to-be love of his life, Gen, get spit-roasted by his two mates.

Then, I was a bystander, a convenient prop on the

outskirts, there to suck him off because he couldn't have the woman he wanted. It was hot as fuck, don't get me wrong, but now I'm the main attraction, the principal plaything, being worked and fucked and filled up and fondled, and it's so perfect I might die. I'm not sure how much more stimulation my body can take, but my *mind* will never, ever tire of this dynamic.

Impossibly, the heat begins to build again, and I moan around Benedict's fingers, my tongue flexing against them.

'Fuck,' he groans. *'Fuck.'* He swells even further in my hand, and then he's covering my hand with his free one, aiming his dick slightly lower before letting rip. His cum hits me right between my tits in hot ropes, and Jesus *Christ,* the feeling of one guy shooting his load all over my skin as another guy ruts into me is everything. It's *everything.*

I move harder, ignoring the screams from my quads and hamstrings as I grind down on this faceless guy whose dick I'm using. I suck harder on Benedict's fingers. The guy fucking me uses my pearl necklace, smearing it across my tits, making my nipples slippery under his touch. Then he's abandoning them altogether so he can grip my waist hard and work me up and down, just the way he needs it.

'Don't come, Athena,' Benedict warns, pulling his fingers out of my mouth as the guy beneath me moves faster and faster, thrusting as though he'll die if he doesn't come right this second. 'If you start to come, I'll pull you off him. Understand?'

I nod, half hearing him, the friction in my core growing fiercer. I barely know which way is up or where I am. As soon as the man has finished shuddering into his condom and biting down on my shoulder so hard I almost come there and then, Benedict is barking at him to hold onto the condom and hauling me off. He takes something—the linen napkin from the wine bucket, maybe—and wipes my chest and stomach down as best he can. His movements feel pragmatic, but they're gentle, too.

'Right, gorgeous,' he says, holding me by the shoulders and turning me around. 'Last one. You're doing great—you're a fucking rockstar.'

It's Gabe. It has to be.

I feel for the last man of the evening, one hand going to his shoulder and the other to his jaw, and as soon as I feel his beard, I know. *It's him.* I straddle him, and he pulls me down with his hands on my hips so I'm balancing on his firm thighs, his sheathed dick trapped between us.

'It's you.' I whisper the words as I stroke his beard.

I can hear his smile. 'It's me, sweetheart.'

Then he's wrapping his arms around me, his fingers finding the rosary beads of my spine like they always do, and the only way I can describe it is as a revelation, a homecoming, the like of which I've never felt. There is nothing else for it but to kiss him, and I'm suddenly glad that none of the other guys have kissed me since he did on that table.

I may be half comatose from orgasms, but the feel of his beard under my fingers and of his lips against mine and of his captive dick twitching angrily against my lower stomach is so perfectly, utterly right, in a way that none of the other men were.

Fucking strangers may be hot, but coming home to a person whose entire body feels as though it was made for yours is prophetic. As our tongues dance, I raise myself up, reaching between us and fondling his sac before positioning him at my entrance so I can slide down. I can tell by the taut pressure of his balls and his insane hardness that he's close to blowing.

Of course he is.

My poor Gabe engineered this whole scene for *me*, the assistant he pays through the nose for the privilege of having my body on retainer for *his* pleasure, and he's had to sit here and watch as man after man gets all the fun.

This is the part where I make it up to him. This is when I show him how grateful and blown away I am.

We rock together, our lips fused. I like to think I have decent stamina, but my legs are tiring after their workout and my orgasms, and I think he can tell. Holding me around the waist, he shunts forward on his chair so he has more leverage. He slides both hands under my bottom to help me move on top of him, and I do.

I'm in a semi-dreamlike state as he fucks me, a little like how I was after our Prima Nocta role play, but I'm conscious that he's growing more agitated, more desperate for release. He thrusts up, and I employ every ounce of strength left to fire my leg muscles. It's not just an altruistic move on my part: that need is still there, deep inside me, and every time he bottoms out in me he hits my cervix and it rejoices in turn.

He releases my mouth. 'She's tired. Help me out, mate.'

Mate is Benedict, I assume, who takes a firm hold of my waist with two large hands and begins to move me up and down. Not only does his gallant assistance relieve my burning muscles, but the very experience of being manhandled in this way, of being bounced up and down on Gabe's dick as if I'm some kind of passive doll has arousal coursing through my body once more. It seems every single variant of this dynamic, in this room, turns me on.

I fasten my weary arms around his neck and hang the hell on as my body processes this deluge of pleasure, bracing myself for a third, cataclysmic orgasm. When it hits, it's with brute force, turning every limb to molasses and my brain to cotton wool. I'm vaguely aware of Gabe coming inside me with fevered thrusts and strangled words of praise, of Benedict stepping away, and of the tears that come suddenly, thickly, flowing from my eyes and seeping into the starched collar of the shirt against which I have my face pressed.

'Hey,' he croons, banding one arm tightly around me and stroking the crown of my head with the other. 'Hey. It's okay, sweetheart. I've got you. You did so unbelievably well. You blow me away.'

'She really did,' someone who's not Benedict says. 'You, Athena, are an incredible woman. And you're a lucky bastard, Sullivan.'

I don't want to acknowledge anyone else. I burrow my face more closely into the crook of Gabe's neck and wrap my arms around him, blocking out the rest of the room. I'm done here —these men blew my nervous system apart in the best possible way, and I'm so grateful, but I have nothing left to give any of them.

'Pass me my jacket, will you?' Gabe murmurs in a low voice. A moment later, one of them drapes his suit jacket over my shoulders, restoring my modesty and providing some kind of physical cocoon in which I can come down. I'm glad of my blindfold. I'm glad to be in the darkness, Gabe still pulsing inside my body.

'We'll see ourselves out,' Benedict says, also in a hushed voice, as if he and the others can sense that the time for jollity has passed and that quiet is now needed.

'Thank you, guys,' I mumble against Gabe's neck, adoring the tender way he's holding me. I'm nowhere near ready to leave my cocoon.

There's the rustle of clothing being fixed and a couple of champagne flutes being drained and set back down before someone unlocks the door.

'No,' one of them says as he passes behind me. 'Thank *you*.'

Gabe

The birthday "dinner" I promised Athena is, in fact, an oversized, over-engineered grazing platter in the splendid isolation of the spa at the Lanesborough Hotel on Hyde Park Corner, which I've rented out for the evening.

While I as good as knew she wouldn't be in a fit state to endure some formal, public meal, I also knew I didn't want her going home alone in whatever state of subspace or overwhelm she was bound to find herself in. This tranquil space strikes the balance, I hope, between privacy and indulgence.

I managed to get her dressed and back down to my office (via the fire escape stairs, so nobody would spot her smudged makeup or mussed hair or borderline drunk smile) before grabbing our things and bundling her into a cab.

The benefits of having exclusive access to a spa are many, and they most definitely include the prospect of naked swimming in the beautiful pool later, if she's up to it and not too sore, but they also include the ability for me to accompany her to the women's changing rooms, help her strip again, and wrap her up in a soft white robe.

She's slowly come back into her body over the past hour, and it seems that working her way through her body weight in brie and charcuterie, figs and fennel-seed-encrusted breadsticks, is helping. After all, it was a serious workout she had back in that meeting room.

We've dragged two white loungers together and are lolling on them in our robes as we graze and drink a lovely crisp Marlborough Sauvignon Blanc. I'm making sure she's mainlining water, too, and she has an ice pack wrapped in a towel tucked under her poor, swollen pussy.

She's bent over the grazing platter, industriously layering ingredients. 'Here. Try this.' She holds a morsel up to my mouth, feeding it to me when I open for her, her fingertips brushing my lips.

This is a perfect little package of pecorino drizzled with honey, layered with a segment of fig and wrapped in prosciutto. I groan with pleasure and she smiles at me, pleased.

'Isn't it incredible?'

'Incredible,' I murmur, looking at her mouth. She removed what was left of her makeup in the changing room, but her face still bears the glow, the flush, of all those orgasms. Her hair, now loose of its bouncy ponytail, cascades over her robed shoulders in big curls. She looks very young and terrifyingly beautiful, and I'm incapable of not staring.

'I'm okay,' she says, reading my stare as concern. 'Honestly, I'm a pro.'

I frown. 'Athena, regardless of what terminology you choose to use, that was a lot for *anyone*. You're only human. Are you sure it wasn't too much?'

She leans in for a kiss, and I oblige.

'It was perfect. Perfect. And the best thing was that I never, ever saw it coming, you devious little bastard.'

I grin, childishly pleased that my diabolical plan worked. 'Really?'

'Really.' She puts her hand on my thigh, stroking the hairs visible where my robe has fallen open. 'And I was much more worried about you in there. How are *you* doing? How did you find it?'

It's impossible to put into words how I found it. I had grave, grave misgivings beforehand, both that Athena would object to being blindsided in such depraved style and that I would be remotely capable of surviving watching her fuck other men in front of me. Contrary to the scenes some of her former employers delighted in roping her into—pun intended—this was very much something for *her*. A gift for *her*.

But amid the depravity and the sinning and the initial rude shock of seeing so many dicks and watching them plough into *my* assistant, watching those men touch *my* assistant, came a cocktail of emotions so heady that the only ones I could truly name were jealousy and arousal, the former most definitely igniting the latter.

'I was fine,' I bluster now. 'I knew what I was getting into.'

'Did you really?' she presses, and I chuckle.

'Nope. No, I had no fucking clue. All I knew was that I had to beat the sex toy birthday you told me about.'

She sidles in closer and lays her head on my shoulder. I tilt my face so I can rest my jaw against those silky tresses.

'Is that what it was about? Did you feel obliged to pull something bigger out of the hat for me? Because if you did, I hate that.'

A question like that deserves a thoughtful answer. *Any* question from her deserves a thoughtful answer.

'No. It wasn't about one-upmanship—at least, I don't think so. But when you told me about that, you were so fucking turned on just recounting it.' I pause. 'I've been very conscious that the things I do with you are relatively vanilla compared to what you're used to, and that you clearly have an appetite for pushing the envelope. I'm no Anton Wolff—I'm well aware of that.'

She sits upright and twists her body so she can look me in the eye, her expression somewhere between distressed and incensed. 'No, not at all! There was nothing vanilla about Prima Nocta, was there?'

I smile, both at her righteous outrage and at the memory of that evening. Of fucking her like a feudal overlord in front of a roaring fire. I let myself stroke her cheek with my thumb. 'No, there was nothing remotely vanilla about that.'

'Gabe.' Her eyes frantically search my face. 'I don't want Anton Wolff, or any facsimile of him. I'm here for *you* and what *you* want. You are a king among men, and everything we do is perfect. You don't ever, *ever* have to prove yourself to me. Surely you can see how affected I am every time we're together.'

'I know, and I can, very much so, and I appreciate that. I just wanted to see...' I huff out a breath. It's harder than I imagined to put my emotions, my motivations, into words. 'I wanted to see if I could set something up that would give you a memory that, when someone asked you about it years later, would have you igniting into flames again.'

Her smile is seductive, but it's genuine. 'Well, mission accomplished.' It grows more mischievous. 'What did you think, really?'

I consider, letting my hand roam over her jaw, down her neck, and through the astonishing silken mass of her hair. 'It was like thinking you know someone and then finding out that they can, I dunno, fly. Or perform aerial trapeze, or speak Japanese.'

She bursts out laughing, but I push through, struggling to articulate as I go. 'It was astounding, watching you perform. You were in your element. Think about it—all those guys, and you were commanding the room. They all wanted you so badly, and you had them wrapped around your little finger. You won't be the only person getting off on that memory for years to come, and I hate that—but I kind of love it, too.'

She leans in as if to kiss me again, stopping when her forehead touches mine. 'Spoken like a true Alchemy member. It's weird—I felt the same. I fucking loved it, don't get me wrong. But the more it went on, the more desperate I got to land on your lap, and when I did, it felt like I'd come home.'

I squeeze my eyes shut for a moment, a torrent of emotion hitting me at her simple confession.

Nothing about this feels transactional.

Nothing about us feels like anything other than an organic, loving relationship.

I've always hoped she'd enjoy this strange, unique role she plays in my life, but *homecoming* is not how you describe fucking a boss you're fond of.

She has a mark on her shoulder. A bite mark. I stroke the skin where her robe has slipped off and exposed it. I fucking hate that one of those dickheads felt he had the right to leave his mark on her.

But it's her birthday. This is not a time for getting heavy. It's a time for ensuring that she feels pampered and appreciated and adored—and *valued.* I reach down the side of my lounger and pull up a gift box.

'I got you something else.'

She stares down at it. 'I think you got me quite enough, didn't you?'

'That one was for your body.' I pause. 'This one is for your mind.'

She takes the lid off the box and pulls off the layer of tissue covering her gift. I hold my breath as she carefully lifts out the book inside. It's no ordinary book, but a beautifully bound early Victorian edition of Seneca's *Letters to Lucilius* with the original Latin and its English translation transcribed next to each other. Its jacket is still wrapped in protective cellophane in a way that allows the book to be opened, and she blows out a breath as she does.

'Oh my God. Oh, Gabe.'

I smile down at her. 'I thought about getting you a Bible or a Book of Hours, but I decided this would get more use.'

'Damn right. It's so beautiful.' She thumbs reverently through the pages, pulling out a plain notecard. On it, I've written the following:

> *Non est ad astra mollis e terris via*
> *Gabe*

She smiles fondly at my use of one of Seneca's most famous quotes: *There is no easy way from the earth to the stars.* It comes not from these letters but from his play, *Hercules.*

'Is this your way of saying that dirty little sinners like me won't make it to heaven?'

'Obviously,' I deadpan. The truth is that there are myriad layers of meaning behind these much-debated words. Perhaps Seneca was talking about man's ability to self-actualise. To self-improve. Perhaps it had a metaphysical meaning, as Athena just suggested. Perhaps it was a commentary on social mobility. We'll never fully know.

But it struck me, as I mused on the right words to tell her how I felt on her birthday without scaring her off, that Seneca could have been commenting directly on our relationship. A contract like ours is as base and transactional and earthly as it's possible to conceive of—in theory, anyway.

But look at us.

The way I see it, we could belong among the stars together if she had enough faith in us to tear down her walls.

It doesn't have to be transactional between us when it could be transcendent instead.

'Well, thank you.' She hugs it to her chest. 'I love it so much. You said it was a gift for my mind, but this is definitely one for my soul.'

'You have a soul? That's actually very reassuring. I have to say, I wasn't sure.'

Her smile is dazzling, her hazel eyes sparkling as she gazes at me. 'Stop it.'

I swallow down the emotion. 'I want you to know, despite everything that went down this evening, your soul is my absolute favourite part of you.'

CHAPTER 42

Gabe

'Your home is far nicer than I expected,' Athena tells me, staring at my enormous open-plan kitchen. 'I thought it would be far more priestly. It's really stunning.'

'I have George to thank for that.' I open the enormous fridge and pull out a bottle of sparkling water. 'He found me this interior designer who seemed to understand me better than I understand myself. She definitely had a knack for knowing what I wanted before I did.'

It's true. While I understood the urgency of departing from what George cuttingly called my parents' "carriage-clock chic" upon taking over this house, I had no real clue what vibe I actually wanted for my home or how to go about achieving it. Laura, the designer he contracted, steered me from a starting point of terms such as *quiet luxury* and *solidity* and *tranquility* to the place I call home today, and the fruits of her labour are astounding.

My home is an unlikely oasis in Central London, masculine and warm. Its lack of gratuitous furnishings feels intentional, the palette of sages and caramels and tans and taupes serene without veering remotely into coldness. It's a sanctuary in the same way my church used to be a sanctuary, but with none of the austerity that came with being an under-funded parish.

Instead, Laura created sensory appeal through layered textures—thick rugs, and reeded oak details, and chunky slabs of marble scored with thick black veins. The lack of clutter allows these details to sing, and the result is that my home provides the space I need to breathe, to think, while cosseting me in the lap of luxury.

It's a Saturday, and Athena has come over to work with me on pulling together the final proposed structure for our foundation. I'm hoping that taking the discussion out of the office will allow us room to be inspired.

I'm also hoping that my chimp brain will move on from the sight of Athena in skin-tight yoga pants and a loose, off-the-shoulder sweater and focus on something more altruistic, though I don't like my chances.

Not when her russet waves are gathered up in a big, messy bun with loose tendrils framing her face.

And certainly not when it's been business as usual over the past week, since I watched a roomful of other guys fuck her before enjoying our blissful non-date-date at the Lanesborough spa.

Athena may think that her actions at work, whether greeting me with a blow job, or anticipating every piece of analysis I need, or acting as my personal pit bull whenever anyone wants a piece of me, are borne out of her desire to excel in this unique hybrid role. But while every aspect of her professional performance is beyond reproach, a small, quiet, hopeful part of me believes that she, too, has caught feelings, even if her cognitive brain isn't yet aware of them.

In any case, she may be here to do overtime as our deadline for firming up the foundation's structure approaches, but she's absolutely *not* on the clock today for sex, and I absolutely *will* keep my hands to myself, and I absolutely will *not* think about how fucking amazing it would be to cup her arse through those lethal yoga pants while I kiss her rosebud mouth.

Unless she initiates something, of course, in which case, I'll be a lost man.

It's a testament to the infectiousness of this woman's energy that I do manage to look beyond her arse. Soon, she has the entire kitchen island covered in a mass of sticky notes clustered in three columns of yellow, pink and green to reflect our three proposed foundation pillars: Urban Community Development, Cultural Heritage, and Environmental Sustainability.

I cast my eye down the notes, letting the headings in Athena's neat handwriting jump out at me. *Affordable Housing Initiatives. Local History Projects. Urban Farming Projects.* So far, so in line with everything we've discussed as a family. The delineation of our focus areas is logical and tidy, and it feels actionable. This is our chance to make an incredible mark on an entire swathe of London.

So why do I feel underwhelmed?

We've been populating and casting our eyes over these for the better part of an hour now. She's watching me, hands on her hips, pacing up and down the length of the island. She glances down at the sticky notes. 'Talk out loud. Tell me what you're thinking.'

'I'm not sure—it's all fine.'

She stops and huffs. The energy coming off her is like crack. 'Well I've sure as hell never aimed for *fine,* and I'm not about to start now. *Fine* is positively offensive in my book. What adjectives would you like it to be?'

I scratch my beard. 'Let's see. Bold. Radical. *Meaningful.*'

'Good.'

'Transformative. Um, profound. Sincere. Borderline insane.'

'Good!' She slaps her hand on the marble. 'Don't filter. Just talk. Tell me more about what *borderline insane* means for you.'

I sigh. 'I suppose it means that other philanthropists look at it and think *those Sullivans are smoking crack.*'

She throws back her head and laughs, delighted. 'I love it! Why would they think you were smoking crack? Because of how much you're giving or what you're doing or the scale of the scope?'

I grin at her. Can't help it. 'All three. Because of the sheer audacity of it, I suppose. I want all those parochial naysayers out there to clutch their pearls and shake their heads and say, "The audacity of it!" when they see our proposal. "Who do those Sullivans think they are?"'

She gasps theatrically. 'Oh my God. *Audacity!* I love it. I love it so much. Yes, yes, yes.' Then she claps her hand to her mouth and stares at me, wide-eyed, and I marvel at how I could ever have found this woman implacable. These days, she allows me a front-row seat to every emotion that plays out on her beautiful face.

She hinges forward, resting her elbows on the island and drumming her fingers on it. I wait, knowing that something incredible is percolating in that terrifying brain of hers. It's not until she slowly straightens up that she speaks. When she does, it's as if she can't believe her own words.

'Fuck, Gabe. You want audacious? What if we've been looking at it all wrong?'

I stiffen in anticipation, watching as she begins to pace again. I swear, this woman could command the entire United Nations and have every delegate eating out of the palm of her hand. 'Go on.'

'The foundation might be looking good, but it's still an

afterthought. The entire Rath Mor model is built around *managing* your wealth, right? It's all very safe, very passive. Preserve the pot first, then give second.'

I nod my agreement. 'Keep talking.'

'What if you completely decimated that? I mean, who the fuck needs eight billion pounds? Not a former priest, that's for sure. Not your parents, not Brendan or Mairead. What if you flipped the entire thing on its head and put the giving first, and everything else comes from that?'

I sit up straighter, the quickening of my heart rate a clue to the excitement that her words are sparking. 'Like an endowment?'

'If you like.' She nods impatiently, as if now is not the time for semantics. 'Rather than it all being about the stewardship of your money, make it about using the money to transform. Every extra pound you guys grow gets funnelled into this insane, *audacious* pot that you pledge to give away. The end goal goes from being the *size* of the pot to the *power* of what that pot can do.'

Fucking hell, she's right. My mind is racing as quickly as my heart. 'We could set a target. Give away, what, seventy-five percent?'

'Whatever you like. Or do it backwards. Say you want to keep two billion for the family. That's more than you or all your heirs could ever need, and you could live off the interest, too. You have eight billion now, give or take. So you ring-fence two billion to manage like you're doing now, for the preservation of wealth, but you commit to giving away everything else, no matter how much it grows, over the next decade. Two decades. However you want to play it.'

Without thinking, I close in on her, my arms going around her waist as I tug her against my body. If it's inappropriate, she doesn't seem to notice. She lays her hands on my biceps and looks up at me, her face shining. 'Give the whole fucking thing away. Old Jim will have a heart attack—we live in hope. And people will say you're crazy. But what do *you* say?'

I know Athena would rather die than admit to any kind of altruism. In fact, I suspect she sees it as a weakness. I also know that she's fully aware of *my* need to be altruistic. She sees it as a point of honour to deliver that for me in a far bigger, bolder version than I could ever dare to dream of.

She elevates me.

She dreams big for both of us.

She's *audacious* enough for both of us.

Since Athena has entered my life, not a single instance of her behaviour has been meek or fearful or apologetic. Whether she's carving out her own take on the career ladder, or standing naked in a room with five aroused men, or proving that women are allowed to be both fiercely intellectual *and* fiercely sexual, she has been nothing *but* audacious.

I smile down at the life force visible on her face. She's aglow with it. 'I'm tempted to say I can't believe I didn't think of this before, but I *can* believe it. I just used the term *parochial* disparagingly, but honestly, I could say the same for my own approach. It is quite literally parochial—how apt. Everything I've done has been at such a small-scale, grass-roots level. It seems my brain is incapable of thinking as big as yours is. It's incredible.'

'Everything about this has you written all over it,' she insists. 'This is *you*, and that grass-roots approach is exactly how it needs to be. All I've done is taken *your* pastoral instincts and scaled them up—pretty dramatically. You've got these amazing, ancient values that are so intrinsic to who you are as a man, and I've got a decent high-level understanding of how modern finance can serve those values in a way that actually works.' She grins cheekily. 'Together, we're unstoppable.'

It may be a quip, but I can't help but think she's spot on.

Bottom up and top down.

Grass roots and high finance.

I ground her, and she elevates me.

I understand people, and she understands business.

I tell her I want to use my wealth to effect real change, and she transforms that mission beyond all belief.

We are the perfect partners. She understands innately the things that drive me at my most profound level, but it feels as though she sees my purpose more clearly than I do.

Non est ad astra mollis e terris via.

There is no easy way from the earth to the stars.

Maybe there is.

Maybe there fucking is.

CHAPTER 43

Athena

Pledging to give away the majority of your ten-figure fortune may be a worthy sentiment, but I'm sure it'll take some serious cajoling on Gabe's part to even remotely get his family on board. That said, to use startup jargon, it's the kind of Big, Hairy, Audacious Goal that's exciting enough, inspiring enough, to give both of us a kick up the arse. Committing to giving as the *starting point* of his estate planning feels intentional in a way the foundation has been lacking so far, and pulling a completely fresh idea from a blank canvas is the ultimate rush.

We mainline coffee and kick ideas around for a few more hours before Gabe suggests that if we wander up Marylebone High Street in search of provisions, then he will cook us supper. I find myself agreeing readily. I have plans to see Marlowe and Tabby tomorrow—Tabs isn't doing great—but have a free evening ahead, and for reasons that feel complicated I'm in no rush to go back to my lovely, lonely flat.

Usually, the office is our bubble, but this bubble, with Weekend Gabe in his grey cashmere sweater and jeans and easy smile, in his beautiful, palatial home, is even more sparkly and lustrous and intoxicating.

We visit a gourmet deli, the kind of place so brimming with delicacies that you can't help but get instant decision paralysis. That probably explains how we come away with everything from fresh ravioli and a block of truffled raclette to smoked salmon mousse and far too many variations on dark chocolate. And when we're back at Gabe's place, I find myself perched on a bar stool with a chilled glass of Provençal rosé, watching my boss potter competently around his kitchen.

This man moves me so much.

He moves me when he speaks and when he smiles. His agile brain and his beautiful soul move me as much as his undeniable physical blessings. He is the most serene person I've ever met, his confidence stemming not from an inflated sense of self, but from a quiet trust that everything is unfolding as it is. His mastery of the art of surrender is Zen-like, just as his energy is intoxicating.

We dine together at the island, glasses filled and thighs brushing and this afternoon's handiwork laid out before us in a host of neon sticky notes. I watch him eat, and he watches me eat, and I suddenly understand that silence and eye contact and proximity can be richer, more nourishing, than any conversation.

It terrifies me, and it enthrals me.

'I bet you were an amazing priest,' I say eventually. It's a statement, something I know viscerally to be true.

He smiles, and it's a little sad. 'I wasn't amazing by any means. But I'd like to think I was decent. I'd like to think I helped some people.'

'And you'll help more now. So many more.'

He's silent before he speaks, his blue eyes fixed on the far wall. 'I hope so.'

'Will it be enough for you, do you think?'

I know he understands what I'm asking. I know he worries that deploying vast, unthinkable sums of money is somehow less worthy than the noble toil of a priest in his parish. I know he believes, deep down, that no matter how hard he works on this foundation, it's some form of cop-out.

His gaze flicks back to me, and it's raw, and it's honest.

'I don't know. I understand intellectually that I don't have to be the one ladling out bowls of soup to make a difference, that what we're proposing is the kind of scale I would have found impossible to comprehend when I was working at the parish level. Still do, as you've seen. But understanding it intellectually and feeling it in my heart are two very different things.'

I nod. He hasn't embodied this yet, hasn't allowed himself to.

'You could argue that Jesus had far more impact after his death than when he was on the ground hanging out with lepers and washing feet.' *Even if Christianity is a total crock of shit from where I'm standing.*

That gets me a rueful smile. 'Good point well made, Miss Davenport. Not sure I'm ready to offer myself up for martyrdom just yet, though.'

Feeling brave, I take the hand resting on his thigh and clasp it, running my thumb over his knuckles. 'Why did you leave?' I whisper.

'There was no great scandal, no dark secrets. I just felt underwhelmed. Spiritually, I suppose, and in terms of my purpose. It was a gradual process—I tried hard for so bloody long, but I tried because I felt obliged, rather than because I had this spiritual zeal in my belly, you know? God, it's so hard to explain.

'I loved the theological side—maybe too much. Sometimes I felt like I was more interested in winning theological arguments than helping people find God.'

I smile. 'I can relate. We're the same like that.'

He squeezes my hand. 'It's all well and good, but the imposter syndrome got worse and worse. I felt like I was behind this curtain, observing and not living. I'd be counselling a couple on marriage and think "what the fuck do I know?" I felt like I was trying so fucking hard but I was just going through the motions.

'Some priests have this natural grace—you can see it literally flowing through them, like God has touched them with His grace—but I just felt nothing. I was getting nothing from Him, and I was constantly in my head about it. I was always trying to prove to myself that I deserved it, and that's not how a true vocation should feel.'

'Of all the things you've said to me about your faith,' I say quietly, 'what you said about grace at The Wolseley resonated the most. You told me you believe we don't need to earn it— that it just flows.'

He smiles sadly. 'I truly believe that. I just couldn't feel it in my own heart. Something was missing for me, so when Dad started making more and more noise about retiring, I threw in the towel. I just couldn't bear that hurt every day of knowing that I was going through the motions and trying my damnedest to serve and to pray and to have faith and simply not cutting it.'

It's so unfair. It's so bloody unfair that a man this good should feel like that, that he should hold himself to such superhuman standards. I bring our conjoined hands to my lips and kiss his knuckles. 'You are the best man I've ever met, and I hope you find whatever's been missing for you. I really, really do.'

When he gazes at me, his eyes are so blue and pure and heartbreaking. 'I think I already have.'

I stiffen, tears springing from absolutely nowhere as I take in his words and his tone and his gaze. He twists on his stool so he's facing me properly and slides his leg between mine.

'Sweetheart.' He pauses as if trying to find the right words. 'The things I feel for you are things no man has any business feeling for his employee, no matter what he's paying her for.'

I swallow. I can't speak. Can't move. He pushes gamely on.

'I didn't leave the priesthood so I could get laid, and I certainly didn't employ you with any agenda beyond what we so clearly outlined, I promise you that. But I have fallen so hard and so fast, and—you are the most spectacular woman I have ever, ever met.' He pauses, and the searing honesty in his eyes nearly kills me. 'And I wonder if you feel the same way— or if I'm deluding myself here.'

I feel so many things, things I never expected to feel, never wanted to feel, things I've fought and denied and dismissed. But regardless of how loath I am to admit them to myself, there's no way in hell I'd ever leave this beautiful man hanging when he's baring his wonderful, wonderful soul.

'I feel the same way.' I can barely hear the admission. Tears are trembling on my lower lids, poised to break free, but I push on. 'And I'm scared.'

His face crumples with compassion as he slides his free hand around my neck. 'Oh my darling. Why are you scared?'

Because my entire plan for my entire career rests precariously on a very specific set of boundaries and behaviours and rules and advancement strategies involving other bosses, and falling for my current boss is not on the cards. At *all*.

I don't quite go with that line. Gabe deserves better.

'Because feelings weren't supposed to come into this,' I stammer, 'and I have absolutely no idea how to marry that with my being the woman you pay to fuck me at work. I don't know how the hell we're supposed to even consider a relationship within that dynamic.'

He blanches at my bluntness, then recovers. 'You are far, far more to me than that. And, in the hope that this doesn't freak you out too much, I think we've both been *in* a relationship for some time.'

I stare at him, horrified. 'What do you mean?'

'Well, you're very, very good at your job—at all the parts of it. But I'd very much like to believe that when you practically fight George to be the one to get my lunch, or when I give you a foot rub just because I can, or when we're lying together in bed in Claridges and it feels like we could lie there quite happily all day—I'd like to think those things are because we're falling for each other and not just because you're a committed assistant and I'm a considerate boss. Because they're also the kinds of things that boyfriends and girlfriends do for each other, you know.'

I'm either going to laugh or cry at that little insight, so I laugh. 'And what the fuck do either of us know about having a boyfriend or girlfriend? The priest and the prostitute? Neither of us are exactly relationship experts.'

He doesn't look like he finds that funny. 'Very little, clearly. Saying that, I know enough about humankind to know that the way you and I look after each other is what most people would consider very loving. Caring.'

He says the final two words carefully, as if they're grenades that might explode upon impact. In reality, their power lies in their accuracy, because I know he's right. If I look at how I approached my working relationships with my previous bosses, it was work and sex. Rinse and repeat. It was transactional. By contrast, Gabe and I have been devoted to each other, consumed by each other, since alarmingly early in my tenure with him, and it would do both of us a huge disservice if I wasn't woman enough to admit that.

'You're right. We've blurred every line going, and I've loved every second of it. And I wasn't totally ignorant of it—I just figured that as long as we let it all happen within the confines of our *working* relationship, we could fudge it.'

'Yeah.' He screws up his face. 'I get that, and it was enough for a while, because it was so much more than I could ever have dreamed of. But I got greedy, and it's not enough anymore. I want you in my bed every night. I want to walk down the street with my arm around you and shout from the fucking rooftops that the most incredible woman I know is *with* me. I want my family to know, and passing you off as my assistant is just bullshit. I want a proper, honest-to-god relationship with you.'

I want to be in his bed, tonight and every night after.

I want his arm around me in public.

I want to claim this man and be by his side and celebrate him and wallow in the miracle of his existence every day. The mere thought of it has a huge smile breaking out on my face, and I drop my forehead to his. 'Oh my God. I want that too.'

'Good.'

'But how the hell do we make it work with my—with the Seraph stuff?' My mind is reeling. I can't date him and let him pay me for sex. Nor can I date him and move firms and let someone else pay me for sex. But—

He's gone silent. I lift my head to see him grimacing. 'What?'

He clears his throat. 'I'm finding it surprisingly difficult to propose to the woman of my dreams that she take a ninety percent pay cut.'

'What the *fuck?*'

'Hear me out.' He's grinning now, and I'm powerless against it. I'm jelly. 'I'm not suggesting this because you and I might be taking this in a new direction, but...'

'But you're going to suggest you should get to fuck me for free.'

His laugh is bright and boyish and gorgeous. 'Ha! You've

got me. I'm definitely not so keen on money changing hands going forward.' His face grows more serious. 'I want to know that when we're together, when we're doing all the amazing things we do, it's because you want to, not because I'm paying you to.'

I nod, blinking back those pesky tears. If I'm honest with myself, I've done an excellent job these past few weeks of ignoring the transactional nature of our relationship at every turn. Everything I do with him is real. Everything we do is because we both want it. 'I understand. Please proceed.'

'Here's the thing. You're obviously ridiculously overqualified to be my assistant. I mean, it's crazy. You're running the show in there.'

'If you want to fire Eleanor and give me her job, I'm game,' I deadpan. In my more self-indulgent moments, I've definitely thought about it. God, I could get my teeth into the Chief of Staff role and then some.

'You're getting warmer than you know. I have to talk to my family about all of this foundation stuff, especially in light of our revelations earlier today, but'—he pauses—'what today did bring home is that not only is yours the most impressive strategic brain I know but that you have my back more than anyone else. You understand my vision, you *elevate* my vision at every turn, you drive me to dream bigger, aim higher, and you care that I achieve it more than anyone else.'

I smile at him adoringly as I lap up his words of praise and appreciation, so much so that I almost miss his next utterance.

'That's why I'd like to propose you to run the foundation.'

CHAPTER 44

Athena

'But I'm twenty-six,' I bluster.

'Oh, no. Nope. Don't pull that crap with me.' He pulls my stool, and me, even closer to him until we're practically kneeing each other in the crotch. 'The Athena Davenport I know would never, ever let anyone play the age card with her. You're the smartest person I've ever met. How do you like that?'

My mind is racing. The kind of financial divestment I'm proposing the Sullivan family commits to making would make the foundation a business with a funding of billions of pounds worth of capital, plural.

That's bigger than the enterprise value of some of the companies I've worked for and analysed.

I change tactics. 'But this is your baby.'

'I have every intention of being all over this project—it's my passion. But I'm not the right person to run it, sweetheart. I just don't have the right skillset. I can't look at a blank piece of paper and see an opportunity the way you can. I can't spot efficiencies and strategies, and I definitely can't hustle the way you can.'

I think of the effortless charm he shows every time we go out on the road. 'I disagree. You can be very persuasive.'

'I'm best when I don't have an agenda. You, in the nicest possible way, are ruthless.'

He's not wrong. He presses on.

'And that's what this thing needs. It needs to be run intelligently and aggressively and hungrily, and you have all those attributes in spades. You may look at yourself and see a twenty-six-year-old, but I see a ferocious business brain and a go-getter.' He peers at me with concern, brushing some stray hairs off my face. 'I've never seen your self-confidence shaken before. I thought you'd jump at the chance to get your teeth into something this juicy—unless this is about the money?'

That makes me start. 'No. God, no. I'm just trying to process it all.'

I'm telling the truth. It's not about the money, not in the slightest. I realise he couldn't possibly justify paying someone seven figures to run a non-profit. It would be the height of corruption. And he's right, of course. What he's dangling over this little pit bull's head is less a carrot and more a big, juicy steak.

A multi-billion-pound juicy steak.

What I'm really attempting to process is this new understanding that Gabe is offering me the most extreme form of validation. He doesn't just look at me and see my body; he sees my MBA brain, and he deems it worthy of *this*.

All this time, I've been harping on about *access*. I've been serving powerful men as a means to an end, climbing my version of the corporate ladder and working on the assumption that access is something you get by swanning into an established company at C-Suite level.

Now he's offering me something far more rare and precious and valuable: the chance to start a business up from scratch with all the backing and stability and *fuel* that comes from a funding source—and a support network—like the Sullivans. He's suggesting I cast aside that transactional ladder altogether and help him build something truly transformational instead.

He's giving me a seat at the head of the table, offering me the chance to wield real power, and to wield it for good.

It's what I always knew I wanted, manifesting in a form my mind didn't know to imagine, and it's come years early from a man so perfect even I could never have dreamed him up.

It may just be that he's handing me my life's purpose in the guise of asking for my help with his.

GABE

This day is so *much*.

Athena, blowing the scope of my hopes and dreams for the foundation sky high.

Athena, admitting to me that she, too, carries feelings for me.

Athena, speechless and incredulous and, eventually, lit up at the mere suggestion that this should all be her show to run.

And, finally, Athena, naked and stripped back and in my bed.

Just as it should be.

We lie on our sides, grinning at each other in exhausted, post-orgasmic euphoria. After everything we've done, making love to her on the clean, crisp sheets of my own bed feels the boldest. The most intentional. She's not here because I'm paying for the privilege. This astonishing woman is curled up facing me, a sexed-out comma the depth of whose feelings seem, miraculously, to mirror mine.

This goddess has an arsenal of weapons so deadly that no man stands a chance against her. But when she lays them down, when she lays herself bare, she is the most intoxicating version of herself.

'Is it weird that I feel shy?' she asks me, and I laugh.

'Shy? You? Yep.'

'Rude.' She screws her face up in thought. 'Maybe *shy* is the wrong word. Maybe *vulnerable* is better.'

I study her. 'That makes sense, I suppose,' I admit slowly. After all, in this career she's carved out for herself the rules of engagement are crystal clear.

This? Us? While the acts we're performing remain similar, there are no rules, there's no prescription—only a multitude of feelings.

It must feel for her like diving off a cliff, unsure whether the sparkling blue sea below is harbouring jagged rocks.

'I don't normally let men in.'

'I know.' I tuck a lock of glossy auburn hair behind her ear and let my hand linger on her jaw. 'That you're willing to let me in is the greatest honour you could give me, and I promise I won't abuse that privilege.'

She echoes my words. 'I know.'

'The more you unravel yourself for me, the harder I fall.' I want her to *know* this, to *feel* it somatically in every square inch of her body. I want her to understand that her vulnerability is a gift to me, a gift I cherish.

'Angel Gabriel.' Her words are whispers. She scratches her fingertips lightly over my beard. 'They don't make many men like you, let me tell you.'

'That helps my odds with you.'

She grins, and it's beautiful.

'You know,' I continue, 'if I'd been a Renaissance artist painting the Madonna, I would have asked you to sit for me.'

Her eye roll may be cutting, but her smile turns pleased. 'Come off it.'

'I'm serious. It's very unlikely that Our Lady looked anything like you—she was Israeli, after all—but so many artists painted her with fair skin and Western European features.'

'That was deliberate, you know,' my little art scholar says, suddenly serious. 'Making religious figures look easily relatable was common practice.'

'Is that a fact? Well, they would have killed to paint you.'

'What is it about Catholics and Our Lady, anyway? Why the obsession?'

Asking a Catholic priest to wax lyrical about the virtues of Our Lady is like holding up a steak to a grizzly bear. 'How long have you got?'

She giggles. 'Minutes, not hours. I have better things to do with my evening.' She trails her fingertips down my neck and between my pecs. 'But I'm genuinely interested.'

I adjust my head on my pillow and blow out a breath. 'Well, she was an eternal virgin, so, you know, she's a symbol of perfect purity. That's always very appealing.'

'Ha ha. You're hilarious.'

'I am, aren't I? But seriously, let me see. First of all, she's the personification of faith. Not everyone would have accepted God's will to impregnate them immaculately. And she was a mother. I think a lot of the devotional focus on Our Lady stems from that. People find that comforting—she's a maternal figure. She's incredibly compassionate—her statues have been documented by the Church as having shed tears on numerous occasions. She understands the burden of human suffering and she's seen as willing to advocate for her spiritual children.'

'Advocate to God?' she asks.

'Yes. Well, Jesus. A lot of people feel safer going to Our Lady with their problems, believing that she has Our Lord's ear and she'll intercede with Him.'

'Do you pray to Our Lady?'

'I do. Every day.'

She frowns. 'I think I'm jealous.'

'I pray to you, too, every day. Don't I? Every time I touch you, I'm praying to you.'

Her eyelids flutter gently closed, as if my confession brings her great contentment. 'Show me how you pray to her. What are the prayers?'

I roll her gently onto her back and brace myself on my elbow so I can stare down at her. 'Well, *Ave Maria* is the most famous prayer—the Hail Mary. That forms the basis of the rosary. But my favourite is *Salve Regina*.'

'Hail, queen.' She gazes up at me.

'The English version is *Hail, holy queen. Mater miseri-cordiæ—Mother of mercy*.'

I stroke back her hair. '*Hail our life, our sweetness, and our hope. To thee do we cry,*'—I bend to kiss her temple—'*poor banished children of Eve. To thee do we send up our sorrows, mourning and weeping in this valley of tears.*'

I climb fully on top of her, bracing on both elbows now. '*Turn then, most gracious advocate, thine eyes of mercy toward us, and after this our exile, show unto us the blessed fruit of thy womb, Jesus.*' Dipping my head, I whisper against her jaw. '*O clement, O loving, O sweet Virgin Mary.*'

'It's beautiful.' She stretches below me, cat-like. 'So melodic, even in English. I can see how it would bring people comfort—it's like they have someone in their corner.'

I appreciate her saying that, given her views on organised religion. 'It is beautiful. And that's exactly right. There's more, but now I have some more pressing business to attend to.'

With that, I turn my head and find her mouth.

Athena

When Gabe sat down with his family, he did it without me or anyone from Rath Mor. This is their money, and it's their decision—an enormous one.

Two incredible things happened over the course of the weekend he spent up in Newmarket.

The first was that the Sullivan family, to a person, got behind his proposal of publicly committing to a figure to give away. It seems my audacious suggestion has struck a chord, that the astonishing wealth they've amassed weighs heavily on these people who've retained their values despise their success.

Apparently his dad, Ronan, commented that if they were at all worried about surviving on five hundred million each for the rest of their lives then that would make them, and I quote, *serious fucking eejits.*

I concur.

I may be a greedy little thing, but that's silly money. Gabe said Mairead was all over the concept and will probably pledge an even greater share of her fortune to the foundation. She said she'd rather be "normal rich" than "will-someone-kidnap-my-kids-rich".

According to Gabe, Brendan was the least amenable, but he came around. He also has a shit-tonne of money—tens of millions at least—tied up in Sullivan Construction stock, too, which isn't on the Rath Mor books.

I don't think he'll starve. I don't think any of them will.

The second incredible thing that happened was that they all apparently lapped up the idea of installing *me* as the CEO of the foundation. Gabe tells me I shouldn't be surprised. After all, I've made various pointed comments in the past about how painful it is to watch do-gooders with fuck-all business sense trying to run charities, and he claims his family feels the same way. Seemingly, my radical ideas and my "aggression" (Gabe's word) around the table at the pitch meeting cast Eleanor's halfhearted efforts to date in a rather unflattering light, and they're all up for taking a chance on some fresh blood. I even had a lovely text from his sister claiming I was a breath of fresh air and exactly what her family needed to shake things up.

I knew I liked her.

My background may fall somewhere between the raw hunger Gabe's father and grandfather's tough upbringing instilled in them and the aristocratic, inbred passivity of Eleanor Whitmore, but I hope my business drive falls somewhere closer to the former. If my results to date resonate with some members of the family, my educational and cultural pedigree is, according to Gabe, pretty much orgasmic from where his mum's standing.

There's no doubt I'm young and green for such a huge job. But this foundation will be a collective effort, an opportunity to draw in leading minds from all over the world. All it needs is an audacious little pit bull like me to pull it all together with my customary tirelessness.

Apparently.

I'm working out my notice period this month. Next month, I will move from being a Seraph contractor to an employee of Rath Mor, under whose umbrella the foundation will sit. Also next month, my salary will drop like a stone. Gabe's actually been pretty concerned about it. He seems to feel terrible, to the extent that he offered to pay a Seraph-level salary out of his own pocket.

I told him, quite eloquently, exactly where he could shove that idea.

You don't take money from your boyfriend.

You don't take a penny from the man you're infatuated with in order to fuck him.

And you certainly don't take it from a man who has looked at you and seen your whole self and said *yes, you*. Who has offered you purpose and opportunity greater than you could ever have imagined. Who has struggled so gravely with his own perceived worthiness of grace and has come from a world of moral absolutes and yet has put the sum total of his faith—a staggering amount—in *you*.

So I'll make do with five figures a month instead of six, and I'll lean into this gift, and I'll even allow myself to revel, like the callous little bitch that I am, in the lowkey schadenfreude as Gabe tells the entire firm about my new positions: professional and romantic. George is ecstatic, bless him, other individuals less so.

My crowning glory, my anointing as a Sullivan WAG and a power player in the family's bold philanthropic efforts, will be a charity gala that takes place next week. Its profoundly ironic title, given that it's being hosted by the ancient Cadogan

Estate, is *The Future of British Philanthropy.* We've taken a table for the Sullivan family and Rath Mor team, and Eleanor is positively orgasmic at the prospect.

The only bright spots are that Gabe is giving the keynote speech during dinner, and that he has insisted on treating me to a very fabulous gown for the evening.

Thus I find myself one lunchtime outside the headquarters of demi-couture brand, Gossamer. I know the brand, of course—I followed it on Instagram long before it was folded into the Wright Holdings stable of luxury brands—but I've never owned a Gossamer piece. Having a designer dress habit is one thing, but demi-couture, with its incredible workmanship, is a whole other ballgame. That said, when your new and extremely generous boyfriend hooks you up with the Creative Director of such a brand, it would be rude to say no.

I know Natalie Bennett's romantic partner and principal investor, the outrageously hot billionaire Adam Wright, is a good friend of Gabe's. It seems I have him to thank for the suggestion that Gabe should give Seraph a spin, in fact. It was he who brought it up one night at Alchemy, prompting Anton and Max to hit my now boyfriend with The Great Athena Pitch.

Clearly, I owe Mr Wright a drink or two. What's less clear is if Natalie, who is hosting me at her studio today, knows the true nature of my and Gabe's working relationship to date.

Whatever she knows, she's delightful. She comes down to the gigantic lobby of Wright Holdings to greet me, a svelte figure in a beautifully tailored black jumpsuit. Her makeup is perfect, the diamonds in her ears and around her wrist absolutely enormous, and her smile is wide.

'Congratulations on the acquisition,' I tell her as we enter the lift. I followed the news on her social media as well as in the financial press. With Gossamer now an official part of Wright's empire, I imagine the sky is the limit.

'Thanks. It helps to sleep with the boss, am I right? Though he insists he bought Gossamer on its merits.'

I throw back my head and laugh, her candour taking me by surprise. I like her instantly. 'I know something about that.'

'I bet you do.' She winks at me, and I know for a fact that she knows. 'I hear congratulations are in order for you, too. The foundation?'

'Thank you. And yes, I apparently got the promotion on *my* own merits, but who really knows?'

'I'm pretty confident they've fallen for our business minds,' she tells me as we trot out into a huge, light-filled room that must stretch the entire width of the building. 'But if they're enamoured of our other attributes too, who are we to argue?'

The studio is incredible. My knowledge of fashion is limited to avid consumption, so it's fascinating to see the banks of desks, and the enormous white tables piled high with rolls of fabric, and the stylish, quirky people who populate the space, each bringing their own brand of cool. It couldn't be more different from most of the places I've worked.

Dotted around the space are mannequins in various states of undress. We pass one that's nothing but a canvas torso on whose décolletage is pinned the most sublime array of pearl beading and tulle.

I could play in this place for hours.

The client area is at the end of the room, set away from the main space.

'Oh, dear Lord,' I murmur as I come face to face with rows and rows of what can only be called frothy paradise. 'This is heaven.' Gabe may have his faith, but I could worship at the altar of Gossamer for hours. If it's a cult Natalie's running here, I'll sign my freedom over without a second thought.

'It really is,' Natalie agrees. 'I'm still not used to it. We've only been in a couple of months, and you should have seen the place we were in before Adam swept in and played fairy godfather. It was a tiny little shithole, there's no other way to describe it.'

Fairy godfather.

Sounds like Gabe.

Although maybe, given the man he is, *patron saint* feels more apt.

'Well, you've certainly put down roots. It feels very established.'

'It still feels like a dream. He brought me to these offices for the first time one Saturday. When I saw Omar Vega's studio downstairs, I could have sat down on that floor and wept. It was so far beyond anything I could have dreamed of.' She smiles, and it's fabulous and victorious and powerful. 'But ours is nicer.'

'Ha! I love that.' I really do. I fucking love it when women exude their natural goddess energy, and Natalie has it going on in spades. 'It's so sumptuous.'

I cast my eyes over the racks and racks of dresses: silk and tulle and lace and feathers arranged in a celestial pastel rainbow. I'm positively itching to get my hands on them.

'So this is for a gala.' She clasps her hands in front of her. 'Do you have any idea what you're looking for?'

'Tasteful but fabulous. I'd like a showstopper, but it can't say *I let men fuck me for money.* It needs to say something like *I'm fully capable of managing one of the biggest foundations in the country but don't for a second think I'll look frumpy doing it.*'

She snorts. 'Gotcha. And I suspect no one could ever accuse you of looking frumpy. You know, if you ever need to borrow something for a big event once you're in the new seat, we'd be happy to oblige. We do it a lot for high profile women.'

High profile women.

I've spent the past four years since Camille recruited me being the soul of discretion, putting on a show only for the men lucky enough to afford me and actively blending in on a wider basis.

That's all about to change.

'Thank you,' I tell her now. 'I could get used to wearing only demi-couture.'

'It's a dangerous precedent to set. I should know. Why do you think I force my team to make every sample in my size?' She jerks her head over to a mannequin standing by the window wearing a frothy black concoction. 'See her? She's literally called Natalie. We got Stockman, the mannequin company, to make her in my exact dimensions.'

I shake my head with a rueful grin. Lucky cow. 'That's genius.'

'Isn't it? Right, we know you need a showstopper. How about something channelling Old Hollywood? With some sleek curls, you could definitely channel a siren of the silver screen.'

'I love that idea,' I admit.

'Do you have any colours in mind?'

There's something about the careful politeness with which she says it that tells me she already has a strong view.

'Why don't you tell me?'

She grins. 'I was hoping you'd say that. We have a dress in this green that's somewhere between mint and pistachio, and I think you'd look *amazing* in it.'

'I love green. Show me.' It's true. Green tends to complement my hair and eyes, no matter what shade I wear, but I don't often gravitate towards the shade she's described. It's not the most practical colour for everyday wear.

She sashays along the rainbow of dresses and stops where blue becomes aqua and then green. The way she presses her lips together in excitement as she carefully lifts a hanger off the rail tells me she has seriously strong feelings about this dress.

She holds it aloft.

Holy fucking shit.

My face must be a picture, because she bursts out laughing. 'My thoughts exactly.'

'It's incredible.'

It's so beautiful that I want to hang it on my wall and gaze at it for ever more, or eat it like a cake, or wear it every single day. It's *perfect.*

'Try it on,' she urges. 'We can adjust it where needed.'

I require no further encouragement. I step into the large changing area, which is softly lit and surrounded by heavy velvet curtains. Once Natalie has drawn them around us, I strip down to my thong and heels. This dress doesn't require a bra. I slip it on with her help, and she zips up the back.

'There.' Her tone is soft and reverent. 'You look like you're going to the Oscars. I could cry—it's as if we made it just for you.'

I gaze at my reflection in the three full-length mirrors. Even in my black heels and workday makeup, she's not wrong.

This gown is *exquisite.*

It's full-length in the palest green, and it shimmers from top to tail whenever I move. While the tiny straps and the bra cups are crafted from satin, the rest consists of tier after tier of silk tassels, impeccably cut to form chevrons. The waist is fitted, the skirt slim with a slit all the way up one side. From the knee to the floor, the chevrons ebb away into hundreds of tiny, ethereal ostrich feathers in the same shade of green that flutter and tremble.

The result, especially with my hair colour, is The Little Mermaid meets old-school, full-wattage glamour. It's classy and sexy and impossibly expensive looking, which is pretty much my personal brand.

It was made for me.

'It fits really well on the breasts and hips, but we can take it in a tiny bit around the waist,' Natalie says, pinching the fabric there slightly. I can see instantly that it improves the silhouette, making it even more streamlined. 'And if you want to buy some ivory satin heels, we can probably get them dyed to match in time for the gala.'

I nod, assessing. Analysing. She releases me, and I turn this way and that, admiring the delicate sway of the tassels and feathers as I do.

As I study myself in the mirror, I can't help but imagine Gabe's reaction when he sees me in this.

I hope he finds it as worthy of its price tag as I've been.

CHAPTER 46

Athena

The great and good of British philanthropy have gathered in the ballroom of The Dorchester Hotel on Park Lane. The agenda? Pretending to care about the future of giving while they get stuck into the twin attractions of free-flowing champagne and mutual back-slapping.

While I'm not particularly looking forward to the event, I'm very much looking forward to a night on the arm of Gabriel Sullivan, Esquire. He made his first foray into my flat tonight when he came to pick me up, resplendent in a Tom Ford tuxedo (George finally got his way on that front).

I'm just glad his aspirations don't run to acting, because the James Bond casting team would kill for this man. This evening, he looks like Sean Connery in his heyday, his dark hair combed back off his face and the snowy white of his dress shirt as good a foil for the olive in his skin tone as it is for the black satin lapels of his dinner jacket.

It seems he was just as blown away by the sight of me as I was by him, because when he saw me in my green mermaid dress, with apricot-coloured lips and the sleekest eyeliner and huge, Hollywood curls, he went quiet, and his face went soft, and he just stared. He stared like he was a man lost in the desert and I was an electrolyte drink.

And then he said, 'You're always beautiful, but this is something else entirely,' and the reverence in his tone and on his face was almost enough to fell me.

I enter the ballroom on the arm of whom I already know to be the handsomest, most decent man in the room. In what is presumably a nod to the theme of environmental sustainability, the entire space is rich with moss-covered plinths and live trees, the latter nested in huge pots and sitting amongst the big round tables. Ivy hangs from the chandeliers, its tendrils swaying as guests waft by. The organisers have opted for table centrepieces in the form of huge silver bowls filled with living orchids and ferns.

And while the overall feel is one of timeless luxury—Edith Wharton and her contemporaries would have swooned over the plethora of ferns—there are modern touches, too. I spot a living wall behind the raised dais from which the dinner speeches will be made, and we pass a gilt-framed digital screen showing the event's sustainability metrics in real time.

'The new head of my foundation is easily the most beautiful woman in the room,' Gabe murmurs in my direction as we saunter between the tables on our trip to the bar.

'I'll bet she's also the easiest,' I observe, my gaze fixed straight ahead. In my peripheral vision, I see him crease up.

'In my book, that's a truly excellent combination.'

If I'm thrilled to be here in my upcoming capacity as the new CEO of the Rath Mor Foundation, then I'm positively ecstatic to be here as Gabe's romantic partner. I could burst with happiness and pride at the way that this man sees me. There's rose-tinted, and then there's Gabe-tinted: that hue tinged with all the goodness and faith in human nature that he possesses so intrinsically.

I will never, ever let his faith in me be in vain. While there's no way on earth my grubby little soul is worthy of his shining one, I can only hope that, with time, even a little of his virtue rubs off on me.

Dame Sarah Blackwood, Director of the Centre for Complex Systems and Societal Change at Oxford, is a force to be reckoned with, and I love her. She wears her white hair short and, if the strong red lip she's sporting is any indication, she's as much of a pro with a lip pencil as she is with driving change. She's in a beautifully cut black tuxedo, but on her feet? A to-die-for pair of Manolo Blahnik Hangisi satin pumps in royal blue satin: utterly stunning and easily a grand a pop.

Maybe philanthropists don't have to be totally boring and worthy.

The five minutes Gabe and I spend chatting with her at the bar is more than enough to give me that intellectual boner I get when I talk to truly dynamic people—especially women. Our conversation is Seraphim-level inspiring, without any of the inappropriate subject matter. And when she lets slip that she consulted on Brooklyn's Industry City, I positively swoon.

'You can always call me,' she says crisply, pressing a thick business card into my hand. 'God knows, I love an excuse for a day trip to London. The shoe shops in Oxford are godawful.' She looks me up and down. 'Good luck to you, Athena. I have a funny feeling you'll be a tonic for us all.'

'I'm getting excited now,' I confess to Gabe after she's bid us a good evening. 'I've been looking forward to the work, but I hadn't really thought through just how many amazing people I might cross paths with, doing this.'

'With the foundation behind you, you should be able to

get a direct line into almost anyone on this side of the pond. I know intelligence is like crack to you—you'll be happy as a pig in shit, I should think. And speaking of farm animals, you ready to go see my family?'

We finish our drinks and make our way across the room to where the Sullivan table is. As we weave between the tables, our fellow guests stop us at regular intervals to greet Gabe. Each time, he introduces me as his girlfriend, and, each time, the light of pride and affection in his eyes as he looks at me makes my innards melt.

The Sullivan table is towards the front of the room, right in front of the living wall. Perfect. I'll be able to ogle my man from up close when he's giving his speech. Most of the family is already seated—apparently Gabe's parents prefer to get settled with their drinks and have people come to them than work the room. It's not a bad game plan.

I spotted his mum earlier. She's in an ornate purple lace gown that I'm pretty sure is Reem Acra, and she looks beautiful. A quick scan of the table reveals Ronan, Mairead next to a man who must be her husband, Peter, Brendan—on his own, shock horror—and Eleanor. Torty's on Brendan's left, and I allow myself a moment to wonder idly if she'll set her sights on him now that Gabe and I have gone public. And on his right is—

Oh my God.

Oh my God.

Fuck fuck fuck fuck fuck.

There isn't even time for me to react, except to clasp Gabe's hand more tightly in what I wish was a warning but which he'll just see as a sign of affection or nerves. As my gaze darts frantically around the table, some part of me registers Mairead's smile and Torty's eyes widening as she takes in our clasped hands. But that's not the threat here.

She's not the threat.

The man sitting next to a bored-looking Brendan, swilling champagne as he recounts some tale, is the threat, because Giles Harrington not only knows exactly who I am.

He also knows exactly what my career of choice is.

CHAPTER 47

Athena

'Evening, all,' my boyfriend says. He squeezes my hand before letting it go, much to my dismay.

'Look at the two of you!' Maeve exclaims. She looks to be well-oiled already. 'Aren't you just the most gorgeous couple! Aren't they, Ro?'

I force myself to smile tightly at her. 'Good evening. It's so nice to be here.' But my gaze locks back on Giles Harrington as if magnetised, and I see the exact moment he recognises me. His jaw hangs slackly open before his mouth stretches into what can only be called a smirk. I stand there, utterly frozen, as Gabe starts speaking beside me.

'I think, Athena, you know everybody, except for Mairead's husband Peter, and one of Brendan's NEDs, Giles Harrington. Giles, Peter, this is my girlfriend, Athena.'

I should be basking in the warmth of my brand, spanking new boyfriend's pride and acknowledgment just now, but instead I am Marie Antoinette, my neck pressed to the rough wood of the guillotine, waiting for the blade to fall.

So that odious dickhead Harrington, who runs a multinational industrial machinery company, is one of Sullivan

Construction's non-executive directors. Who in the world could make this shit up?

He sets down his drink and straightens up in his chair, and I brace myself, turning my head towards Gabe for a single second, silently beseeching him to help me run for the hills or at least press rewind on this evening's progress.

This was supposed to be my night of triumph.

I'm wearing a five-figure dress.

I'm here as the girlfriend of the best man I know.

The role of a lifetime is within reach. More than that—it's *mine*.

But as I watch Harrington open his mouth, I can already feel it all fading, as though it was never anything more than the cruellest of mirages.

'Actually, Athena and I know each other, don't we, Athena?' he says, his pompous voice dripping with condescension. 'She interviewed with me once, didn't you, darling?'

Gabe stiffens next to me, and I know he's clicked. He's a gazelle, standing stock-still in the face of a lion making its presence known.

'I did.' I say nothing more. My only agency lies in how I react in this moment, and I'll be damned if I give a man like him any oxygen at all.

I don't remark on having walked away after the initial, work-focused interview because the mere thought of him getting his hands on me made my skin crawl.

I don't give him an inch, even if I suspect my presence is an unpleasant reminder of the stinging rejection insecure guys like him struggle to shrug off.

'What a small world,' Brendan observes, but he says it lazily, like his interest level in our acquaintance is close to zero.

'Athena's your assistant, is she?' Harrington asks Gabe. When he answers, I can hear the guardedness in his usually open and friendly voice. He takes my hand again and I squeeze it gratefully.

'She was, but she's going to run our foundation for us going forward, and we're all very excited. Anyway, moving on, let's—'

Harrington leans forward, the heavy thud of his forearms on the table telling me he's already had too much of the free-flowing champagne. 'Athena is supposed to be *very* good at what she does. She's pricey, but I bet she's worth every penny.' He leans over and addresses Gabe's mother directly. 'Did you know, Maeve, that Athena offers a very "full" range of services that go far beyond the usual? I wonder if your son was making use of all of them, but—'

'That's enough,' Gabe snaps, but Maeve is looking at Harrington with confusion. I can see her trying very hard to piece together what he's insinuating.

'What do you mean, exactly?' she asks him, squinting in concentration.

Please no please no please no.

'This lovely young *lady*'—he imbues the word *lady* with all of the contempt he can muster—'is a very discreet, *very* expensive whore, and you can bet that if Gabriel here has her on his payroll then she's been making sure the good priest sees heaven every single day of the week. Monday to Friday, anyway.'

He's done it.

He's outed me, just days after I lowered my walls and peeled myself open and laid myself raw for Gabe, days after I decided that vulnerability was a better look than implacability, after choosing to believe that audacity was a good thing, a brave thing that the universe rewarded with dream jobs and good men and legitimacy.

If I wasn't the person upon whose forehead Harrington had just branded with a scarlet *A*, I'd be tempted to laugh at the collective gasp around the table, which is *Bridgerton* level of scandalised.

Ronan looks utterly winded. I'd say Maeve, whose face is turning bright red, is in serious danger of some kind of cardiac episode. Eleanor is staring at me as if I might infect her with syphilis if I so much as pass her the butter dish, while Torty has the triumphant gleam in her eye of someone who's just been passed the winning hand. I have no idea why she looks so pleased with herself. Surely, if I'm a pro, she must suspect that my moves are even more elite than she thought them?

Brendan sits back in his chair with a thump, his tickled expression that of a man who realises his virtuous brother is actually a force to be reckoned with.

'It's not true, is it, son?' Ronan asks, the bewilderment in his voice heartbreakingly evident.

So I do the only thing you can do when you're Icarus, and the wax is melting, dripping, and the beautifully crafted wings that bore you so high into that sun-drenched expanse of possibility and false hope are failing you.

I go to take my leave. To step out of the sun's heat and seek safety in the darkness. I can't stay here, and I can't listen to Gabe trying to defend me. *Us.*

'I'm afraid you'll all have to excuse me,' I say, willing my voice to stay steady as I tug my hand from Gabe's tight grip, drawing on every ounce of training I've had in the cultural and diplomatic circles of Europe to hold myself together. 'I hope you have a lovely evening.'

Before I go, I fix my gaze on Harrington, and only then do I unleash the full force of my freezing cold fury. 'And *you* are in breach of an NDA. I hope you have a good lawyer.'

CHAPTER 48

Gabe

She may talk a good game, but her lovely face is brittle with devastation as she turns away, and righteous indignation hits me with the full force of a tidal wave as I go after her.

'Athena. Wait.'

She doesn't. She keeps walking, an impossibly elegant figure weaving briskly between the half-filled tables. I catch her up as she clears the dining area, my hand going to her arm. 'Sweetheart. Wait.'

'Don't make a scene,' she hisses, avoiding my eye.

'I'm not—I'm—I'm *so* sorry. I'm so, so sorry.'

'I need to get my coat.'

'Please come back.' Even as the plea leaves my mouth, I know it's useless. Of course she's not going to go back there, to the table where some cunt has just insulted her and outed her in front of my entire family.

'Not happening.' She strides over to the cloakroom's hatch, which is deserted except for a lone attendant, and lays her tiny bag down on the counter so she can find her ticket.

Tonight was supposed to be our night. *Her* night. I'm

getting up there to make a speech about our philanthropic commitments over the next decade and beyond, and my plan is—*was*—to name Athena as the new CEO of the foundation.

She's supposed to be basking in this unshakeable belief my family has in her to steward our wealth, and instead she's scurrying to the cloakroom like she has something to be ashamed of.

It's not okay.

If anything, I'm the one who should be called out. I abandoned my calling and hired a woman to fuck me as soon as I got rid of my dog collar. I'm the immoral, despicable miscreant here, not her. And I'm sure my family will reinforce that message to me in style, but I couldn't give a flying fuck.

All I care about is that the woman I've fallen for has been made to feel less than on my watch, because of *my* sins.

'Let me take you home,' I whisper. 'I don't want you going out there alone.'

That gets her to look at me. Her eyes are clear, but it seems to me every nerve ending in her body is vibrating. I know her well enough to see the effort it's costing her merely to hold her shit together for the sake of propriety.

'I am perfectly capable of getting myself home, Gabe, and you have a speech to give.'

'You're more important. Nothing else matters except making sure you're okay.'

She purses her lips as though my lack of backbone is disappointing. Every wall I've had the indescribable pleasure of taking down is back up in force. My goddess has taken up her sword and shield, and she's not about to let a single mortal see the extent of her wounds.

Not even me.

She fiddles with the clasp on her little handbag as she answers. 'That's not true. All this matters. I need to regroup, and you need to go and do some damage limitation with your family. And *then* you need to go and tell that roomful of people exactly what the Sullivans are committed to doing.'

'Athena. Please.' I sigh, sensing defeat. 'Can I come over later?'

'You cannot.' She looks at me, and for just a second, I see the hurt splitting her heart open. 'Leave me alone, Gabe. I'll see you tomorrow.'

I don't know why her request that I leave her alone for the rest of the night hits so hard, but it does. It feels both ridiculous and ominous that she would shut me out like this. There are depths to this woman that still feel fathomless, and it's clear I've only explored the ones she is happy for me to explore. As I make my way back to the table, I channel my anger. Anger is good: it's an active emotion, an empowering emotion.

I can do something with this.

Back at the table, everyone is murmuring, whispering, heads inclined in confidence. Harrington is still there. I take my seat, because I have absolutely not been brought up to make a scene, and I have every interest in containing this scandal as much as humanly possible.

Athena's words come back to me.

Damage limitation.

The only way to approach this is to go on the offensive. If my family has the slightest expectation that they'll receive some kind of apology or explanation from me for my behaviour, they will be sorely disappointed. I need to get on the front foot here.

I lean forward and jab my finger at Harrington.

'You. Get out. You are no longer welcome here. And let

me reiterate Athena's reminder to you—you are in breach of a watertight NDA.' I should know. I signed one before I even saw Athena's portfolio. 'So if you value your solvency, I'd keep your pathetic mouth shut.'

He sneers at me. 'Jesus Christ, she has you wrapped around her little finger. That pussy must be—'

'*Out,*' I say as loudly as I dare.

'You heard my brother,' Brendan says. 'Fuck off. You're a disgrace.'

'Brendan!' Mum says, seemingly more shocked by her sons' indiscretions than her guest's.

'Get out.' Brendan's tone brooks no argument. His eyes slide to me in a silent gesture of support. 'Now.'

Harrington rolls his eyes before pushing away his chair and getting inelegantly to his feet. As soon as he's lumbered off, I put my head in my hands and sigh heavily.

Mum's voice cuts through the stunned silence. 'Gabriel. What in the name of God were—'

The judgement in her voice snaps me out of my defeated slump. I sit up straight.

'*No.* Listen to me very carefully, okay? I'm only going to say this once.' I look around the table, meeting each person's eyes as I do and gathering every remaining ounce of priestly gravitas which, now that my sordid little secret is out, is probably not very much. I take a deep breath.

'I am not discussing this right now. The *only* thing I care about is the wellbeing of my girlfriend, who has just been intimidated and belittled while a guest of this family. I will go up there and make that speech, I will do us proud. But what you heard just now is nobody's business except for mine and Athena's. Do you understand? *Nobody's.*'

I glare extra forcefully at Eleanor and Torty, because I can feel the judgement radiating off the pair of them. 'I swear to

God, if anyone in the office comes to hear about this, I will be forced to assume the leak came from you. Is that clear?'

They both nod, wide-eyed with shock. I have never spoken to any of my employees this way. I turn and address my family.

'You'll have questions. I'll address those another time. For now, I'm going to go and find somewhere quiet to prepare for my speech.'

With that, I get up and go to find one of the organisers. Thank fuck my speech is scheduled to be during the starters, so I don't have too long to wait. The woman I find leads me to an empty room off the ballroom. As she shuts the door behind me and the din from the guests subsides, I collapse gratefully into a chair.

I will pray to the Lord for courage and resilience and wisdom. I will pray to Our Lady, entreating her to have compassion for this wretched sinner and to help him restore the fortunes of the young woman about who he cares so deeply.

It's only the thought of Athena, guarded and brittle and so intent on my forging ahead with my speech, that galvanises me. However unlikely it's now looking that my family will support her spearheading this foundation, I know how disappointed, how disgusted, she'd be if I let this opportunity slide.

I pull my notes out of my jacket pocket and survey them despondently. I cannot name Athena as the foundation's new head tonight; that much is clear.

I can, however, drop the bombshell that the Sullivan family has confirmed its commitment to giving away six billion pounds over the next twenty years.

And I can also announce our proposed rebrand for the Rath Mor Foundation—the rebrand that was supposed to be a surprise for my girlfriend tonight.

The Audacity Foundation.

PART THREE
Communio (Communion)

CHAPTER 49

Athena

I have one day of work to get through before I can permit myself to shatter and regroup over the weekend.

Eight to six.

Ten hours.

I can do this.

The worst part won't even be facing Eleanor and Torty. They can go fuck themselves, for all I care.

No, the worst part will be having to spend the day with the man I've fallen so hard for and know that he will very probably not be strong enough to do what needs to be done. If I know Gabe, he wants to bleed his heart out and fall on his sword and be my saviour. He wants to hope and, let's be honest, pray, for the impossible.

I'll have to be strong for both of us.

I'll have to be the one to pull the plug on all the enchanting things he's promised me for the future and made me want so very badly.

I texted George last night on my way home, alerting him to what had gone down. His reply was every bit as righteously indignant as I could have hoped, and I know he'll do what he can to make today as tolerable as possible.

I also texted Gabe last night. I didn't want to, but I needed to know what I would be dealing with this morning.

> Do I need to worry about this leaking at the office tomorrow?

> No. I've put the fear of God into Eleanor and Torty.

> OK good

> I'm so, so sorry, sweetheart xxx

I reacted to that one with a heart but left it unanswered. There was nothing to say, really.

The only call I placed was to Camille, who reacted exactly how I knew she would and how I needed her to: with a brisk promise to enlist the immediate assistance of Seraph's General Counsel, the inimitable Jenny Baldwin, who would quote-unquote *take that man to the cleaners and make him rue the day he crossed you.*

Despite my shitty night's sleep, I look good. I haven't cried, which is one positive. I haven't allowed myself to.

Tomorrow, I'll fall apart.

Today is about survival.

Thus, my hair is sleek and my makeup perfect and my tailored black shift dress beyond reproach. I'm so refreshed, I look like I spent the evening in a spa. I'm ready to do battle, and I shall emerge victorious as long as I can keep Gabe and his baby blues at arm's length. That man's warm hearted saviour complex is his greatest strength and his greatest weakness, which makes it *my* biggest headache right now.

I'm sitting at my desk when George appears, holding a

small to-go cup that I'm hoping is a double espresso from the heavenly Italian place down the road.

'Liquid courage.' He places it next to this week's beautiful floral arrangement.

'Angel.'

'How are you doing? I hate this for you. Though I love that you are physically embodying *I Can Do It With a Broken Heart* vibes.'

That, I realise, is exactly what I'm embodying, and it makes me feel the tiniest bit better. I'm in good company with this over-functioning martyrdom I've adopted.

'I'm as well as can be expected.'

'You look fabulous. How do you look so fabulous?'

'Under-eye patches this morning. A lot of concealer, then light-reflecting highlighter.'

He nods his approval. 'You've got this, missy. Now, do we think the Angel Gabriel is going to float in here and try to save you?'

'Absolutely. And, of course, you and I both know that what he really needs is to be saved from himself.'

'Ain't that the truth. Buzz me if you need me.'

I blow him a kiss and get down to work. Happily, I have a heavy workload to keep me busy. Only a week remains until I'm due to take my leave as Gabe's EA. The plan has been that I would segue slowly into my new role, with a temporary (non-Seraph) replacement starting after that and my handing the EA work over to him or her gradually. My current plan, formed during the sleepless hours of this morning, is to hand over gradually and remotely once he or she starts. I have no intention of leaving Gabe, or Rath Mor, in the lurch.

I'm deep in a document outlining my workflows, espresso sadly long gone, when the man himself appears in the outer doorway to our office. He most markedly has *not* been employing refreshing under-eye patches this morning. He looks like shit, and my heart cracks in two so violently that I swear I can almost hear a ripping sound.

Our eyes stay locked as he pushes the door shut behind him and comes to stand in front of my desk.

'Hi, sweetheart,' is all he can manage. His eyes rove over me, and I know he's trying to understand how I'm really doing.

'Hi.'

'Can we talk?' He jerks his head to his office, and I rise, smoothing down my dress. 'Of course.' I pick up my notebook.

'You don't need your notebook,' he says with an exhale that sounds downright exasperated.

Fine.

I set it down on my desk and walk through to his office, perching myself on his sofa. I hope to God he goes for the armchair, but he doesn't, of course. He plumps himself right down next to me, the weight of his stare so loaded that I can feel it in my bones. I force myself to meet his eyes.

Oh, shit. Big mistake.

'How are you?' He slides a warm hand over my jaw, and I employ every fibre of willpower in my body not to rub my face against it.

Fine won't cut it here. I'm better off giving him just enough to reassure him that I'm telling the truth.

'I've been better, but nobody's dying. I'll survive.'

I can tell from his frown that he doesn't like that. Not one bit.

'You're allowed to feel furious and let down, you know.'

'Oh, believe me,' I say, ' I feel furious *and* let down.'

'Bren and I kicked Harrington out right after you left. I reiterated what you'd said about the NDA. I'll get our lawyers on it today.'

'Already in motion through Seraph's General Counsel.'

There's a stab of something small and warm at the knowledge that his brother has my back—or Gabe's back. That's something, at least.

He nods, impressed. 'That's my girl.'

'What's the score with your family? Did the speech go well, all things considered?' This I can do: participate in a dispassionate post-mortem of the event and help Gabe to draw up action points.

'I didn't really see them. I basically went back to the table, got rid of Harrington, told everyone else that they'd better keep their traps shut, and locked myself in an empty room to pray until the speech, which was absolutely fine.' He shrugs, and it's forlorn and defeated and boyish, and I feel like I'm bleeding through my skin for this man.

This is why we were so good together. He's too decent for this world, and I'm a merciless little go-getter, but I'm *his* go-getter, and I needed him to save my blackened soul just as he needed me to ensure that the world didn't take advantage of his soul of purest sparkling white. We were an unlikely team, but a perfect one.

'Okay,' I say, focusing on the positives. 'As long as everyone agrees to stay quiet, I can manage this.'

My brain is flipping through potential outcomes at the speed of light. As long as my cover hasn't been blown and Gabe and I don't find ourselves on the front pages of the tabloids this weekend, my future at Seraph is secure. I can go back there and take up another position easily. The thought makes me feel sick to my stomach, but it's a solid Plan B to have in my back pocket, especially since my Plan A has fallen apart quite so spectacularly.

'Seraph can help you with some talking points,' I tell him now. My eyes are darting all over his face and I realise I'm trying to drink in every last, perfect detail of him. 'For your family, I mean. They can help you spin it with them. It's not the first time a client has got caught with his proverbial pants down, and it won't be the last.'

'Sweetheart.' He releases my jaw so he can clasp both my hands on my lap. 'No one is spinning anything. I'll handle my family. At the end of the day, it's not the first time I've morally failed them. It's none of their business what I do on my own dime. Give them time and they'll come around—to our relationship and to the foundation stuff. I just need to let them vent a little. I promise, my darling.'

'Gabe. They're not going to come around to either. I'm telling you now, that plan is dead in the water. There's no point in you wasting any time or energy on it. I can help you find a new candidate, if you like. Someone who's really strategic.'

'*No.*' He shakes his head vehemently. 'Don't think like that. I promise you I'll sort it.'

One thing I've learnt in business is that when the shit hits the fan, the absolute worst things you can do are double down or indulge in any denial. You need to face the problem head-on, rip off that Band-Aid, and do what needs to be done. There's no time to grieve what could have been: you pivot, and you *act*.

Gabe is approaching this like a priest, not a businessman. I know, even if he hasn't uttered them yet, that concepts like *grace* and *redemption* and *forgiveness* are floating around inside that big, gooey heart of his.

I could tell him now that his family certainly isn't embodying *any* of those words. Gabe's excess of emotional intelligence is, in this instance, a blinker, not a benefit.

These are the big leagues. He's running a ten-figure business here. The stakes are sky fucking high, and I'm now dead wood; worse, I'm a liability. I'm blood flowing out of a gaping wound, and he needs to stem that loss *now*, no matter how brutal or painful it is, no matter how anathema to his natural compassion.

But I don't have the chance to explain any of this to him, because he does precisely the worst thing he could do in this moment.

He closes the gap between our faces and kisses me.

I forget for a second—I really do. His lips are so soft and perfect, and his hands, as they come up to cradle my head, are so loving, and my entire nervous system is spilling forth safety cues. *He has me*, it's shouting. *He's your safe place. Just relax and collapse and let him be your person.*

I open for him. His tongue is gentle and warm as he seeks to show me with his mouth what he knows I'm choosing not to hear in his words. For a moment, I allow it. I allow myself this brief, perfect fragment of time where it's just me and him and nothing is more important than the way his mouth feels against mine.

As I do, I can feel how badly my defences want to fall by the roadside. The dams of my eyelids, which have been valiantly fighting for the past twelve or thirteen hours to hold in the weight of my tears, are close to bursting. I recall Gabe speaking that line from his favourite prayer:

To thee do we send up our sorrows, mourning and weeping in this valley of tears.

I could do it. I could let him take it all; I could let someone else in to look after me, and it could feel amazing...

Until it doesn't.

Until his family forces his hand, and I'm out on my ear, having dared to dream outside of this career path I've so meticulously forged for myself, a path that until recently felt like the express lift to the top and whose walls are now closing in around me.

I jerk my head back and wrench myself away from our kiss.

We both speak at once, and I hear his words right as I say my piece.

'I love you,' he whispers, looking at me with a world of pain and joy and adoration in his blue eyes.

But it's too late. The word is already spilling from my lips.

'*Minerva.*'

His face collapses in disbelief. *Grief.* That's the only way I can describe it.

This man has watched me get dicked down by a roomful of guys and not utter a word of complaint.

And now I've safed out over a kiss from the only human being who's ever really seen me as more than a pretty face and a useful brain. The only human who believes my soul may be just as worthy of veneration as my looks and my mind.

The reason?

The raw vulnerability I feel in this moment is more life-threateningly terrifying than I have ever felt in any sexual encounter.

If this isn't rock bottom, I don't know what is.

CHAPTER 50

Athena

I will allow myself precisely one weekend to fall apart.

One.

And then I will assume my armour and sharpen my weapons and go forth in the world like the glittering goddess after who I'm named, and I will be as implacable and impenetrable as I've ever been, and woe betide anyone out there who tries to belittle me.

In the meantime, though, I have some thinking to do as I fall apart, because a call late last night from Jenny Baldwin proved eye-opening in the extreme.

When I threatened that creepy shit, Giles Harrington, it was a matter of principle. You have to learn that you don't get to mouth off and ruin someone's life without serious consequence, no matter how much of an entitled prick you are. In that moment, I lashed out in an attempt to make him feel a fraction of the fear, the disempowerment, he made me feel with his vicious, unnecessary words, and I absolutely intended to follow up and make him pay.

What I hadn't bargained on, really, was that the payout itself could be significant for me.

Not until last night, that was.

'He's the CEO of a FTSE 100 company that's already been dragged through the press for governance issues, and he's a non-exec on three more FTSE 100 boards,' Jenny pointed out with her trademark straightforwardness. 'Believe me, he does *not* want this going to court. Given that his behaviour was deliberate and malicious, I expect you're looking at seven figures, easy. Maybe as much as three million.'

I almost spat out my wine, and I'm still reeling this morning. That's *three years* of a Seraph salary. If I allow myself to press pause on my plans to ascend that express lift right to the top, then that kind of money buys me time and, more importantly, freedom.

I believe in Seraph. I wouldn't do a job like this without the protection a firm like that offers, and the team has proved its mettle over the past thirty-six hours. But, at some point, I'll want to leave and do my own thing. I've always thought that would be in a C-suite somewhere, but perhaps it's time to pull a Taylor Swift and bet on myself, to create my *own* C-Suite where I call the shots and I'm not beholden to the favour or discretion of any man for my success.

Of the many blessings Gabe has given me, one is that self-belief, and another is a taste of how it could feel to be at the helm of something important. To be the key decision maker.

Three million pounds would not only buy me a very long holiday, but it would make for a shitload of seed capital if I wanted to start my own venture. The only question is what kind of venture?

That such a huge payout would financially crucify Harrington makes the entire thing even sweeter.

As the day goes on, I cling to this idea Jenny has planted like a life raft. It's the first development that's allowed me to feel remotely empowered; it's the only thing that stops me from curling up in a ball on the floor of my shower until the water runs cold.

Because every other thing that's happened, from the loss of a dazzling new opportunity to the way I've treated the best man I've ever known, has me aghast and grief-stricken and hollowed out with shame.

Daytime drinking is something I should do more often. I pass the hours with the numbing effect of an excellent Meursault—drowning my sorrows in cheap wine would be an indignity too far. I forsake my usual educational documentaries in favour of *The Parisian Agency*, hoping in vain that the arresting combination of French house porn and French man porn will visually overwrite the image of Gabe's devastation when I safed out and basically ran from the room after his declaration of love.

Around four o'clock, Marlowe joins me on my sofa, having dispatched Tabs to a sleepover party at a friend's house. She has far too much on her plate right now to be worrying about me, but she's here anyway. I don't want to talk about any of it—I just want to watch hot French guys deal with totally contrived drama—but she stays anyway and even helps me drink.

When Sophia turns up around an hour later, looking altogether too healthy and happy and holding a massive bag of takeout from my favourite Lebanese, I'm genuinely surprised. I know for a fact she's been in Athens this week.

'How the hell did you get here?' I ask her as she engulfs me in one of her signature bear hugs.

'Camille called me yesterday morning. That fucking twat.

I knew you wouldn't reach out, you daft cow, so I thought I'd come to you. Thad gave me the jet for the weekend.'

'She and Jenny are on the case,' I mumble, leading her through to the main living area.

'As they should be, but you don't just need lawyers at a time like this. You need *friends*. Oh, hello.'

She stops in the doorway as she spots Marlowe.

'Marlowe, Sophia. Soph, Marlowe. You've heard a lot about each other, obviously. I'm just sorry you've had to meet like this.'

'Hi.' Marlowe unfolds herself elegantly from the sofa and goes to give Sophia a hug. 'It's so nice to meet you finally.'

'Likewise. She talking yet?'

'Not really,' Marlowe says, and I roll my eyes.

'Thought so.' Sophia sets the food down on my coffee table and looks around my home, taking in the trio of French doors overlooking a quiet, South Kensington garden square, the abstract art on the walls and the oversized furniture. 'The pad's looking great. Clearly that priest of yours is paying you far too much.'

'Not any more.'

'The only thing she's been saying is that she feels like Icarus,' my traitorous friend says, strolling over to the drinks cabinet to fetch Sophia a wine glass.

'Oh, excellent. So we've reached the stage of conflating our experience with epic Greek tragedies, have we?' Sophia asks, kneeling to unpack the Lebanese. She's every inch the glamorous jetsetter in her clingy Skims maxi and white trainers. She looks at me pointedly. '*"Never regret thy fall, O Icarus of the fearless flight, For the greatest tragedy of them all, Is never to feel the burning light."* Oscar Wilde, my love. Well, we think it was him. Can't know for sure.'

I roll my eyes again. I see a lot of eye-rolling in my near

future. 'You make it so easy to forget you had a half-decent education.'

'St Paul's Girls and Stanford, baby. Don't for a second think my tits are bigger than my brains.' She cups her boobs to underscore this statement, and I catch Marlowe staring at her as if she's some exotic yet incomprehensible creature in a zoo. 'Anyway, the point is, you *know* we fly high. You *know* we burn bright. We're Seraphim! That's what we do, remember? And when we fall, we may fall hard, but we get the fuck back up again and dust ourselves off and continue on our mission of world domination.'

'You're right, of course,' I say stiffly. I'm not sure I have the emotional capacity for a heart-to-heart with Sophia today. She'll delve too deeply.

'What's with the stunning dress?' she asks. I may have hung the Gossamer dress off the top of a large oil painting in the middle of my living room. It makes my heart ecstatic and devastated all at once to look at it, but I can't bear to put it away in my wardrobe. It's the perfect visual reminder of all I've lost, of quite how fleeting my triumph was.

'That's the dress Gabe bought her,' Marlowe offers unhelpfully. 'The ten grand one.'

Sophia lets out a low whistle. 'Wowzers. It seems we may have a few more emotions going on here than a certain someone is letting on. Okay, honey.' She gets to her feet and steers me to the sofa gently. 'This is where you tell us everything.'

I start with the status of my legal claim, telling her what Jenny told me. She squeals and claps her hands together in glee.

'It's poetic, isn't it?' Marlowe asks.

'That this turd went full patriarchal bullshit on her, and now his patriarchal wealth will free her from more patriarchal control? Um, yes.'

Cue eye-roll number three.

She has a point, though. They both do. In trying to entrap me, to subjugate me, Harrington may just have set me free.

'This is important,' Sophia continues softly. 'It may have felt like checkmate at the time, hon, but it's not. Women like us always have agency. There's always a countermove. We have power, and we have allies. Don't forget that.'

'Thanks,' I mutter. I'm more touched than I'd like to admit, because one of my predominant emotions since the incident has been isolation.

'Why don't we talk about the touchy-feely stuff?' Sophia suggests. 'Have a sip of wine, vomit out the stuff that hurts, and then gorge yourself on kibbeh while Aunt Sophia lectures you on all the things you don't want to hear but absolutely have to, okay?'

'Good luck with that,' Marlowe tells her.

'Oh, I don't need luck. I'm relentless. Now, drink—and purge.'

I drink. 'There's not much to tell. The foundation role isn't on the table anymore, nor is my relationship with Gabe.' The phrase *relationship with Gabe* should be enough to make me giddy, but instead it cuts like a razorblade through my heart. 'I misjudged the situation, and it cost me, so all there is to do is regroup.'

The other two share one of *those* looks.

'Honestly, don't do that or I'll kick you both out.'

'Has Gabe actually dumped you, and has he told you the foundation's off the table?' Sophia wants to know.

No, he told me he loved me and I safed out on him. 'No to both, but I can read a room. This is his family's legacy. You should have seen the way they looked at me—like I was some kind of satanic whore who'd tempted their lovely, golden son.'

On my other side, Marlowe snorts. 'The same golden boy

who left the priesthood and then hired someone to have sex with him at work. Like he's the innocent party here.'

'That's between him and his family. I had them eating out of the palm of my hand, and now it's all undone. They want this foundation to be high profile. There's no way on earth they'll put a woman like me in the seat.'

'*A woman like you.* Wow.' Sophia nudges me with her shoulder. 'Okay, so I see what we're dealing with now. I thought better of you, hon, I really did.'

I give her my best side-eye. 'What do you mean?'

'Did you know,' she begins conversationally, 'that shame is a social emotion? That means it's learnt. It's not inherent, like joy, or fear, or anger. That's why sociopaths tend not to feel shame. It's far harder for them to learn.'

'I know it's a social emotion. That's why I've always been so contemptuous of it.'

'Mmm-hmm. And do you know what else it is?'

'I have a feeling you're about to tell me.'

'I am. If you're feeling shame, then that's because you're internalising *someone else's shit.* Close your eyes.'

I glare at her.

'Go on, close 'em, bish. Okay, good. Now, imagine shame is a horrible, itchy, moth-eaten sweater, but it belongs to someone else. Got it?'

I nod against my will. I'll go along with this charade, if only to get her off my back.

'Right, and imagine they want to get rid of it, because who wouldn't, so they take it off and they make you put it on. But the kicker is, they're not getting rid of their sweater—all they've done is duplicate it. How does it feel?'

'The sweater?'

'Yeah. Describe it.'

I think. 'It's revolting. Scratchy. I don't know where it's

been.' I actually roll my shoulders in disgust. 'I don't want to wear it.'

'*Good*. So what are you going to do? Because no one is making you keep this thing on except you.'

'I'm going to take it off.'

'Show me.'

I mime crossing my arms over my body and tugging the imaginary sweater off over my head.

'And what are you going to say?'

'I don't want it. I won't wear it. This isn't my sweater.'

'Louder.'

'I said, it's not my *fucking* sweater.'

CHAPTER 51

Athena

'So you're really not going to fight for the foundation?' Marlowe asks, a couple of glasses of wine after our little role play. The takeaway has been decimated, and my stomach is uncomfortably bloated. Alas, heartbreak and humiliation haven't hurt my appetite. If anything, I've spent this weekend eating and drinking my feelings.

'No. It was a glimpse of the kind of thing I can set my mind to, if I think outside that very corporate box I've been in. I don't ever want my role to be dependent on other people's goodwill, though.'

'The good thing is that you've got the freedom to choose your next move,' Sophia muses. 'Whatever you do next will come from a position of strength. Hopefully you feel like you still have autonomy.'

I nod. 'I do. I definitely felt like it had been taken from me the other night, and it was the most terrifying feeling in the world. I don't ever want to feel like that again.' Everything I've done in my career at Seraph has been about creating agency. About building a career on *my* terms. I won't jeopardise that again.

'And you really won't give Gabe a chance?'

'It's not about giving him a chance.' I run my fingertip along what's left of the creamy hummus and suck it. 'It's about walking away to save him.'

This is something I've gained enormous clarity on over the course of my navel-gazing this weekend. Walking away from Gabe isn't cowardly—it's noble. It reminds me so poignantly of the most heartbreaking line from one of my all-time favourite books, Edith Wharton's *The Age of Innocence.* In it, Ellen Olenska—a woman as fallen and scandalous as me—tells her own good man, Newland Archer: *'I can't love you unless I let you go'.*

In her case, it alludes to his engagement to her cousin. If he broke it off and eloped with her, he wouldn't be the man of integrity she loved. In my case, it's about bowing out gracefully so that Gabe can step into his own destiny.

This is a man who gave up everything to be deemed *good*, only to admit defeat when he couldn't believe that God's grace extended to him. I sincerely believe that the priesthood was the dress rehearsal for Gabe: it was the laboratory in which he explored his altruism and the gym in which he exercised his pastoral muscles.

Now he's in the big leagues, and he can go forth to win back, in his eyes, the respect of his family and the grace of God. I can see, probably more clearly than he can, how intrinsic the foundation will be to him finding his sense of purpose.

He's finally finding his path, stepping into his power, and I won't let him feel unworthy all over again. I refuse to sully this shining future he has in any way.

If anything, we came into each other's lives at the perfect time. He modelled for me a relationship that transcended the transactional, and his professional faith in me was the kindling that inflamed my imagination, allowing me to scale new heights of ambition.

If I can walk away knowing that I, in some small way, set him on a path that is good and right and true, that is worthy of his hopes and dreams, then I'll consider it an honour.

'So,' I ask Marlowe an hour later. 'What's the latest on Tabs?'

I have to brace myself for her answer. My losing out on a job and love is... whatever. A gut punch. But this is a little girl's life we're talking about.

'She has a heart condition, is that right?' Sophia asks. I can see the reticence on her face, too. Talking about sick children is a whole other level of traumatic.

Marlowe nods slowly. 'Yeah, she was born with it. It's called Tetralogy of Fallot, which is a bit of a mouthful, but it means that the pulmonary valve, or the valve leading from her right ventricle to her lungs, was too narrow when she was born, so she couldn't get enough blood flow to the lungs. She had open heart surgery to insert a new valve when she was born, and another one at three, but she's outgrown that one now.'

The colour has drained from Soph's face. 'Jesus Christ. I'm so, so sorry. That is the absolute worst.'

'Thanks. And yep. It's shit.'

'How do they know she's outgrown it?'

'They have various markers they follow—her ECGs are showing strain across the valve, and her oxygen sats aren't great, especially when she exercises. Which is even more shitty because she really likes sports.'

It sounds ominous when Marlowe says it, but the anecdotal symptoms are even worse. Tabs is getting more and more winded during any physical activity, even play, and she's taking longer to recover. That lack of oxygen is manifesting as everything from headaches and dizziness to a horrible blue tinge around her mouth after exertion. The knowledge that Tabs' little body is unable to provide her with enough oxygenated blood is fucking terrifying.

'Fuck,' Sophia says, pulling her feet up and crossing her legs. She twists sideways on the sofa so she can get a clear view across me to Marlowe. 'So they need to upsize the valve?'

'You've got it.'

'And the NHS can do that?'

Marlowe and I exchange a look.

'They can do it via open heart surgery,' I butt in, 'but some private hospitals in the US could do it laparoscopically at far less risk.'

'And a six figure price tag,' Marlowe points out. 'Mid-six figures, all in.'

Soph sits back, realisation dawning. 'And you don't have that money.'

'Nowhere near.'

'I do,' I point out. 'And she's my goddaughter.'

'I'm not letting Athena fork out that kind of money when she's done what she's done to earn it,' Marlowe insists.

Sophia blows out a breath. 'I'm beginning to feel like a relationship counsellor here, but I have to admit I get that. I also get Athena's frustration.' She turns to Marlowe, looking her up and down. 'There's nothing stopping you from earning that money yourself.'

'What do you mean?' I ask.

She grins. 'Just join Seraph. Easy. Look at you. You're absolutely gorgeous.'

Marlowe takes a huge gulp of wine and promptly chokes on it.

'She doesn't do sex,' I tell Soph.

'I hate to be that person,' she deadpans, 'but the existence of a kid kind of suggests otherwise.'

'She doesn't do sex *because of the kid.*' My stage whisper may be a little loud, but I'm at least a bottle of wine down.

'I had a fling with my professor in my first year of uni,' Marlowe tells Sophia. 'He turned out to be an idiot with bad condom skills, but I got the best thing in my life out of it—Tabs. I don't really do the sex thing anymore, though.'

'Hmm.' Soph sounds like Marlowe is a total conundrum, which, if your attitude to sex is as liberated as hers is, I can understand. I turn my head back to her. Sitting between them is beginning to feel like a tennis match.

'How does the idea of what Athena and I do for a living make you feel?'

'Absolutely physically ill,' Marlowe says immediately.

'Okay then. Not the most promising start. Do you find it morally problematic, or it just gives you the ick?'

'It just gives me the ick,' she insists.

'Ever read spicy romance books?' Soph wonders aloud.

'I'm a single mum. What do you think? I have to get my kicks from somewhere.'

Sophia pounces. 'Aha! So you do have a sex drive?'

'Of course I do. I just don't ever want to do *any* of those things in real life,' Marlowe says, and Sophia cackles.

'Look, babes, I get it. You got messed around and now you've got a sick little girl to look after. None of that would give me the horn, either. But look.' She leans forward, and I sit back so she can have this moment of connection with Marlowe. 'These roles pay like six figures a month. You get twenty-five grand for the first audition, and you get paid up front. You turn tricks for a month or two and then: boom. You're done. Surgery paid for. You can quit.'

I shoot her a disapproving look. Much as I'm Team

Marlowe, I don't approve of anyone sullying the Seraph name by playing the system. Besides, there's no way Marlowe would even last two months. She'd probably clutch her pearls and run out of the audition before letting a guy anywhere near her, bless her.

'I think encouraging Marls to go out for a single date with a nice guy is a more appropriate next step for her love life than throwing her into the Seraph shark tank,' I protest. Talk about a proposed baptism of fire.

But, to my horror, my gorgeous, prudish friend is staring at my gorgeous, sex-obsessed friend as though she holds the key to all the answers of the universe. When Marlowe speaks, her voice is shaky but determined, and I know Soph has somehow unleashed her fiercest inner mama bear. The one that would sell her own soul to save her cub.

'You really think I could do it?'

CHAPTER 52

Gabe

When a former priest realises he needs his very own *come to Jesus* moment, you can be sure it's a low point.

I thought I was done with these revelations. When it came, the epiphany that I needed to—that I *could*—walk away from the priesthood hit me like a cricket bat to the head. Now, though, I face nothing but a muddy brain and nebulous plans and conflict upon conflict when it comes to doing what is right.

The one truth over which I have clarity—the *only* truth, in fairness—is that I love Athena, and I am not prepared to lose her.

Night after night of obsessing and questioning and driving myself crazy, wondering if I did the right thing by abandoning my vows, and the clearest sign God has given me belongs in human form.

Everything I've done has led me to her, and I will not walk away.

The memory of her face as she safed out yesterday is so seared onto my consciousness that it affords me no reprieve. It was so fucking shocking. If she'd kneed me in the balls, kicked me in the stomach, it couldn't have hurt more.

Her show of detachment doesn't fool me for a second, but Athena is a complex woman. On the surface, she's the most self-assured person I know. But I can't quite believe that anyone who knows themselves, at their very core, to be enough, would work so hard. Push so hard. *Fight* so hard.

I need some perspective. The longer I put off speaking to my family, the worse I'm making the situation, but I could use a pep talk from someone who isn't saddled with generations of Catholic guilt.

There is no one *less* saddled with generations of Catholic guilt than Anton Wolff, so I call him and beg him to let me buy him dinner.

God knows, he'll earn it.

It's not until I get to the discreet Italian Anton has suggested in Chelsea that I realise he's rallied the troops. Honestly, I'm relieved to see some friendly faces. I've been sitting on my hands all day in an attempt to respect Athena's need for space, but fuck, has it been hard work.

Anton has roped in his successor, Max, who knows Athena far too well for my taste, Max's husband, Dex, and our mate Adam.

'Christ, you look rough,' Max observes, reaching for one of two open bottles of Brunello. 'Have a drink, mate.'

'Thanks,' I mutter. 'It's been a painful couple of days.' I sink into my seat and run my hand through my hair before blowing out a breath. 'And now I've pissed off most of the Alchemy women, I imagine. They've all been abandoned on a Saturday night.'

'Full disclosure.' Max nudges the bread basket towards me before pouring a generous measure of wine into my glass. 'They're all having a movie night together at Adam's. We were at a loose end, so we thought we'd tag along. As long as you're less tedious than the entire *Pitch Perfect* franchise, you're all good.'

I grimace. 'Not sure I can promise that.'

Anton grins wolfishly. 'If Athena's involved, you can bet it'll be entertaining. Shoot.'

I take a slug of the excellent red before giving a terse synopsis of the main events: Athena and I agreeing to give a proper relationship a go; my suggestion that she lead the foundation; her bold recommendation that we commit to giving away most of our wealth; the gala; Harrington's appearance; Athena's exit; my family's utter moral outrage; and, as a *pièce de résistance*, my declaration of love right as she safed out on me.

While Dex and Adam have the decency to look dismayed on my behalf, Max and Anton howl with laughter at that last part.

'Fuck you,' I tell them.

'Sorry.' Anton attempts unsuccessfully to compose his craggy features into a semblance of sympathy. 'It's just... you're a brave man, mate. Rather you than me. That woman doesn't pull her punches, does she?'

'I've never known Athena to bottle it,' Max adds. 'She's fearless. You must have scared the absolute shit out of her. Rather—this whole situation has scared the shit out of her.'

'It was horrible.' I force myself to relive her happiness, her triumph, as we walked in that night. Her excitement over chatting with Dame Sarah Blackwood. She was on fire—until that slimy bastard went for her. Watching the change in her, the way that fire went instantly out, was fucking horrific. I never, ever want to see her that hurt, that humiliated, again.

'I'm devastated for you both,' Adam says. 'Nat loved her —she hasn't stopped talking about her. Sounds like they got on like a house on fire. She said the dress was perfect on her. I can't believe she got shafted like that on her big night.'

'Speaking as a recovering Catholic,' Dex says with a shudder, 'I'm right there with her. I can't imagine how awful she felt when your entire family looked at her like she was a disgusting little sinner. Jesus Christ, I've been there. That lens is just so toxic.'

'That's the thing, it's just a lens,' Adam points out. 'I've been there too, but in my case I deserved it. I committed a terrible crime. I'm still amazed any of Nat's family give me the time of day. But with you and Athena, who the fuck cares? It's none of their business, at the end of the day. If you love her, be with her. It's very straightforward, from where I'm sitting.'

'I'm still tickled pink that you two have fallen for each other,' Anton admits. 'I thought you might have been a nice, juicy challenge for her. You know, corrupt the former priest who's still stuck in moral purgatory. But she fell hard, by the sounds of it.'

I'm quiet for a moment before I say, 'We both did.' I turn to Adam. 'The reason it's not that straightforward is because of the foundation. I promised her I'd sort it out, but I'm seriously doubtful that my family will give her their blessing now. They're so focused on the image we portray to the world. I suspect Mum would rather die than sit back and let a former sex worker take the reins.

'And because I promised her the earth and now have to renege, I'm bloody petrified that she'll walk and go straight back to Seraph, looking for another client. She's so hurt, and she's so armoured up—you should see her.'

Anton takes a thoughtful sip of his wine. 'Regarding the foundation, who appoints the CEO?'

'Me, in theory. It's a family trust, and everyone should

have a say, but it falls under the Rath Mor umbrella, so it's ultimately my decision.'

'Hmm.' His tone is so ominous that I find myself jumping in to expand.

'This is my chance to prove myself. My mother is still getting over the shame of her son leaving the priesthood. You can imagine.' I look at Dex, who grimaces sympathetically. 'I want to do them proud, but I want to do myself proud, too. I walked away from a vocation that simply didn't feel authentic, no matter how hard I tried, and I came on board to do this. And for the first time in a long time I actually have purpose. I want to do this right.'

'If you want to do it right, you need to get the right person on board,' Max says flatly. 'And you won't find anyone better to run it than Athena. That's the truth.'

'He's right,' Anton offers. 'She's the dog's bollocks. You don't want some ghastly do-gooder running it—you want a fucking shark, and that's what she'll bring to the table.'

I smile, despite myself. 'That's exactly why I offered her the job.'

'It's bloody genius,' Max says. 'Honestly. You realise the universe served you up Athena and solved all your life's problems in one go?'

'Hearing my fiancé talk about the universe is still really weird,' Dex confesses. 'Darcy's really getting to you.'

Darcy is Dex and Max's fiancée and Gen Wolff's younger sister. The guys proposed to her a couple of weeks ago in Como and they're all getting married this summer. I've only met her a handful of times, but she strikes me as far more of a free spirit than either of them.

'Hearing you call me your fiancé is still really fucking amazing,' Max counters, and they grin at each other. The love in their eyes hits me hard. There's something seriously brave about what they're doing. Not only has Dex had to walk away from a relationship with his uber-Catholic father, who cate-gorically would not accept his queerness, but the three of them have embraced their unconventional love in the face of wide-spread scrutiny. After all, Max is the only openly queer CEO in the FTSE 100 currently.

Compared to what they've had to face, my own woes seem relatively immaterial.

I love a woman.

She, I choose to believe, loves me.

We're both free agents.

This problem should not be insurmountable.

'Let's cut to the chase,' Adam says after our main courses have been served, and I'm reminded of the benefit of having your sounding board be made up of serious hitters with excep-tional cognitive abilities. 'And I say this all with the compla-cency of someone who is not in your shoes, mate. But you need to find a way to hold onto her, first and foremost. You love her, it sounds like you're great together, and there's no fucking way you should let an irrelevant dipshit like Harrington ruin your chances of happiness.'

'Amen to that,' Max says through a mouthful of gnocchi.

'Second—go talk some sense into your family. If you can't appeal to whatever Catholic baggage they're holding onto, appeal to their business brains. You say Athena's the best person for the job. Sell them on that. And third.'

He pauses, scrunching up his face. 'For what it's worth, when you talk about the plans you have for the foundation, it strikes me that you've found all that authenticity and purpose you've been searching for for so long. And it sounds like Athena's vision, and all her experience, has been a huge driving factor. So, for God's sake, find a way to do that together and *let yourself enjoy it*, mate.'

I nod soberly. When he puts it like that, it all sounds so sensible. So feasible.

'Can I make an observation?' Dex asks.

'Of course.' I gesture with my fork.

'Some of these blocks you're feeling... that reticence could be coming from a place of feeling like you have to keep on atoning for what you did, so you're playing this role of the dutiful son. But the irony is that if you follow what your heart is telling you—both in your love life and regarding the foundation—you stand a far better chance of stepping into your purpose. Because, let me tell you, otherwise you risk falling into that same trap over and over, and living a quiet, small life, and you'll never feel like you're enough, because everything you do is for the wrong reasons.'

He takes a deep breath. 'One of the things that helped my sister and me finally stand up to our dad was realising that nothing we did would ever be enough. We'd never be pure enough, or devout enough for him. At the end of the day, your parents sound way more rational than my father, but, even if they never come around, it's better to live with their disapproval than your regrets.'

And there's my *come to Jesus* moment.

'At the end of the day,' Max says briskly, 'while we all think you should have a damn good try at changing your family's minds, you can't live for them. Their reactions are not your responsibility, nor are they Athena's, and the sooner that becomes your embodied truth, the sooner you'll be free to live your life.'

'I can't believe you just used the phrase *embodied truth* with a straight face,' Anton quips.

'Texting Darcy right now.' Dex reaches for his phone.

'Let me bring this home in slightly cruder, less beautiful language than Dex here managed,' Anton says. 'One. Athena is hot as fuck and one of the most incredible women I've ever met. I never thought a man would get her to want to settle down, and you have, mate. So don't fuck it up. Two. If she's the best person for the foundation job, which it sounds like she is, then persuade your family of what needs to be done.

'Which brings me to point three. Don't take offence at this, but now's the time to step up and manage this situation like a CEO and not a fucking priest. This is the first real crisis you've had since you took the reins, which makes you luckier than most. You have a very important vision for the future, and you've found the perfect person to execute that vision for you.

'So if some members of your board think they can discriminate based on that individual's sexual choices and not on their actual experience and qualifications, then you have to shut that shit down.'

Max nods his approval. 'Your biggest challenge as a CEO is always going to be making those judgement calls. You need to know that you have what it takes to step up and wield your power when it matters. Athena's not weak. She doesn't need you to protect her. But in this moment, she bloody well needs you to fight for her. So stop trying to be noble and keep everyone happy, and fight for what you know to be right.'

He points his knife at me as he delivers his parting shot. 'And, by the way, mate, the correct moral choice isn't always the one that seems most seemly, or "proper". Life would be very boring if it was.'

CHAPTER 53

Gabe

It's with fire in my belly that I drive up to my parents' for Sunday lunch. Let it never be said that my mother will let her moral outrage get in the way of an opportunity to feed up her children.

As I head out of London, I muse about something Max said towards the end of last night. I asked him if he'd ever thought about backing away from Dex so as to save him from having to tear his family apart. Max stared at me as if I'd lost the plot.

'Christ, no. Not for a single second. I needed to save him from his family—and from himself.'

It makes me wonder why Athena's been so quick to put distance between us, and all I can conclude is that it's some combination of self-protection—the nature with which our secret was revealed and my family's reaction cut her to the core, after all—and a horror of being the person who diverted me further from my journey to find grace and purpose.

After all, she knows I've struggled with both. She knows my life choices, from leaving the priesthood to hiring her— have sat uneasily with me at times. She jokes about my "goodness". In her mind, she seems to have cast herself as Mary Magdalene, and it's as if the fact of seeing herself through my family's eyes has confirmed her worst fears about herself.

The Athena I know, the Athena Max and Anton know, is fearless. Fierce. It makes me wonder if she's willing to walk away because she doesn't think I can handle it if she stakes her claim on me.

It's about time I show her—and my family—that I can.

Max's other indictment rings in my ears now.

Athena's not weak. She doesn't need you to protect her. But in this moment, she bloody well needs you to fight for her. So stop trying to be noble and keep everyone happy, and fight for what you know to be right.

He's quite right.

She's not weak.

She doesn't need my protection, nor should she feel like I need hers.

But what she does need in this moment, and what I can damn well provide, is *vindication*.

I intend to procure this position for her because she's earned it. No more, no less. The vision for the foundation as it stands currently is all hers. It's a sacrilege to think she should have to hand the reins of that beautiful vision over to someone else.

Anton was spot-on, too, when he talked about the importance of recognising the right times to step into one's power.

This is one of those times.

If I'm truly honest, I have yet to fully step into my power since taking up this position. I've said it a million times to Athena, but I'm still thinking small. I'm thinking parochially when I shouldn't be afraid to think like a man who has the stewardship of billions of pounds.

I'm still the caretaker, the appeaser. I tend to my flock, I look outwards, but my *flock* will soon comprise thousands upon thousands of people, and I need to learn to advocate for them fiercely and unashamedly.

As fiercely and unashamedly as Athena approaches everything she does.

I tell myself that my quick pre-lunch trip to the driving range with my brother is born less out of cowardice and more from a strategic desire to get his take before I face the Spanish Inquisition in the form of a Sullivan Sunday lunch. Catholic attitudes to those who "stray" may be less unthinkably cruel these days, but they're still pretty fucking terrifying when you're the so-called transgressor.

Maeve Bernadette Sullivan could have taken Ximinez de Cisneros on as Inquisitor General any day of the week.

Bren greets me in the clubhouse with a bro hug, but that's the only sympathy I get. Instead, he turns his wicked grin on me as we walk to the bay we'll share and shakes his head. 'You dirty, dirty bastard. How the fuck did you pull that off?'

'Well, clearly I didn't, did I?'

'You pulled it off for long enough. What, four months? How the hell did it come about?'

I sigh and look around to make sure I don't recognise anyone. If I shock any of the neighbours, Mum'll have it in for me even more.

'She's from an agency called Seraph. Anton owns it. I can't say much more, but their thing is "full service" EAs. They're all amazing women, apparently.'

'You don't say. And what made you decide you needed to get in on that when you had Alchemy? It wasn't like you didn't have sex on tap already.'

We find our bay. I stand my golf bag up and select my

driver, pulling off its cover. 'I was making up for lost time,' I say drily, 'and I was burning the candle too heavily. After the cleaners found me passed out in one of the rooms, I thought I'd go for a more effective solution.'

He's shaking his head again, like he doesn't even recognise me. He bends and empties out our bucket of balls. 'So all that time you were fucking her, even when you were being all pious at the RA.'

I grimace. 'Guilty.'

'Well, Jesus, mate, I don't blame you. I mean, look at her—'

'Careful.'

He stands and holds his hands up. 'Look. I'm just feeling a bit stupid, that's all. My holier-than-thou brother gets himself an Alchemy membership and then comes by a hooker so he can get his dick wet whenever he fancies at work, and I'm still picking up women in bars like a total muppet.'

'You said it. Honestly, I thought you'd be more enterprising.' I drop my grin. 'But seriously, please do me a solid and don't judge her on that one thing. It's so reductive. She's quite simply the most impressive woman I've ever met, and her having found a way to punch right through the glass ceiling makes her *more* impressive from where I'm standing.'

He nods soberly. 'It's alright, mate. There's nothing I don't agree with there. I don't suppose her mate Marlowe works for the same place? Because that would solve a lot of problems for me.'

That gets a laugh out of me. 'You fucking wish. Anyway, you ruined your chances there when you got all tongue-tied, didn't you?'

His mouth is a grim line. 'Don't remind me. Do you think Athena could put in a good word for me with her?'

Instantly, I see my opening. 'That depends on whether you come through for Athena, doesn't it? Now move back.'

I give my ball a good whack and watch in gratification as it sails cleanly through the blue sky. As it lands in the distance, I step back so Bren can line up his shot.

'If you think I wouldn't come through for you anyway, your opinion of me is even lower than I thought.' He turns and looks out at the driving range, then back down at his ball. I wait as he practices his swing and then takes his hit. Nice.

'You agree she's the best person to run the foundation?' I press.

'Jesus, of course I do. She wiped the floor with Eleanor that time. She's a fucking shark, and that's precisely what we need.'

'I agree. What does Mairead think?' I'm a big coward, so let's start this conversation with the most rational family member.

He snorts. 'What do you think she thinks? She's with me. She thinks sex is just an animalistic act and Mum and Dad are overreacting. Besides, she loves Athena.'

'Good.' That's what I thought. I screw my face up before I ask, 'And Mum and Dad?'

'Well, if you'd had the balls to actually read any of your messages on the family chat you'd know precisely what they think, you spineless tool.'

'Fair. How bad is it?'

I muted the family WhatsApp chat on my way home from the gala on Thursday and haven't dared look at it since. I didn't want my thought process—or my attempts to make things right—being coloured by any parental hysteria.

'Heavy on the slut-shaming from Mum and occasional belligerent outbursts from Dad. You know how he gets. Though I have to say'—he breaks off to chuckle—'she did ask you on the chat if Athena had "gone down that path" because she had a whole gaggle of illegitimate children and desperately needed funds. I was like, "Mum, this isn't *Les Mis*. A woman is allowed to make choices like this because she wants to, not just out of necessity".'

'Jesus. I have to say it'd be disappointing if she had a gaggle of children.'

'Because you want to put all the babies in her, right?'

I glare at him to conceal how badly I do in fact want to put *all* the babies inside Athena.

'I'm not sure she'll give me the chance. She's totally retreated. It's killing me.'

'I don't blame her. Fucking Harrington disrespecting her like that. He's a fucking disgrace. I'm going to see about getting him kicked off the board. I'm pretty sure there's a morality clause in his contract.'

'Good.'

'Is she going to follow up on her threat of legal action?'

'Damn right. Seraph is on the case—she'll take him to the cleaners.'

He nods his approval. 'Like I said, you can't blame her. She's out there living her life and clearly excelling at everything she does. We were all so impressed by her. Now she has Harrington's misogynistic bullshit to deal with *and* probably slut-shaming from all directions. It's fucking horrible. No wonder she's put her walls up.'

I chew on the inside of my cheek as I contemplate my next shot.

'No wonder, indeed. Which is why I have to get this position back on the table for her. It's the only way.'

CHAPTER 54

Gabe

Whsen Bren and I turn up at my parents' house, I busy myself with Mairead's kids, entertaining them over the course of their lunch while Mum and Dad prepare our lunch in the kitchen.

Ideally, we'd have this conversation after eating, but one look at Mum was enough to tell me that the woman is a pressure cooker waiting to blow. Now that she has me in her sights, I'm fair game.

One of the more useful skills I acquired as a priest was that of retaining perspective and compassion under fire. I find myself able to stay more regulated than certain other people in this family. While it doesn't make it any less frustrating to have to engage with people who have spiralled firmly into their sympathetic nervous system, it does make me more mindful of their point of view.

That said, I'm a former priest, not a saint, and I'm not immune to the occasional desire to stir up trouble. I can't, therefore, resist stirring the pot a little. Sometimes a shock is what people need to jolt them out of their blinkers.

Mairead's husband Peter has already made clear his intention to be nowhere near this Sullivan family drama. I wait until he's plated up his lunch and taken it and the kids outside and everyone else has been served their plate of first class roast pork belly with all the trimmings. Once Mum and Dad have picked up their forks, I assume what my siblings used to call my "priest face": some combination of devout and placid.

'I assume you want to talk to me about my role at Rath Mor,' I say pleasantly, spearing a piece of carrot. 'Given you clearly have certain views on solicitation. Are you planning on asking me to step down?'

I smile at Dad, who looks at me as though I've grown an extra head. 'Of course not!' he blusters.

'Oh, good. Because I feel like I've finally got my feet under the table.'

Next to Dad, my sister presses her lips together to halt a smile.

'We're very disappointed in you, Gabriel,' Mum chimes in. 'What you've done is a mortal sin, but we know you've been struggling since you took the reins. It's a big adjustment, that's what it is, but you're a grown man, and it's your business. Yours and God's.'

I smile broadly. 'That's very compassionate of you. I'm glad you feel that way. And I assume the same goes for Athena?'

Mum's fork clatters to her plate, and Bren snorts beside me.

'That little hussy,' she mutters, her eyes fixed on her food. She picks up her fork and carves off a piece of pork with far more venom than is necessary.

'*Wow*,' Mairead says. 'Mum. We've talked about this.'

When someone is operating from a place of fear, not love, meeting fear with fear is counterproductive.

'I understand that what happened the other night came as a shock,' I tell mum as softly as I would have spoken to a vulnerable parishioner. 'The way Giles Harrington behaved was horrible for everyone. I just want to be very clear that Athena was a victim of a particularly damaging and abusive outburst.'

'No one's condoning his behaviour,' Dad offers. 'It was a very ungentlemanly way to behave. But—'

'Hang on.' I put my hand up to stop him, because nothing that comes after that *but* will be okay by me. 'What I was going to say is that it's okay if what you learnt about my and Athena's original working relationship made you feel uneasy. I know it's far outside your comfort zones. You're allowed to dislike it.

'But here's the thing. Your approval of Athena's—or my—sexual activity isn't relevant to either the discussion of whether she's right for me *or* for the foundation. If anything, it's discriminatory.'

Mum's face goes from mulish to outraged in a second flat.

'Of course it's not discrimatory! It's a direct reflection of her character, and nobody who is working as a common prostitute is getting their hands on our foundation.'

Brendan huffs as if this is the final straw and puts down his wine glass. 'Mum, that's such an offensive label. Athena made choices. Gabe made choices. Sex was had. Money changed hands. They're both adults, and no one got hurt. End of story.'

I elbow him softly by way of thanks, and he grunts.

'But this is her *career*,' Mum hisses. 'She sleeps with powerful men like my son to get ahead. That's conniving, and it's a *pattern*. She's trying to ensnare him, and she's blinkered him with her... feminine wiles. Women like her are dangerous.'

'If you're going to cast her as Mary Magdalene, know she's most likely already done that herself. Which makes you just as damning as Simon the Pharisee.' I never speak to my mother so severely, but I can't let her moralistic judgement go unchallenged. 'And if you're so concerned about her morals, remember who Christ chose to stand by him when the time came. Both of these women have seen truths others miss. Athena saw the scale of the potential in this foundation before any of us, the former priest included. Not only that—she was the one who made me see just how effectively we could use our wealth as a force for good.'

God, I'm on a roll here. I'm back in my pulpit, lecturing my parishioners on one of my absolute favourite topics: how moral absolutism and judgement are categorically unchristian.

'And I don't know how you could possibly know so much about Athena's career history, so I'll assume it's all conjecture. But let me set you straight. No one is blinkered. No one is ensnared. And yes, Athena is dangerous, because she's challenging the status quo and using her powers to do things her way. She's unafraid, and she's terrifyingly competent.'

I sit back in my chair and continue more softly, because Mum is looking stricken. I understand the particular concoction of fear and love and ignorance and protectiveness that's driving this extreme scepticism. She's decided Athena is the lion in our midst, and she's hell-bent on taking her down before she causes any imagined damage.

'That's precisely the kind of person we want running the foundation,' I argue. 'Someone brilliant and radical, who doesn't give a damn about what's considered seemly or about doing things the traditional way. If anyone's blinkered, it's you and Dad.'

'How so?' Dad thunders, taking the bait just like I knew he would.

Well, Dad, I'm glad you asked. 'Take Eleanor. The epitome of good breeding and respectability, and, pardon my French, fucking useless.'

'Amen, Father,' my sister pipes up with a wicked smirk.

Mum shoots her her signature *don't make me put you over my knee* glare, to no avail.

'Everything she's done has been mediocre and steeped in snobbery. I'm sorry, but it's true. And I didn't even realise it until Athena opened my eyes to the incredible possibilities of what we could achieve. Athena has a brilliant strategic brain and an exceptional variety of experience—some of which she may have gained in roles that you don't like and don't have to like.

'But, at the end of the day, our fiduciary duty here is to the staggering amount of money we're planning on giving away, and if you compare Athena to Eleanor and find that *Athena* is the one lacking, then I have no earthly clue how to get through to you.'

I've cast the pleasant, pastoral tone aside, I realise. My voice is harder, colder, more authoritative than any tone I've used with my family in a long time. Because I've spent years feeling guilty about this inheritance, overwhelmed by it, and now—thanks to Athena—I finally know how to use it.

I've finally found my calling.

I have felt lost for so long. I felt equally lost during my years as a priest and in the aftermath. All this time, I've bemoaned my ability to be the type of shepherd I believe I should be. The type of *man* I believe I should be.

Managing the Sullivan billions made me feel at worst, uneasy, at best, conflicted.

Stewarding the Sullivan billions takes my innate desire to serve, to shepherd, and reimagines it as a new type of priesthood: ministry on a staggering scale.

There's only one person I know who can transform my purpose into reality, and, God bless her, it's not Eleanor Whitmore.

'I don't disagree on Eleanor. But I worry that we were

shown that young lady's true colours the other night,' Dad says gruffly.

Mairead puts down her cutlery with a huge sigh. 'For God's sake, Dad, the only person who showed their true colours the other night was Harrington. Given what he threw at Athena, I thought she conducted herself in a seriously classy way. And I hope those lawyers of hers take him for every penny he has.'

'They will,' I promise her. I turn to Dad. 'Look, I realise you don't know her very well, but I do.'

'*Very* well,' my brother mutters under his breath, and I turn to frown at him. 'Athena is the least fake person I know,' I tell my parents. 'If she doesn't like you, you'll know about it. She doesn't suffer fools, and she doesn't dissemble. She can't be bothered. In her professional circles, she's supremely self-confident, but the reaction she had from all of you the other night was horrific. I know you were shocked, but think about it from her perspective.

'You don't need to worry about her character. She's withdrawn herself from me, and I know she's making other career plans just now. She's already mentally walked away, and it's not because she's afraid of a good fight. She's really not. I know in my heart that she's walked away because she doesn't want me to have to make a difficult decision, and she doesn't want to put any more pressure on me given my guilt over leaving the priesthood. If that doesn't say *integrity*, I don't know what does.'

'I trust Gabe here,' Bren pipes up. 'I don't think he's blinded. I think he's an excellent judge of character. And from what I've seen of Athena, she's a straight shooter. That's what we need.'

I throw him a grateful look. 'She always expresses horror at being taken for a do-gooder. She's never tried to pretend to anyone that she's an angel. But she gets the job done like no one else I know. We need her.'

Mum pouts, her face like thunder, and my sister goes in for the kill. 'A few weeks ago, we all loved her. We were blown away by her. Absolutely nothing has changed there. She's still every bit as qualified and capable as she was before the gala. Wait.'

She takes a huge gulp of red wine and presses on, her attention going to me. 'I actually think you're the perfect power couple. You've got the pastoral background, but honestly, this lunch aside, I don't ever see you stand up for what you want. Not really. Athena will harness all that goodness and whip you into shape. Together you could be unstoppable—I mean it.'

I smile despite myself. Athena's words from our planning session at my house come back to me. *Together, we're unstoppable.*

Never have I believed something quite so fervently.

I'm done being the gentle priest here.

There's a time for humility. For patience. For lending your ear. My family is used to all those characteristics from me. I dare say they depend on them.

This is not that time.

It's time to advocate for others who deserve it, whether that's the thousands of people we can help or the woman who's been so maligned at the hands of my family.

It's time to step into my power, the power they so readily granted me when they handed me the reins over a year ago.

It's time to stop asking for permission.

'Your belief means a lot, sis,' I tell Mairead.

I fix my eyes squarely on my parents. 'Let me be very clear. As CEO, I have the ultimate say in this appointment. The foundation will be run by the most qualified person. That's

Athena. And, after everything I've said, if either of you still feel you want to cast a stone... Well. You know as well as I do what Christ had to say about that.'

CHAPTER 55

Athena

Rock bottom isn't just freaking out over a kiss. Nor is it telling the man who takes your breath away that you're working from home today and *not* telling him that it's because you can't bear to see his gorgeous, hurt, concerned face.

It's finding yourself singing along to *I Don't Know How to Love Him* on a loop with far too much feeling than is decent.

Fuck Marlowe and her obsession with musical theatre. She and Soph thought it was hilarious to put the *Jesus Christ Superstar* album on after a couple of bottles of wine. And when the line about Mary Magdalene claiming she wouldn't be able to cope if Jesus declared his love, they actually fell about laughing all the while muttering *Minerva*.

Heartless bitches.

Still, the poignancy of her lament has hung over me since the weekend. Andrew Lloyd Webber may have taken some liberties with the plot, but damn that song hits hard. The only part I don't relate to is that I know exactly why he moves me.

He's not just a man.

He's the best man I know.

Which is why I, like Mary, find him fucking terrifying.

He messaged me back with an invitation that scares and intrigues me in equal measure.

GABE:

> I know you needed space this weekend, but I'm desperate to see you.

> Please come to Alchemy this evening.

> There's something I think could help us both xx

If *something* is hot, dirty sex in an actual sex club, then perhaps he's right. Perhaps it would help, if only to give us both closure.

I couldn't handle him kissing me in the unflinching daylight of his office, so maybe the answer is letting him fuck me in a corner of Alchemy so dark that the shadows hide the emotions on our faces.

There's something almost fitting about it.

He hired me on a purely transactional basis, so ending it in a place that literally exists to facilitate transactional sex feels depressingly apt.

I pull out all the stops in my preparations. If I'm back to being the whore, I'll damn well be at my most intoxicating. What's left of my pride demands nothing less.

I sign in as Gabe's guest, leaving my coat with the receptionist and sauntering down the elegant lobby of the Alchemy townhouse in Mayfair. My hair is tonged perfectly, my heels are vertiginous, and almost everything is on display, thanks to a sheer black lace maxi dress that's little more than a body stocking, clinging to absolutely everything.

Beneath it?

Nothing but a nude lace thong.

This may be my first time here, but this is squarely my sphere. Not tonight the humiliation of walking into a gala feeling like a million dollars and leaving feeling like dirt. Here I can own my power, my sexuality.

I push open the double doors and take in the stunning bar area: expensive crystal chandeliers and polished floor and a back-lit pink onyx bar that takes up the entire far wall.

And leaning against it, his face grave, his eyes fixed only on me?

My priest.

In full clerical attire, he's the man from the photo, and he's every bit as arresting, as solemn, as he was then. Only now, I know what lies beneath. Now, he's a million times more handsome than the holy man I drooled over on my laptop.

I walk towards him, suddenly conscious of my near-nakedness in the face of his austere all-black outfit and white dog collar, no bigger than a postage stamp but significant in the extreme.

Is this the first time he's donned it since he left the priesthood?

Has he brought me here for a *role play?*

He's standing alone, though the two women to his right can't stop staring at him. As I walk across what feels like the endless expanse of floor, a guy approaches me. I put up a hand to ward him off without even looking at him, and I keep moving. Gabe is still staring at me, his eyes roving over my face and my untethered tits and everything else I've put on display for him tonight.

'I didn't know it was Vicars and Tarts Night,' I say lamely as I reach him. 'Good job we both dressed for it.'

He grins tiredly, sliding a hand under my hair and around my neck.

'Is this okay?'

He's back to asking if he can touch me.

I was his girlfriend for a few, blissful days, and now he's back to asking.

I did that.

I nod, blinking away the moisture in my eyes. 'Of course,' I whisper, and then he's tugging me into his arms and wrapping them around me, and *God*, I needed this. I needed to be in his arms so badly. I belong here, and I don't deserve to belong here, and I can't bear it.

I hug him back, and we stand there for a moment, swaying slowly together. His body heat permeates my ineffectual dress, and his scent permeates my nostrils, and every fucking thing permeates my porous, broken heart. The heart that was once so strong and fierce and which now bleeds for this man.

'I missed you,' he whispers against my hair.

'I missed you.'

After a couple of moments, he releases me and turns away, regretfully, it seems, to request two glasses of champagne from the server behind the bar.

'*Non est ad astra mollis e terris via,*' he says as we clink, and I smile sadly.

'Amen to that.'

'I finally made a Catholic of her.' He shakes his head.

'You look stunning,' he tells me as we drink. 'Will you come downstairs with me in a minute? There's something I want to show you.'

I nod, though I really hope it's his dick and not his own bleeding heart, because I can't handle that at all.

'Before we do, I have something to tell you,' he says. 'I saw my family yesterday, and we had a long conversation. The foundation job is yours, just as it should be.'

I stare at him in amazement. What the actual *fuck?* 'There's no way your parents are okay with me running it now that they know what I do for a living.'

'Did,' he corrects. 'And I wouldn't say they're thrilled, exactly, but trust me when I say they *are* on board.'

I only have one word. 'How?'

He purses his lips. 'Conversations were had around various points: your suitability for the role, which has never been in dispute, your character, to which Mairead and Brendan and I all attested, your superiority to Mum's so-called respectable choice—Eleanor—and, let's see, the double standards of them judging you and not me.'

His voice is sharper than usual. More commanding, less tolerant. He smiles, but it's grim. 'I reminded them that this bold new vision for the foundation came from you. And, for good measure, I threw in a reminder that I have the ultimate say as CEO.' He shrugs. 'I can't do this without you, and I don't want to. Simple as that. You and I are so opposite in our natures as to coincide perfectly. And, like I said, they came around. They even admitted that they may have judged you unnecessarily harshly, once I'd thrown a few Bible verses around to really ram the point home.'

I'm dumbfounded. This isn't the priestly, mild-mannered Gabe we're all used to. What he's recounting sounds a lot like he's just flexed his considerable power for the first time. Except, of course, that this is Gabe we're talking about, which means that he hasn't done it in the usual alpha-hole billionaire kind of way.

He's done it in an inimitably *Gabe* way, from the sounds of it, combining that pastoral wisdom with this newfound sense of authority in a manner that's so uniquely him.

'And it worked? They caved?' I ask incredulously.

This time, his smile is beatific. 'I like to think I cemented my argument as I left with a politely-but-firmly-delivered reminder that they'd do well to stay on the good side of my future children's mother. But yes, they rolled over eventually, and with a pleasantly surprising amount of grace.'

'I can't believe this,' I murmur, rapidly shelving his comment about my bearing his children. There's no way I'm going *there*. Still, my head is spinning with outcomes and possibilities. At no point over the past four days did I imagine the Sullivans would sign off on this. It sounds like Maeve and Ronan are far from my biggest fans, but whatever. Plenty of people dislike me. Plenty distrust me. The only way to win his parents over will be with results. Even if they hate me, they'll be on board with my methods.

'Don't make any decisions yet,' he urges. 'I don't want you feeling obligated to rush into anything. I just needed you to have all the facts before I took you downstairs.'

'What about Eleanor? And Torty?' I had precisely one run-in with the latter on Friday, when she came by to drop off some irrelevant folder in the hope of seeing Gabe. She said precisely nothing about the events of the previous night, but the supercilious nature of her smile left her perceived triumph in no doubt whatsoever.

I can handle people like them. I certainly don't feel sexually threatened by a woman who's likely oblivious that the term *pearl necklace* has more than one meaning. Still, I want to know what I'm dealing with here.

He smirks, and it's decidedly unpriestly. 'They will be in precisely zero uncertainty as to where my loyalties lie: to you, and to the foundation. If you come back, my darling, it will be in a blaze of glory. Believe me when I say I have no qualms about you being the person I want by my side through it all.'

The openly adoring look in his eyes tells me he's not fibbing, and once again, the power of Gabriel Sullivan's heart to heal and protect and empower hits me with full force.

Once we've finished our drinks, he leads me through more double doors into what he tells me is The Playroom, and holy fuck, is it hot. The place seems quiet—I suppose Monday night is not a night to party—but the sights of people naked and fucking instantly have my arousal levels ratcheting up. As he grips my hand tightly, I point at the trio of empty St Andrew's crosses with my free hand.

'Five months, and you've never brought me here? Please tell me you're going to string me up on one of those.'

He shudders. 'A bit above my pay grade, I think.'

I suppose if you're a priest, crucifixion play might seem a little *too* taboo, now I think about it.

We pass through a door and down a staircase to a corridor of closed doors and elegant hurricane lanterns. With a cryptic grimace, Gabe opens one of the doors and gestures for me to precede him.

I stop dead just inside the door. There are thick, creamy candles galore standing on the shelves and around the edges of the room, their flames flickering softly. Red rose petals in their thousands litter the wooden floor. If that all screams *romance* and the large bed, covered in black satin sheets, screams *sex*, then I have no clue what the fucking *enormous* wooden confessional, its dark wood carved and gleaming, is supposed to signify. I've been to enough Catholic churches on my cultural pilgrimages around Italy to know that this is the real deal.

'Holy fuck,' I say, staring at it blankly. 'How the hell did that thing get in here?'

He shuts and locks the door with a quiet chuckle. 'Logistically speaking, I have no idea, but its origin story is that my mate Rafe, who's one of the founders here, had it installed. His wife, Belle, had a pretty full-on Catholic upbringing and apparently it gave her a thing for priests.'

'I know how she feels.' I turn to him. His face is watchful. 'Are we doing a scene?'

'Kind of. Possibly not the kind you're thinking of, though.' He pauses. 'I didn't want to assume anything.'

I swear another piece of my heart rips off. 'I'm so sorry about...' I trail off.

'You have nothing to apologise for. You hear me? Now, you ever been inside one of these?'

'Absolutely not,' I say with a shudder. 'I can't believe Catholics actually go to confession in these things. Isn't it utterly terrifying?'

He laughs softly and moves around to open the far right of the three doors. 'Why don't you find out for yourself?'

I peer in. It's dark, and tiny, and really foreboding, some-how. I have no clue what Gabe's game is here, but if he's aiming to distract me from our issues by activating low-level claustrophobia, then it's working.

There's a narrow seat and also a leather-covered kneeler that unhelpfully recalls the prayer room off his office where he's fucked me so often. 'Should I sit or kneel?' I ask him.

'Whichever you prefer, sweetheart.' I'm not sure whether the endearment or the gentle smile with which he delivers it slays me more.

'Where are you going to be?'

'I'll be right here, in the middle. You'll be able to see me through the grille.' He points. Sure enough, there's a wooden grille through which I can see the shadows of another little box.

This is getting weirder and weirder.

'Okay,' I say, and I allow him to shut the door on me. I opt for kneeling—it feels more on brand for me, and it gets me closer to him.

I wait as he enters the middle chamber, and sure enough, I can see his outline as he sits down. His face is higher than mine and in profile. He doesn't turn it to look at me when he starts to speak in a low, reassuring tone.

His priest voice.

'Thank you for being open to this, sweetheart.' He pauses as if searching for his words. 'It strikes me that there's a lot to say, and that you didn't feel particularly comfortable discussing any of it in my office on Friday. I've been thinking about how to create a safe space for you to share your feelings, because I know how vulnerable my family made you feel on Thursday night, and I'm so, so sorry.'

'They did,' I admit, because it strikes me as unnecessarily harsh to not only wall up but then pretend I'm not hiding anything. I may want to protect myself, but I never, ever want this man to think I'm not hurting over him. Not when he's been so intensely vulnerable and generous with me.

'I know, and I hate that. Believe me when I say nothing could make me more outraged.' Another pause. 'The thing is that this whole confessional may seem seriously bizarre to you, but it's very oddness can be a kind of comfort. My parishioners could confess things to me in here—could bare their souls in a way they certainly never could out in the open. So I wondered if you'd be open to exploring that.'

My jaw drops open, because I've belatedly realised what his endgame is here.

'You want to hear my *confession*?'

CHAPTER 56

Athena

He laughs softly. 'Not in the traditional sense of the word, no. Of course not. This isn't about me trying to make you feel in any way exposed.'

I squint through the grille, drinking up every shadowed fragment of his profile as he speaks.

'What is it about, then?'

'These days, the act of confession is known as the Sacrament of Reconciliation. I've always far preferred that term. It's less about exposing sins and more about restoring harmony and communion when there's been a rupture. And it's pretty clear there's been a rupture between us, my darling, even if neither of us are to blame in the slightest.'

I'm quiet. His priest voice is soft and reassuring. It makes me feel safe and warm, even in this alien space, and his choice of words soothes me, even if he's spot on about the rupture element.

Harmony. Communion. Restoring.

For the first time, I can see how speaking one's truth in an enclosed space like this can lead one to feel less claustrophobic and more cloistered.

'I know.' My voice is small. I'm aware that he blames himself for what happened on Thursday, yet I'm the one who's walled myself off and frozen him out. Just as Gabe has confessed to rallying his inner alpha male to advocate to his family for me, all my actions have been to protect him. To save him.

'Are you willing to try something?' He shifts again in his seat.

'Why not?' I know this man. I trust this man with my life. Taking a leap of faith on him in this moment, in this wooden, womb-like space, feels more like a baby step than a giant leap.

'Okay, let's try something.' He clears his throat. 'Athena, I'm Father Gabriel. I thank the Lord for your courage in coming here today and in seeking to open your heart.' A weighty pause, during which I'm unsure whether to speak. But he continues in the softest voice: 'I hear you've been having some troubles with your partner, and I wondered if you would feel comfortable telling me what scared you on Friday.'

So this is his game.

He's not asking me to talk *to* him.

He's asking me to talk *about* him.

I blow out a breath, my innate scepticism warring with a desire to try this for Gabe's sake.

'I've never done this before... Father.'

'There's no wrong way,' he says gently. 'Just speak what's in your heart.'

He's firmly back in priest mode, and I can already see how fully he embodies all those years of pastoral care. 'He wanted to be'—I stumble over the words—'intimate, and vulnerable. He kissed me, and he told me he loved me, and I wasn't ready.'

'Good. That's good. Why do you think you weren't ready?'

I squeeze my eyes shut, reliving that moment, trying to

understand what it was about that conversation with the man of my dreams that felt like falling backwards off a cliff.

'It was the way he looked at me. Like—like I was this precious, sacred thing, right at the time that I was feeling at my most humiliated and shamed and—'

I stop dead, my eyes flying open.

He waits, but his silence feels less unnerving than accepting, as if he's holding space for me.

'Unworthy,' I admit, hating the word while knowing it's the truth.

'What exactly did you feel unworthy of?'

'Everything. The job he'd offered me. His love. *Him.*'

He's perfectly still and composed in profile, as if he's merely a compassionate ear and not the subject of my revelations.

I push on. It feels as though the truth is unravelling itself in my heart like a great ball of yarn. 'The thing is, Father, this man knows everything about me. All the things I've done, that other people find so shameful. And yet he still looks at me like that.'

'You know, Athena, that word *worthy* is very subjective. We're all worthy of love, just as we're all worthy of God's grace. Both are freely given in abundance, but it's up to us to build our capacity to accept them. That's the key.'

'I can think of a man who'd do well to remind himself of that,' I say, and he laughs softly.

'Yes, well, sometimes we have far greater clarity over the worthiness of others than ourselves. But I can tell you, you are worthy of this man's love. He's chosen you not despite of what you believe you've done, but precisely because of who you are. He loves all of you, your entire being, and he sees you fully.'

He hasn't glanced in my direction once, and I know it's his way of giving me as much space, as much safety, to purge myself. I'm quiet for a moment as I process. It strikes me that his point about our having to build our capacity to accept love is something that warrants further thought.

'Okay,' I say. 'I hear what you're saying.'

'What do you think scares you most about being loved?'

I consider. I'm someone who has a pretty high opinion of myself. I'm used to being desired, respected, feared, even.

'It's being loved by *him* that scares me.'

'Because...'

'Because he's the best man I've ever known, and I love him so, so much, and I'll do anything to protect him.'

He inhales raggedly, and I'm so happy I could give him this, at the very least. It suddenly feels so urgent that he knows how very indelibly he's written his name on my heart.

When he speaks again, his voice is thick with emotion. 'Why on earth would you think he needs you to protect him from loving you?'

'Because he's so good and pure, and he doesn't see it. He's been struggling with his sense of worth, too, and he's already given up so much—his vocation, and his family's approval, and he's been on a journey to get all that back.' I pause. 'I don't want to be the person who jeopardises all that for him.'

'Why do you think you would jeopardise it?'

'Because he's chosen someone who's the precise opposite of who he was trained to be or to want.'

'I see. So you think you need to protect him from his own desires, is that it?' He sounds weary, but the slow way he speaks those words tells me he's finally beginning to under-stand what prompted my hissy fit in his office.

'Yes.'

'Because that's your job. That's what you've always done —you've had to run the show throughout your career. And he's been leaning on you, so you have no faith in his ability to look after himself.'

'I have faith in *him*,' I say quickly, because he's making it sound like I have a low opinion of him. 'I just—I've always been the strong one, and I was happy to be that for him while he was going through so much uncertainty in his life. I don't want to be a complication for him.'

He hangs his head for a long moment. Then he turns and looks directly at me through the grille. 'Will you still feel comfortable talking to me if I take you out of there?'

'Of course,' I say. It's true. I will. This scene he so cleverly created has had its desired effect of opening my heart and loosening my tongue, but there are things Gabe and I need to say *to* each other.

This confessional has served its purpose.

He stands and exits his little box, swinging open my door a moment later. As he holds out his hand to me, I gaze up at him. He's so beautiful, and I feel honoured to see him like this. His priest outfit is objectively very sexy, but it's not only a uniform. It's clear that he's embodying his former office with all of his being, and it's wonderful to behold.

We sit together on the bed, side by side, and he clasps my hand on his thigh as I lay my head on his shoulder, inhaling the scent of him like an addict.

'What you said in there was so brave,' he tells me. 'Do you think that's what really scares you? Not just feeling unworthy of love, but having to put all your trust in someone else to be strong for you, even when it gets hard?'

I mull his words over. I am an island; there's no doubt about it. I have my support system, but at the end of the day, if you want to build a safety net that can catch you when you fall, you have to build it yourself. That's the only way you'll know it's secure.

'I would say that's absolutely terrifying,' I admit with a little shudder, and he laughs softly, as if that's no surprise to him.

'What if I told you,' he asks softly, 'that I truly believe I can be that for you? I'll admit, when you met me I was flailing. I was purposeless and out of my depth and shame-filled. And out of all that came you and me, and you blew me away. Your confidence is so infectious, you know that? You pulled me along with you, and suddenly I found I could swim on my own. Everything I'm fired up about in life is down to you, sweetheart, and I know, I just know, I'm strong enough to be the man you need.'

I turn my head and press my face into his shoulder, not trusting myself to speak. God, how are he and I so good at seeing the best in each other and so bad at seeing it in ourselves?

'I have to say,' he continues, wrapping an arm around me, 'I find it quite ironic that you're scared of weakening me, when you're the one who helped me find my true strength.'

I groan my acknowledgement, my tears dampening the fabric of his shirt. 'The fallen priest and the fallen woman. Are we a punchline?'

'No. I'd say we're pretty fucking magical together. May I propose a different narrative?'

'Ugh. Please do.'

'What if... we both stand down and stop trying to be such martyrs for each other? I expect it of myself, but from someone who doesn't have a religious bone in her body I'd expect more self respect.'

I manage a laugh at that. 'The only religious bone I have in my body tends to be your dick.'

'And there she is.' He sighs. 'Look. What if we stop trying to protect each other and just focus on loving each other? Celebrating each other? What if we accept that we deserve a bit of happiness, hmm? And that we're both strong, but together we're unstoppable.'

'I said that in your kitchen,' I mumble. I feel completely

drained. That confessional was one hell of an emotional wringer.

'Mairead said it about us yesterday, too. That's what put it in my mind.'

'Your sister thinks we're unstoppable?'

'She *knows* we're unstoppable. And I think my parents do too, deep down.'

I raise my head and look at him through teary eyes. 'I love you so much I can barely breathe, and I love you so much it's terrifying.'

His smile breaks my heart. 'I love you too, and I agree. It is terrifying. But I knew we'd find the stars together, even if the way wasn't easy.'

Fuck, nothing about ripping your heart open for another human is easy, but I know it will be worth it.

My good, kind man.

My very own saint.

I'm just grateful he prefers playing the sinner in the bedroom.

Epilogue - Athena

FOUR YEARS LATER

Nat and her team are magicians.

The green Gossamer dress that's hung in my wardrobe all these years, taunting me with its perfection, its expense, its *memories*, is getting a second shot at glory tonight.

The only snag?

After growing and delivering two babies, I've gone up at least a dress size.

Enter the magicians. They've somehow reengineered it, expanding those endless rows of tasseled chevrons horizontally so that it skims my curves just as beautifully as it did that night.

That night.

I have mixed feelings about it now as I look back. I was so happy, and then so shattered. I truly believed I'd overreached. Dreamt too big. Dared too greatly.

For a few days, a few years ago, I was almost stricken

enough to believe that audacity was a bad thing, a character flaw that was both unseemly and bound to bite you in the arse.

To that version of myself I say:

Look at me now.

Once my hair and makeup team have left, I take a final look in the full-length mirror in my and Gabe's bedroom. Before we got married, we rented out the Manchester Square townhouse and instead bought a gorgeous Georgian pile in Ham, near Richmond, whose old walled garden had us both falling at first sight. It's less convenient for town, but it gives us more space to dream.

As I walk down the corridor towards Gaia's nursery, I'm struck by the sheer volume of photos on the walls. I'm only thirty, but my life is so rich with memories already. There's our safari in the Kruger. Gus's birth. Gaia's birth. Multiple shots of my bump. And, of course, my favourite selfie of us bathed in a pink sunset at Cape Sounion, seconds after Gabe proposed. Behind us stand the stunning ruins of the Temple of Athena Sounias and the rose-hued Aegean Sea.

When he asked me to marry him, he said he wanted to pay homage to the most incredible goddess he'd ever met in front of an ancient temple honouring her glory.

Pretty romantic for a guy who only believes in one true God.

I creep into the nursery, which is lit by a rotating night-light that casts an endless cascade of stars across the walls. Our nanny, Agnes, gives me and my dress an approving thumbs-up from the rocking chair in which she's sitting, and I grin at her as I make my way across the room to peer into my daughter's cot.

We named our son Gus for St Augustine, and our daughter Gaia for the goddess of the earth. (It's called compromise.) The six months of data we have for her have confirmed unequivocally that the goddess energy is strong with this one.

But you wouldn't know it right now. She's flat on her back in her white embroidered gro-bag, mouth pursed and arms raised cactus-style and eyelashes feathery arcs against her pink cheeks.

She's simply the most exquisite sight I've ever seen.

I blow her a kiss and mouth goodbye to Agnes before descending the wide staircase and locating my boys in the den where they're snuggled up watching some show about diggers together. My husband is looking dangerously hot in his tuxedo, our two-and-a-half-year-old son in his favourite pair of brushed cotton fire engine pyjamas. His dark hair is fluffy and his thumb is in his mouth, his index finger stroking his cheek: a dead giveaway that he's knackered. Agnes will have no problems getting him down tonight.

They both look up as I enter the room. My husband's eyebrows shoot up. 'Holy... cow. Doesn't Mummy look every inch the goddess tonight, Gus?'

He's so charming. And he looks like he wants to eat me for dinner. I smile at him and smooth my hands over my hips. I'm thrilled to be getting another chance to give this dress a whirl. I couldn't care less that I'm still carrying a little baby weight—I didn't build my appeal by being the thinnest woman in the room, and I'm not about to start now. 'Thank you, darling.'

'So. Fucking. Hot,' Gabe mouths silently over Gus's head, and my smile turns seductive.

'So pretty, Mummy,' Gus chirps, having unplugged his thumb. My heart melts again.

'Merci, mon coeur.' I bend and cup his little face in my hands as we gaze at each other. *'T'as fait pipi? T'as bien brossé tes quenottes?' Have you done a wee-wee? Have you brushed your teeth properly?*

'Oui, Maman.'

'C'est bien mon petit loup.' That's my good little wolf.

I speak French and German around Gus whenever I can. I'll leave Italian for another couple of years. Gabe accuses me of being a tiger mother, but this is the best age for him to learn. He's like a sponge.

Gabe extracts his arm from behind Gus's warm little body and plants a kiss on the crown of his head. 'Night, little man. I love you, but we've got to head out. Mummy has an award to accept.'

The ballroom at The Dorchester is even more resplendent than usual. The botanical gardens at Kew have helped to create a greenhouse air with the loan of a staggering amount of stunning potted trees and plants for the evening.

I should know. I'm on the organising committee for this event, for my sins.

The Audacity Foundation has taken its usual two tables near the front of the room, which is handy, given I'm a keynote speaker again this year. Notably absent is Giles Harrington. While the mere thought of him makes me shudder, his dirty money is doing very nicely. I ploughed it all into starting up that platform I designed back at business school for matching female entrepreneurs with female angel investors.

It's been a real joy to watch an army of women thriving thanks to his misogyny.

Next to our table are the usual representatives from The Wolff Foundation. Having shamelessly copied our model over the past couple of years, Anton and Max are runners up for the award for British Philanthropist of the Year.

Sometimes bad girls do finish first.

'Show me my grandbabies,' Maeve demands almost as soon as we've sat down at the table. I pretend to sigh, when really, I love showing my kids off. If they weren't the most accomplished, advanced children on the planet, I probably wouldn't be so bothered, but they are. I hand over my phone to show her a video of Gus, in full fireman costume, singing *Frère Jacques*. Both his pronunciation and his pitch are perfect.

Since they made the decision to judge me on my merits and not on an arbitrary label that apparently put the fear of God into them, Maeve and Ronan and I have got on famously. I find it fascinating that we humans have such a ready fear response. We armour up so quickly when something or someone feels strange or unfamiliar or in any way unsafe. But when we take the time to get to know people, much as it irks me to admit it, most of us aren't as awful as we seem.

'I bloody love that you're wearing that dress,' Mairead tells me from across the table. 'You make vindication look really, really great.'

'You certainly do, love.' Maeve lifts her glass to me, and I get a little misty-eyed until I remember I'm a badass business-woman who has far better things to do than get weepy over a sentimentality or two.

Mairead and I have become firm allies. She had a gigantic fight with Brendan a few years ago over some land that his company had earmarked for a new mall. It will surprise no one to learn that Mairead won, and the result is a beautiful equestrian centre with stables, a decent-sized paddock for an urban area, and an indoor arena. The equine therapy it offers is spearheaded by some experts she knows and funded by us.

The Audacity Foundation is quite the family affair.

As the initial speeches drone on, my husband is happy to provide some entertainment of his own. His arm draped languorously over the back of my chair, he proceeds to pour a steady stream of love and filth into my ear.

'The things I'm going to do to you when you get home.' His fingertips brush my shoulder oh so lightly. 'You're a fucking vision, and I've never been more proud of what you've achieved.'

'Tell me I'm a good person and I'll stab you with my fork,' I say under my breath while staring straight ahead. If this award paints me as some do-gooder, I'll be furious. Happily, the foundation's PR agency has enough interviews lined up with the broadsheets, financial press, and glossy magazines over the next month for me to set the record straight.

'I'm not that foolhardy. But your competence has been my kink since I met you, and I'm going to show you just how much your talents turn me on as soon as we can get out of here.'

'It was my competence you liked in that Seraph photo, was it?'

He groans against my jaw. He still has such a boner for that photo. There's a reason we have a random bar stool in our bedroom. 'You're competent at *everything.*'

I turn my head and cup his face. 'Don't get too starstruck,' I whisper in his ear. 'I want you to treat me like a whore tonight and get me on my knees as soon as we get home.'

There was a time when I felt typecast by my background. Limited. I felt that the stars, in all their dazzling celestial glory, weren't mine to reach for.

Now that I'm there, I enjoy nothing more than embracing my past. My unique, perverted, crazy past that led me to this man.

When my name is called, I find myself hoping I haven't turned Gabe on *too* much. Given this is his award as much as mine, I've insisted that he join me on stage, and no one likes a philanthropist with a boner.

His grip is firm on my hand as we weave through the tables to thunderous applause. At the next table, Anton stands and shakes Gabe's hand before planting a kiss on my cheek.

'That's my girl,' he says with a wink.

Max, Dex and their wife Darcy are applauding, too. Darcy, who's in a gold dress that's definitely not appropriate for an event this formal and utterly fucking fantastic, puts her fingers in her mouth and wolf-whistles at me.

'Thanks, babe,' I mouth with a grin.

Gen looks disapprovingly at her sister before blowing me a kiss.

The Alchemy women are the best.

I have a short, punchy speech planned. It will remind the great and good of British philanthropy that running a successful non-profit doesn't automatically arise from a desire to do good. Success comes from running it just like a business. From adhering religiously to KPIs. From obsessing over efficiencies as aggressively as any hedge fund and being as bold with your experiments as any self-respecting laboratory. And from being as shameless as possible when it comes to harnessing the incredible expertise of people far smarter, far more knowledgeable, than you are around the world.

I will remind them, most importantly, that every commercial shark like me will benefit from having someone of vision and decency and unwavering faith standing beside them.

Someone like Gabriel Sullivan.

As I ascend the stage, my husband's hands linger lightly on my hips.

'Up you get, sweetheart. Show them all what you've got.'

THE END

I have a **bonus epilogue** you won't want to miss with a lot of Alchemy Easter Eggs... oh, and Athena has a bun in the oven: https://geni.us/audacity_bonus

If you haven't yet encountered Alchemy, start with **Unfurl** - **MAJOR PRIEST KINK ALERT** - or dive straight into Gen and Anton's story in **Unveil**.

Brendan and Marlowe are up next! Preorder **Duplicity**: https://geni.us/duplicity_seraph

**TURN THE PAGE
FOR DUPLICITY!**

Hi, and thank you for reading!

Well, you've just had a pretty detailed insight into what's occupied my brain for the past eighteen months…

Athena wasn't supposed to be a character of note in *Unveil*. Anton Wolff absolutely was not supposed to have a threesome with his BFF and his EA in Chapter 2 of *Unveil*. It just… happened, and Athena was born.

I thought about her so much after I published *Unveil*. Way too much. I thought about Seraph, and what an intoxicatingly taboo concept it was.

And then other people started asking about her. About Seraph. Wondering if she would get a book. And I realised it wasn't just me whose interest she'd piqued.

It was obvious to me from the start that Athena was far less submissive than Anton liked to think she was. I think she had him right where she wanted him, frankly.

Gabe, though… Gabe was supposed to be far more of an alpha hole, or at the very least, far more dysfunctional, but he came streaming onto the page as a man of such integrity and decency that there was nothing I could do about it. And it turned out to be far more fun watching Athena, master manipulator and ice queen, falling for the priestly cinnamon roll (is that a thing? It should be a thing). I like to think that, just like Jesus and Mary Magdalene, they saw each other truly and fully and perfectly.

This book was also my way of showing the Catholic Church, which, let's face it, has had a bit of a bashing in *Unfurl* and *Unstitch*, in a slightly more positive light through a man with true faith and a boatload of compassion.

A final note - the itchy sweater analogy for shame was borrowed from Sarah Baldwin, a nervous system expert and somatic coach whose courses are changing my life. I thought it was such a beautiful way to describe how we can choose to internalise or reject shame when others try to foist it upon us.

Now bring on Bren and Marlowe! Oh - and Sophia is getting Book Three - you heard it here first...

Elodie x

Acknowledgments

I love this community!

Thank you to my ARC readers, who are the loveliest cheerleaders and the nicest place for my brand new book babies to land before they go out into the big, scary world of nasty Goodreads reviewers. Thank you for the rapturous receptions you always give my ARCs, and for your eagle-eyed typo spots.

A special thank you to my beta reader and proof reader for this one, Jennifer Brooks Brown. She read a highly serialised version of this book, always graciously dropping everything to read the latest salacious instalment, and unfailingly fluffed me up. She also had some delicious suggestions for tying up loose ends, especially Giles Harrington's settlement!

A massive thank you to my FB reader group aka my Nerds, who are always there for me (even when I go deep into the writing cave).

Thank you also to all the influencers and readers who support me on IG and TT, especially my sister from another mister, Tierney Page, who is the most unfailingly generous champion.

Finally, thank you to my fairy godfather, Bobby Kim, for navigating the stormy seas of marketing and advertising with such aplomb. If he ever decides to prioritise his sleep, I'll be in trouble.

Elodie x

www.ingramcontent.com/pod-product-compliance
Lightning Source LLC
Chambersburg PA
CBHW031739180726
48283CB00005B/1573